HER
WILD
HERO

PAIGE TYLER

sourcebooks
casablanca

Published by Sourcebooks Casablanca, an imprint of Sourcebooks, Inc.
P.O. Box 4410, Naperville, Illinois 60567-4410
(630) 961-3900
Fax: (630) 961-2168
www.sourcebooks.com

Printed and bound in the United States of America.
RRD 10 9 8 7 6 5 4 3

With special thanks to my extremely patient and understanding husband. Without your help and support, I couldn't have pursued my dream job of becoming a writer. You're my sounding board, my idea man, my critique partner, and the absolute best research assistant any girl could ask for.

Love you!

Prologue

DECLAN MACBRIDE GAZED THROUGH HIS BINOCULARS at the rolling mountains stretching in every direction around him. Nothing out there but fresh air, wild animals, trees, and solitude—make that lots of trees and lots of solitude. And that was exactly the way he liked it.

When he'd told his boss at the regional U.S. Forest Service office in Portland he was fine with a full-time post out here, the guy had looked at him like he was insane. Silver Butte was the most isolated fire tower in the area—no one wanted to get assigned here. There weren't any trails nearby, so you could easily go days without seeing another human being. It was also too far from civilization for the ranger on duty to go home between shifts, which meant you had to stay out here for the entire tour of duty—usually a week at a time. Put those two things together and it was a tough place to keep manned, even during the critical days of fire season. The only forest rangers who got sent here were the newbies and the screwups.

Volunteering to stay at the tower for the rest of the summer had confused the hell out of Declan's boss. But the man wasn't going to look a gift horse in the mouth. As soon as Chet made sure Declan knew he wasn't going to get any bonus pay, he'd given the okay. The other rangers thought he was nuts, too. They couldn't understand why anyone would willingly isolate themselves from human contact. But Declan had his reasons, and he didn't care to go into them.

Declan moved around the interior of the tower, scanning in all directions for any sign of trouble. Fire was the big concern at this time of year, but he was looking for anything out of the ordinary: poachers, circling buzzards, campers in distress.

He'd just set down his binoculars and grabbed his book when he picked up the sound of footsteps approaching the tower. He sniffed the air before he could stop himself, then bit back a growl. He rarely relied on his sense of smell. It was better than a normal person's—way better—but he went out of his way to ignore what his nose told him. He didn't feel comfortable experiencing the world that way. It made him feel too much like an animal.

Fortunately, his sense of hearing—which seemed far more acceptable to depend on—was good enough to compensate for refusing to use his nose. And right now, his ears were telling him there was someone about five hundred feet to the north of the tower and moving this way.

Declan sat down and went back to his book. It was probably just an adventurous hiker who'd wandered off the trail. Once the guy saw the chain across the bottom of the stairs with a sign saying the tower was off limits to the public, he'd go on his way.

A few moments later, boots were pounding up the steps. Declan frowned. *What the hell?*

He tossed his book on the table and walked outside

to look over the railing. "Sorry, Mister, but this tower is government property. It's off-limits to the public."

The man glanced up as he climbed, grinning at Declan. "I'm well aware of that, Mr. MacBride. That's why I got permission from your boss before coming out here to see you."

Declan did a double take. How the hell did this guy know his name? More importantly, why hadn't Chet called him on the satellite phone to tell him the guy was coming out here?

"Nice to finally meet you, Mr. MacBride," the man said when he got to the landing. He held out his hand. "I'm John Loughlin."

Declan tried to ignore his nose as he shook the man's hand, but it was hard—Loughlin's clothes smelled like they'd just come off the rack at the nearest outdoor store. His boots weren't even broken in for Pete's sake. If the brand-new duds weren't enough to tell him the guy wasn't a hiker, the fact that he wasn't carrying a pack would have been a dead giveaway. Who hiked all this way without food or water?

"How do you know my name?" Declan asked.

"I know a great deal about you Mr. MacBride." Loughlin smiled up at him. "Though I have to say your personnel record doesn't do you justice. You are a very large man."

Declan's eyes narrowed. He didn't like anyone knowing too much about him. "You mean my Forest Service records? How did you get access to those?"

Loughlin motioned toward the tower. "Perhaps we could sit down and talk about this inside? It's rather complicated and might take a while."

Declan didn't like the sound of that. But he led the guy inside the tight area that served as both an observation tower and living space. He grabbed a bottle of water from the small camping fridge that ran off rechargeable batteries tied to the solar panels on the roof and held it out to the man.

"Okay, so talk," he said. "Who are you, how did you get into my personnel records, and what do you want with me?"

John took a deep drink of water, then saluted Declan with the bottle and sat down in one of the room's two chairs. "As I said, my name is John Loughlin. And I didn't look at your Forest Service records. The organization I'm with has its own folder on you already. To put it simply, I'm here to offer you a job."

Declan leaned back against the wall and folded his arms. He had a feeling this conversation wasn't going to take nearly as long as Loughlin thought. "Someone sent a headhunter all the way out here to scoop up a ranger from the Forest Service? I didn't realize we were in such high demand."

He didn't bother to hide the sarcasm.

John laughed and took another swallow of water. "I'm sure you're a very good forest ranger, Mr. MacBride, but those skills aren't the ones my organization is interested in—as I'm sure you know."

Declan swore under his breath. He should have known. The guy had "corporate manager" written all over him.

"Sorry you wasted your time coming all the way out here, Mr. Loughlin, but if you'd dug a little deeper, you would have learned I never finished that engineering program I started—or the design from my thesis you're so interested in." Damn, he hadn't thought about that part of his life in a long time. "Besides, I'm not involved in that kind of work anymore. I'm a forest ranger. If you leave now, you can probably get back to your car before dark. Feel free to take another bottle of water with you when you go."

Declan started for the door when Loughlin's voice stopped him cold.

"Your engineering acumen—even if garnered at MIT—isn't the skill set my organization is interested in."

Declan wasn't sure why, but alarm bells went off in his head. He eyed the door. There was nothing between him and that exit. And for someone his size, he could be damn fast when he wanted to be.

But he didn't run. Instead, he turned to face Loughlin. Clearly, the man was more dangerous than he appeared. "What other skills do you think I have?"

Loughlin slowly put the cap back on the plastic bottle. "My organization is very interested in your talents as a shifter."

Declan had never heard the word *shifter*, but it wasn't hard to connect the term with the monster he had inside him. The only confusing part was how the man—and his organization—had learned about his secret. And what they wanted from him.

He glanced at the door again. It didn't sound like there was anyone else nearby, but that didn't mean there wasn't anyone out there—just that they were being careful. Declan might be a fast runner when he wanted to be, but he couldn't outrun a gun.

Declan swung his gaze back to Loughlin, looking for

a distinctive bulge that told him the man was carrying a weapon. He didn't see anything, but...

"I'm not carrying a weapon, Mr. MacBride, if that's what you're concerned about," he said as if reading Declan's mind. Loughlin motioned his head toward the door. "And there's no one waiting below with a weapon, either. I'm not here to harass you, hurt you, or try to force you into anything you don't want to do. I simply want to talk to you about a job that can put your unique abilities to good use—in a place where you won't have to feel like you have to hide who you are. If you're not interested in my offer by the time I'm done, I'll walk out of here and forget I ever saw you. I'm just asking for a chance to talk to you."

Declan didn't answer. He hated that Loughlin had walked out of the woods and screwed up the carefully constructed facade that was his so-called life, but curiosity kept him from telling the man to get the hell out. Declan needed to ascertain just how much Loughlin and his organization knew about him. He'd likely have to leave Oregon as soon as Loughlin hiked out of here anyway, of course. Which really sucked because he liked it here.

He sat down on the stool by the map table. "How did you find out about me? Was it Marissa?"

"Your former fiancée?" Loughlin shook his head. "No, we've never talked to her. We didn't think you'd appreciate that."

That was true. Declan didn't want to think she'd rat out his secret to strangers, but then again, things hadn't ended well with his former fiancée—hence the *former*. If the organization Loughlin represented hoped to employ him, using the woman who had ripped out his heart probably wasn't a smart way to gather information on him.

"So, how did you learn that I'm a…monster then?"

Loughlin unscrewed the top from the bottle and downed the rest of the water in a few deep gulps. "First off, you're far from a monster—"

Declan snorted. "Marissa would disagree with you on that."

"Probably," Loughlin agreed. "But that's only because, for all her intelligence, Marissa couldn't have known your talents are purely the result of a genetic mutation that occurs in an extremely tiny portion of the population. In your case, the blending of human DNA with that of an ancient member of the genus *Ursus*. As far as how I found you, it wasn't easy. But if a person knows what to look for, he can pick up on little clues here and there. Physical feats you demonstrated through middle and early high school, the way other animals react around you, police reports that read just a little too strange. From there, it was a matter of getting some of your DNA and knowing what to look for."

Declan hadn't realized his jaw had dropped until it snapped shut. Forget about how they got his DNA. The only thing he cared about was one word. "*Ursus*?"

"Yes, *Ursus*—a bear." John frowned. "You didn't recognize that when you shift, you take on certain obvious bearlike qualities? The size, the strength, the shape of your face and teeth?"

Declan shook his head. "I've never really seen myself when it…happens. I've just seen the horror on other people's faces. I thought I was a werewolf or something."

Loughlin laughed. "While there are a lot of wolf shifters out there, you're definitely not one of them."

It was Declan's turn to frown. "There are others like me?"

"Other shifters? Yes. Several of them work for me. You're the first bear shifter we've found, though. For reasons unknown to us, higher-order canids and felids seem to predominate the shifter ranks."

Declan's mind whirled a thousand miles an hour. He'd spent every minute of his life, or at least every moment since he was fifteen—when he'd started changing—thinking he was some kind of freaking monster. Now this guy walks in here out of nowhere and tells him that not only is there a rational scientific explanation for what he was, but there were other people like him.

"These other shifters—they work for you?"

Loughlin stood and walked over to the small fridge. He opened it and took out another bottle of water. "You mind? That walk out here didn't look so bad on my GPS."

When Declan shook his head, Loughlin took a long swallow, then went back to his seat.

"Yes, these shifters work for me, along with other less unique, but no less valuable people. We partner them up in small teams that accentuate the strengths and skills of each member, then have them carry out missions that best suit those skills."

The idea of being able to work with a team of people who wouldn't view him as a monster when they discovered his secret was damn enticing.

"Okay, you have my attention," he told Loughlin. "What kind of work would I be doing? I mean, I might be one of these shifters you're talking about, but I don't have any special skills that I know of."

Not unless you counted being able to throw someone through a wall.

"You have more skills than you realize—you simply need training to bring them out," Loughlin said. "We won't ask you to do anything that's beyond your capability. Or outside the boundary of your moral compass."

"I'm still listening," Declan said.

"Good. Because I have a new team I'm putting together. You would be working with three other men that I consider to be some of the finest people I've ever had the privilege of meeting." He shook his head. "I won't sugarcoat it. This team will have a very difficult job. You'll be responsible for tracking down and capturing—or killing if necessary—some of the worst predators in the world. Killers, rapists, terrorists, and worse. Some will be everyday, run-of-the-mill psychopaths. But others will be shifters who have gone rogue."

Damn. "Does that happen a lot?"

"Not too often, but when it does, the average cop, federal agent, or soldier isn't prepared to handle it. That's where you and your team will come in."

Declan shifted on the stool. "I'm not sure I could kill someone—shifter or otherwise—no matter what they've done."

Loughlin regarded him thoughtfully. "I know what happened the night Marissa left you, Declan. You exposed yourself to protect her, even though you knew it might cost you."

Declan didn't say anything.

"Something tells me you would have done the same

thing if it hadn't been Marissa—if it'd just been some random stranger," Loughlin said. "Am I right?"

Declan didn't even have to think about it. "Yes."

"That's all I'll ever ask you to do—save a person you might not even know, regardless of what it might cost you."

When Loughlin put it that way, the job didn't sound half-bad. And maybe helping people would be a way to atone for what he'd done that night when he'd protected Marissa. He weighed the pros and cons of the job offer, going back and forth between them while Loughlin patiently sat there drinking his water. This was a big decision and he should sleep on it for a couple days, but it wasn't the kind of choice that could be made with his head. He had to go with his gut, and it was telling him that this was the right thing to do.

"Okay," he finally said. "I'm in."

Loughlin smiled. "And I didn't even have to mention benefits and pay—both of which are damn good, by the way."

Neither of those things had even occurred to Declan.

Loughlin walked over and held out his hand. "Welcome to the Department of Covert Operations, Mr. MacBride."

Chapter 1

Seven Years Later

AFTER TEN YEARS OF WRITING PERFORMANCE REVIEWS, training schedules, and after-action reports, Kendra Carlsen was finally going on a mission. She was so excited, she was practically bouncing in her chair. But getting all geeked up wasn't going to get the work on her desk done—and she had a ton to do before she left.

She was just finishing up the semiannual performance evaluation on Trevor Maxwell's team—outstanding as usual—when intel specialist Evan Lloyd stuck his head in her office.

"Some of us are heading out for lunch. Want to come?"

Kendra was sorely tempted, but she was heading to the airport in—she looked at her watch—three hours. Yikes!

She shook her head as she kept typing. "Thanks for the invite, but I can't. I have way too much to do before I leave."

Evan frowned. "You going on vacation?"

Kendra had a hard time keeping the silly grin off her face. "Mission in Costa Rica."

His eyes went wide. "Seriously?"

"Uh-huh. John wants me to evaluate a big international, interagency training exercise down there."

"You're going down there alone?"

She printed out the report on Trevor's team and signed it, then attached the secret cover page on it and slid the document into an envelope. "Of course not. I'm going with Tate's team. They're taking part in the exercise."

"Oh." Evan shook his head. "Damn, that sounds cool."

Kendra grinned. "Yeah, it does, doesn't it?"

"Well, I'd better let you go then," Evan said. "Watch yourself out there, okay?"

"I will."

Kendra checked her email once more before logging off and thumbing the power button. It felt weird to shut down her computer. The only time she ever did it was when she went on vacation. And running around the hot, sweaty Costa Rican jungle for two weeks was going to be anything but a vacation. But she'd been begging her boss, John Loughlin, for months to go into the field, and now that he'd finally agreed, she was damn well going to make the most of the opportunity. Sure, she would have preferred if her first real mission had been going with Ivy and Landon to check out a hybrid research lab. Or maybe tagging along with Clayne and Danica to serve as backup the next time they took down a bad guy.

But John wasn't ready to go that far…yet. He probably thought that if he sent her into the hot, humid, bug-ridden Costa Rican jungle, she'd hate it so much she'd never bother him about going into the field again. He was wrong. She was going to kick butt out there.

Kendra grabbed her purse and was heading for the door when her cell phone rang. She dug it out of her bag, putting it to her ear as she locked her office. "Hello."

"Hey, Kendra, it's Layla Halliwell," the caller said,

then added, "Ivy's sister? I don't know if you remember me, but we met at her wedding."

Kendra almost laughed. She doubted there were many people who could forget Ivy's younger sister. The girl had the kind of personality that made you smile just thinking about her. She and Layla had both been in the wedding party, so they'd hung out and talked—when the other woman hadn't been hip deep in conversation with Landon's Special Forces buddy, Jayson Harmon.

"Of course I remember you." Kendra started down the hall toward John's office. "What's up?"

"Ivy told me to call you if I ever needed help, and well...I need help."

Kendra frowned. "What's wrong? Are you in trouble or something?"

"No, it's nothing like that," Layla assured her. "I'm looking for a job and was hoping you might be able to get me an interview at the DCO."

Kendra stopped mid-step. *Crap*. If there was one thing Ivy was dead set against, it was her little sister working at the Department of Covert Operations. They might call shifters like Ivy and Layla extremely valuable assets—EVAs for short—but they also gave their human counterparts permission to kill them if they ever got compromised on a mission rather than let them fall into enemy hands. Ivy had been lucky enough to be paired with a partner who would die himself before hurting her; Layla might not be so fortunate. Why couldn't Layla be like Kendra's other friends and call asking to borrow money or something?

"You know, I'd love to, but the DCO isn't really hiring right now," Kendra said slowly.

There was silence on the other end of the line. "Ivy told you to say that, didn't she?"

"What? No, of course not."

"Yes, she did. Damn her." Layla growled in exasperation. "She thinks I want to be a field agent like her, which is ridiculous. I don't know the first thing about guns and spies and covert operations. I'm a psychologist. All I want is to work with other shifters like me. I don't understand why she's so against that."

Kendra felt for Layla, she really did. Being told that someone knew better than you what was good for you and what you should or shouldn't do was tough to handle. It was even tougher for Layla. Knowing there was a whole world of shifters like her out there and being told she couldn't associate with them? Ivy was wrong to do that.

Besides, the DCO could use a person with Layla's education and personal familiarity with the shifter mind. The psychologists the DCO had on staff—both of whom were human—were overwhelmed with the workload and not all that great when it came to helping shifters anyway.

"Kendra, please," Layla begged. "Ivy won't even know you set up the interview."

Right. And how else would Layla get a job with a super-secret organization like the DCO? It wasn't as if Layla could just walk into the personnel office and fill out an application.

"Okay," she said. "I'll get you an interview with the director."

Silence. Then, "Seriously?"

"Seriously. I'll text you the directions to the main office in DC."

"Thanks," Layla said. "I owe you big for this, Kendra."

"It's only an interview," Kendra said. "You have to get the job."

Though something told Kendra that wouldn't be a problem. She stifled a groan as she hung up. Ivy was going to kill her.

She dropped her phone back in her purse and walked into John's office. As she'd suspected, he was more than willing to talk to Layla.

"Just because she's a shifter doesn't mean she's a field operative, John," Kendra reminded him.

He peered at her over his reading glasses, his mouth quirking. "I heard you the first two times you told me. Don't worry. I won't ask her to do anything she doesn't want to do. Now go before you miss your flight."

Actually, Kendra still had an hour before she had to meet Tate and his team at the airfield, but she could take a hint. Telling John she'd see him in two weeks, she left and headed over to the lab. The facility had gotten a complete makeover, thanks to the DCO's new fascination with hybrids.

Six months ago, nobody knew what a hybrid was. There were the DCO's natural-born shifters and that was it. Kendra's very best friend in the whole world, Ivy Donovan, was a feline shifter, but no one would know it just from looking at her. Sure, when Ivy wanted to, the claws and fangs came out and she could be deadly as hell. But most of the time she was a normal woman. The other DCO shifters were like that, too—Clayne Buchanan and his wolf traits, Trevor Maxwell with his coyote abilities, Declan MacBride and his massive physique to match his bear DNA.

Then Ivy and her husband, Landon Donovan, had investigated Keegan Stutmeir, the former East German intelligence officer turned arms dealer. Everyone had thought he'd been kidnapping scientists and doctors to make a new bioweapon. They'd been wrong. He'd been creating man-made shifters, using science to shove animal DNA into humans. Everyone called them hybrids.

While they might share animal traits, hybrids were nothing like shifters. Shifters blended perfectly into normal society. You'd never notice them if they didn't want you to. Hybrids, on the other hand, were bloodthirsty, violent, enraged creatures almost all the time. It had taken a small army of DCO agents along with a group of completely unauthorized Special Forces soldiers from Landon's former team to take down Stutmeir and the pack of hybrids he'd created out in Washington State.

Unfortunately, two of the doctors responsible for creating the process had gotten away. Everyone knew it was only a matter of time before the DCO ran up against the hybrids again.

The official company line was that all the new high-tech equipment at the DCO training complex was to help them "understand" the threat the DCO faced, but that was crap. The assistant director, Dick Coleman, was pushing their doctors not only to understand how Stutmeir had created his hybrids, but to also replicate the process.

All Kendra could say was thank God for Zarina Sokolov. She'd been one of the doctors Stutmeir kidnapped, and had decided to work for the DCO to make sure people like Dick could never replicate Stutmeir's hybrid process—without anyone realizing it, of course.

The Russian doctor looked up from her microscope as Kendra walked in, her reading glasses perched on her nose and a pencil stuck in her messy blond bun. Zarina said something to the gray-haired man beside her, then slid off the stool and came over.

Kendra shivered. "I don't know how you all put up with this place all day. It's freezing in here."

Zarina laughed as she pushed her reading glasses up on her head. "Is that your subtle way of asking if we can do the status briefing outside?"

"If you don't mind?"

"I don't mind." The doctor grabbed her coat from the wooden rack beside the door. "I could use a break."

Once outside the lab, she and Zarina walked along the sidewalk until they were too far from the building for anyone to overhear—although with shifters on the property who had exceptional ears, there could always be someone listening in. They stopped at a section that overlooked one of the complex's training areas. Even though it was November, the sun was out and it was an unseasonably mild day. Certainly warmer than it had been in the lab.

"The last of the DNA from the teenage girl found in Canada has been corrupted," Zarina said softly.

Kendra let out the breath she didn't know she'd been holding. "Ivy will be able to sleep better knowing that."

Ivy and Landon had found the girl three months ago in a farmhouse outside Saskatchewan, Canada— yet another victim of the hybrid program Stutmeir had started before his death at Landon's hands. The fact that the two doctors who'd worked for Stutmeir were continuing to develop the hybrid process after his death was bad enough. That they were using kids as their test subjects was even worse. After Zarina had examined the girl's body, she'd confirmed Ivy's worst fear: her DNA had been used in an attempt to turn the teen into a better hybrid.

Ivy had been terrified the DCO would find out her DNA had been taken, and that Landon had violated the DCO's number-one rule and hadn't killed his shifter partner when it looked like she'd be compromised. Once the DCO figured that out, it wouldn't be too hard to piece together that Ivy and Landon were married, which was in violation of rule number two.

Luckily, Zarina was running the lab now. She'd muddied the waters so much the DCO doctors would never be able to even duplicate Stutmeir's work, much less improve on it.

Kendra watched a group of people navigating the confidence course in the distance for a moment before turning back to Zarina. The Russian doctor was staring off into the distance, too, but she wasn't looking at the team navigating the course. She was focused on the tall, long-haired man standing off to the side watching. Kendra smiled. She didn't have to see the guy's face to know who he was. Just the fact that Zarina was looking at him so intently told her everything she needed to know. It was Tanner Howland, the DCO's resident hybrid. The former Army Ranger had been experimented on by Stutmeir's doctors, and while he was a hybrid, he possessed at least some control over the rage that had consumed the others. At Zarina's insistence, the DCO was trying to help him get his life back together.

She turned back to Zarina. "How's Tanner?"

A blush colored the woman's cheeks. "Amazing."

Oh yeah, the good doctor was all detached professionalism there. Nobody at the DCO understood how Zarina could talk Tanner down from one of his rages with a gentle touch and a few softly spoken words. They all thought she was some kind of hybrid whisperer, but it was obvious Zarina and Tanner had a serious thing for each other. And Kendra for one was damn happy to have her around. Tanner was a sweet guy when he was in control of his hybrid half. When he wasn't, then look the hell out.

"No problems with anger management?" she asked.

Zarina pushed the hair that had escaped from her bun back behind her ear. "Not since that live-fire training exercise he and Clayne took part in during the summer. I think all those counseling sessions with Dr. Anders are helping. The other day I actually found him meditating."

The DCO's psychiatrist, Marlon Anders, had been talking to Tanner three times a week, but Kendra doubted that was the reason the hybrid was calmer these days. No, this was a case of beauty soothing the savage beast. Even Dick had figured that out. Which made Zarina that much more valuable to him. Because if there was one thing that excited Dick more than the prospect of the DCO having hybrids of their own one day, it was having one of their own right now.

"Have you figured out why Tanner acts differently than other hybrids yet?" Kendra asked.

Zarina hesitated. "Maybe. But I don't want to say anything until I'm sure."

Kendra was tempted to push, but didn't. Zarina would tell her once she knew more. They talked for a little while longer about what Zarina was doing to slow down the DCO's work on the hybrid front before Kendra left to go to the cafeteria.

"Be careful," Zarina said. "I've heard they have bugs as big as your head down in Central America."

Kendra shuddered. "Thank you. Now I won't be sleeping for the next two weeks."

She picked up the pace as she neared the cafeteria. She didn't want to be late for her first mission.

She sagged with relief when she spotted Declan MacBride on the far side of the crowded room. At six foot eight, he was hard to miss. It didn't look like he and his team were leaving yet, so she grabbed a cheeseburger and a plate of fries, then hurried over to their table.

Two of Declan's teammates, Brent Wilkins and Gavin Barlow, were arguing about baseball—again. The World Series was over, and neither the Yankees nor the Red Sox had played in it, but the two former homicide detectives had made trash-talking about each other's hometown team a sport all its own.

She pulled out the chair beside Declan and sat down. "Hey."

He barely glanced at her before pushing away his empty plate. "I'm going to get a couple more cheese-burgers. Anybody want anything?"

On the other side of the table, Brent looked at the big bear shifter like he'd just announced he was taking up ballet. "A couple more? You just ate four."

Declan shrugged his broad shoulders. "They're small burgers."

Kendra looked down at her own cheeseburger. It took up half the plate.

Tate Evers let out a snort. At forty, he was the oldest guy on the team, but you'd never know it by looking at him. "You do realize you're going on a mission, not into hibernation, right?"

"Yeah, I know. That's why I'm getting something else to eat. It's a long flight to Costa Rica."

Gavin shook his blond head as Declan walked over to the counter. "A real grizzly bear thinks the amount of food Declan puts away is freaking ridiculous."

Kendra laughed. Poor Declan. His teammates were always teasing him about how much he ate. She was just jealous all that food turned to pure muscle. If she ate half of what he did, she'd roll out of the cafeteria.

She picked up the bottle of ketchup and poured some on her fries. "I was afraid I wouldn't be able to get something to eat before we left."

"No worries there." Tate picked up his fork and dug into a slice of apple pie. "Military flights always run a little late."

She'd picked up her burger and already taken a couple bites when she realized that Brent and Gavin were eyeing her funny.

"Did we miss something?" Gavin asked Tate in his Boston accent.

Kendra frowned. Tate hadn't mentioned she was going with them?

"Tate?" Brent prompted when he didn't answer.

"Kendra's going to Costa Rica with us," he said casually.

"What?"

Kendra turned to see Declan standing there with a big plate of food and a pissed-off look on his handsome face.

"Remember I mentioned John was sending an observer down with us?" Tate said. "Kendra's the observer."

The muscle in Declan's jaw ticked under his perpetual stubble. "No, you didn't mention that."

"I didn't? Huh." Tate shrugged and ate another forkful of pie. "I'm telling you now, then."

Declan let out a grunt that Kendra couldn't translate as either acceptance or disagreement. It was just a grunt.

"John finally decided to let you go into the field, huh?" Gavin asked. "Good for you."

He leaned forward and gave her a fist bump. Kendra laughed as Brent did the same, but her amusement quickly died when she caught sight of Declan. He was sitting beside her, glowering at the cheeseburgers on his plate like he wanted to pound them flat. She stared down at her own burger, not nearly as hungry now. Maybe these next two weeks weren't going to be as much fun as she'd thought.

The flight down to Costa Rico was pure hell. Instead of the roomy C-17 or C-5 Declan had expected, they'd been stuck in the cargo area of a smaller C-130 that had most of the available space filled with pallets of equipment and supplies. He and the rest of the team were relegated to two sets of drop-down benches wedged between stacks of bottled water. Worse, the two rows of uncomfortable seats were facing each other. Brent, Gavin, and Kendra were on one side while he and Tate were on the other. Which meant he had to look at her the whole way. There was a time when he would have thought spending a whole day gazing at Kendra was time well spent, but being forced into close proximity with her now made him mad as hell.

Or maybe he was still pissed off at Tate. He and the former U.S. Marshal had gotten into it pretty good before leaving the tarmac at Anacostia-Bolling.

"Why the hell is Kendra coming with us?" Declan demanded when he finally got Tate alone. "There's no reason for us to be going down there, but there's even less for her. She doesn't even add anything to the team."

Unless you counted long, blond hair, big blue eyes, and the sexiest butt he'd ever seen.

"Look, I know you don't want to be around Kendra," Tate said, his mouth tightening under his mustache. "I'm not thrilled at the idea of her tagging along with us either, but John wants her to get some field time on a low-risk mission—sort of a reward for all the hard work she's been doing."

Declan swore. "You know that's crazy, right? There's no such thing as a low-risk mission, not when every third person in the place we're going carries a weapon. Is John willing to let her—or one of us—get killed just so he can give her a freaking *reward*?"

"No one's going to get killed," Tate shot back. "And unless you want to quit the DCO in protest, there's only one option—shut up and soldier on."

"I was a forest ranger, not a soldier."

"Yeah? Well, go over there and take a look in your rucksack. I'm pretty sure forest rangers don't carry the amount of weaponry you have shoved in that bag."

Tate was right, but Declan still growled in frustration.

His friend sighed. "I know the situation sucks, but it is what it is. You have to get your head right or somebody is going to get hurt. But it won't be because of Kendra; it'll be because of you."

That had pretty much been the end of the conversation. Tate had left Declan there, staring at the cracked asphalt of the runway, wondering how he was going to handle two weeks in the same jungle as Kendra.

But no answer had been forthcoming then, and now, as he sat wedged into a seat that was way too small for him, he still didn't have one.

Being so close to her shouldn't bother him. He'd gotten over his crush on her and moved on. As he stole occasional glances at her, he knew that was a crock of shit. He'd tried; he really had. But since deciding four months ago that enough was enough and it was past time he stop pining for a woman who refused to even acknowledge his existence, he'd been miserable as hell.

He bit back a growl. Damn, he was pathetic. But there was something about Kendra that attracted him like a bear to honey. He might have chuckled at the analogy if it wasn't so damn fitting.

Kendra had already been firmly established with the DCO when he'd shown up seven years ago. Back then, she'd mostly shadowed the training officers and watched—taking notes, making her quiet observations and recommendations directly to the trainers. At the time, Declan had been coming off the disaster that was his relationship with Marissa, so he hadn't been interested in getting involved with any woman. Plus, he'd been consumed with trying to fit in with his team

and learn everything they had to teach him. He had no
military training to fall back on, so there'd been a lot to
learn. By the time he'd gotten his head above water, he
already had it bad for the behavioral scientist.

Unfortunately, he couldn't string together two sen-
tences whenever he was around her. He wasn't a Romeo
with the ladies by any stretch of the imagination, but
he'd never gotten tongue-tied around women—not even
his former fiancée. But it wasn't hard to see why Kendra
had that effect on him. She was beautiful and smart,
made him smile like no other woman ever had, made the
camouflage uniform she was wearing look way sexier
than it should, and she smelled delicious as hell.

His nose usually wasn't that good—mostly because
he never used it—except when it came to Kendra. Then
it worked just fine. Sometimes he could pick up her
scent from the far side of the DCO training complex.
Sitting this close to her now, it was the only thing he
could smell, and it was overwhelming. He closed his
eyes, hoping to block out her scent, but it was useless.
Her pheromones surrounded him, holding him prisoner
and refusing to let go.

He'd tried to catch Kendra's eye for years and fallen
flat on his face every time—because she was too busy
obsessing over that jerk Clayne Buchanan. It had taken
Declan a while, but he finally realized he was wasting
his time—and his life—waiting for her and had decided
to move on.

And it had been working. He'd gotten to the point
where he didn't think about her 24/7, didn't subcon-
sciously sniff the air to catch her scent the minute
he drove onto the DCO complex. He'd even dated a

few women he'd thought might have had long-term potential. There might not have been that same animal attraction he felt with Kendra, and he'd have to hide his shifter side, but that wasn't too high a price to pay to be normal, right?

Before today he thought he'd been well on his way to forgetting about Kendra and getting on with his so-called life. Then John had decided to send her on this mission and everything Declan thought was in the past came right back and smacked him in the face.

For the first time in forever, he wanted to put his fist through a wall. But as he felt his anger rise again, he realized he wasn't angry at John or Tate or even Kendra. He was mad at himself for being so screwed up that the mere thought of being in the same jungle as the blond-haired, blue-eyed beauty could get him so twisted up in knots.

Damn, he really was pathetic.

Chapter 2

KENDRA WAS READY TO ADMIT THIS FIELD THING hadn't been one of her brightest ideas. So far, all she'd officially observed was the color green—as in the endless jungle that threatened to grow over anything that stopped moving for more than five minutes—and that this whole thing was stupid—as in stomping through the undergrowth, scouting objectives and choke points, setting up landing sites for helicopters that were never going to be coming, and generally wasting their time.

Of course, maybe she wouldn't have felt nearly as foolish stumbling around in the jungle if she were carrying a weapon. But Tate had pointed out that her official task for this exercise was to observe—and that didn't require a weapon. At least he'd given her one of the GPS units and a map, so she could track their movement through the jungle. If not for that, she would have lost her mind already.

It wasn't long after they'd arrived at the airport outside San Jose that she'd thought maybe the rest of the mission wasn't going to be as thrilling as the covert flight down. First, she and the guys had been herded directly from the aircraft into the back of a covered cargo truck. Then they'd driven south for the next seven hours, stopping only once to get gas. When she'd wondered out loud if the truck was going to drive them all the way to Panama, Tate told her that Costa Rica didn't have a military of their own, so having heavily armed Americans close to the cities was bad for public relations.

"The government prefers to keep us out of sight as much as possible," Tate added.

"I thought we were invited down here," she'd said.

He shrugged. "Invited is a relative term. They want the U.S. here to help train the police, but they don't want to be too obvious about it."

From the reading she'd done on the local politics, Kendra understood that, but it posed an even bigger question. "If they want to keep this as a small operation, why is the DCO sending people?"

Tate let out a short laugh. "They don't know we're DCO, remember? To them, we're Homeland Security down here teaching their law enforcement how to protect the country from terrorist organizations and internal threats."

"If that's the case, why isn't there a real team of experts from Homeland Security down here instead of us?"

"Rumors are that the first DCO team sent down here used the exercise as a cover to get into the country to rescue some congressman's son from a group of rebels who'd kidnapped him for ransom," Tate explained. "Since then, I think it was just a case of us getting stuck with the job because Homeland doesn't want it."

When they'd reached the base camp deep in the mountainous jungles of the huge La Amistad National Reserve and met the other people they'd be working with, Kendra had immediately understood why John and some of the Committee members wanted this exercise reevaluated. It wasn't exactly a well-run operation. In fact, it seemed sort of like a hot mess.

There were twenty of them in all—eight local cops, eight marines, and four drug enforcement agents. It was obvious from the get-go that nobody trusted or liked anyone else, and most of them didn't want to be there. The DEA agents in charge of the training exercise didn't appreciate the marines encroaching on their territory. The marines, who seemed to be there simply because they were part of the bargain that came with using the navy helicopters that would be part of the exercise, didn't seem to appreciate being involved in the operation. And both groups looked down their noses at the odd team supposedly from Homeland Security. They probably thought Kendra and the guys were CIA spies. The local police officers wouldn't talk to anyone, clearly wishing they didn't have to be included in an exercise that had apparently devolved into more of a political hot potato than useful training.

Kendra glanced at Declan as they trudged through the undergrowth. She knew he was upset about her tagging along, but he hadn't said two words to her since they'd gotten to Costa Rica. Figures. The moment she decided to give Declan a shot, he didn't so much as notice her anymore.

Did she have luck with men or what?

She'd wasted years fixating on Clayne, only to discover there was absolutely zero chemistry between them. The worst part? Her damn compatibility software had told her she and Clayne weren't a match years ago. Instead, it had correctly identified Danica as the woman he was supposed to be with. But did she pay attention to her own damn matchmaking program? No. She only wished she'd realized they were so completely incompatible before they'd slept together. Fortunately, Clayne was just as eager to forget the indiscretion as she was, and they'd sworn to never tell a soul about it. Well, Ivy knew, but that didn't count.

As Kendra climbed over a huge fallen tree, she looked for Declan and realized he'd disappeared again. For a big guy, he could move like a ghost. She had no idea where he went, but he'd been slipping off like this the entire day. Recon, she guessed, though she didn't know what he was looking for. Other than about a million monkeys, sloths, birds, and reptiles of every variety, they hadn't seen another soul out here.

No surprise there. Not only was La Amistad a pristine nature preserve, but their training exercise had taken them into the very deepest, most inhospitable sections of the park, close to the border with Panama. Plus, it turned out that November was the rainiest time of the year for this part of the country. Not exactly the peak of the eco-tourism season. That meant they had the whole jungle to wander around in without worrying about running into another person. And considering what Tate had told her about the government being a little uncomfortable with their presence, the timing and location for this exercise probably wasn't an accident.

But if that was the case, why did Declan disappear every thirty minutes or so?

Kendra searched the surrounding forest again and caught sight of the bear shifter jogging into the clearing. She sighed as he brushed past her to catch up with Tate. Now that she'd started looking at Declan as something more than a coworker, she couldn't help but notice he was a lot more attractive than she'd realized. Last night, she'd seen him in nothing but his uniform pants as he'd rinsed off in a stream after they'd stopped to make camp, and damn, he was scrumptious. Why hadn't she ever noticed how hunky that body of his was?

She was starting to think she was really slow when it came to seeing what was right in front of her face.

They spent the next fifteen minutes skirting a rocky ridge that was too steep to go over. Even going around it was hard work and everyone was breathing heavy by the time the group leader—a gruff DEA agent named Carmichael—called for a break. Kendra opened her canteen and took a long drink. She had no idea this part of the world had such rough country. One second they were climbing up the side of a five-hundred-foot ridgeline, the next, they found themselves slopping their way through swampy marshes. And the moment they dragged themselves out of the mud, they'd be in the middle of a thick jungle where it seemed like the foliage clung to them every step they took. It was beautiful, but it was hard not being intimidated by the sheer wildness of it all.

At least it wasn't hot. Even though she'd read all the weather profiles for Costa Rica, some part of her still thought the jungle would be hot and steamy—like in the movies. But it hardly ever got much warmer than seventy during the day, and at night it was down in the fifties.

The worst part was the rain. Most of it didn't make it through the thick jungle canopy, but water constantly dripped off every branch and leaf. Within two days, she didn't have a single piece of clothing that was completely dry, and sleeping turned into more of an exercise in finding a dry spot than in getting any actual rest.

Voices drifted her way as she screwed the cap back on her canteen. She looked up to see Declan and Tate deep in conversation. From the looks on their faces, they were worried about something. She stowed her canteen and walked over to join them. Brent and Gavin followed.

"What's wrong?" she asked quietly.

Tate hesitated. "I'm not sure. But I'm getting a funny feeling that someone has us out here playing human mine detector."

That didn't sound good. "What does that mean?"

"Pull out your map," Declan said.

She pulled the carefully folded laminated map out of one of the cargo pockets of her pants and opened it. She'd taken the readings from the GPS Tate had given her and logged their position every few hours. Declan stepped closer and pointed at the dots she'd made on the map.

"I know it doesn't look like it because someone is trying to make it hard to see, but we're not stomping around aimlessly. We're being run through a loose search pattern. Somebody has us looking for something."

Studying the map while standing so close to all that muscle was difficult and Kendra had to force herself to focus. Looking at the placement of the dots on the map, she could see how they might seem like a search pattern. She'd simply thought they were supposed to move back and forth through the region like this.

"Maybe it's just easier to have us move in a relative straight back and forth pattern?" she suggested.

Declan shook his head. "I'd agree if we weren't occasionally pulled off our path and routed through specific areas. Like that sheltered valley we just left. Or that big bend in the river we passed this morning."

Kendra followed along as he pointed them out on the map with his long fingers, then looked up at him. "What do you think we're supposed to be looking for?"

"I don't know," Tate said. "But I'm not comfortable knowing we're only going to find out the answer after we've stepped into the middle of something."

Hence the human-mine-detector reference.

Kendra glanced at Declan to see him looking off into the jungle again.

"What aren't you guys telling me?" she asked. "Declan, where have you been disappearing to all day?"

It was Tate who answered. "Declan thinks someone's following us and has been since late last night."

She pinned Declan with a look. "You *think*? Or you know?"

He met her gaze. "There's definitely someone out there, but they're quiet—too quiet. And they're keeping their distance most of the time. Every once in a while though, I'll hear them move closer, but they disappear whenever I try to get a look at them."

Kendra glanced at each of the guys. She knew they trusted Declan's instincts, so that meant she did, too. "Should we tell the others?"

"Tell them what?" Tate asked. "That we're suspicious about the coordinates we've been following for the last three days? That the bear shifter on our team is certain he's heard someone following us, but that they're a couple miles away? Would you believe any of that if you didn't work for the DCO?"

He had a point. "So, what do we do?"

"We keep our eyes open and be ready if the shit hits the fan," Declan said.

Great.

"Declan, if things get ugly," Tate added, "I want you to get Kendra out of here."

Declan didn't look happy about that, but he nodded.

Kendra clenched her jaw. They were talking like she wasn't even there. "I can take care of myself."

"Not without a weapon, you can't," Tate said.

"That's because you didn't give me one."

"You're right, I didn't. Which means you can't take care of yourself, can you?"

Kendra opened her mouth to argue, but DEA Agent Carmichael shouted for everyone to get back on the trail. Declan and Tate walked away, leaving Kendra with nothing to do but follow and fume. If she could just tell them how she'd handled herself in Washington State, or how calm, cool, and collected she'd been under pressure breaking into the DCO's record repository, they'd change their tune. But she couldn't say anything about either of those things, so they thought she was nothing more than a mild-mannered behavioral scientist who occasionally helped out by setting up training for the DCO field teams.

Regardless of how she felt, though, she kept close to the guys—Declan in particular. She might be mad, but she wasn't stupid. If anything happened, she wanted to be right next to the big shifter.

They'd barely made it fifteen minutes down the path when Declan came to a sudden halt and held up his arm, signaling them to stop.

"What is it?" Tate demanded, immediately at their side. He'd already flipped the safety off his M4 carbine.

"They've moved in front of us now, and to either side

of our line of travel." Declan tested the breeze with his nose. "They're not even trying to hide it now. We're being surrounded."

Carmichael strode over, an annoyed look on his face. "What the hell are you saying?"

"He's saying we're about to be attacked," Tate said softly. He took up a defensive position several steps away from Declan's left shoulder while Gavin and Brent quickly moved up behind Kendra, putting her in the middle of a protective box.

"And how the hell does he know that?" Carmichael demanded.

Tate gave him a sidelong glance. "You don't surround a group of armed people if you want to ask them to play poker."

Carmichael opened his mouth to reply when a rifle grenade hit the ground a few feet from where they stood.

Declan shoved Kendra to the ground the second he heard the pop of the rifle grenade's projecting cartridge go off. He didn't have to look to know the rest of his team would be on the ground, too. He had no idea if the other men took cover, and there wasn't much he could do to warn them. They weren't going to believe they were in trouble until it'd been rammed up their asses sideways.

There was a sharp crack of an explosion, followed by small fragments smacking into the trees and dirt around him and Kendra. Men shouted, some cursed, then bullets started flying. Damn, he hated being right sometimes.

He'd woken up around 0200 last night with the

feeling that someone was watching their camp. He'd gone to check it out, running out into the rain-soaked jungle in just his pants and boots with his M4, only to hear whoever it was slip away before he'd gotten close. That had really worried him. Whoever was out there was really frigging fast. They'd been playing with Declan the entire day, like they were testing him, just to see if he'd know they were there. But when Declan had heard approaching movement from three different sides a few minutes ago—including the direction they'd been heading—he knew playtime was over.

He heard feet crashing over the jungle floor before the rumble of the initial explosion died down. There were a lot of them, and they were coming fast.

Declan's first thought was to run straight toward the force attacking from the north, which was most likely where he'd find their leader. Take him out and the rest of the men would be lost.

But Declan couldn't do what his gut and his training shouted at him to do. He had to protect Kendra and get her the hell out of there.

He jumped up, scooped Kendra into his arms, and ran in the only direction that seemed to be clear to them— south. He hated being herded anywhere, but it was the best option available.

Behind him, he heard Tate, Brent, and Gavin trying to get their ragtag group to work together in an organized retreat. Declan had a pretty good sense of the numbers they were up against. If Tate couldn't make that happen, there was a good possibility no one was going to make it out of this jungle alive.

"What happened?" Kendra asked.

Declan expected her to be freaking out or shouting for him to put her down. But instead she was holding on tightly while trying to see over his shoulder. Hell, she was probably calmer than most of the men around them.

"Whoever has been shadowing us all day finally decided it was time to start the ambush."

He jumped a small stream. Carrying Kendra, his weapon, and his rucksack, he couldn't move as fast as he normally would, but he still could have outrun the others if he wanted to. But running off into the jungle wouldn't help keep her safe. Even now, he could hear the bad guys sprinting hard to get ahead of them, repositioning themselves to keep the jaws of the ambush clamped closed.

Tate must have succeeded in getting everyone going in the same direction because Brent, Gavin, and several of the marines and DEA agents moved in front of Declan, creating a wedge that'd hopefully break through the attackers' line.

Declan finally got a visual on the enemy, and what he saw shocked the hell out of him. He assumed they'd stumbled across a drug cartel farming site or perhaps a small group of revolutionaries—FARC maybe—hiding out in the huge, uninhabited tracts of the La Amistad Park. But while he saw a few faces that looked local, most looked European. He'd bet some were even American. They all wore military-style uniforms and carried state-of-the-art military weaponry. This wasn't some lightly armed guerilla camp they'd stumbled on. He didn't know what the hell it was.

The marine right beside them got hit and went down hard. Declan grimaced as their effort to escape the ambush started to slow. He needed to be able to shoot back, and he couldn't do that with Kendra in his arms. He set her down and pulled his weapon off his back.

But instead of cowering behind him like he expected her to do, Kendra surprised him by scrambling over to the body of the downed marine and pulling the man's M4 out of his lifeless hands. As Declan watched, she dropped the magazine, checked to see how many rounds were left in it, then expertly reloaded the weapon and eyeballed the ejection port to make sure a round was chambered. Then she took it a step further and searched the man's body for extra magazines and ammo.

Where the hell had she learned how to do all that?

"Don't shoot unless you have a target right in front of you," he told her. "The way our people are running around like chickens with their heads cut off, you have a better chance of hitting one of ours than one of theirs."

She nodded and kept herself positioned right on his shoulder as they started moving forward again.

Tate caught up to them, dragging less than a dozen stragglers with him. Damn. Their guys were going down fast.

"I was able to get a call to the base camp on the satellite phone," Tate yelled. "They're not too happy about it, but they've agreed to pull two Seahawks off interdiction duty to evac us out of here. They're coming into that landing zone we cleared a few hours back. We just have to stay alive long enough to get there."

Someone fired a weapon beside Declan and he jerked his head around to see Kendra aiming her M4 at a man just barely visible in the branches of a tree twenty feet away. Declan lifted his weapon in that direction, but the camouflaged sniper was already falling to the ground.

Well, shit.

With Tate leading the way, they started moving toward their goal, picking up stragglers and wounded as they went.

—〰〰—

It had taken them the better part of the day to traverse the rough terrain between the site of the ambush and the landing zone. On the trip out, they'd covered at least two swampy areas, a practically vertical ridgeline, and about three miles of thick jungles in that time. It had been exhausting even when they'd been moving slowly. Now they had to do it again faster, all the while being hounded every step of the way by a group of men intent on killing them.

Kendra had saved her ammo as long as she could, but their attackers were relentless and wouldn't let them have a foot of real estate without extracting a price in blood. She'd just killed men. This wasn't like being out in Washington State, where she'd been facing monsters. These had been men. But she'd had no choice. It was what she had to do if they were going to get out of this alive.

As good as she was at protecting herself, she would have been dead three times over if it wasn't for Declan, Tate, Gavin, and Brent. She'd known they were good— she'd evaluated their training and read their after-action reports for years. But she hadn't known just how truly skilled they really were.

To say that they worked like a well-oiled machine

was an understatement. It was more like their minds were linked as one. They never spoke, never even gestured. But they covered each other's backs—and those of the people depending on them—like nothing she'd ever imagined. And yet even as good as they were, they couldn't protect every single person with them. Not when their attackers seemed willing to die to get to them.

They were still about half a mile from the landing zone when the ambushers suddenly broke off the attack.

"What the hell are they doing?" one of the marines gasped out. He was half carrying, half dragging a lance corporal who was already bleeding through the pressure dressings wrapped around the wound in his right thigh. "They had us on the ropes. Why the hell would they stop now?"

"I don't know, but we're almost there," Tate called. "Just hold this pace for ten more minutes and we'll make it."

"Tate, someone's coming," Declan said urgently from beside Kendra. He hadn't moved from that position the entire time. And while she'd taken down a few of their attackers, he'd taken down a whole lot more.

"Are they coming back?" Tate asked. "Which direction?"

"Not them. Someone else, moving fast—too fast."

Declan turned in a circle, while the marines and cops eyed him in confusion. Kendra was already getting a queasy sensation in her stomach when the bear shifter's attention locked in one direction.

"There," he said. "They're coming at us like a shot."

Tate and the others aimed their weapons in that direction. Seconds later, the underbrush exploded in movement. Three men came through, moving so fast they were almost a blur. Gunfire erupted, but even with all the shooting, they didn't go down right away.

Crap.

"They're hybrids!" Kendra shouted, aiming her M4 straight into a creature's chest and emptying the entire magazine into it.

Declan and the other men took down another, but that still left one hybrid, and it was running straight at her. With her weapon empty and no time to reload, she knew she was done for. The thing's glowing red eyes filled her vision.

Then a roar so loud that it literally shook the trees around her filled the air and Declan charged in front of her, wrapping the hybrid in a crushing bear hug. Declan had known bullets weren't going to put this thing down in time to save her, she realized, so he'd shifted right there in front of everyone.

Kendra's eyes widened as the normally gentle shifter squeezed the hybrid so hard she heard the creature's ribs snap over its growls and snarls. Declan roared again and slammed the hybrid into the trunk of a tree so hard that everything else in the hybrid snapped.

Declan turned to face them, his elongated canine teeth visible to everyone. "More are coming."

Tate, Brent, and Gavin took the scene in stride, but it proved too much for most of the others. They freaked out and lost it, babbling about not signing up for this crap. Kendra couldn't blame them. It wasn't every day that a person realized everything they thought they knew was a lie—that monsters really did exist.

Tate did his best to keep everyone moving again, but

it was hard. The hybrids hit them three more times as they ran for the landing zone. And taking them out went through what little ammo they had left at an alarming rate. Kendra quickly reloaded her last magazine in her carbine. They were all short on ammo.

Worse, there were more injured men than healthy ones to carry them, and Gavin and Brent were forced to help keep everyone moving at the cost of defending the group. If it wasn't for Declan and his shifter strength, they would have all been wiped out. Of course, now many of the men, especially the locals, were just as frightened of Declan as they were of the hybrids.

She wasn't sure how, but they made it to the landing zone to find the two navy helicopters waiting, their rotors thumping at half speed, ready to take off. Kendra and Declan ended up on one of the Seahawks with a wounded DEA agent, two local cops, and two wounded marines. The marines were in bad shape—the hybrids had torn into them with claws and fangs, causing far more damage than any bullet would. Both were slipping in and out of unconsciousness. If they didn't get them to a hospital soon, they weren't going to make it.

"Get us the hell out here!" Declan shouted to the pilot. "They're coming back!"

The crew chief of their evac bird didn't have a clue who Declan was talking about, but he obviously recognized a serious situation when he saw it. He strapped the two local cops having trouble with their lap restraints into their seats, then ordered the pilot to lift off.

Bullets hit the helicopter the second it left the ground.

The navy pilot knew his stuff, though. He dipped the Seahawk in a sideways tilt, slipping them across the landing zone away from the direction of the incoming fire, all while flying no more than five feet off the ground. Once out of immediate danger, the pilot leveled off and started to climb. Kendra could already see the other helicopter clearing the treetops. She let out the breath she'd been holding. They hadn't started to gain altitude themselves yet, but they would be any second. They were all going to make it.

"What the hell...?" the crew chief shouted from his position at the open side door.

Kendra didn't have to wonder what he was talking about, not when the crew chief drew his pistol from a chest holster and started shooting out the open door. A moment later, a snarling hybrid jumped onto the helicopter. *Crap!* The pilot had kept them too low for too long.

Seeing a ravaging monster with red eyes, fangs, and claws was just too much to take for the pilot and copilot. Kendra was shocked the helicopter didn't go down on the spot. Luckily, the pilot got himself back together and steadied the Seahawk. The crew chief hit the hybrid at least three times in the chest and abdomen, but as Kendra knew from experience, the damn things were slow to react to even life-ending injuries.

Declan launched himself at the hybrid, yanking the creature off the crew chief and slamming the thing against the side door frame, smashing its head repeatedly against the metal supports there.

Kendra tried to get out of her seat to help, but the helicopter was spinning around so wildly she couldn't get her seat belt undone. Even if she could, there were so many flying arms, legs, and claws, she knew she'd be risking her life just getting near them.

But she couldn't just sit there and watch Declan fight this thing on his own.

She finally got her lap restraint undone and clambered around the bench seats, almost slipping on the huge amount of blood spilling on the floor of the cabin from the dead crew chief. But she made it to Declan's side, spreading her legs wide in an attempt to keep from being thrown out the open door of the almost out-of-control helicopter.

Declan must have seen her out of the corner of his eye because he let out a growl and shoved the hybrid against the interior wall of the bird, pinning its head and one arm at the same time. The move left Declan open to the hybrid's claws, but Kendra jumped in before the creature had a chance to do any damage, pushing the barrel of her M4 into the thing's chest right over his heart and unloading the five remaining rounds.

The bullets ripped right through the hybrid's body and out the side of the helicopter. Thank God there wasn't anything critical in that part of the airframe. But it had been worth the risk—even a hybrid needed a heart to pump its blood.

Declan flung the creature out the door with a growl. They were a good hundred feet above the ground now, and the crash the hybrid made as it slammed into the treetops was audible even over the thump of the rotors.

Kendra sagged against one of the seats. Holy crap, they'd done it. They were going to get out of here.

Then something slammed into the underside of the Seahawk like a bull had kicked it. Kendra would have fallen out the open door if Declan hadn't grabbed her and pushed her toward the bench seats. As she scrambled to get a grip on something solid, the torn, lifeless body of the crew chief tumbled out of the helicopter, leaving a trail of blood on the floor in its wake.

Crap. She'd jinxed them. Whatever had just hit them was way bigger than small arms fire. The helicopter bucked and spun out of control, alarm buzzers screaming in warning as smoke filled the cargo compartment. Kendra was so disoriented, she could barely tell up from down.

The pilot and copilot shouted at each other, fighting the controls to keep the aircraft up in the air. But she knew their heroics were in vain. They were going down—right back into the middle of the pack of hybrids and soldiers who had been trying their damndest to kill every one of them for the last three hours.

Declan had known they were going to crash even before the rocket-propelled grenade had slammed into the belly of the copter. The damage they'd taken right after lifting off had done something to the controls. Worse, the pilot had been hit and was barely able to keep the aircraft flying straight and level. By the time the hybrid had jumped on board to tear anyone he could reach to shreds, Declan was wondering what the hell they'd done to deserve this. It was like some force was acting against them, doing everything in its power to make sure they never got out of this jungle.

He'd read all the reports that Landon and Ivy had written about hybrids, but it was one thing reading about them and a completely different thing fighting them. He couldn't believe the amount of damage it took to put

down one of those things. It was as if they were too
stupid to know when they'd been mortally wounded. Or
maybe they simply didn't care.

If he hadn't been so worried about the helicopter
spinning madly out of control and that they were probably going to be dead in a few seconds, he would have
told Kendra how well she'd handled herself. She'd
stayed calm throughout the long march to the landing
zone, taking out soldiers and hybrids like she'd been
born to do it. And her actions in the helicopter when
she'd put down that hybrid to save his life? That had
been impressive.

Of course, none of that mattered. Because in a fight
with gravity, gravity won every time.

Nevertheless, that pragmatic outlook didn't keep
him from throwing his body over Kendra's when the
helicopter lurched and took a header toward the ground.
He shifted just before they hit, tensing every muscle
in his body in an attempt to create a protective barrier
around her.

He told himself he was doing it because it'd been
Tate's last orders, but a voice in the back of his head told
him that was bullshit.

The impact was horrendous, the sound of crushing
metal, snapping rotor blades, and breaking trees overwhelming everything else—even the screams of pain
and fear.

He was actually surprised after it was all over that
he was still alive. Movement beneath him told him that
Kendra was, too. Damn, she was one tough woman.
Thank God.

Acrid smoke began to fill what was left of the

helicopter, and his thoughts immediately turned to fear of a fire. It would be just their luck to survive the crash only to die in the flames.

There was another reason to get out of the helicopter—the smoke would draw the soldiers and hybrids to come finish the job they'd started. They'd been in the air for a few minutes after getting hit, but he had no idea how far they'd traveled from the landing zone. He knew they didn't have long.

He pulled back to look down at Kendra. Some of her long hair had come free of her ponytail to hang down in her face, and he had to fight the urge to push it back. "You okay?"

She coughed. "Yeah. You?"

"I'm good. But we need to get out of here."

He looked around, trying to orient himself in the hazy smoke-filled mess that had been the main section of the helicopter. It took a second for him to figure out which way was up—the Seahawk had landed on its side, blocking the door he'd recently tossed the hybrid out. But it didn't matter because the whole front of the helicopter was gone. It must have been ripped off as they'd crashed through the trees. He didn't want to think about what had happened to the pilot and copilot.

Declan turned to see what remained of the other occupants only to find Kendra already checking on the two wounded marines. Declan crawled over the debris to kneel beside her. What he saw turned his stomach. The hybrid's claws had gotten to one marine, while the impact had gotten to the other. Declan knew their deaths had been anything but painless.

Noise came from the back of the helicopter and

Declan lifted his head to see the two local cops slowly coming their way. Declan got them moving in the right direction, then came back to help Kendra pull the DEA agent out of his seat. The guy was unconscious and had a dark purple bruise across his face and temple. He didn't look good, but Declan carried him outside and gently set him down on the ground anyway. The man's heart beat with an unsteady rhythm. Declan swore. He hadn't had a chance to learn the guy's name, and now it looked like he never would.

He heard a crashing sound behind him and looked over his shoulder to see Kendra dragging out one of the dead marines. When he moved to help her, she waved him off.

"I've got him," she said. "Go get the other guy."

Declan nodded and ducked inside. The helicopter might not have caught fire, but it still didn't seem right to leave them in there.

He'd just gotten the second marine positioned respectfully away from the downed bird when he heard more noise coming from the wreck. Kendra was tossing stuff out of the helicopter—weapons, ammo, a ruck-sack, extra canteens, what looked like ration bars, and a first-aid kit. Okay, it was official. She was a whole lot calmer in a stressful situation than he'd ever imagined she would be. If he wasn't already hopelessly in love with her, he would be now.

A few moments later, she came stumbling out, coughing and hacking. Declan grabbed one of the canteens and held it out to her.

"You okay?" he asked.

She nodded, taking a big gulp of water, then put the cap back on the canteen. "How far away did we get?"

"Not far enough," he said. "We flew farther than I thought before the crash, maybe two miles. But I can already hear them coming. They'll probably be able to hone right in on the smoke coming off the crash."

"Then we need to get moving."

As Kendra started gathering up the gear she'd tossed out of the smoldering wreck, Declan checked on the other survivors. The two locals were whispering to each other as he approached the injured DEA agent. He could hear them clearly, but they were speaking in Spanish, so it really didn't matter that he could overhear everything they said. But while he didn't understand the words, he got the gist of their tone—they were scared to death and wondering if staying with Declan and Kendra was their best bet.

He knelt down beside the DEA agent, preparing to carry him—at least until they had enough time to rig up some kind of travois or litter—but the man was already dead. Between all the blood he'd lost, shock, and head trauma, there was no way of telling what had done him in.

Declan pulled the DEA agent's rain jacket off to cover his face. Hopefully the soldiers and hybrids wouldn't disturb the man's body or those of the dead marines. But it was anyone's guess what hybrids considered an acceptable way to honor the dead.

"Where the hell are they going?" Kendra asked.

Declan spun around just in time to see the two police officers slip into a dense section of jungle and disappear.

"I guess they figure they have better odds on their own than staying here with a monster as bad as the things trying to kill them."

Kendra swore and shouldered one of the packs loaded with extra supplies. "What about the pilot and copilot? Should we go look for them?"

He winced as he envisioned the violence that had ripped apart the front of the Seahawk. Neither of those men were still alive. "No. Come on, we need to be well away from this place before the hybrids show up."

Declan shouldered the other pack and the M4, then took off at a steady trot he hoped Kendra would be able to hold for a while. He didn't really have a plan, other than to keep both of them alive long enough to get out of the immediate area so he'd have a chance to come up with something better. Right now, that was about the best he could hope for. If the rest of his team were here, it would be different. But with just the two of them going up against what seemed like an impossible number of trained soldiers and hybrid killing machines, he wasn't holding out much hope.

Chapter 3

ANGELO RIOS INHALED DEEPLY, ALMOST GROANING IN appreciation as the aroma from the grill wafted across the terrace. His former captain might not be in charge of their Special Forces A-Team anymore, but the man still knew how to take care of them. Landon and Ivy had literally emptied the freezer for him and fellow Special Forces operator Derek Mickens. And the weather today was perfect for grilling.

"So, why's the army sending you guys to a place like Tajikistan?" Clayne asked. "Not exactly a name you see in the news a lot."

Angelo grabbed another handful of tortilla chips and sat back in his chair. He'd asked his first sergeant the same thing when the operational order had come down.

"Tajikistan's proximity to Afghanistan makes it an ideal location for terrorist safe havens," he explained. "According to the State Department, the amount of fighters, weapons, and drugs flowing back and forth across the border finally got bad enough for them to ask for help. We're going in to help conduct counterterrorism training."

"How long are you guys going to be there?" Landon asked as he flipped the burgers, steaks, and chicken on the grill—in that order.

"Probably two or three months, but it could be as long as six." Derek frowned down at his bottle of beer. "So, why is Kendra in Costa Rica again?"

Angelo almost laughed. Derek never was a subtle guy. While the medic liked hanging out with Landon as much as Angelo did, Derek had mainly come on the impromptu vacation with the hope of seeing Kendra again. According to him, they'd hit it off at Landon and Ivy's wedding.

Landon moved the chicken to a cooler part of the grill. "I think it's the boss's way of showing his appreciation for all the hard work she does for him."

Derek frowned. "By sending her to Costa Rica? Couldn't he just give her a few extra days of leave?"

Landon chuckled. "John probably would have, but Kendra has her own idea of fun. She wanted to go."

"I don't think fun had anything to do with it." Angelo grinned as he reached for his bottle of beer. "She probably heard Derek was coming up here and figured getting out of town was the best way to avoid having to tell him she's not interested."

Derek gave him a sour look. "You just don't want to admit that Kendra and I made a connection. Admit it. We're meant to be together."

Angelo almost choked on his beer. "You made a connection? All you did was dance with her, dude."

"There's dancing, and then there's *dancing*, Tex-Mex." Derek shook his head with a snort. "Why am I bothering? You're not even qualified to evaluate my relationship with Kendra. You've never connected with a woman in your life."

That wasn't exactly true. Angelo had connected with a lot of women over the years, just not in the way Derek was talking about. But that was by choice. He'd learned long ago that women, long-term relationships, and Army

Special Forces didn't mix. Never had and never would. He'd seen firsthand what endless deployments and dangerous missions could do to a wife a Special Forces operator left behind. Every time his father shipped out, his mother had died a little inside until it finally destroyed her. Angelo had vowed then to never get married, or even involved seriously with a woman until he got out of the military. Since he intended to make a career of being a soldier, that was going to be a long time.

Landon opened the sliding glass door and leaned in. "Protein's just about ready out here, hon."

"We're almost done in here, too," Ivy called.

"Keep your shirts on," said Clayne's fiancée, Danica Beckett. "Or don't. Ivy and I won't complain."

The two women laughed at the joke, while Clayne let out a snort. Angelo still wasn't sure how the gruff wolf shifter—man, it was going to take a while to get used to the idea that there were people who had animal DNA— had landed an amazing woman like Danica.

"When are you two getting married?" Angelo asked.

"I'd get married today, but Danica says we have to do it right." Clayne grabbed another beer out of the cooler by the deck railing. "By that, she means get married in a church."

Landon straddled the bottom of a lounge chair and sat down. He'd always worn his hair shorter than the rest of the guys on the team, but since going to work for the DCO, he'd let it grow some. "Isn't that where most people get married?"

"Yeah, I guess, but I don't do churches." The words were practically a growl. "I thought we'd just go to Vegas or something."

Derek shook his head. "Man, you know less about women than Angelo does."

Clayne grunted. "Don't even get me started on the other stuff. Between invitations, gift registries, flowers, cake, and DJs, my head is about to explode."

Landon chuckled and started to reply when his cell phone rang. He dug it out of his pocket and put it to his ear. "Donovan."

As Landon moved to the other side of the terrace to take the call, Angelo opened his mouth to ask Clayne if Danica was going to make him wear a tux to the wedding, but closed it when he realized the wolf shifter was staring intently at Landon, almost as if he could hear what the person on the other end of the line was saying from fifteen feet away. Of course, if half of what Landon had told him about shifters was true, Clayne probably *could* hear what the person was saying.

Angelo looked closer at his former captain and noticed that Landon's mouth had tightened into that familiar grim line whenever there was trouble. Whatever it was, it involved Ivy and Danica because Landon opened the sliding glass door and asked them to come outside.

"It's Tate," he said when the two women got there. "Tate, I'm putting you on speaker. Go ahead."

"I'll keep it simple," Tate said. "The training exercise we were down here for just got a whole hell of a lot more real. We got ambushed by a bunch of damn hybrids. Brent, Gavin, and I made it out with a few scrapes, but the rest of the guys with us weren't so lucky. Neither were Declan and Kendra. The helicopter they were on got shot down a few hours ago. Best we can tell the bird ended up right in the middle of those bastards. We're going to need help with a rescue."

Ivy's perfect complexion went pale at the mention of hybrids. Derek didn't look much better. Who could blame him? The guy had practically just professed his love for Kendra and now she was missing—or worse. Damn.

"Ivy and I are on the first plane John can get us on," Landon said.

There was silence on the other end of the line. If it weren't for the background noise in the distance, Angelo would think the guy had hung up.

"I'd rather you didn't involve John," Tate finally said.

"Why not?" Landon asked.

"We're not sure we can trust him. Or anyone else in the DCO except you and Ivy. This was a setup from day one, and John is the guy who sent us down here."

Landon exchanged looks with Ivy. She nodded at him. *What the hell was that about?*

"Tate, I know you don't want to spend time going over details you don't think are important, but if you're going to drop a bomb on us like this—that you think John set up your whole team to get slaughtered—you're going to have to give us something more to go on."

There was another long pause before Tate answered. The more the guy talked, the more stunned Angelo was. While he didn't know John personally and couldn't say if he was the one who'd set up Tate's team, he was pretty damn sure Tate was right about the whole thing being an ambush in waiting from the start.

"And you can't get any support from the American forces down there?" Ivy asked. "I mean, with all those marines who got killed, you'd think they'd be ripping the place apart to get out there and track down the people responsible."

"They wanted to, but the political shit hit the fan the moment we told them there were dead marines and a downed navy helicopter out there in the jungle," Tate said. "The local government reps shouted foul, claiming we'd violated the use-of-force restraints placed on the U.S. military assets they'd allowed into their country. The Costa Rican president and legislative deputies shut everything down and put a hold on all operations while they investigate. There's no way we're getting help from anyone down here, which is why we need you and Landon, and we need you down here fast. Buchanan, too, if he's available."

"Count me in," Clayne said.

Landon and Ivy asked a few more detailed questions— like whether they knew the coordinates where Declan and Kendra had gone down and most importantly, how many hybrids they might be facing.

Like Derek, Angelo kept quiet. This guy Tate was tense enough. Knowing two guys he'd never met were listening in on the conversation wasn't going to make things better.

"Regardless of what you believe, you know I'm going to have to bring John into this," Landon said.

"No way," Tate said.

"I know you don't trust him, and I understand why. But if we're going to rescue Declan and Kendra, we need John's help to get us into the country and set us up with the equipment we need. If we try to do this on our own, it could take us days to get there, and Kendra and Declan may pay with their lives. Are you willing to risk that?"

Tate muttered something Angelo didn't catch, then let out a heavy sigh. "Okay, I hear what you're saying. But I need you to control the operation—marginalize his influence as much as you can. And I want your word that you'll handpick the team that comes down here. If you don't trust someone, don't let John send them."

"You have my word," Landon assured him. "I'll select the team myself. They'll be people I know and trust personally."

While Landon discussed the details they needed in order to link up with Tate, Ivy pulled out her cell phone and began making calls. By the time Landon hung up, Ivy was putting down her phone, too.

"John is at the main office in town," she said. "I'm not sure what he's doing there on a Saturday, but I told him we need to talk to him immediately. He's waiting for us."

Landon nodded, then looked at Angelo. "I hate to do this to you guys, but—"

"We're both in," Angelo said.

"In? As in going with us?" Landon shook his head. "No way. You guys are on leave. I can't ask you to fly down to Central America and risk your lives."

"Then don't ask," Angelo said. "Kendra is a friend—not to mention a possible soul mate for Derek. We're going."

Landon looked from him to Derek and back again. "Thanks."

Ivy ran her hand through her waist-length, dark hair. "Okay, that makes six of us."

"Five," Danica corrected. "I'm supposed to go undercover at Chadwick-Thorn on Monday. It's taken weeks for the Bureau to get me in there. If we pull out, we may not get another shot at them."

"Good," Clayne said. "I don't want you going."

Danica's dark eyes narrowed. "Excuse me?"

"I'm sorry, babe, but I don't want you within a hundred miles of a damn hybrid. They're too dangerous."

"But I'm supposed to be okay with you going up against them, right?"

"That's different. I can handle myself," Clayne told her.

Angelo winced. He might not be able to *connect* with women, as Derek put it, but he knew that probably wasn't the best thing to say.

"Excuse us," Danica said, grabbing Clayne's hand and dragging him inside.

Angelo frowned as Danica slammed the door closed. "Do we need to run interference in there with those two?"

Ivy shook her head. "No. Clayne may have the sensitivity of a bucket of mud, but his heart is in the right place. He's as afraid for her as she is for him."

Angelo shook his head. That only confirmed serious relationships and dangerous fieldwork didn't mesh. He never wanted to be in the position of seeing the woman he loved having to deal with him deploying to dangerous places over and over, or worrying about her while he was on the other side of the world. That was something else he'd learned a long time ago. A soldier's wife wasn't the only one who paid the price when he went on a mission.

Derek leaned back in his chair so he could see through the glass door into the living room where Clayne and Danica were arguing. "Things look pretty tense in there to me."

"They're fine," Ivy said. "Right now, we have a bigger problem. Like who else we're going to recruit for this little search-and-rescue mission."

Angelo took another look at Clayne and Danica and saw them hugging. Apparently, Ivy knew what she was talking about when it came to men and women.

—⁓⁓⁓—

Angelo was thoroughly unimpressed with the DCO offices. He didn't know what he'd expected, but an unmarked set of glass doors in the parking garage of the Environmental Protection Agency wasn't it.

"This is just the place where the politics are played," Landon explained as Clayne opened the door for them. "All the real work happens out at the training complex near Quantico."

Angelo made no comment. Any organization that needed to have a separate set of offices just so politicians would have a place to play wasn't an organization he wanted to work for. He looked around the lobby and grimaced at the white walls, generic DC tourist pics, and marble accents. How the hell did Landon put up with this crap?

The click-clack of high heels coming down the hall interrupted his musings. Angelo dragged his attention away from the framed photo of the White House and did a double take. For a second, he thought it was Ivy — though he had no idea how she could have gotten here before them when she was with Derek and Danica getting their personal gear together — but then he realized it was her equally beautiful sister, Layla. If she wasn't ten years younger than he was and already hung up on his former lieutenant, Jayson Harmon, he definitely would have done some serious flirting when he'd met her at Landon and Ivy's wedding.

Her dark eyes widened when she saw them. "Landon." She did a quick scan of the lobby. "Is Ivy with you?"

"No. She's at home." Landon frowned. "What are you doing here?"

Layla's fingers toyed with the strap on her shoulder bag. "I had a job interview."

Landon's frown deepened. "A job interview?"

"Uh-huh. I got it, too. John wants me to start on Monday." She caught her lower lip between her teeth, looking at each of them in turn. "Please don't say anything to Ivy, okay? I want to be the one to tell her."

"Yeah," Landon said. "Sure."

"Awesome. Thank you." She grinned. "Okay, I'm outta here. Jayson and I are going to celebrate. Nice seeing you again, Angelo. Clayne."

Angelo barely had time to return the greeting before she hurried out the door, her high heels echoing behind her.

"I'm guessing Ivy isn't going to be happy about her sister working here?" Angelo asked.

Clayne snorted. "Understatement."

Considering how the DCO treated shifters, Angelo wasn't surprised Ivy didn't want her sister involved with them. Angelo had two sisters he was extremely protective of, so he knew where Ivy was coming from. He didn't say anything as he followed Landon and Clayne down the hall, though.

Halfway down, Landon stopped at one of the offices and knocked on the already open door, then walked in.

The director of the DCO wasn't at all how Angelo'd pictured him. He expected a slick, politician type, but instead the man fit the bill of a battalion or group commander. He might dress like the head of a Fortune 500 company, but he looked like he could definitely handle himself in a fight if he had to.

The man's gaze lingered curiously on Angelo briefly before settling on Landon. "What's the problem? Ivy said there was something important you wanted to see me about that couldn't wait until Monday."

"It can't," Landon agreed, then glanced at Angelo. "John, this is a good friend of mine, Sergeant First Class Angelo Rios from my old A-Team. Angelo, my boss, John Loughlin."

John held out his hand. "Nice to meet you, Sergeant. Would it be too presumptuous to hope you're here because Landon recruited you to join our ranks?"

Angelo smiled. "I'm happy where I am, sir, but thank you."

"I thought you might say that."

John regarded Landon with a calculating look in his eyes, and Angelo suddenly had the feeling that the director wasn't a man you screwed with. He had enough clout to grab Landon out of Special Forces in the middle of a deployment. He hoped Landon knew what the hell he was doing.

John gestured to the small conference table. "Have a seat."

If the director of the DCO was behind the ambush in Costa Rica, he was a damn good actor because he looked genuinely stunned—not to mention concerned—when Landon outlined the situation.

"Why am I hearing this from you and not from Tate?" John asked when Landon finished.

"Because Tate thinks you sold them out and walked them right into that hybrid ambush," Clayne said.

Shit. Subtle wasn't in Clayne's vocabulary. Now John would get pissed off, then Clayne would go into beast mode, and they'd never get anywhere. But instead John regarded them calmly.

"And what do you think?" John asked, looking at Landon.

"I don't think anything. I just know the facts," Landon said. "You sent a DCO team on an exercise. They were ambushed. Tate, Brent, and Gavin barely escaped with their lives, and Kendra and Declan are missing, maybe even dead. And a pack of hybrids are at the center of it."

A muscle in John's jaw flexed. "This exercise has been on the schedule every year for the past decade. Other than choosing the team the DCO sends, I don't have any involvement."

Clayne's eyes flashed gold. "You expect us to believe that Tate's team just stumbled into those hybrids by chance?"

Angelo frowned. Okay, what hadn't Landon told him? Because there was way more going on here than his friend had let on. Landon and Clayne wouldn't be leaning on their boss this hard if they didn't already have a reason to distrust him.

"I don't believe in coincidences any more than you

do, Clayne," John said. "Someone obviously set this whole thing up, but I can assure you it wasn't me."

Landon and Clayne exchanged looks, though Angelo'd be damned if he could tell whether either of them believed their boss.

John swore under his breath. "I can see that nothing I say is going to sway you one way or the other. What's important right now is getting Declan and Kendra out of that jungle in one piece. Agreed?"

"Agreed," Landon said.

"Then let's table the discussion of whether you trust me or not for another time, and get down to business. What do you need from me to get a search-and-rescue mission going?"

"Weapons and equipment for an eight-person team, not counting Tate, Gavin, and Brent, as well as immediate transport and entry into Costa Rica," Landon said without hesitation. "According to Tate, politics down there are dicey, so I'm going to need you to make sure no one tries to stop us."

John's gaze went from Landon to Clayne to Angelo, then back again. "Eight?"

Landon didn't flinch. "If you expect us to trust you, you need to trust us."

John regarded Landon in silence for a long time before the corner of his mouth edged up. "I knew bringing you into the DCO was going to change everything."

Angelo's mouth twitched. He and Landon had a lot of conversations over the years while sitting out in the middle of nowhere wondering if they were going to die. But one topic that kept coming up over and over was Landon's self-doubt about whether the men he led would follow him into danger. Landon might be like a brother to him, but sometimes he was freaking stupid. Men would follow him anywhere, anytime, into any kind of danger. Because he was a leader, born and bred.

"Be at Bolling in two hours," John said. "I'll get you, your team, and your gear down there. It will be up to you to get everyone back out."

Landon nodded. "I'll get them out."

"And, Landon," John said as they headed for the door. "When you get back, we need to talk."

Landon just nodded.

"Eight of us?" Clayne asked when they got to the lobby.

Angelo was wondering the same thing. It couldn't be any of the guys from the A-Team because they were all out in Monterey brushing up on their Tajik before the deployment.

"Eight," Landon confirmed as he led the way to the parking garage.

Clayne grunted. "Whoever these other guys are, they'd better be damn good because we're already going to be seriously outgunned."

"Don't worry," Landon said. "They're good."

Now Angelo was even more curious.

Chapter 4

"DON'T MOVE," DECLAN WHISPERED SOFTLY IN Kendra's ear.

She nodded, but otherwise remained motionless—as much as she could, considering she was probably freezing to death. Being submerged to your neck in cold water and even colder mud could do that. It didn't help that the temperature had dropped ten degrees after the sun had gone down. But while the mud was uncomfortable as hell, it was the only thing keeping them alive right now.

The hybrids had chased them nonstop since he and Kendra had crawled out of the helicopter wreckage. It had taken every skill he'd ever learned as a forest ranger just to stay ahead of the bastards. If he hadn't stumbled across a patch of tulip orchids and recognized them for what they were, he and Kendra would have been dead hours ago. Luckily, the hybrids' sense of smell wasn't much better than Declan's, so rubbing the pungent cinnamon-scented flowers all over their skin and clothes had masked their scent.

Unfortunately, it didn't trick the creatures entirely. Since the hybrids couldn't seem to track them by scent, they formed a noose around the area and slowly tightened it until he and Kendra had nowhere left to run but into the stream. Instead of a shallow crossing, they found themselves hip deep in thick mud.

As the hybrids converged on their location, Declan

did the only thing he could think of—he pulled Kendra against him and sank down into the slime that lined the edge of the water until only their heads were above it. Thankfully, there were enough ferns growing near the bank to hide them.

He hoped the hybrids would sniff around awhile, then leave, but almost half an hour later, there were still nearly a dozen hybrids prowling around, snarling at each other about who'd let the quarry slip through the trap.

Kendra shivered as two of the beasts moved nearer, their eyes glowing scarlet in the darkness. Declan pulled her closer underneath the water. He didn't blame her for being terrified. Not even hanging around Tanner had prepared him for just how rabid these things could be. The reports Ivy and Landon had written didn't do them justice.

Around them, the hybrids suddenly fell silent. A moment later, the human soldiers with them did the same.

Declan tensed. *What the hell…?*

A huge hybrid moved into the thin slice of moonlight along the shore barely fifteen feet from him and Kendra. *Damn.*

The dark-haired hybrid on the far side of the stream was at least a half foot taller than Declan and a good fifty or sixty pounds heavier. He was more animalistic than the other hybrids, too. His upper fangs were so long they almost hung below his jawline, like some kind of freaking saber-toothed tiger. His claws were just as big, nearly as long as his fingers. But it was the thing's eyes that were freaky. They didn't simply glow red. They burned like fire. Hell, they even flickered.

"Where are they?" the monster demanded.

Every hybrid in the clearing ducked his head and stared at the ground—except one. The beast nearest the big guy stepped forward with a quick nod.

"They've slipped through our line. We've lost them, Marcus."

The big hybrid—Marcus—turned to scowl at the other creature. But the monster giving the report didn't back down and instead stood his ground like a man used to delivering bad news. If Declan had to guess, this hybrid was Marcus's second-in-command.

Marcus looked mad enough to rip off someone's head, but the second-in-command didn't say anything else to provoke his boss. One of the men standing behind them wasn't as wary.

"You didn't cast the net wide enough to start with, Captain," he said, taking a step forward. "These agents aren't morons like the locals around here. They know what they're up against, and I guarantee they made a beeline for the Panama border the second they got out of that chopper. You've let them get a good head start on us. If you would've just listened to me—"

The man never finished his thought because Marcus raked his big-ass claws across the man's neck and upper chest in a strike so fast it was nearly impossible to follow the movement.

Kendra jerked in horror and probably would have lurched out of the mud if Declan hadn't been holding her.

The captain regarded the man's lifeless body coldly before turning on his second-in-command with a growl. "Widen the search grid to fifteen miles."

"Sir, our ranks will be stretched thin if we do

that," the hybrid said. "There will be gaps they could slip through."

The leader's eyes narrowed as if he was contemplating whether to kill someone else today. Lucky for the lower-ranking hybrid, he decided against it. "Not if I tell the doctor to accelerate his process on the other men. Send most of the soldiers south. I want that route blocked first. I'll send reinforcements as soon as they're ready."

The hybrids and their human counterparts disappeared into the jungle, leaving the dead man and the hulking hybrid captain behind. The creature scanned the surrounding jungle with his red eyes before looking right at them—or rather the ferns they were hiding underneath.

Kendra's breath hitched. Declan squeezed her tighter. *Shit*. What if the monster had an intuitive sense that told him something wasn't right, like Ivy did?

But after glancing down at the body of the man lying twisted on the ground, the hybrid turned and loped off into the darkness like the predator he was.

Declan didn't move for a full five minutes, worried the hybrids had tricked them and were still out there waiting. Even though Kendra was shivering, she stayed where she was.

When his ears finally convinced him there wasn't a hybrid or human within miles, he slowly eased them both out of the mud. The stuff clung to them like a living thing, refusing to let go, and he swore under his breath as he led Kendra upstream. He resisted the urge to take her in his arms and started cleaning his M4 instead. If they got caught with their weapons plugged up with mud, they were screwed. Beside him, Kendra did the same.

As soon as their essential gear was clean enough to

function, they started on their rucksacks and clothes, scraping the worst of the gunk off, then using water from the stream to get the rest. On the downside, that made them wetter and colder than they were before. Within a few minutes, Kendra was shaking so badly she could barely control her hands.

"Here," Declan said. "Let me do that."

He worked fast, refusing to think too much about where he was putting his hands as he rinsed the mud out of Kendra's hair and the parts of her clothes she couldn't reach. Even the darkness couldn't hide the fact that her lips were turning blue by the time he was done. But she didn't complain.

"Let's get away from the stream and find a place to hole up for the night," he said softly. He didn't think there were any hybrids nearby, but why chance it?

Kendra shook her head. "No. We need to keep going."

"What we need is rest." He didn't tell her that hiking through the jungle for another three or four hours would likely kill her. She didn't need to hear that. "Besides, that'll give them some time to spread themselves out, so we can escape through those gaps they mentioned."

When she opened her mouth to protest, Declan took her hand and led her away. She didn't try to resist or even put on her night vision goggles—NVGs—convincing him more than ever she was starting to show early signs of hypothermia.

He grabbed another handful of orchids as they walked. The flowers were everywhere. After being submerged in mud and water, there wouldn't be much of the scent left on them.

Declan found a thick cluster of shrubs and brambles

growing near a cliff face about a mile from the stream. While Kendra stood guard—she refused to just sit there and rest—he bulled his way into the foliage until he was up against the rock. He ripped a few of the bigger plants out by the roots, then bulldozed with his shoulders until he made a space large enough for the two of them to lie down. When he was done, he looked at the space.

The plants around the makeshift shelter were at least six feet thick in every direction, including over their heads. Someone could walk right by them and never even know they were there. He tossed the orchids on the ground. At least the flowers would cover their scent enough until he could rub them both down again.

Kendra was kneeling where he'd left her, covering the approaches to the area like their lives depended on it. She was shivering like crazy, yet she was still stubbornly holding her weapon up, ready to shoot anything that came at them.

He shook his head as he guided her into the dark hole in the brush. He really had underestimated her. Not only had she moved quickly and quietly the entire day, but she'd also displayed a talent with her M4 that made him think she'd been doing a lot more at the DCO complex than evaluating training. When the sun went down, she'd donned her night vision goggles and kept pace with him. He was impressed she knew how to use her gear.

There wasn't a lot of space in the little hiding spot, but there was enough room to spread his poncho on the ground. Kendra sank down wordlessly on it. Declan debated whether they should change into something drier, but neither of them had much in the way of dry clothes to change into—four days in the Costa Rican jungle during rainy season had seen to that. Instead, he stretched out beside Kendra and pulled her against his chest, hoping to warm her up with the heat of his body. He might hate the idea of cuddling with her, but if he didn't do something, she'd freeze to death.

Her icy skin started warming up within minutes. If the situation weren't so screwed up, he would have laughed. If he'd known that this was all he needed to do to get her hot, he would have done it years ago. Well, without the hybrids.

"I'm sorry." Kendra's voice was so soft it was barely audible.

Declan stiffened. "About what?"

"That I'm such a mess. I guess I'm not as good at this field thing as I thought."

For a moment he thought she was going to apologize for failing to notice he existed for the past seven years. "You're doing better than I did the first time I was in the field."

She let out a tiny snort. "I doubt that. An hour ago, I couldn't stop shivering. I'm just glad I didn't have to actually shoot anything. I'm not sure my frozen finger could have pulled the trigger."

"You've been running all day without food, it's rained on us half a dozen times in the last six hours, and we just sat in a freezing-cold swamp for freaking ever," Declan said. "You got cold. It can happen to anyone."

She leaned back into the warmth of his body. "You don't seem that cold."

"I'm half-bear," he pointed out. "And I consumed about twenty thousand calories in the days leading up to this exercise. I could go out naked in a snowstorm."

She laughed. "That's quite the image."

Despite his discomfort, Declan chuckled, too.

"I read the profile for Costa Rica before we left, but I never expected it to be this cold," she said, serious again.

Most people didn't think about that in the jungle, but with the temperatures in the fifties, the exhaustion, the intermittent rains, and thirty minutes in the icy-cold mud, it was pretty damn easy for the body's core temperature to sink to dangerous levels.

"The jungle canopy makes it worse. The sun rarely gets a chance to penetrate down to the ground level and heat things up," he explained. "You feel like eating something?"

She nodded and sat up, putting some blessed distance between them and pushing the hair that had come loose from her ponytail behind her ear. He rummaged in his pack and pulled out an energy bar, then handed it to her.

"Brent and Gavin had the good camp food in their packs, so we're stuck with the survival stuff we had in ours and whatever we can forage until we get out of here."

But Kendra didn't seem to care that the energy bar had the consistency and taste of shoe leather. She tore into it and took a big bite. She chewed, then frowned.

"Aren't you going to eat?" she asked.

He shook his head. "Nah. I wasn't kidding about all the food I ate before coming down here. I can go without eating for a few days if I have to."

Declan didn't tell her the real reason he wasn't eating was because they hardly had any food in their packs. Foraging for food sounded like a good idea, but it wasn't going to be that easy with hybrids on their tails. Thankfully, Kendra didn't press the issue. He picked up a few of the cinnamon-scented flowers and rubbed down her pack while she ate.

"Those smell nice, kind of like spiced apple cider. How did you know it'd fool the hybrids?"

He shrugged. "I didn't know. But the odor has always been overpowering for me, so I hoped it'd be as bad for them. It's so strong that it could trick a shifter with a good nose—like Ivy. And based on how little the hybrids used their noses back there at the stream, I think their sense of smell is worse than mine."

She regarded him thoughtfully. "I've always wondered about that. Why do bears generally have such an amazing sense of smell, but you don't?"

Declan set down her pack and picked up his. "I don't know. It's just not something I'm good at."

He tried to keep his voice casual, but it actually came out sharper than he intended. Maybe because it was Kendra asking and he knew she'd take it as one more reason to think he didn't measure up.

"Guess that makes sense," she said. "How did you learn so much about flowers? Is it something you picked up when you were a forest ranger?"

The question caught him off guard. He would have thought that since she had access to his personnel record, she already knew everything there was to know about him, including where he'd learned about flowers.

"My mother has a huge greenhouse. She raises all kinds of exotic plants and flowers, but orchids are her favorite. I used to help her when I was a kid—planting, watering, weeding, that kind of stuff."

Kendra smiled. "Sounds like you and your mom are close."

Declan grunted. He wasn't going to tell her that his mom had all but disowned him when he'd dropped out of MIT.

Kendra finished her energy bar and shoved the wrapper in her pack, then took a quick drink of water from her canteen before digging around for a small canvas pouch. He watched in surprise as she picked up her M4 and started breaking it down. They'd gotten the worst of the mud off their weapons, but the M4s would need a detailed cleaning to keep them from malfunctioning later. That she was cleaning her weapon now wasn't nearly as surprising as the fact that she was doing it in the near darkness of their shelter. Sure, he could see fine—he was a shifter—but she was doing it all by feel. Just another indication that she was way more comfortable handling a weapon than he'd realized.

"Something tells me you've done that before," he remarked.

She didn't say anything.

"Don't take this wrong," he continued, "but I watched you kill several men today, and I'm pretty sure it wasn't the first time you've done that, either."

Her hands stilled on the M4, then went back to work, moving with more determination this time. When she didn't answer, he thought about pushing but changed his mind. He was the last guy to complain about someone keeping secrets. He had his share.

Declan picked up his own weapon. He'd pulled out the rear takedown pin and had the bolt halfway removed before her soft voice stopped him.

"It's not the first time I've killed. The first time I've killed a man, yes, but not a hybrid. I've killed them before."

How was that possible? "When? The DCO only learned about hybrids when Ivy and Landon found them out in Washington State."

"I know," she said. "I was there."

Declan was glad it was dark or Kendra would have seen how stupid he looked with his mouth hanging open. He'd seen the reports. Ivy and Landon had taken on more than forty hybrids and lived to tell about it. Except now it turned out that Kendra had been there, too.

It certainly explained a lot. Like how she'd identified the hybrids on sight while the rest of them had been caught staring at the moving blurs. It also explained why she'd been able to calmly fight something out of most people's nightmares.

"Is that why John sent you with us?" he asked. "Did he know there were hybrids down here?"

Kendra dropped the bolt of the M4 back in the upper receiver, then ran the carbine through a function check, reloaded it, and flipped on the safety before setting it aside.

"He doesn't know I went to Washington. No one knows. There are people whose lives will be ruined if it comes out, so no one can ever know." Though it was impossible for her to see in the darkness, she looked right at him anyway. "Promise me that you won't tell anyone."

She didn't say who she was protecting, but it wasn't that hard to figure out she was talking about Ivy. The two women were as close as sisters. If there was anyone Kendra would keep a secret for, it would be the feline shifter. He could respect that.

"I won't tell anyone," Declan assured her. "You

didn't answer my other question. Did John know there were hybrids down here?"

"No. We had no idea there were hybrids."

"That's not what I meant." He took a deep breath. He couldn't even believe he was thinking this. John had brought him into the DCO. "I don't think we just stumbled across these things, Kendra. Remember how I said earlier today that it was like we were being run through a search grid?" She nodded. "Well, I think it's pretty obvious we found what they had us searching for."

"That's crazy," she said. "If you're right—and someone had us looking for hybrids—they had to know we'd all be killed."

Declan nodded. "My guess is that they were willing to sacrifice us to find them. Only someone high up in the DCO could have made it happen."

"It doesn't mean it was John," she protested. "It could just as easily have been Dick."

"How many times has Dick ever gotten involved in a field operation? I don't think he even knows how to arrange an ambush."

Kendra didn't answer.

Declan finished cleaning his weapon in silence. He could hear a lot of animals, but none of them sounded like hybrids.

"What are we going to do?" Kendra asked as he set down his weapon.

"We survive," he told her.

"I mean about John...or whoever set us up."

"We'll worry about that later. Right now, we focus on getting out of this jungle and away from these things."

She took a deep breath as if composing herself. The

same steely resolve he'd seen all day came back into her eyes. "Okay. So, what's the plan?"

"First, we lie down and get some rest," he said.

Declan shifted a little to make room for her. She got the idea and crawled in close, her back against his chest. He automatically wrapped her in his arms. Her clothes were drier, but she'd get cold again as the night chill crept in. He needed her fully functional tomorrow. If she stayed close to him, she'd be warm—it was that simple.

"Tomorrow, we head northwest, back across the same general area we spent the last four days covering," he continued. "It's the shortest route out of the jungle."

"Won't that be like crossing right through their territory?"

"Pretty much, but that may actually be our best chance. The hybrid leader sent a lot of his men south toward the border, so going that way would be too dangerous. East'll take us deeper into the Talamanca mountain range, which would slow us down to a crawl and keep us in the jungle for weeks. We're not left with a lot of options and I'd rather do the unexpected and go where they don't think we'll go. With so many of them going south, the hybrids in the northwest will be spread thin. If we're careful, we should be able to slip through without them knowing."

"Being careful means going slowly," she pointed out. "It could take a week or more to get back to civilization. Can we make it that long on our own?"

"I'm hoping we won't have to. Tate, Brent, and Gavin are already out looking for us. We just have to hold on until they find us."

Kendra didn't say anything for a while, and when she spoke again, her voice was soft. "How do we know they even made it out? Our helicopter got hit so fast, I never had a chance to see what was happening with the other one. What if they went down, too?"

Declan's chest tightened. He'd been teamed with Tate, Brent, and Gavin since he started working at the DCO, and they were more like his family than his real family. They weren't dead. He'd know if they were.

"They made it out. I know that in my gut," he told Kendra firmly. "They'll find us."

Kendra sighed. "Okay, we have a plan. All we have to do is sneak right through the middle of a valley filled with vicious hybrids, not to mention the regular soldiers they had with them. Then we somehow have to let Tate, Gavin, and Brent know where we are. Once we do that, it's just a simple matter of the five of us fighting our way out of the jungle against a hundred bad guys. Doesn't sound hard at all."

He chuckled. "Exactly. You know what they say— the simplest plans are the best plans. Now get some rest. I'll wake you in a couple of hours to stand watch."

She must have been pretty beat, because she didn't even try to argue with him. Instead, she snuggled closer to his chest and fell asleep.

Declan closed his eyes, carefully listening for the sounds of hybrids sniffing around, but he didn't hear anything. He still couldn't believe they hadn't smelled him and Kendra in the stream. Thank God they had a crappy sense of smell like him.

But at the moment his nose was working just fine. Unfortunately, the only scent he could pick up was Kendra's. Even sweaty and dirty, she smelled good— too good.

He ground his jaw. Why the hell was it so hard to ignore her scent? He wasn't even attracted to her anymore.

Okay, so that was a lie, at least as far as his nose — and other parts of his body — were concerned. This close to her, he couldn't deny it, not even to himself.

Declan shifted a little to get some separation between them, but Kendra only groaned and wiggled closer. Thank God she was asleep. It would be damn embarrassing if she asked him what the hell was poking her in the ass.

Of course, thinking about what his hard-on was poking just made it worse. Shit, this was irritating. He'd worked hard over the last few months to mentally distance himself from her. Now, here he was with a nose full of her scent driving him crazy and an erection that had a mind of its own.

The really sad part? If she woke up right then, she'd move away from him in disgust and continue to ignore him. Because even if he was the last non-hybrid creature in the jungle, she still wouldn't be interested in him.

He bit back a growl and moved again. She shifted with him.

Damn, this is going to be a long freaking night.

—⁓—

Without the DCO director's clout, Angelo was convinced they'd still be sitting on their rucksacks back in Washington right now instead of standing in the middle of the camp where Tate and his team had set up. Not only had John arranged to have a fueled C-17 waiting for them at Bolling, but he also had two trucks of ammo and supplies waiting for them on the runway in Costa Rica. The rest of the op should go as smoothly.

Unfortunately, Tate and his team hadn't been thrilled to see Landon and Ivy show up with the rest of them in tow. Angelo supposed he could understand their reluctance. Going into hostile territory with people you didn't know and didn't trust would make anyone uncomfortable.

Angelo still wasn't sure when Landon had found a chance to slip away and call in a favor, but when they'd touched down in Costa Rica, there were two other Special Forces operators already waiting for them—Sergeant First Class Nik Carter and Lieutenant Zane Butler, both out of the 7th Special Forces Group from Florida. They'd been down in Panama training antinarcotic forces when Landon reached out to them. Angelo didn't know them personally, but they'd put their own mission on hold to help Landon, and that told him everything he needed to know. Special Forces was one big family. When family called and needed help, you dropped what you were doing and went to help.

"These guys don't even know Declan and Kendra, and you expect them to risk their lives to save them?" Tate demanded.

"They risk their lives every day for people they've never met," Landon shot back. "You asked me to hand-pick a team and that's what I did. They wouldn't be here if I didn't trust them with my life, with Ivy's life, and with Declan's and Kendra's lives."

Angelo saw Derek's mouth tighten. No doubt the medic wanted to point out that both he and Angelo knew Kendra, but admitting that would mean mentioning what happened out in Washington State, and that was classified.

"Do they know what we're going up against?" Tate asked.

"Some of them do," Landon told him. "Angelo and Derek have fought hybrids before. Carter and Butler will keep it together once they find out."

Tate considered that. "Okay, I get that you're comfortable working with guys from Special Forces. But Tanner? Shit, Landon. Why the hell would you bring him?"

Angelo grimaced—not only because Tanner was standing right there, but also because he wasn't exactly sure why Landon had insisted on bringing the DCO's pet hybrid, either. Putting a guy with a short fuse on the team didn't seem like a good idea. But Landon and Clayne insisted the former Army Ranger could do the job. More importantly, the team needed him.

Behind Tate, Gavin and Brent looked like they'd rather go out in the jungle again without their weapons than fight alongside Tanner.

"If we're going up against as many hybrids as you think, we'll need Tanner," Landon said. "He could be the difference maker for us."

"More like the straw that breaks the camel's back," Tate muttered. "I've seen how he reacts in stressful situations. He can't be trusted out here."

"I trust him," Landon said softly.

Angelo knew that tone. His former commanding officer was about to get seriously pissed. Angelo was getting pissed, too. They should be looking for their missing teammates, not arguing about who was going to be included in the rescue party.

"Well, I don't trust him," Tate said. "He's not going with us."

"Then you're going on your own," Landon said.

Tate frowned, wondering if Landon was bluffing.

Angelo could have told the man he wasn't. Landon never had a problem standing his ground. Angelo had learned that the first day of basic training. Tate must have figured that out, too, because he turned to Ivy.

"This is your best friend we're talking about, and mine. Are you honestly telling me you're okay with putting their lives in Tanner's hands?" Tate asked.

Ivy nodded. "I am. Landon is right, Tate. We need Tanner. I wouldn't have agreed to bring him if he wasn't ready."

Tate looked at Gavin and Brent. Both men shrugged.

"Fine, we'll do it your way," Tate told Landon. "But if things go south, it's on you, and I'll be coming for payback." He turned and strode off toward the big tent they were using as a makeshift headquarters, but stopped and glared at Landon again. "Keeping Tanner under control is your problem. Don't expect any help when he loses it. And if he takes off, you're going after him this time."

With that, he ducked inside, Gavin and Brent on his heels.

"Don't pay any attention to Tate," Ivy told Landon. "He's just worried."

"Not to mention pissed that Tanner ran his whole team ragged for weeks before they brought him in," Clayne added.

Landon didn't say anything. If Angelo knew his friend, Landon had already dismissed what Tate'd said. His mind was focused on the next problem.

"So, why don't they want to work with you?"

Angelo turned to see Carter regarding Tanner, his dark eyes wary. Angelo didn't blame him. With the long, blond hair and beard, the hybrid looked a little like the wild animal he sometimes turned into.

"I have anger management issues," Tanner said. "I tend to go nuts and kill people at the slightest provocation."

If Tanner expected the comment to scare off the two Special Forces guys, it didn't work.

"Must be a bitch getting through a holiday with your in-laws," Carter said. "Ever consider meditation?"

Tanner stared at the sergeant for what seemed like forever before he finally cracked a smile. It was small, but it was there.

"My doctor has me doing it now and then."

"Yeah?" Carter said. "Is it working?"

"Not so much."

"Then maybe you should think about getting a new doctor," Butler suggested.

The telltale red glow that came with a shift flashed in Tanner's eyes. Angelo tensed. Had Carter and Butler seen it, too? Maybe he could say it was the reflection of the setting sun in the hybrid's eyes. Right. That excuse would only last until Tanner fully flipped the switch and went nuts. What the hell had set him off anyway?

Angelo looked around for a little help, but Ivy and Landon were nowhere to be seen. Clayne was leaning against a nearby tree watching the scene unfold like it was a damn movie. And Derek was standing there with a pissed-off expression on his face, no doubt wondering why the hell everyone was screwing around with these stupid-ass macho games when Kendra was out there in the jungle with numerous monsters chasing her.

Shit.

Angelo took a step toward the hybrid. "Tanner,

before you lose your temper and kill Lieutenant Butler, I think you should consider how disappointed Zarina would be."

According to Landon, Zarina had a magical ability to calm the DCO's one and only hybrid. Hopefully invoking her name would snap Tanner out of the rage that was starting to build.

It worked like a freaking charm. Tanner blinked several times, took a deep breath, then nodded. The red slowly receded from the hybrid's eyes. But not before the two soldiers saw it.

"What the hell…?" Carter muttered.

Angelo stifled a groan. Why couldn't Landon have made things easy on everyone and filled Carter and Butler in on what a hybrid was?

"Okay," he said. "Time for a security briefing. Landon told you this mission would involve some strange shit, right?" Both men nodded. "Good, because the strange shit just started. Consider anything you see and hear over the next few days to be top secret. It goes to the grave with you. Hooah?"

"Hooah," Butler and Carter said in unison. No shock there—Special Forces guys saw so much classified crap, they flushed it without too much thought.

"The people we're going up against are…well, they've been genetically modified to make them meaner and nastier. When they're in control of themselves, they're your basic hair-trigger soldier. But once they start fighting, they go into a battle lust like nothing you've ever seen. Bottom line, at that point, they're essentially berserkers, pure and simple." Angelo jerked his head in Tanner's direction. "He's one of them, except he's on our side. If he lost his temper and accidently killed you, he'd feel really bad about it later. The ones we're going to be running into out there in the jungle, not so much."

Butler's gaze swung back and forth between Angelo and Tanner. No doubt the lieutenant was trying to convince himself that the red glow he'd seen a few seconds ago had been nothing but a reflection of light, or that maybe he hadn't seen anything at all.

"You're shitting us, right?"

Angelo should have known they wouldn't believe him. The whole thing sounded like something out of a sci-fi movie. Hell, he probably wouldn't have believed it if he hadn't seen those hybrids out in Washington State with his own eyes. But if Carter and Butler waited until they came face-to-face with a real-life nasty-ass hybrid, there was a good chance they wouldn't live long enough to help rescue anyone.

He glanced at Tanner. "This has to come out sooner or later, and sooner would be better. Could you show them, so we can get on with this?"

Tanner didn't move.

"Well?" Angelo prompted. "You gonna, you know, go a little tooth and nail for me?"

"I can't. It doesn't work that way. I can't control it." The look Tanner gave him was almost apologetic. "It's an all-or-nothing thing. And you really don't want me cutting loose here in camp."

Carter chuckled. "Okay, real funny. I like a good joke as much as the next guy, but it's time to get serious. Who are we going up against? Drug runners, Revolutionary Commandos, People's Vanguard, what?"

Angelo swore under his breath. He was just about to

say the hell with it and let the two of them find out the hard way, but Clayne pushed away from the tree and came over.

"We call them hybrids," he said. "And they look a little like this."

Clayne had his back to Angelo but whatever he did got the Special Forces guys' attention. Both men almost fell on their asses they stepped back so fast. That had been Angelo's reaction the first time Clayne had gone all shifter on him, too.

"Holy shit," Carter muttered.

The wolf shifter let his claws and fangs retract. Carter and Butler were still staring at him as if they were wondering what the hell they'd gotten themselves into.

"It's like Angelo tried to tell you, only a bit more complicated," Clayne explained. "I have a few animal-like traits. Tanner has a lot more. He occasionally needs a little help with his control, but he's dealing with it. The things you'll be facing once we get out in the bush are rabid animals with a few human traits. They're vicious, psychotic, and would rather rip out your throat with their fangs or claws than shoot you—though they probably won't have a problem with shooting you, either. They'll go down if you put a round through their heads or their hearts, but anything less will leave them standing long enough to finish you."

Butler exchanged looks with Carter. "How many of these things do you think we're up against?"

"Based on what Tate told us, there could be as many as thirty of forty of them," Angelo said.

Butler let out a low whistle. "Forty against eleven? Not real good odds."

"No, it isn't," Angelo agreed. Understatement there. "But when the sun comes up in the morning, we're going out in that jungle anyway."

Chapter 5

KENDRA COULDN'T BELIEVE SHE'D SLEPT SO WELL. SHE definitely had Declan to thank for that. Not only had sleeping in those big, strong arms of his allowed her to completely forget the dangers existing outside the confines of their shelter, but the warm cocoon he'd created had kept her snug and dry the whole night. It might have been her imagination, but she swore she could still feel the heat of his body, and they'd been on the move for a couple hours already this morning. That was the kind of warmth she could definitely get used to—she was a sucker for a warm, muscular guy to put her cold feet on at night.

She kept her gaze moving from side to side as they crossed a semi-open patch of jungle. It was nice to actually feel the sun on her skin, even if it was only for a short time. Between the trees and the rain showers, there wasn't a whole lot of sun. But on the upside, they hadn't caught a whiff of any hybrids. Maybe Declan's plan was going to work. Maybe all they had to do was slip through the perimeter the bad guys had set up and they'd be home free. They were still being careful anyway. Declan kept his ears open for any sign of trouble while she depended on her eyes. She appreciated that he took her contribution to their protection seriously, checking every few minutes to see what she thought and letting her know what his ears were telling him. She just wished he would have treated her as his equal last night. She was still miffed that he hadn't woken her up to take her turn standing guard.

"The sun came up before I realized it," he'd said.

As excuses went, it was pretty lame. It was more likely he hadn't wanted to wake her because he knew how zonked out she'd been last night. She hadn't called him on the oversight though, mostly because he was probably right. She had needed the rest. She hadn't realized how crappy she'd been sleeping out here until last night. And whether she liked admitting it or not, she had to keep herself fresh if she was going to keep up with Declan.

"I'll pull extra duty tonight," she told him before they left the shelter.

He just grunted in that typically male fashion that meant *I heard you; I just don't really agree with you.*

As they moved back into the deeper confines of the jungle, the early day sun disappeared again to be blocked almost entirely by the thick canopy over their heads. She shivered at the sudden drop in temperature. It only served to remind her how warm she'd been snuggled in Declan's arms.

She glanced at him as they walked. How the heck had she been so wrong about him? She'd thought because he was quiet and introspective that he was boring. But that wasn't true. The conversation they'd had last night had been the most insightful she'd had with a guy in a long time. And, okay, the topic of their conversation wasn't the stuff of first dates, but neither was the situation they were in. But she couldn't think of anyone she'd rather be stranded with than Declan.

Kendra glanced at him again, her gaze lingering a little longer this time. Since they'd started out that morning, she'd spent as much time sneaking peeks at him as she had keeping an eye out for hybrids. It was dangerous, but she wanted to make up for lost time. Even covered in the remnants of their impromptu mud bath yesterday, he was still a sight to behold. Dark blond hair that looked as if he ran his fingers through it all the time, captivating blue eyes, and a square jaw with the perfect amount of scruff. Not to mention a body that wouldn't quit. Even now, his thigh muscles bunched and flexed under his uniform pants. She'd never noticed how graceful he was for a man his size.

She was still marveling at that when Declan suddenly stopped and held up his hand, fist closed in the universal sign for halt. Kendra immediately dropped to one knee behind the closest tree, her finger curling around the trigger of her M4. She followed Declan's gaze but didn't see anything except trees. That was when she realized he wasn't really looking at anything. Instead, his eyes had that unfocused look he got when he was listening intently. She remembered Ivy telling her once that shifters could get so absorbed in what they were doing that they literally lost connection with the real world.

Crap. If Declan did that in the middle of hostile territory, what the hell was she going to do? Somehow, she didn't think that smacking him across the face would be a very good idea.

She was just about to softly call his name when he spoke.

"There's a small group of hybrids moving in this direction. We need to find cover."

Declan started through the jungle. She immediately

followed, checking to both their left and right as he focused on finding them another place to hide.

"Any chance we could just circle wide around them?" she asked.

He shook his head as he veered left and headed up the side of a rocky slope. She had to run to keep up with his long strides.

"There are at least two separate groups out there, maybe three," he told her. "They're scattered pretty wide, but we'd have to essentially thread the needle to get past them. We think the hybrids' sense of smell isn't very good, but I don't have a clue what their hearing is like. It's too risky to try to move past them in broad daylight until we know more about them."

That answered the other question she'd been about to ask—whether Declan thought they could fight their way through the hybrids. God, she hoped the orchids they'd rubbed all over their clothes this morning still covered their scents.

Declan stopped when they got to a group of palm trees. Low growing, they had thick, brownish fronds hanging down to the ground. It wasn't as good a hiding place as they'd had the previous night, but based on how fast Declan was moving, the hybrids were too close to give him time to find anything better.

They pushed their way into the palm trees carefully, trying not to break or dislodge any of the hanging grass. There wasn't much space inside, so she and Declan were forced to crouch side by side.

Kendra slipped the muzzle of her M4 through the cover of their hiding spot, ready to shoot. "How close are they?"

He pointed toward the bottom of the slope they'd just climbed.

As if on cue, three figures came into view. She didn't have to see the red in their eyes to know they were hybrids. They prowled more than walked, swinging their heads back and forth, noses in the air as if sniffing for something. *Crap.* One of them was the captain who'd killed his own man on the bank of the stream the night before simply for challenging his authority. The automatic weapon he carried looked like a toy in his hands, a waste of time compared to the claws he possessed.

She and Declan were barely a hundred feet away and upwind, as best she could tell. There was no way the hybrids wouldn't be able to smell them, no matter how crappy their noses were, orchid perfume or not.

Her heart racing, Kendra slowly sighted the lead hybrid, ready to shoot the second he swung in their direction. Out of the corner of her eye, she saw Declan doing the same. They had to put down the captain first— and fast—or they wouldn't live long enough to worry about the other two. But even if they somehow managed to kill all three of them, the sound of gunfire was sure to bring every other hybrid in the area running.

This so wasn't the kind of action she'd wanted to see on her first official DCO mission.

But while the creatures continued to sniff the air, they never moved any closer. After a few minutes, all three of them disappeared into the jungle.

Kendra slowly let out the breath she'd been holding. Carefully lowering her M4, she leaned back against Declan's shoulder, the fear she'd been keeping in flowing out of her until she was shaking all over. That had been too close.

She closed her eyes, feeling Declan's solid strength and warmth behind her. She didn't care if he thought less of her because of it. She needed to steal some courage from him. He didn't say anything or pull away from her. Instead, he sat there quietly and gave her time to get herself together. She sat up but didn't look at him.

"We should probably get going," she said.

"We'll stay here a little while longer," he told her. "Let the hybrids move completely out of the area."

Kendra suspected the real reason Declan wanted them to wait was because he didn't think she was ready to go back out there yet. She wanted to tell him he was wrong, but honestly, she wasn't so sure. She peeked between the palm fronds to make sure the hybrids hadn't come back, then relaxed.

"Does your family know you're out here?" Declan asked quietly.

She turned a little so she could look at him. Her thigh pressed up against his and she could feel the heat of his skin through her pants.

"No way," Kendra answered. "I mean, my parents know I work for Homeland Security, but they think I have a nice, safe desk job. Which I did up until a few days ago." She gave him a small smile. "I told them I was going on a business trip for a couple weeks and that I'd call them when I got back. They'd be terrified if they knew I was running around the jungles of Central America with an automatic weapon in my hands."

"Do they live in the DC area?" he asked.

She nodded. "Virginia. My mom teaches eighth grade history and my dad is a dentist."

"Any brothers and sisters?"

"Just me." Kendra pulled her knees up and wrapped her arms around them. "What about you? Does your family know you work for Homeland?"

Declan shook his head. "My parents don't know what I do for a living. They don't even know I'm a shifter."

She tried not to let her jaw drop, but she wasn't sure she succeeded. "How is that possible?"

He parted the palm fronds enough so he could see the surrounding jungle, then let them drop into place. "My family is…well, reserved is probably the best way to put it. Image has always been very important to them. My mom teaches at Rhode Island College and my dad is the senior scientist for an independent bio research lab. Having letters after your name is a big deal where I come from."

Kendra frowned. "So what does that have to do with your mom and dad not knowing you're a shifter? They're your parents. How could they miss something like that?"

He shrugged. "I was home alone when I changed the first time and by the time my parents came in, I was back to normal. What was I going to say? *'Hey, Mom; hey, Dad. While you were out, I turned into a werewolf'?*"

"You thought you were a werewolf?"

"I was seventeen and sprouted claws and fangs. Plus, I watched a lot of TV. What was I supposed to think?"

Okay, back before she knew about shifters, she probably would have thought the same thing. "And it honestly didn't occur to you that maybe you should tell your parents?"

"I thought about it," he said. "But then at the dinner table that night, while I sat there eating everything in sight, I listened to my mom explain how shocked she was that one of the other professors at the college had worn white after Labor Day. She literally went on about it for thirty minutes."

His mother would really have a problem with Kendra's clothing choices. She wore whatever she felt like, whenever she felt like it, including white in the middle of winter. "What about after she finished going on about that?"

"I figured that if my mom got worked up about something as stupid as that, she'd probably pass out if she discovered her youngest son was a monster. And what if other people found out what I was? How would my parents deal with it? The longer I sat there, the surer I was that they wouldn't handle it well."

"So you never told them."

He shook his head. "Six months later, I went off to college, so it wasn't all that hard to keep hiding it from them."

She sighed. "So, what do they think you do for a living?"

"They think I work for the USDA, tracking various conservation programs. Let's just say they're not exactly thrilled with my career choices. Which is why my mom and I don't talk much anymore."

Wow was the only word that came to mind. She couldn't imagine going through the changes a shifter did that first time and not having someone to confide in. "What about your dad? Or your brothers and sisters?"

"We still talk occasionally, but we're not as close as we used to be," he admitted.

Well, that sucked. Her parents might not know what she did for a living, but at least they were still proud of her. It sounded as if Declan's family had turned their backs on him because he hadn't followed the career path they'd wanted him to. God, she wanted to smack every one of them.

Since she couldn't do that, she placed her hand on his thigh and gave it a gentle squeeze. "Well, your family might not like your career choices, but if you didn't work for the DCO, I probably wouldn't be alive right now. So, thank you."

Before she could stop herself, Kendra leaned over and brushed his cheek with her lips. The kiss was nothing more than a peck, and yet it sent a little quiver through her. Declan stared at her, surprise in his blue eyes. Had he felt it, too?

"You're…um…you're welcome." He cleared his throat. "We should get going."

She nodded, and just that fast, the thought that she and Declan had experienced a cosmic connection disappeared, replaced by more practical matters. Like getting out of this jungle in one piece.

——ww——

He and Kendra were forced to hide to avoid groups of hybrids three more times in the space of an hour. The first two times, they'd hidden in more palms. This third time, they'd been fortunate enough to find a huge cluster of shrubs and brambles growing along the side of a stream. It was thick enough to hide them from sight and the gurgling water helped cover any sound they might make.

Stopping to hide every fifteen minutes made it seem like they weren't getting any closer to freedom, but it was better than having to fight their way through numerous hybrids. And there were a hell of a lot more roaming around today than there'd been last night. No human soldiers, though. That was a damn scary thought. Had the hybrids killed their own soldiers, or just turned them into monsters like them?

Declan moved slightly, careful not to rustle the shrubs around him and Kendra too much. If there were enough hybrids to both maintain a perimeter and scout the area, that meant there could be as many as a hundred of them out there. To say this had the potential to end badly was an understatement.

But one look at Kendra was enough to make him say to hell with that shit. She was depending on him to get them out of this, and that's exactly what he was going to do.

She was sitting cross-legged beside him, more strands of hair coming loose from her ponytail, a smudge of dirt on her cheek. Take away the cammies and the M4, and put her in a tank top and cutoffs, and she'd look like the quintessential girl next door. And for years, that's how he'd thought of her. But there was so much more to her that he'd never given her credit for.

It wasn't only the courage she'd shown facing the hybrids, though that was damn impressive. What amazed him the most was how mentally tough she'd been. She'd seen things in the last few days that would make the strongest person curl into a ball and give up, but she kept shaking it off and pushing forward.

Kendra was turning out to be full of surprises. Like

the way she'd been able to get him talking about his family—where the hell had that come from? He went out of his way not to talk about them with anyone, but she'd asked and the next thing he knew, he was telling her stuff he'd never told a soul. The worst part was that he'd liked confiding in her. And when she'd kissed him on the cheek? Well, he damn near thought he'd died and gone to heaven.

For one insane moment, he'd let himself believe it had meant something to her, too. But then he realized she would have done the same thing if she'd been out here with Tate, Gavin, or Brent. Or Clayne. Definitely Clayne. But while it hadn't been a big deal for her, it had been for him. One little kiss and he'd been ready to say to hell with the hybrids and spend the rest of the day making love to her.

His hand tightened reflexively around his weapon. It pissed him off that she could make him lose control like he was some kind of hormonal teenager. It convinced him more than ever that he needed to be extra careful around her. In some ways, she was more dangerous to his health than those damn hybrids. At least he was able to keep his head screwed on straight when it came to them.

But five minutes later, he was still thinking about that little kiss and how soft her lips had felt against his cheek. Before he even knew what he was doing, he found himself leaning close to her, breathing deeply through his nose and inhaling her delicious scent. It really wasn't fair. His nose didn't work worth a shit when he needed it to, but when it came to Kendra, it worked like a frigging bloodhound's.

He ran his hand through his hair. He needed a distraction quick or he was going to be nuzzling her neck in a minute.

"So, is your first official DCO field mission living up to you expectations?" he asked.

She parted a few branches and tried to see out of their shelter. He knew she wouldn't be able to, and after a few moments she gave up and sat back again.

"Honestly, there was a certain part of me that was hoping for a little excitement on this mission." She gave him a sheepish look. "Would you consider it whining if I admitted this is way more than I wanted?"

His mouth edged up. "I wouldn't consider it whining at all. But it does make me wonder why you wanted to come on this mission in the first place. Why risk your life if you don't have to?"

She looked away. "You wouldn't understand."

"Try me."

She toyed with the laces on her boot. "Watching the rest of you go out on mission after mission, year after year, seeing places and doing things I'd only dreamed about really sucked. I guess I wanted to be a part of the conversation instead of always being the one on the outside."

After spending all those years in high school and college feeling like an outsider, he understood how that felt. "None of us ever thought less of you because you work behind the scenes. You know that, right? We couldn't do our jobs without the stuff you do at the DCO. You're amazing."

Her face colored with the cutest blush he'd ever seen. "Thanks, but it's not the same. You might not think less of me, but I've always thought less of myself for never risking my life like you do all the time."

When she put it that way, it sounded insane. But he respected her for it.

"How long have you been trying to get John to send you on missions?" he asked.

"About three years, I guess. But the itch has gotten really bad since—"

"Since you fought the hybrids with Ivy and Landon out in Washington State," he finished.

Kendra nodded. "That's when I realized this was something I could do. And it's when I discovered how good it felt to be part of a team and not be the one who stays at home while everyone else risks their lives. It made me feel like I was doing something important." She tilted her head to look at him. "Does that make any sense at all?"

He grinned. "Yeah, actually it makes a lot of sense."

She returned his smile with a small one of her own that lit up his little piece of the world. *Dammit*. Declan mentally kicked himself for asking her something personal. He'd been trying to get her off his mind so he could get his defenses back up, but it hadn't worked out that way at all. She'd opened up and told him something she probably hadn't told another soul. Now, instead of reestablishing a safe distance between them, she'd somehow weaseled herself in even closer.

He was fighting tooth and nail, but Kendra was making it damn near impossible for him to not feel something for her.

Declan was so wrapped up in his own stupidity that he made the decision to leave the shelter without checking to make sure the area was clear. And it was why he didn't hear the pack of hybrids moving along the edge of the stream until he and Kendra walked right into them. He didn't even have time to berate himself before the three hybrids jumped them.

He tried to shove Kendra out of the way, but he was too late. She went down with one of the snarling creatures on her back, her scream echoing in his ears. All Declan could do was pray she lasted until he got to her. And the other two weren't going to make that easy.

He'd barely lifted the barrel of his M4 when both creatures hit him like a ton of bricks, sending his weapon and rucksack flying. Declan let his body shift as he went down, cursing that he didn't have the superlong claws and fangs like other shifters in the DCO. But then again, he probably wouldn't have known what to do with them if he did. Fortunately, he did know how to use the one shifter ability he'd always depended on—his strength. And he needed that strength now to get the two psycho monsters away from him so he could help Kendra.

He got a hand around one hybrid's throat while he used his free arm to deflect the creature's long-ass claws. Or tried to anyway. The beast found his target a couple times, slicing into his chest and shoulder.

Declan bit back a growl and tightened his grip on the hybrid's throat, squeezing until he felt something squish. He shoved the first attacker away and sent a kick toward the knee of the second one. It didn't land, but it made the thing skip back a step.

That was the opening Declan needed. He lunged to his feet and darted over to Kendra. His heart lurched. The hybrid was on her back, both hands clawing at her rucksack like a creature possessed. Hunks of the pack and its contents were flying everywhere, but Declan couldn't tell if the beast's claws had hit anything vulnerable yet. He threw himself at the hybrid, knocking it off Kendra and sending it tumbling.

Declan came down on top of the creature, hoping to get his arms around it and crush the damn thing to death, but it was too fast. The beast slipped out from under him like it was greased, swiping at him the same maniacal way it had gone at Kendra. The thing worked itself into a rage trying to reach him. Declan desperately wanted to get back to Kendra's side, but at the moment, it was all he could do to just keep the hybrid from sinking its teeth into him.

He shot a quick glance past his attacker and saw Kendra scrambling backward like a crab in an effort to reach her weapon, where it lay on the ground. He swore as the hybrid whose windpipe he crushed advanced on her. What the hell did it take to put these things down?

Declan couldn't count on Kendra reaching her weapon in time. He had to get to her.

He roared, gathering himself to charge the frenzied creature in front of him. He'd probably take a shot or two from those razor-sharp claws as he bulled past the thing, but it'd be worth it if it meant saving Kendra's life.

But then a little voice in the back of his head reminded him that he hadn't seen the third hybrid in freaking forever.

He turned just as a blur darted toward him.

He caught an arm and twisted, hearing a satisfying crunch as he took down the hybrid. He'd crush every bone in its body if he had to.

But when Declan moved to go in for the killing blow, the hypodermic syringe in the hybrid's grip froze him in place. As big around as his wrist, it had a four-inch needle with yellow goo dripping from the tip.

What the fuck?

He didn't have time to consider why the hybrid had just tried to stick him with a needle because the rabid creature he'd been about to charge earlier leaped on him. But instead of going for Declan's throat, the beast reached for the needle. The three of them went down in a rolling ball of claws, fangs, and muscles as they all fought for control of the syringe.

Declan was so focused on trying to keep whatever was in the needle out of his body, he barely registered the sound when a weapon rattled off three-round bursts right over his head. The hybrid holding the needle flinched, giving Declan the opportunity he needed to get the heel of one hand under the thing's chin and shove—hard enough to snap its neck and make the back of its head connect with his shoulder blades. He didn't wait to see what effect that had on the creature. If it survived a neck broken that badly, Declan was beyond screwed.

Ripping the syringe out of the dead hybrid's hand, he jabbed it into the neck of the other hybrid. He hadn't really intended to inject the thing. He just wanted that big-ass needle someplace out of the way.

Declan shoved the hybrid away, praying he wasn't too late to help Kendra. But as he rolled to his feet, he realized she didn't need his help. She aimed her M4 at the hybrid he'd stuck with the syringe and shot the thing in the head.

He put his hand on her arm. "Are you okay? Did that thing get you?"

Declan didn't wait for an answer, but instead spun her around to check for himself. Her uniform top was torn in a few places, but the skin underneath appeared beautifully unmarred.

"I'm okay," she said. "It was close, but you got it off me in time."

Thank God. Declan was so relieved he felt like hugging her. He probably would have if her eyes hadn't gone wide with horror. *Oh, shit. What now?*

"You're bleeding!" she said.

Declan looked down at the gash on his chest. "It's just a scratch. He barely got me."

She swung her M4 over her shoulder. "Let me check."

The urge to feel her hands on him was way more tempting than it should have been given the circumstances. But right now, he had to get his head screwed back on right and get them out of here, and he couldn't do that with Kendra playing nursemaid.

He caught her hands. "Later. We need to get out of here before more hybrids show up. The gunfire is bound to draw them like flies."

She frowned, her gaze lingering on his wounds, but then she nodded. "You're right. Sorry. I had to shoot. I couldn't figure out any other way to put them down."

"You don't hear me complaining." He gave her hands a squeeze. "Let's get our stuff and get going."

Unfortunately, getting their stuff turned out to be more difficult than anticipated. Kendra's pack was a goner, as was most of the stuff in it. She ran around, trying to pick up what she could salvage—ammo, protein bars, and the gun cleaning, survival, and first-aid kits. Her clothes were scattered and shredded, but she still checked to see if any of them were usable.

"Forget about those," he said. "You can make do with the uniform you're wearing."

She put her hands on her hips, pinning him with a look as he dropped to one knee beside a dead hybrid and began going through its cargo pockets. "And what am I supposed to do about underwear?" she demanded.

"I don't know." He moved to the second hybrid. "Can't you just do without?"

Declan was sorry he'd said it the second the words were out of his mouth because the image it brought to mind—of Kendra running around the jungle bare-ass naked—was seriously distracting.

She bent to rummage through another pile of clothing. "I'm not even going to answer that."

Thank God. Because if she'd said yes, he really would have been in trouble.

Once Kendra found what she was looking for, she ran over to his rucksack and crammed the remains of her belongings into any space she could find in the stuffed bag. What didn't fit in his bag went into the cargo pockets of her uniform pants.

Declan didn't find anything of value on the first two hybrids. No food or water, no survival gear beyond two cheap knives, not even a map that might have told him where the hybrid camp was located. There was a handheld radio, but it had been smashed to pieces in the fight, so there was no chance eavesdropping on any communications. As for weapons, the hybrids had been carrying heavier FN SCAR assault rifles, so even the small amount of ammo that went with them was worthless to Declan and Kendra—it wasn't 5.56 mm, so it wouldn't fit in their M4s.

He walked over to where Kendra was standing beside the third body—the hybrid he'd stabbed with the syringe and she'd shot.

"What the hell is that?" she asked, pointing at the hypodermic needle.

"It's a syringe."

She gave him an impatient look. "Really? I never would have guessed. I meant, what was a hybrid doing with it?"

"They were trying to stick me with it."

She kneeled down and yanked the syringe out of the hybrid's neck, then depressed the plunger the last few millimeters until glistening, yellow goo squirted from the tip. She seemed so fascinated Declan almost asked if she was going to taste it like they did on TV shows.

"What do you think is in it?" she asked.

"I'm pretty sure it's not vitamin B. I wasn't going to let him stick me so I could find out."

When she leaned close and sniffed the needle, Declan decided he'd had enough. He pulled the syringe out of her hand and tossed it to the ground, then reached down and pulled her to her feet. "We have to go."

"Hope the stuff I added to your pack didn't add too much weight," she said as he slung it onto his shoulder.

He chuckled. "I think I can handle a few spare magazines and some shredded undies."

That last part prompted yet another unwanted image, this time of Kendra prowling around the jungle wearing nothing but a sexy smile and some strategically ripped underwear. He shoved that thought aside and focused his attention outward as he started to run through the trees.

"I should have had you carry my stuff all along," she said as she pulled even with him. "We probably would have moved faster that way."

He only grunted and picked up the pace. But a part of his mind rebelled and painted a nice picture of him digging through his rucksack looking for ammo and finding her cute little panties instead.

Damn, he had issues.

Chapter 6

"YOU SURE SHE'S LEADING US THE RIGHT WAY?" Carter asked softly. "How the hell does she know where the crash site is without a GPS or compass?"

Angelo chuckled as he stepped over a downed tree. "She knows where she's going, trust me. And she doesn't need toys to tell her."

"I don't know." Carter gave him a sidelong glance. "I'm not being sexist or anything, but I'm not sure I'm too comfortable with her leading the group."

Behind Angelo, Derek snorted. "I wouldn't let her hear you say that. She might decide to come back here and gut you like a fish."

Carter threw Ivy a quick look. She was fifty yards ahead of them on point. "It's not like she can hear me. Besides, all I'm saying is that I've never met a single woman who was any good at land nav."

"Good thing I'm not single then," Ivy called out from up front, her eyes never leaving the jungle ahead of them. "Or I might get us lost out here."

The sergeant first class stumbled, almost losing his footing. He gave Angelo a chagrined look. "Oh, shit. She's one of those things, isn't she?"

Angelo laughed. "Yeah, she's a shifter. And when things get bad, you'll be glad she's with us."

Carter frowned and glanced at his lieutenant.

"Don't look at me," Butler said. "You opened your piehole and put your foot in. Deal with it."

Carter swore again and moved faster to catch up to the group ahead. Angelo chuckled again. No doubt it was so he could talk to Ivy and make sure they were good. Smart guy. You didn't want to go into a firefight with things left unsaid.

Up front, Ivy and Landon were breaking trail and making sure they didn't walk into an ambush. Tate, Brent, and Gavin followed in a loose cluster behind them, doing their best to try and push the pace as hard as they could. That explained why Landon hadn't let Tate take the lead. The guy was so worried about Declan and Kendra, he wasn't exactly thinking straight. Angelo couldn't fault the guy. If he were in Tate's place, he probably wouldn't be firing on all cylinders right now either.

Angelo glanced over his shoulder, checking on Derek and Butler off to either side, then back at Tanner and Clayne, pulling trail position about twenty yards behind them. Even as he watched, Tanner disappeared into the jungle, moving so quickly it was hard to track him. He and Clayne had been disappearing on and off like that for the last hour, constantly checking along their flanks to make sure they didn't get caught by surprise from that direction.

Angelo swore as the gathering gloom started to darken the jungle. The light would be completely gone in thirty minutes. It had taken them a hell of a lot longer than expected to get to the original landing zone that Tate and the others had been evacuated from.

Last night, Landon had fought to get them military air support, but even with John and the DCO's considerable pull, they hadn't been able to swing it. The political powers that be—both in Costa Rica and the United States—had every military and federal asset in the country on full lockdown until somebody could figure out exactly what had happened in the jungle. The fact that there was a good chance there were still more than half a dozen Americans and Costa Ricans out there somewhere in need of rescue didn't appear to be on anyone's list of concerns. Angelo ground his jaw. Typical politicians.

It had been well past midday before John had finally come through and secured them helicopter transport to where they needed to be, in the form of three old tourist choppers that looked as if their best days were long since passed. Even though John had already paid a king's ransom for a quick one-way trip to the landing zone coordinates, they'd still had to pass a hat around to collect money to pay the pilots. After hearing rumors around the camp about monsters in the jungle with fangs and claws and glowing red eyes, the pilots had given the money to the helicopter mechanics with instructions to make sure their families got it if they didn't come back. Angelo suspected the mechanics would probably pocket the money if that happened, but he didn't say anything. Not that he had the chance. When they'd reached the landing zone, the pilots had practically torn the rotors off their birds trying to get off the ground and back home. Catching sight of the smoldering remains of the U.S. military chopper out in the jungle as they'd come in probably had something to do with that.

"We're here," Landon called from ahead, jerking Angelo out of his thoughts and bringing all of them up short.

This was the part Angelo had been dreading—checking

the helicopter for remains. He wanted to believe Declan and Kendra were still alive, but one look at the smashed Seahawk told him otherwise. The bird had come down hard, then partially burned. Not many people could survive that.

The three bodies on the ground only confirmed his worst fears. Angelo was too far away to make out who they were, but beside him, Derek went pale.

"It might not be them," Angelo told him. "There were other people on that chopper with Kendra and Declan."

Derek nodded but didn't say anything. He made no move to check, though.

Giving Derek a nod, Angelo walked over to the bodies. Tate fell into step beside him while Landon climbed into the helicopter. Two of the dead men wore marine uniforms, so it was obvious who they were. A rain slicker had been draped over the third, and Angelo held his breath as he crouched down and moved it aside.

"He was DEA," Tate said, his face a mix a relief and sorrow as he gazed down at the dead man.

Angelo knew how he felt. Covering the man with the slicker again, he stood up. A few feet away, Derek breathed a sigh of relief.

Landon came out of the helicopter shaking his head. "No one in there."

"That's good," Tate said. "That means two other people made it out with Declan and Kendra, along with the crew from the chopper."

Clayne jogged up. "Cut the list of possible survivors by two. I found the pilot and copilot…they didn't make it through the crash."

Tate swore. Angelo couldn't blame him. They'd

come out here looking for survivors and so far they'd already found five bodies.

"I know it looks bad, but at least we know that Kendra, Declan, and at least three of the others made it out," Angelo reminded him. "We're going to find them."

Clayne disappeared into the jungle with Ivy and Tanner without a word. Probably searching for some sign or scent of which way Kendra and Declan had gone. Even though the shifters were circling the site a mere fifty feet away, Angelo could barely see them.

"Damn it gets dark fast out here," Derek said, as if reading his mind.

"You guys from the 5th spend too much time in the desert," Carter said as he pulled out his NVGs. "You forget what it's like in the jungle. The sun probably won't go completely down for another thirty minutes, but under this canopy it might as well be midnight."

Angelo rummaged in his pack for his own goggles. As soon as Ivy and the other shifters found a trail, they'd be on the move, and he wanted to be ready. Now that they knew Declan and Kendra were alive, there was no time to waste.

"What are they doing out there?" Butler asked as he attached his goggles to the Ops-Core Ballistic helmet he'd pulled out of his rucksack.

"They're tracing all the different scents around here." Landon quickly put on his own gear. "They'll be able to tell how many of our people left this site, which way they went, if any of them were injured, and most importantly, if they were followed."

Carter let out a low whistle. "They can do all that?"

Angelo flicked on his goggles and adjusted his helmet

straps just in time to see Landon nod. "They can do all that. And they can do it damn fast. So let's make sure we're ready to go when they are."

While they waited, Angelo pulled out his poncho, then glanced at Derek. "Give me a hand, would you?"

Derek didn't ask what he needed a hand with, but he quickly figured it out when Angelo crouched down beside one of the dead marines and wrapped the poncho around the body. When they were finished, Derek took out his poncho and covered the other marine. Carter did the same to the DEA agent. It wouldn't protect the remains as well as burying them, but it was all they had time to do and it might keep animals away for a time. They'd barely finished when Ivy, Clayne, and Tanner came back. Their eyes glowed in the darkness.

"What's the situation?" Landon asked.

"Four people walked out of here," Ivy said. "Declan and Kendra, and two others. Locals probably."

Tate let out a breath. "What about the third crewman?"

Clayne shrugged. "No sign of him."

"Kendra and Declan were okay after the crash, right?" Derek asked.

"Looks like it," Clayne said. "They didn't hang around here for long, though."

"Declan would know the smoke from the wreckage would draw the hybrids like flies. He would have gotten everyone away from it as fast as he could," Tate said. "Do you know which way they went?"

Ivy exchanged looks with Clayne. "Declan and Kendra headed out going due west, directly away from the landing zone."

Landon frowned. "Kendra and Declan? Not the others?"

Clayne shared another look with Ivy. "The other two headed out on their own, going almost due south."

"Why didn't they all stay together?" Butler asked.

Tate swore softly. "Because they saw Declan shift during the ambush. From their point of view, there isn't much difference between him and the hybrids."

"So what do we do?" Carter asked. "I know you brought us in primarily to rescue your friends, Captain, but we aren't just going to abandon the other two, are we?"

Everyone turned to Landon, and Angelo was once again struck by how people naturally turned to him for leadership. Always had, always would.

"No," Landon said. "A couple of us will track down the locals while the rest of us focus on finding Declan and Kendra." He looked at Ivy, then Clayne. "But any team I send out will need a shifter to help track them."

Angelo knew Landon well enough to know he didn't want Ivy running around the jungle without him, but the alternative was pointing at Clayne and saying, "Tag, you're it." Landon wouldn't do that, if for no other reason than Ivy wouldn't put up with it.

"I'll do it."

Angelo turned to see Tanner standing there with his eyes glowing in the green light of the NVGs.

Landon hesitated. "Can you use your nose well enough to track them?"

Tanner nodded. "My nose isn't as good as Ivy's or Clayne's, but now that I have a good bead on their scents, I can find them."

"I'll go with him," Carter said.

Tanner shook his head. "I can travel faster alone."

"I'm sure you can," Carter agreed. "But what are you

going to do once you find them? Club them senseless and
force them to do as you tell them? I speak the language,
remember? I can get them to come with us willingly."

"I'll go, too," Gavin said quietly.

Tate's mouth tightened. "Like hell. We're out here to
find Declan and Kendra."

"I know that. But there are two locals out there who
are as good as dead if they run into those damn hybrids,"
Gavin said. "Someone has to go after them. If Declan
were here, he'd say the same thing."

"For all we know, the two locals could already be
dead," Tate ground out. "And as far as Declan agree-
ing with you, he was the one who let them go off on
their own."

"Because you told him to get Kendra out of here
safely," Gavin shot back.

In the green glow of the NVGs, Angelo could see
Tate's jaw clench. For a minute, Angelo thought he
might have to get between the two men.

"Dammit, don't you think I know that?" Tate finally
said. Cursing, he turned and stormed off.

In the silence, Angelo let his gaze follow the man,
half-afraid Tate would be stupid enough to go out looking for his missing teammate on his own. But the DCO
operative stopped on the edge of the clearing to stare
off into the jungle. Tate might not have come out and
said it, but it was obvious that he felt responsible for
what happened to Declan and Kendra. If they died, Tate
would carry the weight of that with him for the rest of
his life, and nothing anyone said would ease the pain or
the memory. Unfortunately, Angelo had some experience with that.

Angelo gave himself a mental shake and turned his attention back to Landon, listening in as they hammered out what Tanner's team would do if they found the locals, as well as if they didn't. The details took a while to work out, but they finally decided that if they found the locals, they'd head in whichever direction seemed the safest. If they didn't, Tanner and the other men would backtrack and link up with them again. A few minutes later, Tanner and his group went south while Angelo and the others headed west.

"Do you really think it was okay to let Tanner lead the other team?" Ivy asked Landon as they walked.

Angelo had been wondering that, too. He didn't know much about Tanner, but if half the stuff Landon told him was true, they'd just let a ticking time bomb take charge of a three-person rescue team.

"We didn't have any other choice," Landon answered.

Not exactly a ringing endorsement, Angelo thought.

Ivy gave Landon's hand a squeeze; then she and Clayne ran ahead, tracking Declan's and Kendra's scents. They set a fast pace, which forced the rest of the team to commit almost all their attention to keeping up. But Angelo trusted the shifters to alert them if any hybrids got close enough to be a threat.

Clayne came back fifteen minutes later to report that Declan and Kendra had been moving fast, running whenever the terrain would allow it. A few minutes later, Ivy materialized out of the darkened jungle to tell them why they'd been in such a hurry—there'd been a lot of hybrids on their trail.

Angelo swore. He hated thinking of Kendra running through the jungle while a pack of bloodthirsty hybrids

nipped at her heels. He'd liked her from the moment
they'd met in Washington State and couldn't stand the
thought of something happening to her. She was smart,
resourceful, and loyal to her friends. But she wasn't a
soldier, and she wasn't used to the stress of being hunted
like an animal. Angelo prayed Declan could keep her
safe long enough for the rescue party to catch up to
them. At the pace Ivy and Clayne were setting, that
shouldn't be too long.

But two hours later, their pace slowed considerably
until finally the two shifters up front came to a complete
stop. Clayne disappeared into the jungle while Ivy dou-
bled back to let them know what the hell was going on.

"We've lost Declan's and Kendra's scents."

Derek frowned. "What do you mean, lost them? Like
they were captured?"

Ivy shook her head. "No. It just disappeared. I think
Declan is using something to cover their scent, but
I'll be damned if I know what it is. Clayne is trying
to follow them using their physical tracks instead, but
that's hard to do in the jungle at night. It's going to slow
us way down."

"If you two are having problems tracking them,
maybe the hybrids will, too," Angelo said.

As they waited for Clayne to return, Angelo grabbed
a quick bite to eat. He was just putting away a half-eaten
energy bar when Ivy's head snapped up.

Six weapons swung in the direction she was looking
as if they had a mind of their own.

"What's wrong?" Landon whispered.

"Clayne's headed back, and he's not alone," she
said softly.

"Declan and Kendra?" Derek asked hopefully.

"Hybrids—a lot of them."

Angelo's hands tightened around his weapon. *Shit.*

Landon quickly positioned them for a hasty ambush, spreading everyone out in a loose line. He put Angelo on security, along with Brent and Butler. Their job would be to not only lay fire into the kill zone, but also to act as a reaction force in the event that any of the hybrids tried to slip around their flanks.

"Wait for Clayne to come through here before you open fire," Landon ordered. "Initiate on my signal unless compromised."

Thirty seconds later, Clayne came running so fast he was almost a blur, a pack of snarling hybrids on his heels.

Landon put a three-round burst through the chest of the first. Angelo took that as his signal and started shooting. Everyone else around him did, too, and the jungle came alive with the sound of gunfire and the glowing zip of tracer rounds.

One big-ass hybrid with blood pouring out of at least four holes in his chest and stomach charged Angelo. He switched to full auto, hoping it would bring the damn thing down, but it didn't even seem to faze the creature. Then Clayne was beside them, his .45 blasting into the hybrid at point-blank range. The beast reached for Butler even as it fell. The lieutenant pulled his sidearm and put one more round through the thing's head for insurance's sake.

"What the fuck are these things?" Butler took aim at another hybrid inches before it reached Brent, who was in the middle of reloading. "Zombies would go down easier."

Angelo was too busy burning through clip after clip of ammo to answer. He had to say one thing about the hybrids—they didn't lack for balls. They attacked like nothing he'd ever seen.

If there was any saving grace to the hybrids' aggressive style, it was that they did it without any finesse or thought. They threw themselves at whoever was shooting at them without flanking the ambush, retreating, or any other option Angelo would have considered had he been in the same situation. When the hybrids ran out of ammo, they didn't even try to reload. They simply tossed their weapons aside and attacked with fangs and claws.

It seemed to take forever to finish them off. Landon moved among them, checking for injuries and the status of ammo. The smell of smokeless powder and hot metal warred with the near-overwhelming stench of blood. Angelo breathed through his mouth, trying to avoid the worst of it, but it didn't help much. All around him, the jungle was deathly still, as if every animal within a mile was waiting to see what happened next.

Butler shook his head at the dead hybrids scattered throughout the kill zone. "Holy shit. There are only ten of these damn things. I thought there were at least twice that."

"Ten's enough." Clayne bent down to take a closer look at one of the hybrids. "Damn, look at the fangs on this one. They're as long as my fingers."

Landon took out his flashlight. "Turn off your NVGs."

When they'd done as he ordered, he turned on the flashlight and swept it over the dead bodies. Angelo flipped up his goggles and joined his former captain as Landon leaned down to look at one body, then the next.

"What's up?" Angelo asked.

"These hybrids are different than the ones we fought in Washington." He shined the flashlight straight into the hybrid's mouth. "Damn. Is that a second row of teeth coming in? Ivy, take a look at this."

But Ivy wasn't paying attention to her husband. She had her eyes closed and her face turned up, sniffing the air.

"Shit," Clayne muttered. He dropped his pack and started digging in it.

"Ivy?" Landon said.

Ivy finally turned her attention to him. "I heard you. And I'd love to take a look at the dead hybrids, but later. Right now, I'm more concerned with the live hybrids coming this way."

Angelo swore and reloaded his magazines. Butler did the same. On the far side of the clearing Tate and Brent picked up the dead hybrids' weapons and raided their ammo pouches. Probably not a bad idea.

Beside Angelo, Clayne was reloading his M4 magazines faster than Angelo had ever seen anyone reload. Then he did the same to his .45 clips.

"I swear that if we get out of this alive, Danica can have her wedding in any damn church she likes," Clayne said. "That includes the Vatican."

Angelo laughed. "I'm going to tell her you said that. Though I think there might be a long waiting list of people ahead of you."

Clayne slammed a fresh clip into his .45 with a growl. "I have a way of dealing with waiting lists."

"Stop wiggling around like such a baby," Kendra said. "It's just an antiseptic wipe. Sheesh, I'd have thought someone your size would be tougher."

Declan chuckled. "It doesn't hurt. It's cold."

"Oh." She cringed. "Sorry."

She fell silent as she went back to cleaning the three long, ragged wounds that started at the top of his left shoulder and ran diagonally across his chest. She'd already cleaned the other claw marks on his chest, but the ones on his shoulder concerned her the most. They were deep. She thought about putting on her NVGs so she could see better, but she hated those things — everything looked so green and washed out. She'd do a better job working by feel.

Declan had attempted to tell her he didn't need her to fuss over him, but she wasn't putting up with any of that. The moment they'd gotten far enough away from the attack site and found a good hiding place, she'd ordered him to take off his shredded uniform top and T-shirt.

She'd been really worried about his wounds; there'd been a lot of blood on his clothes. She had no idea what kind of nasty jungle crud those hybrids had been carrying under their claws. The last thing she needed was for Declan to get some kind of hybrid-induced infection while they were out here fighting for their lives. And working at the DCO had taught her one thing — shifters healed quickly. She had to get his wounds cleaned before they started closing over and trapped dirt and possible infection inside. Fortunately, after she'd gotten his top off and wiped away the worst of the blood, she realized they weren't nearly as bad as she'd thought.

"That was a lot of shooting we heard before," she

said as she ran the wipe over his skin. "Was it as close as it sounded?"

Declan growled a little as she hit a tender spot but shook his head when she asked if she should stop. "I'm okay. Keep going. As for the shooting, it might have been only a few miles away, or it could have been fifteen. All the valleys, canyons, and cliffs around here can do crazy things to sound. But I agree with you. There were a lot of people—or hybrids—shooting."

She'd hoped his shifter hearing would be able to pinpoint the source of the gun battle. But she still had reason to hope the sound might bode well for them. "Do you think it was a rescue party looking for us?"

Declan was silent as he considered that. As she waited for him to answer, she let her fingers trail along his ribs and abs, looking for other damage. She didn't think he'd gotten scratched anywhere else, but she wanted to check and make sure. The act of slowly and gently cleaning his muscular body, checking for other wounds, running her fingers here and there was extremely mesmerizing for some reason. At first she told herself she was doing it to be thorough, but as she continued to trail her fingers over places she knew the hybrids had never gotten near, she finally admitted she was touching him because she liked it.

She blushed, but she didn't stop what she was doing. Declan had a really nice body—even with the ragged claw marks. It was dark in the shelter, so she couldn't see much, but she didn't need to see his body to enjoy it. The sensation of his warm skin under her fingers was enough.

"It might be a rescue party," he answered, his voice

soft. "But it's just as likely those shots were from a pack of hybrids executing a random group of hikers or eco-tourists they stumbled across."

Kendra shuddered. God, she didn't want to think about that. Instead she focused on the positive. "But there's still a chance it was Tate and the other guys. Shouldn't we try to rendezvous with them?"

He pondered the question before answering. Kendra took the opportunity to let her fingers wander farther, from his thick, muscular neck, down across both broad shoulders, and around his big biceps and finally his forearms. Declan didn't seem to mind her ministrations, and she sure didn't mind doing them. If she closed her eyes and blocked out all the plant smells and animal sounds, she could almost imagine they were back home in her bedroom, enjoying a leisurely massage instead of fighting for their lives in the hybrid-filled jungles of Costa Rica.

"Before we started running into all these hybrids, I would have been the first to say we should be heading in that direction," Declan said, pulling her back to the here and now. "But now, we can't take the risk. There are just too many bad guys running around the jungle right now. And all that shooting is bound to draw even more hybrids in that direction. We'd literally be walking ourselves right into their hands, then end up having to fight our way through who knows how many of them, exposing ourselves and likely using up what little ammo we have left. And what do we do if we get there only to find out that it wasn't Tate and the guys? It'd be over for us."

She sighed, knowing that he was right. "Sorry. I was just hoping. Silly, I know."

Declan put one of his big hands on her leg and gave it a soft squeeze. The squeeze was nice but not nearly as nice as the warmth of his touch. "There's nothing to be sorry about, and it wasn't silly. I had the exact same thought when I heard those shots. If I thought the risk was worth it, we'd be heading there right now. But I really think our best bet is to use the distraction offered by whoever was doing that shooting and keep moving northwest as fast as we can."

Kendra moved her hands up his well-muscled arms to his equally chiseled chest. She had a thing for really muscular chests. Or maybe she just had a thing for Declan's muscular chest. Either way, she kept swiping here and there with one of the medicated wipes, using the flimsy prop to justify what was really nothing more than a massage now.

Declan didn't complain. In fact, she was pretty sure his eyes were closed. No shock there. He'd just fought off three hybrids, not to mention hadn't eaten for the last two days. He was probably wiped out, and her gentle touches were likely putting him to sleep. She smiled in the dark. She was glad she could do something simple like this for him in return for the amazing job he was doing keeping her alive.

But as she glided her fingers down the center of his abs and along the light happy trail of fine hair toward his belly button, Declan stiffened. "I think I'm good, Kendra. I don't think any of those hybrids got me that low."

Kendra flinched at the sudden harshness in his tone. Apparently, he didn't appreciate her touch quite as much as she'd thought. It hurt her feelings more than a little, but she supposed she shouldn't be surprised. He'd been avoiding all contact with her for months, so he probably didn't appreciate it now.

"I was just checking," she explained softly. "Even a little scratch can get infected out here."

"I know…and…thanks."

Kendra took her hands away as he slowly sat up, already missing the contact with his skin and the sense of calm that had come with it. As she scooted back to make room for him, she abruptly felt foolish, both for letting herself get so emotionally invested in something as impersonal as cleaning a guy's wounds and for feeling so hurt by his rejection.

She mentally slapped herself. She needed to stop acting like a hormonal teenager on prom night and focus on the here and now. They had bigger crap to worry about than hurt feelings and unrequited interest. As Declan pulled his pack over and dug out a semi-clean T-shirt, she focused on the one issue that had been bothering her since the hybrids had attacked them earlier.

"You know that needle meant the hybrids were trying to take you alive, don't you?" she asked.

He pulled on his shirt. "I've been thinking the same thing, but why? They sure as hell didn't have a problem shooting at me that first day. What could they want with me?"

Kendra had a pretty good idea why the hybrids might be trying to take him alive, but she wasn't sure how to tell him without spilling all of Ivy's secrets—and those weren't hers to spill. She could try and mince words, maybe say enough to get him to recognize the risk he was facing. But that wouldn't be fair. She'd be risking Declan's life if she didn't give him the whole truth. She had to make sure he understood the kind of psychos he was up against.

"They don't want you," she said. "They want your shifter DNA."

Declan frowned. "How the hell do you know that? Oh wait, let me guess. You can't tell me. It's a secret, right?"

"It's a secret all right…a big one. But you need to hear it because I need you to realize how serious this is."

Declan was silent. "This involves Ivy again, doesn't it?"

She nodded. "Yes. So when I tell you that you can never breathe a word of what I'm about to tell you to another soul, you know why."

"Okay. I understand."

Kendra took a moment to collect her thoughts, trying to figure out what to say that wouldn't require at least an hour of backstory. Finally, she decided to stick to the important facts that mattered the most right now.

"You know those two doctors the DCO has been hunting for months?" she asked.

Of course he did—everyone in the DCO was aware that they'd been after the architects of the hybrid program since Ivy and Landon had filed their report on the two insane doctors. But she needed somewhere to start and that seemed as good as anywhere else. When Declan nodded, she jumped in with both feet.

"They grabbed Ivy out in Washington State and experimented on her. The one big thing they were after were DNA samples—all kinds of samples."

Declan swore. "How the hell did this not come out?"

"It didn't come out because Ivy and Landon never told anyone."

Silence, then another curse. "Because then everyone would have known Landon didn't follow the DCO's first standing order and kill Ivy when it looked like she was going to be captured."

"Exactly," she said.

Hopefully Declan wouldn't ask the next obvious question: *Why* had Landon refused to follow the most rigid DCO order? Telling Declan that Ivy had been experimented on was bad enough; telling him that she had fallen in love with — and married — her partner? That was a whole different level of complicated.

But Declan was more interested in something else. "So Ivy was captured and instead of calling the DCO for help, Landon called...you?"

"Sheesh, you don't have to make it sound like I'm that far down on the list," she said wryly. "But you're right. Landon initially wanted you and your team, but you were out chasing down Tanner. Landon wanted someone he could trust. That ended up being me."

She wasn't going to mention Clayne or the entire Special Forces team Landon had called in. No need to draw anyone else into this story. She was already violating so many promises it wasn't even funny.

"And these doctors — they experimented on Ivy. Took DNA samples?"

This was the part she really needed to hammer home. She needed Declan to understand the kind of vicious psychos they were up against.

"*Experimented* is putting it mildly. *Tortured* would be a better word. They wanted DNA samples and they didn't care how they got them. At the same time, the doctors wanted to evaluate Ivy's pain threshold. They used scalpels, drills, and worse. If we hadn't found her when we did…" She shuddered. "They were planning to take brain tissue samples next."

Declan was growling before Kendra was halfway finished, and she looked up to see his eyes glowing a soft rose color. She'd never seen Declan's eyes glow, even when they'd been moving around at night. But while the glow was reddish, it was completely different than that of the hybrids. Nevertheless, to know that his eyes did that when he got angry was a little… scary. She couldn't believe in all the years she'd worked with him, she'd never seen that part of his shifter nature.

But the glow disappeared just as fast as it had appeared, leaving her to wonder if she'd really seen it at all.

"Is Ivy okay now?" Declan asked, his voice a little thick, and Kendra knew he was fighting to get his fangs and jaw to shift back to normal.

"Yes. As okay as one could expect after what happened to her. But she'll never forget what they did to her or what they took from her. And when she finds them, they'll pay."

"Is that what she and Landon have been doing all those times when their missions ran over or they got delayed in transit, trying to find those doctors?"

Kendra tried not to look shocked, and thought she'd managed it, until Declan chuckled. "I'll take that as a yes."

"How long have you noticed this going on? Have you told anyone else?" she asked.

If Declan had noticed—or pointed out—what Landon and Ivy were doing, they were screwed. Did John know?

Or worse, Dick? If so, the Committee almost certainly knew as well. Her pulse began to beat out of control.

"Relax and breathe." Declan reached out to place his big hands on her shoulders. "I noticed a while ago, but I haven't told anyone. And I'm pretty sure no one else has realized what's going on, so you can calm down before you start to hyperventilate."

She took a deep breath, then another while Declan sat there with his hands on her shoulders, waiting patiently.

"How did you figure out what was going on?" she finally asked.

He took his hands away. "I'm big, but that doesn't mean I'm stupid. I pay attention to the little things most people could care less about. Like when I noticed Landon chewing a piece of gum from a pack with airport markings for a tiny island in the Philippines, even though they were supposed to have been in Japan. Or that box of real Belgian chocolate Ivy left on your desk a couple of weeks ago, though they'd supposedly just come back from Moscow. Little things, but I noticed them often enough to figure out the two of them were doing some off-the-books traveling. I figured it was none of my business, so I didn't tell anyone about it."

Kendra was shocked—and embarrassed. She'd never thought of Declan as being that perceptive. Stupid of her. She knew he was smart—MIT smart. It shouldn't be surprising he used that intelligence to see things around him other people missed. And since he was so quiet, it wasn't like he'd broadcast what he picked up on. Had he already figured out Ivy and Landon were a couple, too?

"Do you think anybody else noticed the same things

you did and figured out what Ivy and Landon are up to?"
she asked.

"Like John? I doubt it. He is way too busy keeping
the DCO going. He's so big picture that the day-to-day
stuff isn't even on his radar."

"What about Dick?"

Declan snorted. "Dick isn't around any of us field
agents enough to notice stuff like that. He's too busy
spending all his time in the offices up on the Hill. He's
the least of our worries. No, the only one who might be
on to you is that Russian doctor—Zarina. She's sharper
than anyone realizes. She runs around with her nose
stuck in her lab notes, but trust me, she sees everything.
If there's someone you need to worry about, it's her."

Kendra smiled. Nice to know that while Declan
was observant enough to see some things, he didn't
see everything. "Don't worry about Zarina. She's not
a problem."

"More secrets?" he asked, then held up his hands.
"Never mind. I don't want to know. Let's just focus on
why those hybrids were trying to stick that needle in me."

Good idea. She didn't want to spill any more of her
friends' secrets. "That needle tells me it's likely the doctors who tortured Ivy are here in Costa Rica looking for
DNA material from more real shifters to improve their
hybrid process."

Declan frowned, considering that. "Maybe that's
why we were ambushed—so they could get their hands
on me."

"I thought that, too, but then why shoot at you
when they first came after us? I don't think you were
their target."

"Okay, but then what changed?" he asked. "The doctors Ivy and Landon have been chasing certainly have the intel to let them know I was out here. Why go from trying to kill me to wanting to grab me?"

She shook her head. "I don't know. There's obviously something going on here we don't know about."

"Well, there's one thing we do know."

"What's that?"

"That I sure as hell don't want to fall into their hands. I like my DNA exactly where it is."

She laughed. "Me, too."

Declan pulled his pack closer and dug around inside it, then held out an energy bar. "Here. You haven't eaten anything since this morning."

Kendra made a face. "God, I hate these things. It's like eating tub and tile caulk."

He lifted a brow. "And you have experience eating tub and tile caulk?"

"After eating these things, the answer is yes, I do."

"Just eat it," he said gently. "If you do, I promise to take you out to a real restaurant when we get back and buy you anything you want."

She eyed him thoughtfully as she tore open the wrapper. "Anywhere I want to go, and anything I want to eat?"

He chuckled. "Yes and yes. But you have to eat the whole bar."

"If I have to eat, so do you."

"I'm not hungry," he said. "I loaded up before the mission, remember? I'm still good for a couple more days."

Kendra knew that was bull. She hadn't seen Declan eat anything since the day before the ambush—over forty-eight hours ago. There was no way he could keep going as hard as he had been with absolutely no fuel in his system, bear shifter or not.

She wrapped the bar back up. "Well, in that case, I'm not hungry either. I'll wait until tomorrow."

He growled but reached into his pack and pulled out another bar. "Fine, you stubborn woman, I'll eat one. But we don't have many of them left. This will have to be my last one for a while."

She waited until he unwrapped his bar and took a bite. Only then did she nibble her own. Yuck, she really had grown tired of these things. But she was starving.

"I want to go to P.F. Chang's," she said in between small bites.

"What?"

"You said you'd take me to any restaurant I wanted and that's where I want to go. It's my favorite place to eat."

He thought about that, then shrugged. "Okay. If that's where you want to go, that's where I'll take you." Declan took another bite, devouring more than half of the remaining bar in a single chomp. "So, what do you want to eat?"

She didn't even have to think about it. "Spring rolls."

"That's it?" He finished his bar, then stuffed the wrapper in his pack. "I'm taking you to your favorite place for dinner after a week in the jungle, and all you want is spring rolls?"

She laughed. "They make really good spring rolls, but no, that's not all I want. The spring rolls are just the appetizer."

"Tell me what else you want." He gestured to the bar in her hand. "Just don't forget to eat while you do."

She looked down to see that she hadn't eaten much of the bar at all. When she took another bite, it just reminded her why energy bars weren't on the menu at P.F. Chang's. She forced herself to eat. Declan was right. If she didn't keep up her strength, she was going to weaken at the worst possible moment. She opened her canteen and took a swallow to wash it down. Chang's had about five or six dishes she loved, so it was hard to decide what she wanted—even if this was just in her head.

"Does it take you this long to make up your mind about what you want to eat when you're actually in the restaurant?" Declan asked.

She grinned. "Most of the time. I don't know why I have such a hard time making some of the simplest decisions. It's crazy."

He let out a deep chuckle. "I'll remember to eat before we go to dinner, so I won't rush you."

That was when it hit her. Declan really intended to take her out...like on a date. The thought warmed her right down to the tips of her combat boots. Would it be too much to hope that it might be the start of something?

Declan took a drink from his own canteen. "If it helps, for the duration of this conversation, the food is calorie free, so don't feel you have to limit yourself to just one thing."

She laughed. That would be really cool, wouldn't it? "Well, in that case, I'll start with the spicy chicken. You can absolutely never go wrong starting with that."

He leaned back on one elbow, getting more comfortable and looking sexy as hell. "Go on."

"From there—since I'm not worrying about calories—I'll have the Mongolian beef, then the sweet and sour pork. And to finish up, their famous lettuce wraps."

"Because that's what everyone has after eating three entrées—another appetizer. What happened to dessert?"

She laughed. If it wasn't for the fact that they were sitting in a pile of prickly brambles, surrounded by monsters that wanted to kill her and cut up Declan for his DNA, she'd say this was the best date she'd been on in…well…forever.

"Is the no-calorie offer still in effect?" she asked.

"Of course."

"Then I'll have the Great Wall of Chocolate." She almost shivered at the thought of all that deliciousness.

"Damn," he said. "You must be hungrier than I thought."

"It's cake, silly." She frowned. "Wait a minute. Haven't you ever been to Chang's before?"

He shook his head. "I tend to eat mostly at the DCO cafeteria at the training complex."

Was he serious? "Well, that just isn't right. The moment we get home, we're going to Chang's and I'm going to order you the Great Wall. It's a huge slice of chocolate cake smothered in raspberry sauce. I promise you'll love it."

He grinned. "I do like chocolate cake. You've got yourself a date."

Declan probably didn't mean it in the literal sense of the word, but the thought of going on a date with him made her pulse kick into a whole other gear.

He suddenly sat up and leaned in close; for one wild moment, Kendra was sure that he was going to kiss her—and she was more than willing to let him. But he only reached out and gently brushed his thumb over the corner of her mouth.

"You, um, had a crumb sticking to you." The back of his knuckles lingered ever so briefly on her cheek before he took his hand away. "I figured you wouldn't want something nibbling on you while you're sleeping."

She didn't want to even think about that. Unless Declan was the one doing the nibbling, of course. That prompted all sorts of erotic images, and she bit her lip.

"Thanks," she murmured.

He cleared his throat. "Speaking of sleep, we should get some rest if we're going to get an early start in the morning."

Like she could sleep with the feel of his fingers lingering on her skin. It didn't help that Declan lay down behind her, placing one of his big arms over her in what he probably thought was a very nonsexual manner. Okay, so having his big forearm and bicep lying across her hip and stomach wasn't necessarily sexual, but it sure was nice as hell. She could definitely get used to snuggling with him like this every night. She was already getting warm all over and her body hadn't really come in contact with his...yet. She was tempted to wiggle her bottom back against him, but resisted the urge. This was not the time or place for that, no matter how much her body wished it were. No, she'd just lay here like she was. Thinking that was one thing, but doing it was another.

Declan must have mistaken her restlessness to mean she couldn't sleep because he leaned closer to her ear. "Get some rest. I'll stay awake and keep an ear out for any hybrids."

Having his warm breath that close to her ear certainly wasn't going to help her stop fidgeting. "Are you going wake me when it's my turn to stand guard tonight?"

"Yeah, of course," he said. "I'll wake you up in a couple hours."

Kendra didn't believe that for a second, but she didn't call him on it. The night had gone too well to end it with an argument. She stifled a groan. *Was this sad or what?* It took a screwed-up mission with both their lives at risk for her to finally realize how good she and Declan were together. She'd never be able to kick herself hard enough for how stupid she'd been. The guy she'd been looking for all these years had been right in front of her the entire time. Unfortunately, it was too late to do anything about it.

Declan had been cordial tonight, even warm. And he would probably keep his promise and take her out to dinner if they got out of this alive. But she couldn't miss the huge gulf existing between them. Declan still had his walls up higher than ever. Even now, while his arm was close enough to provide a sense of comfort and warmth, he was being careful not to touch her.

She'd been banging her head against the wall trying to figure out why Declan had shut her out so completely and could only come up with one reason. He'd found out she'd slept with the one person he couldn't stand—Clayne.

Kendra lay there with him almost touching her but not quite, feeling like she wanted to cry. Part of her wanted to tell Declan that Clayne wasn't the one she wanted. But then she cringed. She refused to be the girl who said that stupid line, *Yeah, I slept with someone else, but it didn't mean anything*.

Because it would mean something to Declan. It would mean she'd chosen Clayne over him. Chosen the loud, in-your-face, aggressive shifter who embraced his inner animal without apology. If there was one man who was the one-hundred-and-eighty-degree opposite of Declan, who acted in every way different than the introspective, calm, quiet bear shifter, it was Clayne.

And she'd slept with him.

Tears stung Kendra's eyes and she wiggled, pressing herself closer to Declan, as if that would somehow make everything better. But Declan moved away, silently confirming her worst fear. Even if they made it out of this jungle alive, there was just no way he could ever get past what she'd done to him.

Chapter 7

"OKAY, I THINK THEY'VE MOVED FAR ENOUGH AWAY," Declan said softly in Kendra's ear, then immediately wished he hadn't done it. He didn't regret the words—he really felt the damn hybrids who'd literally forced them up a tree an hour ago were finally far enough away for him and Kendra to climb down. No, what he regretted was leaning in close to say those words. Even after running around the jungle for four days, she smelled so damn good he could barely keep himself from licking her.

Fortunately, Kendra removed the temptation by grabbing a branch and lowering herself to the ground. Declan found himself dropping his head back against the trunk of the big tree, breathing deep as he tried to get her scent out of his head.

Why the hell was this happening to him now, when they were in the middle of the jungle, surrounded by hybrids who wanted them dead?

They'd scrambled up the big tree when he'd heard two groups of hybrids converging on their location. It had been a dangerous place to hide, but there hadn't been any other options. So, after he'd rubbed a few of the orchids he'd had in his cargo pants' pocket on the lower trunk, up the tree they'd gone. The hybrids had passed by without even looking up. Still, he and Kendra had stayed in that tree just to make sure it wasn't a trick.

Declan had his nose back under control by the time he hit the ground beside Kendra, but just barely. It seemed to be getting harder and harder to ignore her as the hours passed. By the time they got out of here, he'd probably be drooling on her.

"Well, all those supposedly smart people who say adult grizzlies can't climb trees have obviously never watched you do it," Kendra said as he straightened his rucksack. "There are monkeys out in the jungle right now hanging their heads in shame."

He couldn't help but let out a snort of laughter, even if he did want to yell at her to stop being so sweet and nice to him all the time. "Anyone can climb fast when they're properly motivated."

"I'm not so sure about that. I had just as much motivation as you and still would've never gotten up there if you hadn't given me a boost."

Oh crap. That boost brought back more memories he'd rather forget—mostly the one that involved his hand pushing against her ass as he helped her get up in the tree.

"Yeah, sure," he mumbled, not looking at her. "No problem."

Damn, her ass had been really nice—firm, but soft, too.

Stop thinking those thoughts, you stupid idiot. But it was too late. His cock had started to harden again in his uniform. *Shit.* He'd spent most of the time in that tree thinking about anything and everything he could just to get the thing to go down. Now he was going to have to walk around the jungle with a tree branch in his pants.

"You hear anything?" she asked, completely oblivious to the torture she was putting him through.

Declan forced his attention outward, glad to have something else to focus on. He picked up a hundred individual sounds—small animals moving across the jungle floor, monkeys and birds hooting and screeching, leaves and branches rustling against each other—but nothing that made him think hybrids were nearby.

"Nothing right now," he told her.

"Good because my butt is so numb from sitting on that branch, I'm not going to be able to move fast for a while."

She started off ahead of him, but he quickly passed her so he wouldn't have to go through the torture of watching her massaging her ass as she walked.

"How can there still be so many hybrids around?" she asked from behind him. "I thought they were supposed to be spreading out."

He'd thought so too, but Kendra was right. The area had been crawling with hybrids since 0500 that morning. They'd been ducking and diving nearly every twenty minutes as the creatures appeared. It was destroying his plan to keep them traveling in a generally northwest direction. No matter what he did to correct for it, every encounter forced them to move east and deeper into the mountains. He liked to think that all the hybrids moving through this part of the jungle was random, but his instincts told him different.

"The way I see it, there are two possibilities that can explain why we're seeing so many of them right now—one good and one not so good. Which would you like to hear first?"

Declan looked over his shoulder to see Kendra smiling. Then she laughed as she caught up and started walking beside him. At least she wasn't rubbing her butt anymore.

"Give me the good news first," she said. "If I really like it, we can skip the bad news completely."

He chuckled, too. She always knew what to say to make him laugh. "Well, if we're lucky, the reason we're seeing all these hybrids this morning is because we've reached the edge of their perimeter and the noose they've been tightening around us. If that's the case, once we're through them, it'll be clear sailing all the way back to base camp."

"Okay, let's just go with that," Kendra said. "But that's probably not what's really going on, is it?" When Declan shook his head, she sighed. "Thought so. Let me hear the bad news then."

He hesitated, wondering just how much he should tell her. He decided to only go with the really bad, instead of the really, *really* bad.

"The bad news is that I think my biggest fear has come true—that the intermittent gunfire we heard last night and early this morning is the rescue party trying to track us down."

A glimmer of hope flashed in her eyes. "But isn't that a good thing? If it's the rescue party, don't we want them to find us?"

"Sure. Except, every time they fire their weapons, they're drawing every hybrid within a twenty-mile radius to us. We may not survive their rescue if this gets any worse."

She thought about that for a while, and he felt bad to burst her bubble like that. But what could he do?

"You think it's Tate leading the rescue party, with Brent and Gavin?"

"I'm not sure anyone else would willingly come looking for us," he said. "Not after going up against those hybrids in the dark. But it's likely there's a shifter with them, too. Tate and the guys wouldn't be able to track us, especially at night."

Kendra's eyes went wide. "You mean Clayne?"

Hearing her say the shifter's name made him want to growl. Kendra might know what to say to make him laugh, but she also knew exactly what to say to piss him off. And it usually had to do with bringing up Clayne's name in the worst possible moment.

"Maybe." Declan tried to keep his voice even. "But it could be Ivy, Trevor, even Lucy," he added, thinking of the other female feline shifter at the DCO. "There are a couple others who could do it."

Even though she had this irritating habit of bringing up Clayne's name all the time, which usually snapped at least a little sense into him, Declan knew he was falling for Kendra all over again. As stupid as that was, it was happening, and he couldn't seem to stop it. Lying close to her last night had been pure misery. But it had also been one of the best nights of his life. That was sad.

Fortunately, Kendra didn't mention Clayne again. If she'd started going on about how the wolf shifter might ride to their rescue, Declan was going to be sick.

They made use of the relatively hybrid-free moment and tried to get some distance between them and the tree they'd just climbed out of. They even found some berries and mangoes growing along their path and had an impromptu snack. Eating something other than energy bars was too much of a morale booster to pass up. And, even though it probably wasn't the wisest thing to do, they talked softly as they moved through the jungle. He had a feeling it was Kendra's way of dealing with the stress, so he was okay with it.

At first, Kendra's questions were pretty general—where did he hang out when he wasn't working, what kind of movies did he like, what were his favorite foods? Declan didn't mind answering those types of questions and even asked a few of his own—how much time did she spend with her family, and how often did she go out to eat at her favorite restaurant? But then she hit him with a seriously personal question that left him at a complete loss for words and no clue how to answer. Hell, he was pretty sure he didn't even want to answer that kind of question.

He fumbled over his words, finally spitting out an extremely unintelligent sounding, "What?"

"Have you ever been in a long-term serious relationship?" she asked. "You're such a great guy. I have a hard time believing no woman has ever tried to tie you down."

Declan ground his jaw. *If I'm such a great guy, why haven't you ever shown any interest in me?*

"I'm sorry if that was too personal," she said when he didn't answer. "You don't have to answer that."

He was tempted not to, but then she'd think he was hiding something, which he was. But he didn't want her to think he was some kind of pathetic loser. The fact that he'd been engaged wasn't a big deal. Anyone who'd read his personnel file already knew.

"There was someone…a long time ago," he told her. "We were engaged."

When Kendra didn't say anything, he glanced at her and found her gaping at him.

"You should really close your mouth," he said dryly. "Any number of nasty things could fly in."

She closed her mouth with a snap.

"Is it that frigging hard to believe a woman wanted to marry me?" he grumbled.

Kendra shook her head. "No, of course not. It's just that, if you were engaged, how come you're not married? I don't see you as the kind of guy who'd leave a woman at the altar, and I sure as hell don't see any sane woman leaving you there."

He supposed there was a compliment buried somewhere in all that twisted logic, but he had a hard time seeing it.

"When was this?" she prompted.

"It was during my senior year at MIT."

Her brow scrunched up. "You were in some technical engineering program there, right?"

At least she'd read that much of his personnel file. "Yeah. I was a dual major, electrical and mechanical engineering."

"Was your fiancée an engineering student, too?"

He shook his head. "Marissa was a political science major. Her family was very rich and very deep into the political scene in Massachusetts. She wanted to get into politics as well. She appreciated my brains and rational outlook on things. I loved her passion and social savvy. We might have been complete opposites, but we were crazy about each other."

Back then everything had looked so bright and possible.

"I'm not completely sure her family was as thrilled about the pairing as we were," he continued. "Probably thought her future political career would fare better if she married another politician—or at least someone just as rich as she was. But we didn't care about any of that. Marissa always said I was the one decision in her life that wasn't about her future career or her family's image."

"Why didn't it work out?" Kendra asked.

"We were planning our wedding most of our final semester. Late one night, after class, we were in downtown Cambridge, going over some of the last-minute details with the wedding planner. We were having so much fun that time got away from us, and before we knew it, we were walking down completely empty streets at almost midnight."

"Oh God," Kendra breathed. "I don't think I like where this is heading."

Declan strained his ears, listening to make sure no hybrids had snuck up on them. So far, so good.

"We were still a half-dozen blocks from the car, walking across a parking lot to save time, when two guys stepped out of the shadows and approached us."

He remembered every detail like it had happened yesterday. He remembered smelling something he'd never remembered smelling before—fear. Marissa had been exuding it like a perfume.

"At first I thought they were just planning to rob us," he murmured. "I was already reaching for my wallet to give it to them."

"But?" Kendra prompted when he stopped.

"They were looking for more than money. I heard them saying what they were going to do to Marissa after they killed me."

"Oh no," Kendra whispered. "Did you shift?"

Declan lifted a low-hanging branch for Kendra, then

stepped underneath it himself. "What choice did I have? I hadn't shifted more than once or twice since that first time. I'd completely boxed up that part of me and put it away in the closet, never intending to bring it out again. But when they came at us, one with a knife, the other with a gun, all I could think about was what they were going to do to Marissa."

Declan took a deep breath. He couldn't believe that after this long, the memory was getting to him. Maybe saying it was harder than thinking about it.

"I tried to keep my claws and fangs in, but I didn't have enough experience with controlling my shift because I'd refused to ever let it happen. So when it happened, it was pretty bad."

"But you said one of them had a gun," Kendra said. "How did you…?"

He shook his head. "I don't even remember exactly what I did. I just shifted and charged the one with the gun. The guy with the knife slashed me, but I didn't pay any attention. I hit the first one so hard I think he was out cold before he landed on the ground. I turned on the other one, roaring at him so loud he almost crapped himself, but he came at me anyway. I broke his arm and threw him through a car window."

"What about Marissa? How did she react?"

Stopping right there in the middle of the jungle even for a few minutes was dangerous, but Declan needed a moment to get himself together. "She didn't handle it well. While she knew the two men were violent, she hadn't heard them whispering about what they were going to do to her. She didn't even know there was a gun until it was all over. She just saw her fiancé turn into a snarling monster and beat two guys to bloody pulps. When I turned to check on her, she screamed and ran."

Kendra's hand came up to cover her mouth, her eyes full of pain.

"I tried to go after her, but she only screamed louder and ran faster, so I stopped." He swallowed hard. "Someone heard the screams and called the cops. They found me there waiting beside the two unconscious men. It took another fifteen minutes to find Marissa. She was hiding behind a Dumpster nearly a quarter mile away. She was so freaked out they couldn't even get a statement from her."

"How did you keep the cops from figuring out what happened?"

He shrugged. "I really didn't have to do anything special. The pair had hit several other people over the last few days. Exact same MO, including one sexual assault. The cops took one look at my size and assumed I'd kicked their asses the old-fashioned way. When the punks finally woke up and started talking, everyone thought they were on drugs. Who'd believe a story about an MIT engineering student turning into a monster?"

Kendra shook her head. "And Marissa?"

"The cops assumed I told her to run when the attack started and she never told them differently. Actually, she never gave a statement at all. Claimed she couldn't remember any of it—total PTSD blackout."

"What did you tell her?" Kendra asked. "Didn't she have a million questions?"

"She didn't have any questions." He snorted. "I never saw her again after that night. Her father came over to my apartment the next morning, thanked me for saving his daughter's life, then gave me Marissa's engagement ring back and told me she no longer wanted to marry me."

Kendra's jaw dropped. "You're kidding right? You save her life and she dumped you over something as stupid as you being a shifter?"

Declan tried not to let the words hurt, but they did, because that was exactly why Marissa had left him. "You didn't see her face when she looked at me…when she saw the real me. The monster she saw terrified her more than the idea of anything those men might have done to her."

"That's crap." Kendra didn't even bother hiding her anger. "Did you try to talk some sense into her, remind her you were still the same man she fell in love with, the same man she'd been about to marry?"

"Of course I did." This part of the story didn't hurt nearly as much. Maybe because he had more calluses from it. "After I got everything settled with the police, I drove out to her parents' place to talk to her, but her father wouldn't let me see her. One of the maids took pity on me and led me outside to the trash cans. Marissa had thrown out her wedding gown, the invitations, and the wedding favors. I dug a little deeper and found a bag full of all the stuff I'd given her over the previous two years we'd been together. The Valentine's and Christmas presents, the silly knickknacks guys give their girls, pressed flowers…everything. Any thought I had about us getting back together disappeared right then. I knew it was over."

"I'm so sorry," Kendra whispered. "I never knew."

"How could you know?" His mouth curved into a wry smile. "I don't talk about it much…for obvious reasons."

For one crazy second, he thought she was going to hug him, but she only took his hand in hers and gave it a squeeze. "No one should have to deal with that. I don't think I would have handled it nearly as well."

Declan looked down at her hand wrapped around his. It felt nice. "I didn't handle it all that well." He scanned the area around them for sounds of trouble, then got her moving again. "I drove straight back to MIT, dropped out, and ran away from the world. My parents thought I was insane when I moved out to Oregon and became a forest ranger."

Kendra gave him a sidelong glance. "Why did you move out to Oregon and become a forest ranger? With your engineering background, I thought you'd find something technical."

He shrugged as he kept moving. "I didn't consider myself fit to be around people. I figured if I was going to be an animal, I might as well find a job that allowed me to live with them. And keep me away from humans as much as possible."

Kendra moved around in front of him and put her hand on his chest. "You're still human."

"There are times when I'm not so sure of that."

Before he realized what he was doing, Kendra went up on her toes and kissed him on the cheek. She stepped back and smiled at him. "I'm sure."

Then she was walking ahead of him, leaving him unsure about what the hell had just happened. He wasn't unsure about the effect the little kiss had on him, though. His cheek tingled from the touch of her lips, his heart was thudding, and from the way his vision had tightened all of a sudden, he knew his eyes had shifted. Damn,

how was it possible for one little kiss to completely dis-
combobulate him? It wasn't fair. His head was frigging
spinning as he followed her.

Why the hell had he spilled his whole life story to
Kendra? He'd never told a soul about what had happened between him and Marissa.

Kendra glanced over her shoulder at him. "This is
probably a silly question, but do you still love Marissa?"

"She was a big part of my life…first love and all that,"
he admitted. "But no, I'm not in love with her anymore."

That was the first time he'd said those words out
loud—it felt good. He was still thinking about that when
the sounds of crunching leaves and branches pulled
him back to the present. *Shit*. He grabbed Kendra and
held his finger to his lips, then urged her away from the
approaching hybrids, pulling her behind a pile of boulders that weren't much taller than he was. He breathed a
sigh of relief as the sound of boots crossing rock and soil
receded steadily, then finally disappeared in the distance.

"Dammit, I wish we could come up with a better way
of dealing with these things than hiding every thirty
minutes," he growled.

Kendra leaned against one of the rocks, a smile curv-
ing her all-too-kissable lips.

"What's so funny?" he asked.

"Nothing. I just had this crazy image of Clayne hiding
behind this pile of rocks while two hybrids walked by.
Something tells me he'd opt for shooting them—or
something equally violent."

She laughed, as if the picture in her head was the
funniest damn thing she'd ever imagined.

Declan didn't laugh. He sure as hell didn't find the

comparison funny. It might be juvenile as hell, but he hated when she compared him to Clayne. He was nothing like the other shifter. Which explained why Kendra had never been attracted to him.

He clenched his jaw so tight, he thought his teeth were going to shatter. He'd been looking for something to get Kendra out of his head, and bringing up Clayne had done the trick.

Declan fought the urge to stand up and start moving again, anything to get his mind on another subject. But he couldn't do that with the hybrids so close. Instead, he had to sit there and stew in the knowledge that Kendra was obsessed with the damn wolf shifter. Unbidden, his mind went to the one place he'd always refused to let it go: wondering how many times Kendra had slept with Clayne. God, he hated thinking about the two of them together. It literally made him see red to picture her with Clayne—or any man.

But as they hid behind the rocks, that's the only thing he could think about.

Kendra was never going to understand Declan's mood swings. After spending a good part of last night and this morning connecting with each other, he'd suddenly shut down on her, as if someone had hit a switch and changed his channel on her. And she had absolutely no idea why. She'd retraced their conversation and her actions over the last few hours but couldn't identify anything she'd said or done that might have provoked him to pull away from her and drop that damn wall of his back into place.

And they *had* been getting closer; she'd felt the wall coming down. Nothing else explained the willingness Declan had shown in opening up about that bitch who'd dumped him. She'd almost cried more than once during his story. It was either that or shoot something. She'd never met Marissa, and she hated her. What sort of idiot walked away from someone as special as Declan just because he'd flashed some fangs and claws while in the process of saving her life? The woman must be the dumbest twit on the planet.

Then again, she could say the same thing about herself. She might not have dumped Declan, but she'd ignored him for years, which was just as bad. Maybe worse.

But while she might not get his mood swings, Kendra now completely understood one very important thing about Declan. His ex-fiancée was the reason he kept a wall up around himself. He wasn't going to let anyone get close enough to hurt him like that again. She only wished there was some way to make him see she was different from Marissa.

She glanced at him as they weaved through the trees covering the mountainous slope. "You know, I've been thinking about something—"

Declan held up his hand, cocking his head to the side in a posture she was growing to really dislike. "Hold on."

Not again.

"Hybrids heading this way," he said. "And they're coming in fast."

Kendra raced up the hillside as quickly as she could while at the same time picking her path carefully, so she wouldn't kick loose any rocks. This was a big ridge to get over with nowhere to hide. If the hybrids caught them out here, it was over.

By the time they crested the ridge, she was gasping for air. Thank God she wasn't still wearing her pack or she would've been in even more trouble. The cumulative effect of little food, hardly any sleep, and days spent running for her life were finally catching up to her. But there was no rest just because they'd gotten to the top. Declan hurried her right down the other side, urging her to go even faster as they approached the thick jungle growth covering the ravine at the bottom.

Kendra groaned when she saw there was another ridge waiting for them. This one was even steeper and more thickly overgrown than the one they'd just traversed. There was no way she could make it up that at anything approaching a full run.

"We have to keep moving," Declan said, grabbing her hand and pulling her after him. "They're just on the other side of the ridge we crossed. I think they have our scent."

Crap. She was in no condition to get into a footrace with a pack of hybrids.

"How many of them are there?" she asked, working fast to catch her breath. "Can we fight them?"

He shook his head. "Too many. We can't fight them. Not out in the open like this."

Dammit. She picked up speed, psyching herself up for the climb, when Declan suddenly changed direction, running parallel to the slope instead of up it.

"What are we doing?" she demanded as he hustled her through the jungle.

"Change of plans." He pushed her ahead of him. "Keep running straight ahead."

She didn't have a clue what he was up to, but she liked any plan that didn't involve running up the side of a mountain. She started rethinking that idea a few minutes later, when their route led straight to a swiftly moving stream and Declan dragged her into it with him.

God, it's cold!

Biting her lip, she lifted her weapon high and let Declan lead the way upstream through the freezing, knee-deep water. The stream was moving fast, and the bottom was filled with big rocks that rolled out from under her feet as she moved. Hitting them at a stumbling run made it hard to keep upright. If Declan hadn't been holding her hand, she would have fallen a dozen times.

Kendra was so numb from the cold, she barely realized the tree-lined banks had transitioned into steep, rocky cliffs. Her eyes went wide. If the hybrids followed them in here, there'd be nowhere to go but up those cliffs, and she'd never be able to climb them. She and Declan would be trapped. Her panic kicked up a notch when he abruptly changed direction and headed for the nearly vertical cliff on their right. What the hell was he thinking?

But when they got to the stone wall, Declan didn't order her to climb as if her life depended on it. Instead, he shoved some hanging vines out of the way to reveal a wide diagonal gash in the rock that was almost four feet wide and ten feet high.

A cave?

"How did you know this was here?" she asked.

His mouth quirked. "I'm a bear, remember? Finding caves is in my nature."

Kendra would have marveled at that if hybrids hadn't been on their tail. She dropped to her hands and knees and crawled into the cave. The opening was jagged and rough, but within a few feet, it leveled out. Loose dirt covered much of the floor, making the place feel almost...cozy.

As soon as Declan climbed in, the vines fell back into position, cloaking the cave in shadows. Kendra was about to head deeper into the cavern, but Declan stopped her with a touch on the shoulder.

"Stay here and cover the entrance while I go check out the rest of the cave," he said. "I want to make sure we're the only ones who thought this was a great place to hide."

She hadn't even thought of that. The cold water had obviously frozen more than her legs—her head was pretty numb, too.

While Declan looked around, she took up position just inside the mouth of the cave and aimed her M4 toward the rapids. She waited, tense and nervous, expecting to see a pack of hybrids stomping their way up the stream toward them at any second. Would they be able to see the cave? She hadn't seen it even when Declan had been leading her toward it, so she hoped the hybrids wouldn't be able to either.

She almost jumped out of her skin when Declan came up beside her. "We have the place to ourselves. You see anything yet?"

"Nothing. Can you hear anything?"

"Not over the sound of the water."

"Do you think they followed us up the stream?" she asked.

After the sprint over the ridge, then the slog up the rapids, she was beat, and crouching there in her wet clothes was exhausting her even more. If she took off her boots right then, her toes would probably be blue.

"I don't think so. If they had, they would've gotten here already. I think we're okay for now," he said. "Come on. The cave opens up a little back here. We can get dry and warm."

Kendra wasn't sure she remembered what being dry and warm felt like. Between the almost-constant rain and the frequent treks through one body of water or another, she'd been wet and cold for almost a week.

As Declan promised, the cave opened up into an area that was fairly spacious. There wasn't much light, but she couldn't have cared less. It wasn't dark enough to worry about pulling out the NVGs. Besides, she was so tired, all she felt like doing was throwing herself on the stone floor and sleeping for a week. But there was no way she could sleep in these soaking wet clothes. She'd wake up with hypothermia—if she woke up at all.

She threw Declan a quick glance over her shoulder as she started unbuttoning her uniform top. "You think you have a dry T-shirt in your pack I can wear while my stuff dries out? The extra ones I have are wet."

He looked confused for a second, and she wondered if maybe she wasn't the only one affected by the cold.

"Um, yeah. I think I have one left I haven't worn." He propped his weapon against the cave wall and dug through it. "Hold on a second."

The idea of getting out of her wet clothes and into something dry was too enticing to resist, so she yanked off her uniform top and immediately started in on her boots. If it meant getting warm and dry, she was willing to strip naked in front of the big bear shifter. But the stupid laces were all knotted up and her soggy, cold fingers couldn't seem to get them loose.

"I told you to hold on a second," Declan scolded. "Here, let me get those. Your hands are shaking too much to do it. Hold this."

He gave her a T-shirt—oh God, it was completely dry—then sat down in front of her. She felt silly sitting there with her wet boots in his lap, but Declan got the laces undone much faster than she would have been able to. He had her boots and socks off in seconds instead of minutes.

While Declan spread out a poncho for them to sit on, Kendra turned her back and shucked her wet T-shirt. She pulled Declan's on and almost laughed when it fell all the way to her knees. She imagined she looked a little goofy, but who cared? She was warmer already.

It took a bit of work to get her pants off, but thankfully Declan didn't ask if she needed help with those. That would have been too embarrassing.

She arranged all her wet clothes on the rocks littering the cave floor, then went back to dig a pair of her panties out of Declan's pack. It wasn't too hard to work those on under his big T-shirt, and a few minutes later, she was seated comfortably on Declan's poncho.

"You think we're safe here for a while?" she asked.

"Yeah, I don't think there's any way for the hybrids to track us through the stream, and I doubt they're going to stumble on this cave."

Declan had pulled off his T-shirt, pants, and boots, and was sitting across from her in nothing but his boxer briefs, facing the cave entrance. His crossed-legged position gave her a nice view of rippling abs, defined pecs, and bulging thighs. And speaking of bulging, those tight underwear looked like they were hiding a serious bulge of their own. She'd never seen this much of him before and he looked good—really good.

Kendra tried not to stare at all that nakedness, but he caught her. "You don't mind, do you? My stuff is soaked, too, and the T-shirt you have on is the last dry thing I had in my bag. I can put my clothes back on if it bothers you."

She shook her head, forcing herself to focus on anything other than all that exposed skin. "No problem. You're fine."

Yeah, you're fine all right.

She pulled her knees up to her chest and tugged the bottom of the shirt down to her ankles. The thing was so big on her it was like wearing a bathrobe. "Sorry to steal your last dry shirt."

He chuckled. "Don't be. It looks better on you than it does on me."

And you look better without it. But she kept that to herself.

As they settled into a comfortable silence, Kendra wanted to laugh. Here she was, sitting half-naked in a cave while a gorgeous, equally naked guy sat only a few feet away. This would have been a sexy scenario if it wasn't for two simple facts: one, Declan wasn't interested in her, and two, there were dozens of hybrids out there right now who would love to come charging in here and tear them apart. It was difficult to focus too much on sexy thoughts with things like that hanging over her head.

Chapter 8

SHE PULLED OUT HER PONYTAIL HOLDER AND RAN HER fingers through her hair, shaking it out around her shoulders. "How far do you think we got today?"

Declan snorted. "With the early start, I thought we'd get at least ten miles in, but we barely made five. Worse, we've been driven way off course, so half of those five miles were in the wrong direction. Bottom line, it was a wasted morning."

As long as they were safe, Kendra was willing to deal with the delays, but she knew that all this hiding was driving Declan crazy. "Do you think we should try and go a little farther today or just hole up here?"

"My gut says to get out of here as soon as we can, so we can get a few more miles between us and the hybrids roaming this general area. But…"

"But?" she prompted.

"I'm worried if we head right back out, we'll run right into the arms of that same pack of hybrids that chased us in here. It would probably be better to stay hidden until later—nightfall maybe—then try and slip out of here when they're not expecting it."

Kendra sure as hell wasn't going to complain about resting for a while—she could use it—and this cave was the most secure place they'd stumbled on since this nightmare had started.

"How did you know this cave was here?" she asked.

Declan frowned and shifted on the poncho. "It's kind of hard to put into words, but I always know whenever I'm near a place where I can hide or lay low for a while if I have to. It's just this feeling I get. Like a sense of security. I know it sounds crazy."

Actually, being a bear shifter who instinctively knew when a good hibernating place was nearby made perfect sense. The thing she didn't understand was why having a talent like that seemed to disturb Declan.

She'd been evaluating Declan and his team for many years, and while they were certainly amazing in the field, she'd noticed that Declan depended on his natural shifter abilities the least of all the shifters at the DCO. She'd always thought it was because he didn't have as much shifter DNA as they did, but maybe that wasn't it at all. Maybe Declan didn't use his shifter skills because he didn't want to.

"It doesn't sound crazy," she told him. "Bears have to hibernate, so it makes sense that they have a natural talent for finding safe places to do it. You're a bear shifter, so it makes sense that you have the same talent."

"If you say so. It never seemed like a worthwhile talent to me."

She gave him a smile. "It sure came in handy today."

Declan grunted and reached for his pack. He pulled out another energy bar and split it, then handed her half. "I know you won't eat unless I do, so I'm not going to waste my breath."

"Good. If I have to eat these, so do you."

She took a bite and slowly chewed, pretending it was a candy bar instead. If they ever got out of here, she was never going to eat another one of these dry, tasteless things again. To distract herself while she ate, she spent the time checking out Declan's body. But she could only gaze at his fine-looking body for so long. It was like dreaming about dessert when you were on a diet; it only frustrated you in the long run.

She turned her thoughts back to why Declan didn't embrace his shifter side instead. No doubt it had something to do with what had happened with Marissa.

Kendra put her chin on her T-shirt-covered knees and dragged her eyes away from those killer abs to focus on his beautiful blue eyes. "You mind if I ask you a personal question?"

He leaned back on his hands, showing off more of those perfect abs. "I suppose that depends on how personal the question is."

"Fair enough," she said. "You don't have to answer if you don't want to, but I sometimes get the feeling that you're keeping your shifter nature under wraps."

His eyes narrowed. "What do you mean?"

"I didn't mean to offend you," she said quickly. "It's just that in all the time I've known you, I've never seen you cut loose and shift all the way. In fact, up until two nights ago, when I was telling you about Ivy being tortured by Stutmeir's doctors, I'd never even seen your eyes glow red like they did. And just now, when I asked you how you found this cave, you seemed as if you were uncomfortable admitting it was one of your shifter talents. If I'm out of bounds here, just say the word, and I'll drop it. But I really am curious."

Declan closed his eyes. When he opened them again, they were filled with a pain that tore at her heart.

"My eyes were red?"

Kendra nodded.

He swallowed hard. "You mean like a hybrid's?"

"No. They're nothing like a hybrid's." She scooted closer. "Hybrid eyes are a red full of anger and violence. Yours are a beautiful rose red, like the glow of a setting sun. Yours hold nothing but warmth." She let out a sigh. "But the fact that you just asked the question only reinforces my point. You didn't even know your eyes glowed, and when you found out, you jumped to the worst possible conclusion—that you're like a hybrid. Why would you even assume that?"

If anyone else took as long to reply as Declan, it'd probably mean they weren't going to answer at all. But after all the time they'd spent together over the past few days, she realized he simply liked to think before he spoke. While there was nothing wrong with that, it irritated her that he felt he had to filter every word that came out of his mouth.

"I hate being a shifter," he said softly.

Kendra stared at him, too stunned to do anything else. She knew a lot of shifters and had never heard any of them utter the words Declan had just whispered.

"Declan, being a shifter is a big part of what makes you the person you are."

"Yeah, unfortunately that's true." He shrugged his broad shoulders. "I can't help but wonder how my life would have turned out differently if I'd never changed in the first place."

So that was it. "Meaning, you wonder how things would have worked out with you and Marissa?"

"Can you blame me? We probably would have had a couple kids by now. What would they be like?

Where would we be living? Where would I be working? Would I still be close to my family? There are so many possibilities to think about. My life could have been completely different."

It hurt to hear Declan talking about the kids he'd never had the chance to have, but she couldn't sit there and commiserate with him—not when the whole fantasy was built on a lie.

"Yes, your life would have been different," she agreed. "For one thing, you and Marissa would be dead now. Or maybe you'd be dead, and Marissa would have just been raped and beaten. Unless your do-over fantasy includes those two men in Cambridge never attacking you?"

Okay, that was harsh. But it was true.

His jaw tightened. "I could still have fought them off if I wasn't a shifter."

She sighed. "You know how unlikely that is, right? One had a knife, the other had a gun. You've been in the DCO long enough to know how odds like that usually turn out."

"I know, but that doesn't keep me from dreaming about the possibilities anyway."

Kendra hugged her knees tighter. "That's why you resist using or even developing your shifter abilities, isn't it? Because you blame yourself for what happened that night?"

"I suppose," he admitted. "I've never felt right depending—or even accepting—the talents that have brought me so much pain. I never asked to have them, and if I choose to make my way in the world without them, that's my call."

"You're right," she agreed. "If you don't want to use the abilities that come with your DNA, you have every right. People do it every day. But there's one big difference between those people and you. You're in the DCO. Refusing to embrace your shifter side and use your God-given talents might get someone you care about killed some day."

"Let's not bring God into this," he said wryly. "I'm sure He's taking a nonparticipatory role in the lives of shifters in general, and my life in particular."

She held up her hand. "Okay, fine. I'll agree to drop the unintended philosophical part of the question if you agree to answer the real part. Aren't you worried someone on your team could get hurt because you won't let go and allow your true self out?"

Declan swore under his breath. "You don't think I haven't thought about that? I think about it all the time." His eyes flashed light red for just the briefest moment before going back to their usual, beautiful blue. "Hell, I probably could have gotten you out of this mess already if I were more of a shifter."

She frowned. "What are you talking about? You've done an amazing job keeping me safe out here."

He let out a half snort, half laugh. "Maybe. But I know what holding back has cost me. My sense of smell is complete crap. I probably hear half of what I should. My strength is reduced. My claws and fangs are barely useable as weapons."

She swung her legs around to the side. "If you know all that, why do you continue to turn your back on your own abilities? Why haven't you tried to accept that these talents are just part of who you are and connect with them?"

Declan blew out a loud breath and flopped down until he was lying flat on his back. "I've been neglecting the shifter part of me for so long, I don't even know how to connect with it anymore."

She hadn't thought about that. "Have you ever tried? I mean *really* tried?"

He stared up at the ceiling of the cave. "Yeah, once or twice. But it was no good. It's like trying to speak a language you've never even heard."

Kendra almost laughed, and would have if the whole thing didn't make her want to cry. "Maybe you just need to be in the right situation. Or maybe you need a session with the DCO's psychologist. Better yet, Clayne. If anyone could give you lessons on how to get in touch with your inner shifter, it's him."

Declan shot up. "What did you say?"

"That Clayne could give you lessons on how to be more like him."

She didn't realize she'd stuck her foot in her mouth again until Declan's eyes suddenly glowed red. *What the hell have I said this time?*

"I bet you'd like it if I were more like him, wouldn't you?" Declan growled.

She'd never heard Declan growl like that—ever. It shocked her. Then made her angry. She didn't know what she'd said to piss him off, but it obviously had something to do with Clayne. Well, she was too cold, too worn out, and too damn tired of Declan snapping at her every time she stepped over a line she couldn't see.

"What the hell is it with you?" she demanded. "Every time I mention Clayne's name, you act like I slapped you with a cold fish."

Red swirled in Declan's eyes. "I don't like him."

"Why not? He's a shifter like you."

"He's nothing like me," Declan shouted. "And I don't like him because you do."

That knocked her off balance for a second. "Of course I like him," she said, trying to sound casual. "We're friends."

His lips twisted in a sarcastic smile. "Friends? Right."

"Why is that so hard for you to believe?"

Declan took a deep breath, and then let it out slowly, the reddish glow fading from his eyes. She knew it sounded crazy, but it seemed that some of his life had drained out as well.

"It's hard to believe you're friends because I know you've always wanted it to be more than that," Declan said softly. "Am I stupid to think that it never went any further than that?"

Damn. There it was. The thing she'd been concerned about all along. Declan had figured out she'd been obsessed with Clayne for years and realized the wolf shifter was the reason she'd never given him the time of day. She didn't know exactly how to handle this, but Kendra was damn sure never going to admit she slept with Clayne. That was one mistake she was never going to even think about again. If Declan called her on it, she wouldn't deny it, but she wouldn't volunteer it either. He deserved an honest answer though, at least as honest as she could give him.

She tucked her hair behind her ear and met his gaze. "You're right. I spent a lot of time trying to get beyond the friend stage with Clayne, and it worked. Thing is, when we finally went out a few months back, we bombed out."

Declan frowned. "What do you mean *bombed out*?"

"As in we had zero chemistry," she clarified. "It wasn't the worst date I'd ever been on, but it wasn't a date that either one of us had any interest in repeating."

"Wait a minute." Declan's frown deepened. "You only went out with him for the first time a few months ago?"

She nodded. "Pretty sad, huh? I moon over a guy for nearly six years before he finally asks me out and the date turns out to be a complete disaster."

Declan's whole posture changed as he gave her a wry smile. "I know a guy who mooned over a girl for nearly seven years before he gave up. And he never even got to go out with her. So, in the contest of who's more pathetic, he wins."

Kendra blinked. "Wait. What?"

He laughed harshly. "I must be worse at asking you out than I thought if you didn't even notice."

Her face colored. "Of course I noticed."

"Could have fooled me."

The words stung. "Why did you stop asking me out?"

He gave her an incredulous look. "Why do you think? Because I finally figured out you were never going to say yes."

Kendra remembered all those times he'd asked her out and she'd blown him off. Her heart hurt to think about it. God, she'd been such a fool. "I know it won't help to say I'm sorry, but I am. I was stupid. Really, really stupid." Tears blurred her vision and she blinked. "Crappy timing, huh? I finally get my head screwed on straight enough to realize how stupid I was, and you decide to move on."

He draped his arms over his knees. "Yeah, well I may have decided it was time to move on, but that doesn't mean I was able to."

Her breath hitched. "What are you saying?"

"I'm saying that I'm still hung up on you," he muttered. "I don't know why. Maybe I'm a masochist."

Hope surged inside her. Could there still be a chance for them? She pushed herself up on her knees and moved a little closer to him. "Maybe because you knew I'd come around."

Declan raised a brow. "Come around?"

He wasn't going to make this easy on her, was he? Not that she blamed him.

"It took me a while—okay, years—but I've finally realized the man I've been looking for my whole life has been right here in front of me the whole time," she said softly.

Declan didn't say anything, and as the silence stretched on, she thought he wasn't ever going to. But then he reached out and gently cupped her face in his big hand. "You don't know how long I've waited to hear you say that. What made you figure it out?"

She smiled. "I guess I was just waiting for you to sweep me off my feet and steal me away to the perfect romantic locale."

Declan chuckled at her lame attempt at a joke, but there was still a sadness in his eyes. As if he was afraid to open up and let her in for fear of being rejected again.

Kendra covered his hand with hers. "Declan, I've spent more time with you in the past three days than I have in the past seven years. You're exactly what I've always wanted in a guy: brave, strong, warm, gentle, caring…romantic."

He looked embarrassed. "I don't know about the romantic part."

"Well, I do. And you are." Her lips curved. "And, if you don't mind me saying so, you're damn easy to look at—especially sitting there in just your underwear."

He laughed, and if possible, looked even more embarrassed.

"Can we put the past seven years behind us and start fresh?" she asked. "Forget about Marissa and Clayne, and all the times you asked me out and I said no?"

She knew neither of them could forget it entirely, but if he could forgive her for all the wasted time, maybe she could forgive herself, and they could both move forward.

Declan didn't answer. This close to him, it was impossible not to focus on his lips. Knowing there was never going to be a better time than right now, she leaned closer, fully intending to kiss him before he could stop her.

She never got the chance. He moved faster, his mouth closing the distance between them and coming down on hers.

The kiss was soft and tentative at first, seeking confirmation. She gave it by sliding her fingers into the thick tangle of hair at the back of his head, pulling his mouth against hers harder.

The tentativeness disappeared and Kendra almost gasped when she felt Declan's warm, wet tongue slip into her mouth. He threaded a hand in her hair with a soft, sexy growl. Her whole body hummed with pleasure. She was pretty sure she'd have found goose bumps on her arms if she'd checked.

This was what had been missing with Clayne and every other man she'd ever been with. That zip—that spark—that convinced her she was finally with the guy she was meant to be with. The realization was so sweet, she almost cried.

Declan must have felt her surprise because he pulled back to give her a worried look. "Is everything okay?"

She laughed. "Everything is perfect. I'm just mad at myself for waiting this long to kiss you."

Heat flared in his eyes, warming her all over. "Then I suppose we'll just have to make up for it."

He pulled her close, covering her mouth with his again. She closed her eyes and moaned as one sensation after another flooded her senses—the taste of his tongue, the roughness of his scruff against her chin, the feel of his strong fingers in her hair. All of those came together in an intoxicating blend that made her dizzy.

Almost with a will of their own, her hands slid down his neck, stopping momentarily to squeeze those powerful shoulders before continuing across his muscular chest. She let her fingers trace back and forth across his rippling muscles, enjoying the feel of so much strength and power there.

Declan pulled back with a throaty growl, effortlessly pulling her on top of his chest as he lay down. She let herself go, knowing he wouldn't be doing this if he didn't feel they were safe in the cave.

As she positioned herself comfortably astride him, she felt something nice and firm poking her in the tummy. "Why the hell did we wait so long to get to this point?"

He gently brushed her lower lip with his thumb.

"Let's stop worrying about all the stupid things that got in our way and just focus on the fact that we're finally here."

Hadn't she just said the same thing a few minutes ago? So why wasn't she doing it? She smiled and nibbled on his lower lip. "I can do that."

He kissed her, his hands once again tangling in her hair, holding her close. She found his tongue with hers, moaning at how good he tasted. She rocked against him, unable to help herself. The friction of his hard-on pressing against her through his boxer briefs had heat pooling between her thighs, and she had to drag her mouth away from his to catch her breath.

Declan tilted her head back, nibbling his way from her mouth, along her jaw, and all the way to her ear, bringing sighs of pleasure from her. How did he know she liked to have her earlobes played with? He caught the right one firmly in his mouth as if to hold her in place—like she would try to get away—then let those big, warm hands roam up and down her body.

She groaned. "Let me take off my shirt. I need to feel your hands on my skin."

He released her long enough for her to sit up and whip off her T-shirt. She dropped it onto the poncho beside them, then made quick work of her sports bra. She really wished she were wearing something sexier for their first time together, but Declan didn't seem to mind. The moment she bared her breasts, his eyes began to glow. Between the cool air in the cave and the undisguised hunger on his face, her nipples were practically throbbing. Then he licked his lips, which only made her poor nipples tingle even more.

She sat back a little to give him a better view, and immediately noticed that his cock had hardened considerably since she'd stripped down to her panties. She could feel it wedged firmly between her thighs, rubbing perfectly along her panty-covered pussy.

If it felt this good already, what would it feel like when they were both completely naked? She glanced down and saw that he was almost there anyway. His underwear could no longer contain his erection—several inches were already peeking above the waistband. The part she could see was thick, long, and beautiful. She bit her lip to keep from moaning out loud. It was as if he'd been built just to please her.

She rested her hands on her thighs and wiggled back and forth on his cock, watching the dim light coming from the mouth of the cave play over his strong, muscular body. It was crazy that she was getting so hot already—they'd just been chased by hybrids only a couple of hours ago—but now that she'd figured out he was what she wanted, she wanted him badly.

He ran his hands along her inner thighs, causing her to shiver. "Do you know how beautiful you are?"

She snuck a finger down and traced it along the ridge on the underside of his exposed penis. "After a week in the jungle without a bath, makeup, or my straightening iron, I have to wonder about your judgment. But if you want to keep telling me, I certainly won't mind."

She teased the tip of his shaft with her fingertips as she continued sliding herself up and down his hard length. She was already imagining about how good he was going to feel inside her when he interrupted her daydreaming.

"I really hate to bring this up, but I think one of us

has to," he said. "I didn't bring any condoms with me, so unless you did, this isn't going to lead to anything more."

Kendra stilled her fingers. Yikes, she hadn't even thought of protection. That showed just how much she wanted him. Thank God Declan still had enough wits left to think about it. But not having any protection didn't necessarily mean they weren't protected.

She caught her bottom lip between her teeth. "I haven't had unprotected sex with a man in…well…ever, so I know I'm clean. How about you?"

"No. I haven't had unprotected sex with any woman since…in a really long time. I've been checked since then, so I know I'm clean. But that's only half the issue here. There's that little matter of pregnancy to consider, too."

She stopped teasing him and slid forward, pressing her breasts to his bare chest. Her nipples immediately tingled on contact. "I'm on a long-term birth control. I can't get pregnant."

He looked confused for a second, then his eyes widened. "Long-term?"

She nodded. "I never knew when I would find Mr. Right, but when I did, I wanted to be ready."

He reached around to cup her ass. Her bottom felt so small in those big hands of his. He squeezed her cheeks and she whimpered.

"So, are you saying you're ready for Mr. Right… right now?"

She kissed him long and slow. "That's what I'm saying. Just you, me, and my long-term birth control—if that works for you?"

He tightened his hold on her ass, pulling her down snuggly against him. "That works for me."

She smiled, kissing him again as she went back to grinding against his erection. If she kept doing this for a while longer, she might just come from the foreplay alone.

But as she got hotter and hotter, she realized she didn't have nearly the control Declan did. Ultimately, she was the one who broke first and came up for air. "Maybe we can get the rest of our clothes off now?"

Declan slid his hands around from her ass, along her sides, and up to cup her breasts. He gave her a wicked grin as he tweaked her nipples. "I don't know. I think I could stay like this, touching you all over, for hours."

She gasped as his fingers sent shock waves through her sensitive nipples. "As much fun as that sounds, I'm a little worried it might drive me insane. I'm not sure I can wait any longer."

He chuckled softly. "Well, we can't have that."

Kendra reluctantly climbed off his lap to peel off her soaking wet panties, then watched in anticipation as he stripped off his underwear. The big reveal was everything she'd hoped for and more.

She would have immediately dived down to get her lips wrapped around his beautiful penis, but he caught her hand and urged her on top of him into the same position she'd been in before. She couldn't complain too much. What woman wouldn't want to straddle a gorgeous hunk like Declan and slowly slide down on that long, perfect shaft?

She sighed audibly as her wet pussy came into contact with his hard cock. She wasn't sure how she did it, but somehow she managed to control the urge to take him inside her and instead went back to the gentle rocking she'd been doing before.

Declan lightly traced a finger along her cheek. His touch was so gentle, it almost brought tears to her eyes.

"You don't have any idea how long I've waited and dreamed about this moment, do you?" he whispered huskily.

She turned her face into his hand, kissing his palm. "If you say you've been dreaming about me since the day we first met, I'm going to start crying."

"Please don't." He pressed his mouth to hers. "I don't ever want to make you cry." He said something else, but it was lost as he trailed hot kisses along her jaw and down her neck, then up to her ear again.

"God, I love when you do that," she breathed. "It makes me shiver."

He nipped at her ear. "I do love to make you shiver."

Kendra was so focused on what he was doing with his mouth that she didn't even realize he'd moved a hand down to her ass until he slid her up his body and positioned the head of his cock right at her wet opening. She pulled back so she could see his face, and their eyes locked as he paused, on the edge of sliding in.

"Are you ready?" he asked softly.

Her whole body quivered from this tiny touch. She might just die if she couldn't have the rest of him. "I'm more ready than I've ever been in my life."

He slid his other hand down to her ass, squeezing and rocking her against his thickness. "No screaming, okay? We don't want to be in the middle of this when the hybrids hear you and come running."

She gave him a teasing smile. "You think you can make me scream in pleasure, huh?"

He squeezed her derriere even tighter. "I guess we'll find out."

Kendra didn't scream, but she sure let out one hell of a groan as he spread her wide and slid in deep. She was soaking wet from all the foreplay, but he was so big that she still felt every inch of him as he entered her. She buried her face in his warm neck as he rocked her up and down, going a little deeper each time.

Maybe she was going to scream. Nothing was supposed to feel this good. And he hadn't even started thrusting yet. She slipped her hand under his shoulders, getting a good firm grip as Declan started to pump into her gently.

She tried to thrust back onto him harder, wanting to drive his cock all the way inside her at once, but the tight hold he had on her butt wouldn't allow that. He completely controlled the pace and the depth of her movements.

"Faster," she demanded. Tingles were already spreading out from her pussy to envelop her body. "Please."

He chuckled softly in her ear. "Not yet. Be patient. We just started."

His length speared her a little deeper, making her groan even louder. "You might be just starting, but I'm already halfway there. You better catch up."

He laughed again, deeper and huskier this time. "If you think you're halfway there, sweetheart, you're in for one hell of a surprise."

That's when Declan finally took pity on her and really started thrusting. Not hard yet, but definitely deeper. And when that big, perfect cock of his bottomed out inside her, she knew with even more certainty that the two of them were meant to be together. No man had ever felt this good inside her.

She grabbed more tightly onto his shoulders and pushed back, urging him to take her faster, but he refused, instead driving slow and deep into her, making sparks fly with every thrust. One hand stayed on her ass, controlling her movements, but the other slid up her side to massage one breast and tweak the nipple in time with his steady pumping.

Tingles were racing all over her body, and her pussy was clenching so hard she thought she might go insane. She was so close already. All she needed was a little push.

She lifted her head to gaze at him. "Stop teasing me," she begged. "Please."

He didn't reply, but he did move faster, pumping into her harder and harder.

Kendra dropped her head to his shoulder and bit down on the muscles. It was either that or scream as she went over the edge. Declan wrapped his arms around her, holding her close as he growled his pleasure. When she felt his warmth pour into her, she exploded.

There were no words to describe how hard she came. She'd never ever experienced anything like it, so she had nothing for comparison.

She only knew it was magical.

When the cave stopped sparkling and spinning, Kendra opened her eyes to find her cheek resting on Declan's broad chest, his arms around her, keeping her warm. He was still inside her, though not nearly as hard and rigid as he had been. It felt good, though, and she had no interest in letting him go anywhere.

She pressed a kiss to his chest. "That was beautiful."

He ran his fingers gently through her hair. "I wasn't too…rough?"

"Of course you weren't too rough. You were amazing." To prove it, she lifted her head and kissed him on the mouth. "Better than amazing, even. You were perfect."

Declan grinned. "Perfect, huh? And to think, we're just getting started."

She quivered as she felt his cock harden inside her. *Mmm, this is going to be good.*

Chapter 9

ANGELO FROWNED AS DEREK WRAPPED LAYER AFTER layer of bandages around Landon's left forearm. The four scratches weren't too deep, but they were ragged and going to leave some serious scars. Ivy crouched beside her husband as he leaned against his rucksack, concern in her eyes.

Landon had gotten his latest collection of conversation starters when six hybrids hit them from behind while Clayne and Ivy had been out in front, trying to get a bead on Declan and Kendra's trail. It hadn't been a chance encounter with a bunch of scouts like the previous attacks. No, these damn hybrids had lain submerged in a muddy stream along the path until Angelo and the others had moved past, then had come at them in a flat-out kamikaze ambush meant to take out as many of them as possible before Ivy and Clayne could get back to help. The first part of their plan had worked to perfection, and they'd come damn close to accomplishing the second part as well.

Angelo ground his jaw. There wasn't a single one of them that wasn't bleeding from somewhere on their body. Derek's medic bag was practically running on empty as he tried to patch everyone up and get them back into fighting condition. Thank God Tanner, Gavin, and Carter had shown up, or they'd all probably be dead right now. If the eleven of them could barely fight off a pack of hybrids, how the hell was it possible for Declan and Kendra to still be alive?

"How far did the locals make it before the hybrids caught up to them?" Ivy asked Carter as Derek applied antiseptic cream to the sergeant's ribs.

Carter had tackled one of the hybrids during the assault. His lightweight Kevlar vest had absorbed most of the damage as the creature tore into him, but his chest and stomach looked like he'd gone ten rounds with a cat on steroids. Angelo was pretty sure the guy had a few cracked ribs, too, but he was dealing with it.

"Fifteen miles, give or take," Tanner said. "They put up a fight, that's for sure. If we'd gotten there sooner, we might have been able to save them."

Tanner's voice was tinged with regret. Angelo got that. In battle, you always wondered if things would have ended differently if you'd only pushed a little harder, gotten there a little sooner.

Clayne strode into the small defensive position they'd set up so Derek could tend to the wounded. The wolf shifter was pissed the hybrids had slipped past him and had been out roaming the perimeter for the last hour. Clayne stopped in front of Landon and tossed a handful of something on the ground at his feet. It was dark, but Angelo was pretty sure they were flowers.

Landon regarded the flowers for a moment, then looked at Clayne. "And I didn't get you anything."

Clayne growled. "Funny, but it's not a present. It's the reason we haven't been able to find Declan and Kendra."

Ivy bent down and picked up the flowers. She held them at arm's length and sniffed, then groaned. "Dammit."

Landon frowned, looking from his wife to Clayne and back again. "What am I missing here?"

Angelo wanted to know the answer to that, too.

"Declan and Kendra have been rubbing these damn flowers all over themselves for days," Clayne explained. "To you guys, they probably smell nice, but to us, they're overpowering as hell. A shifter—or a hybrid—wouldn't be able to smell anything cloaked by this fragrance."

"Then how do you know Declan and Kendra used them to mask their scent?" Angelo asked.

"It wasn't too hard to figure out once I realized a plant shouldn't leave a trail through the forest like this." Clayne jerked his head toward the trees. "I went back about a mile or so and checked. This flower's scent follows right along with the prints we've been following. Declan covered their tracks with a fucking flower, and it took us almost three days to figure it out. I'm not sure if I should be impressed with him or pissed at myself. But it's them, I know it."

Ivy picked up her pack. "Let's get going. If we're lucky, we might be able to catch up with them tonight."

"No," Landon said.

She swung around to face him, her eyes glowing. "What do you mean, no?"

Landon moved to put his hands on her shoulders, but stopped himself. Angelo felt for his friend. God, it really sucked that Landon couldn't touch his wife in front of other people simply because the DCO had some stupid policy that said they weren't supposed to be married.

"I want to find Declan and Kendra as much as you do, but we can't go after them right now," Landon said gently. "Derek needs more time to finish patching everybody up and we all need to rest some after that attack. Besides, we can't go charging around the jungle willy-nilly anymore. We'll have to move much slower now that we know the hybrids are trying to ambush us."

Ivy looked like she wanted to argue, but she didn't. Even in the dark, the frustration on her face was clear as she nodded. "You're right." She fingered the wedding rings Angelo knew she wore on a necklace beneath her shirt as she looked at Landon, then turned to Clayne. "Get something to eat. I'll cover the perimeter."

Landon started to go after her, but thought better of it. Instead, he stood there and watched her disappear into the jungle.

"Should I go with her?" Tanner asked.

Landon shook his head, tossing him an MRE—meal ready to eat—from his pack. "No. I'll head out in a little while. Right now, she needs some time to herself. She has a lot on her mind."

Tanner frowned, but sat down beside Angelo and tore into the MRE. "Did I miss something while I was gone?"

Angelo dug in his own pack and pulled out some food. Unlike Landon, he didn't have any complete MRE pouches—the things took up too much space. Instead, he'd raided an extra case of rations back at the base camp, taking only the best parts—the main entrées and the cheese—which in his opinion was the best thing the food nerds had ever invented. Angelo tore the corner of an entrée at random and squished the stuff into his mouth like toothpaste. Chicken and egg noodles…maybe.

"We've been hit a few times by hybrids since you took off to look for those locals," Landon replied to

Tanner's question as he sat down on the ground opposite them. "Nothing like the ambush they just pulled on us, but bad enough to slow us down."

"Is that why Ivy's upset?" Tanner opened the MRE. "Because she feels like we aren't getting any closer to her friend?"

"That's some of it," Landon admitted, digging out another MRE. "But I'm guessing she's still freaked out by the three hybrids we stumbled across earlier today."

Tanner looked up from the mystery goo he was spooning into his mouth, his eyes sharp. "Why? What happened?"

Angelo picked up the story so his former captain could eat. "It wasn't anything that happened. It was how they acted. One was a lookout, while the other two crawled around on their hands and knees, sniffing the ground like a couple of freaking bloodhounds."

Tanner's brow furrowed. "That's strange."

"No shit," Angelo agreed. "They were so intent on sniffing the ground, they didn't even notice us until we were practically right in front of them. It wasn't until we put them down that we noticed the two bloodhounds had been carrying ripped up pieces of Kendra's clothing."

"Oh, shit," Tanner murmured.

"Yeah, it's not good. But we're all trying to stay positive." Landon took a ration bar out of its wrapper and bit into it. "It wouldn't make sense for the hybrids to use pieces of Kendra's clothing to track her if she wasn't still out here somewhere."

"But Ivy still doesn't like the idea of the hybrids being close enough to Kendra to get pieces of her clothing," Angelo added. "And just because we think Kendra might still be out there, that doesn't mean Declan is. They didn't have any of his clothing."

"So, Ivy is wondering if Declan might already be dead and Kendra is out there on her own," Tanner finished.

Angelo nodded. Regardless of what Landon said about not thinking the worst, they were all worried about the same thing.

"Tanner, did Zarina tell you about what happened to Ivy out in Washington State?" Landon asked, opening his canteen and taking a swallow of water.

Tanner dug around in the bottom of his MRE pouch, came out with the small tan packet of cheese, and wordlessly passed it to Angelo. "She told me those doctors took DNA samples from Ivy and that Ivy is terrified they'll use it to create a hybrid-shifter blend." He frowned. "I hope it wasn't wrong of Zarina to tell me that?"

Landon shook his head. "No. Ivy and I trust Zarina completely. If she felt it necessary for you to know about it, that's good enough for us."

Tanner relaxed. "I think she wanted me to understand how horrible the people behind the hybrid program are." He snorted. "As if I needed a reminder. She forgets I'm living proof of what they're willing to do."

"Then you probably understand better than anyone what Ivy is going through," Landon said. "It's bad enough she has to worry about her friends being dead, but the thing that has her pacing around out there in the jungle right now is the thought that they might be dead at the hands of hybrids who were created from her DNA. If that happens, and Kendra and Declan truly are dead, I don't think she'll be able to handle it."

"She'll blame herself," Tanner said.

"Yeah." Landon dug in his pack and came out with another MRE pouch. "I'm going to go spend some time with Ivy—see if I can get her to eat something."

Angelo leaned forward and handed him the pack of cheese Tanner had given him. "Here, take this. Everything tastes better with MRE cheese on it."

Landon shook his head as he stood up and adjusted his NVGs. "I think there's a T-shirt somewhere with that slogan on it."

Angelo grinned. "And if there isn't, there should be."

As Landon moved off quietly into the bush and disappeared from sight, Angelo wondered how he'd find Ivy out there in the jungle, but decided she'd probably find him first.

"You two seem like you're tight," Tanner observed.

"We've known each other for a long time," Angelo said. "We went through a lot of crap together in Special Forces. Before he got pulled into the DCO."

"Looks like you're still going through a lot of crap together, regardless of the fact that he's in the DCO."

Angelo chuckled. "You got that right. Although it seems like the crap's a lot weirder now."

"Amen to that," Tanner agreed. "I saw a lot of strange stuff while I was in the army, but nothing like this."

Angelo swallowed some water from his canteen. "Landon told me you used to be in the Rangers. How long were you in for?"

Tanner was slow to answer, and when he did, the words were so soft Angelo had a tough time hearing him. "Eight years. But it was so long ago it sometimes seems like it was all a dream."

Landon hadn't told him why Tanner left the army,

but Angelo was familiar with the story of how Stutmeir had grabbed the former Ranger from the forests of Washington State and turned him into the hybrid he was now. It wasn't too hard to imagine how a soldier could go from the battlefield one day to being an outcast in his own country the next. Unfortunately, Angelo had seen it far too often in the past few years. He loved serving his country, but facts were facts. The military was good at a lot of things—killing people and breaking things being at the top of the list—but taking care of soldiers who couldn't fight anymore wasn't one of them. Veterans like that usually ended up on the street, where they didn't fit in and weren't understood. If the Veterans Administration safety net didn't catch them— and there were a lot of holes in that net—they ended up like Tanner. Alone and on their own.

"When did you get out?" Angelo asked.

Tanner's brow creased as he tried to remember. "Maybe two years ago? With all the hybrid crap, and the other stuff, it's hard to remember the details. But I do remember spending a full summer and winter out in the forest before I got grabbed by those bastards."

Angelo wanted to ask Tanner if he'd ever talked to anyone from the VA, but he guessed things had progressed a little bit beyond the point where they could do anything for him.

"The DCO is helping you, though, right? With your hybrid problem…and the other stuff?"

Angelo didn't know for sure, but if he had to guess what that "other stuff" was, he'd say it was probably PTSD. He'd seen a lot of that, too.

"The DCO probably thinks they're helping, but I'm

smart enough to know that some of the people there are only interested in how I can be turned into another weapon in their arsenal." Tanner shook his head. "Nah. Most of the real help I get comes from Zarina."

Angelo didn't miss the fleeting smile that snuck across the hybrid's face as he said her name. He'd be damned. Tanner had a thing for Zarina. He couldn't blame the guy. Zarina Sokolov was a beautiful woman.

"She doesn't exactly fit the image I have of a cold, detached Russian scientist," Angelo said.

Tanner's grin broadened. "No, she doesn't, does she? Underneath that beautiful exterior is the smartest person I've ever met."

Angelo screwed the cap back on his canteen. "Does she know you like her?"

Tanner's eyes narrowed. "How did you know?"

Angelo laughed. Did Tanner really think he could hide something like that? Anyone could see it. "Well, for one thing, I've met her, and it's hard not to notice how attractive she is. And then there's that goofy-ass grin you get on your face every time you say her name. It's sort of a dead giveaway."

Tanner looked stunned, but then he gave Angelo that aforementioned goofy-ass grin. "I guess I do smile a lot when I think about her. It's hard not to. She's amazing."

The poor guy had it bad. But at least Tanner had one thing going right in his life.

"You didn't answer my question," Angelo pointed out. "About whether she knows how you feel."

Tanner grimaced. "As if a woman like her would be interested in a screwed-up mess like me."

"You're a basket case for sure, and she's miles out

of your league," Angelo agreed. "But women seem to have their own set of criteria when it comes to evaluating men."

"You sound like you speak from experience."

"Me? Nah," Angelo said. "But I have two sisters, and the guys they date sometimes make me scratch my head and wonder what the hell they're thinking."

Tanner snorted but was silent as he considered that. "Sometimes I wonder if Zarina is spending so much time with me because I'm such a scientific curiosity—a genetic freak of a hybrid with the barest modicum of restraint."

Angelo chuckled. "It's nice to finally meet a man who's even more clueless about women than I am. Dude, women like Zarina don't waste time playing games with men they're not interested in. They don't have to. If she's taking a personal interest in you and all the crap you're going through, it's because she's into you."

Tanner grabbed his canteen but didn't open it. "I'd like to believe that. She's sure as hell the best thing in my life right now. But even if she was interested in me before, she won't be after I took off to come down here with you guys."

Angelo leaned back and pulled a ration bar out of his pack. He was still hungry and they probably weren't going to get a chance to eat again for a while. "Did you get in an argument with her before you left?"

"I didn't get to talk to her," Tanner said. "She wasn't there when I stopped by the lab to tell her I was going, so I just left a note."

"Ouch," Angelo said. "You're right, that is worse. What did you say in the note?"

"Landon didn't want me to give her any details, so I

was a little vague. I told her I was going on a mission with him, Ivy, and Clayne, that I'd be back soon, and that she shouldn't worry."

Angelo grimaced.

"That bad, huh?" Tanner asked.

Angelo thought about sugarcoating it but changed his mind. "Pretty much. Zarina's trying to help you learn how to control your rage, right? Well, she's not going to be thrilled that you're down here getting into it with a bunch of hybrids. Hell, if I'm right and she actually cares about you, she's probably going to be worried out of her mind."

Tanner's brows furrowed. "I never thought about that. Landon said Declan and Kendra were in trouble, and I just went with it."

"A guy like me would find your willingness to risk your life for your friends as something admirable. A woman who cares about you? Probably not so much."

Tanner swore. "I'm screwed, aren't I?"

Angelo just looked at him.

Tanner stared at the ground as if contemplating exactly how screwed he was. After a moment, he lifted his head. "What would you do in this situation?"

Angelo laughed as he took another swig from his canteen. "Dude, I'm the last one you should be asking. I suck when it comes to knowing what women want to hear. Which is why I don't have one waiting back at home worrying about me."

The panicked look on Tanner's face was painful to see. Angelo swore under his breath. *Great. Just what we need out here. Another guy who's distracted.* He had to get Tanner's head back in the game, and quick.

"Okay, I'm not sure how much this will help, but if I were you, the first thing I'd do when I got back would be to show up at her door with a gift of some kind," Angelo advised. "Flowers. Chocolates. Hell, I don't know—a plush tree sloth if you can find a store that sells them. Anything like that. Then make sure the first words out of your mouth are, *I'm sorry for making you worry*. Women like a man who can apologize when he's wrong."

Or so his mom had always told him.

Tanner thought about that. "You really think it will work?"

"I have absolutely no idea. I suck pond water when it comes to charming women. But on the bright side, if this rescue goes south, we'll probably all get killed and you won't have to worry about what to say to her."

It really wasn't that funny when Angelo said it out loud, but Tanner grinned anyway, the worry disappearing from his face. "I'll use that as my backup plan. Until then, I'll keep my eyes open for a plush tree sloth."

———

Declan lay on the sand-covered cave floor with nothing but a poncho separating him from the ground, and decided it was the most comfortable place he'd ever slept. Of course, the beautiful woman draped over his chest probably had something to do with that. Kendra had spent the whole night on top of him—first making love to him like a vixen, then sleeping like an angel, and he'd loved every second of it. Actually, he'd loved her more and more every second of it. Further resistance was futile. He was completely, one hundred percent in love with her.

Discovering Kendra felt the same way about him was what had finally pushed him over the edge. Okay, so maybe the word *love* hadn't come up last night, but there was no mistaking the fact that Kendra cared for him. Right now, that was enough.

He grinned at the rock ceiling. To say last night had been incredible didn't even begin to cover it. He'd never dreamed sex could be so good. He realized now that what he used to consider great sex had been barely average compared to what being with Kendra felt like. It almost hurt to think how hard—and how many times—he'd come. He was already dreaming of how much better it was going to be when he got her in a nice, soft bed.

A moan from beneath his chin let him know that his princess was finally waking up. Kendra lifted her head and gave him a sexy smile that made his cock start to harden. Or maybe it was simply the fact that she was naked.

He brushed her hair back. "Morning, beautiful."

She wiggled up his body to kiss him, nudging even more life into his sleeping cock. "Morning, my hunky teddy bear."

Declan laughed and pulled her down for another kiss, only to freeze when she suddenly looked around in a panic.

"What's wrong?" he asked, trying to sit up with her on his chest.

Shit. Had the hybrids found them? He didn't hear anything.

But Kendra pressed a hand on his chest. "Stay. I just need to…um, how far back does this cave go?"

He frowned, trying to figure out why she wanted to know. Then it struck him. She had to go.

"It keeps going back about twenty more feet," he said. "The ceiling dips down in a couple of places and it's dark, so take a flashlight."

She was off his chest and digging through his pack in a flash. She came out with her flashlight, her canteen, and the small hygiene kit she'd saved from the last hybrid attack. Then she was running for the back of the cave, giving him an incredible view of her perfect ass.

Declan groaned. Maybe doing something mundane like checking to see if their clothes were still wet would distract him. Their T-shirts were just about dry. Their uniforms and boots, on the other hand, were still damp. It was probably about as dry as they'd get in here, but he shook everything out and flipped them over so the back side could dry some more. Of course, the moment they left the cave, their clothes were going to get soaked all over again. Or at least his would. He could carry Kendra and keep her out of the worst of the water.

While he waited for her to come back, he looked out of the cave opening, using his nose as well as he could to verify there weren't any hybrids nearby. He was back on the poncho eating an energy bar—sex with Kendra had made him hungrier than running around the jungle and fighting hybrids—when she materialized out of the darkness, naked and beautiful. The sight of her damn near took his breath away.

She shoved her hygiene bag back in his pack. "Sorry for the unsexy dash to the back of the cave."

He chuckled, ditching the half-eaten ration bar to grab her hand and pull her down on his lap for a long, slow kiss. When that urge was satisfied, he slid one hand down to caress her ass. "Unsexy, huh? I don't know what you're talking about. Watching this bottom of yours bounce as you ran off was about the sexiest thing I've ever seen."

That earned him a gorgeous smile and another kiss. Pulling her onto his lap had seemed like a good idea, but all this skin-on-skin contact wasn't helping the situation with his growing hard-on.

Kendra grinned. "You didn't get enough last night, huh?"

"I don't think I'm ever going to be able to get enough of you." Declan nuzzled her neck with a soft growl, then tried unsuccessfully to position her in some manner that didn't involve her warm, soft skin touching his cock. "And if we were in my bed, I wouldn't let you out of it until I made love to you in every position I could think of." He grinned. "And I can think of a lot."

She laughed, and maybe even blushed a little too, he couldn't be sure. But then she sighed, the amusement fading from her eyes. "Last night was so perfect that I almost forgot where we are."

And he had to be the insensitive jerk who reminded her. As far as he knew, there weren't any hybrids around right now, so they really should get going while the coast was clear. But he made no move to get up. Instead, he trailed his fingers over the curve of her breast.

"Staying here a little while longer won't hurt," he told her softly.

Her breath hitched as his thumb brushed her nipple. "Are you sure?"

Declan wasn't sure of anything at the moment except

how badly he wanted to be inside her. For the first time in days, they were safe. If they had enough food and water, they could stay here like this forever.

He kissed her, gently sucking on her lower lip. "I'm sure."

She didn't ask him again. Instead, she let out a breathy sigh and slid a hand down his chest to wrap her fingers around his very erect shaft.

He slipped his hand in her hair, holding her captive as he kissed her. Her hand tightened around him, and he groaned.

She broke the kiss and licked her lips, like she was reveling in the taste he'd left on her mouth. The blatantly erotic gesture made him remember what her tongue had felt like on his cock last night. She moved her hand up and down on him as if reading his mind. Damn, she knew how to get him going, didn't she?

"Do you like that?" she asked.

Declan could only growl softly in answer. Obviously, he liked it. She had amazing hands. But two could play at that game. He bent to nuzzle her neck as he slipped a hand between her legs and ran his finger up and down her slick folds.

She gasped.

He chuckled. "Do you like that?"

Kendra moaned.

He dipped his finger into her wetness. "Is that a yes?"

She clutched his shoulders. "Yes!"

He rewarded her by sliding his finger even deeper, pressing the palm of his hand against her clit at the same time. Kendra wiggled against his palm. Remembering how much she'd liked when he kissed her neck last night, he used the hand in her hair to tip her head gently to the side so he could get access to that sensitive part of her body.

He played with different techniques, hungry to learn everything he could about what turned her on. He discovered that when it came to her neck and ears, there didn't seem to be anything she didn't like—gentle kissing, light nibbling, sharp bites. She moaned no matter what he did. And the longer he nuzzled her neck, the wetter her pussy got. It wasn't long before her hips began to undulate, which told him she was going to come soon.

He pressed his lips against her ear, breathing softly on her skin as he moved his hand faster against her clit. "Come for me, Kendra. Right now."

As if following his orders, she dropped her head against his shoulder and let out a low, shuddering moan. Her thighs clamped down hard on his hand and she trembled against him like a beautiful flower in the wind. A red blush colored her cheeks, her breath coming in rapid, shallow pants as her nipples tightened to hard peaks. He could watch her come like this for the rest of his life.

It was so beautiful.

She was so beautiful.

He continued to make slow circles between her legs, not applying too much pressure but simply letting her ride her orgasm as long as it lasted. Which turned out to be almost a whole minute. That was pretty damn incredible. If he ever came that hard for that long, he'd probably explode.

When he carefully slid his hand from between her thighs, Kendra rested her cheek in the curve of his neck.

Her breath was warm against his skin, and he reached up to smooth her hair. Damn, how did it smell so wonderful out here in the jungle?

He was still trying to figure that out when he felt Kendra's hand moving on his erection. He fully expected her to return the manual favor—he was completely up for that—but when she slipped off his lap and spun around, he realized he was in line for something way better than a hand job. He might have growled as her warm mouth enveloped his cock, but he wasn't sure. He was too focused on how good it felt.

As she worked, Kendra slid one hand to his chest, urging him onto his back. He liked the view just fine from where he was, but since he was currently in a very giving mood, he acquiesced and lay back on his elbows to watch. The view of her long hair draped across his thighs, not to mention the sight of those beautiful lips of hers wrapped around his shaft, was an extremely erotic sight.

She worked slowly, letting her hand travel up and down his length in time with her mouth. It was clear she had no interest in rushing. No, she was taking her time. He have mentioned they needed to get back on the move, but for some reason, he couldn't get his lips to form the right words. Instead, the only things that came out were unintelligible groans and growls.

Kendra worked her tongue around the head of his penis, driving him crazy with each swirl. Just when he was sure it couldn't get any better, she gently ran her teeth over that extremely sensitive part of his cock. *Daaaaammn*.

It felt so unbelievable that he started thinking maybe he wasn't going to last nearly as long as he'd hoped. But just when the tingle started to really build, she took her mouth off him with an audible pop and sat back on her heels.

He opened his mouth to ask her what she was up to, but she put a finger on his lips, shushing him. "I promise the next time I start doing that, I won't stop. But right now, I need you inside me."

When Kendra put it that way, Declan couldn't be too disappointed she'd put the blow job on hold. Being inside her again more than made up for it.

He grinned. "Climb on."

She bit her lip. "Actually, I have another position in mind."

He was about to ask her what it was, but she was already motioning him to slide over and make room for her in the middle of the poncho. The moment he did, she scooted onto her back and spread her legs, curling her fingers in a come-hither motion.

The impulse to throw himself between those sexy, toned thighs of hers was hard to resist, but somehow, he did.

"I want to." He shook his head with an audible growl. "God, you don't know how much I want to, but I can't. The ground is way too hard, and I've got more than a hundred pounds on you. I could squish you or something."

Kendra laughed. "Declan, I'm not made of porcelain." When he didn't move, she sighed. "I love that you're so worried about me, I really do, but I won't break. If you keep most of your weight on those big, strong arms of yours, I'll be fine. Now get over here."

Declan wasn't so sure, but Kendra didn't look like she was in the mood to argue. And seeing her lying there with her legs spread like they were was making it hard to remember what he'd been worried about just a few seconds ago.

He moved forward until he was kneeling right between her thighs. She looked so gorgeous lying there, completely confident he'd never hurt her. But one little slip while he was in the throes of orgasm and he could seriously damage her. Figuring the best way to avoid that was to kneel between her legs, he moved closer and teased the head of his cock up and down her wet folds. She felt so hot.

Kendra wrapped her legs casually around his hips and whimpered softly, clearly enjoying the slow friction of his penis against her clit.

He could have teased her like that all day, but they didn't have all day. Silencing a groan, he moved back and angled his erection down just enough to wedge the head in the entrance of her incredible heat.

Kendra gasped, then bit her lip as he rocked back and forth, going a little deeper with each motion. He wouldn't be able to drive as deep in this kneeling position, but that was fine with him. It still felt amazing.

Kendra lifted her legs, hooking her ankles around his back, jerking him forward. Then she grabbed his shoulders with both hands and pulled him on top of her. "Don't even think about not coming down here."

He locked his arms on either side of her body, refusing to put any more of his weight on her, but she seemed satisfied. Her quick move had forced him deep inside her, which appeared to be what she was going after. He had to admit, it felt pretty damn amazing.

She repositioned her legs around his hips, digging her heels into his ass as she smiled up at him. "See? Told you I wouldn't break." She ran her fingernails across his tensed shoulders and down his arms. "Now, why don't you stop acting like I'm going to shatter the moment you start moving, and come down here and kiss me?"

She'd been right up to this point, so maybe she was better at knowing which sex positions would work for them than he was. Still moving carefully, he lowered himself to his forearms. She felt tight around him.

"Okay, you were right," he admitted as he settled comfortably between her legs. "This works pretty good."

"Glad you think so."

She got a hand in his hair and pulled him in for a kiss, slipping her tongue in his mouth. He growled, kissing her back as he began to slowly move inside her. She murmured her approval against his mouth, her heels pressing rhythmically into his ass, urging him to move faster.

But he refused. She felt so hot and tight in this position that if he didn't go slowly, this would end up being over before they got started.

He took his time, staying buried deep inside her, then only moving an inch or two in and out before plunging in again. To keep his mind off how unbelievable it felt, he focused on kissing her, nibbling her neck and ears, and generally anything else except how much he wanted to come.

"That's perfect right there," she breathed, pulling her knees higher and crossing her ankles over his lower back. "Don't stop. Please don't stop."

So Kendra had a perfect spot she liked touched just like this? That was something he would keep in mind.

Declan toyed with her, changing the angle of his thrusts as well as the speeds, just to see what she liked best. She definitely enjoyed it when he thrust slow and hard the most, if the way she gasped was any indication. Could he make her come from moving this slow and steady?

"Faster," she begged. "Right there, but faster!"

As much as he wanted to find out if his theory was correct, he couldn't deny Kendra anything she wanted, especially when he wanted it just as badly. He thrust faster, slapping into her spread thighs with every pump.

Kendra's head fell back and her mouth opened in a soundless expression of pleasure. Her fingernails bit into his shoulders and back as she bucked under him. Seeing her climax was the most beautiful thing he'd ever witnessed, and he thrust harder, pushing her further into ecstasy.

When she finally went completely over the edge, it was so damn sexy that he didn't bother to hide his growl. But he didn't come. Not yet. He wanted to make sure she experienced every single ounce of her pleasure before he did, because he didn't want to miss a second of it.

When her body had started to relax just the slightest little bit, he drove into her, drawing a gasp from her as he held himself there and exploded.

Her eyes held his captive the entire time he pumped his essence deep inside her, never losing focus, never looking away. They stayed locked together through it all…as locked together as he knew their hearts to be.

When the last spasm passed through him, he let himself relax. As they lay together, arms and legs entwined, Kendra kissed him, first on the lips, then on his scruffy jaw, and finally his neck. Then she placed her mouth beside his ear, her breath warm and moist on his skin. Her scent filled him, almost overwhelming him.

"That was the hottest sex I've ever had in my life," she whispered. "And watching you come inside me like that was seriously the most amazing thing I've ever seen." He would have thrown a few compliments her way in return, but she continued. "You want to know what the best part of it was? The way your eyes flared that beautiful shade of rose when you came. It let me know that I made you come really, really hard. I love that flash of color."

There was a time when the thought of shifting during sex would have freaked the hell out of him. But doing it with Kendra didn't bother him because she didn't care.

For the first time, he really believed that.

"Only for you," he growled, kissing her neck.

"Damn straight."

As if to show him how serious she was, she gently nipped him on the muscular junction of his neck and shoulder with her perfect teeth.

He liked when she bit him.

Chapter 10

As Kendra pulled on her almost-dry socks, she finally got the courage to ask the question that had been on her mind since she and Declan had finally crawled out of each other's arms.

"The stuff you said—that you don't like being a shifter—it made me wonder something."

He looked up from pulling on his boots. "What's that?"

His eyes were so warm and captivating that she found it hard to speak. When she finally found her voice, she could barely remember what she'd been going to say. Wow, she was falling fast. She'd spent the last week berating herself for being stupid enough to miss what had been right in front of her all along, but that was over. She was focused on the future now, and when they got home, she promised herself she was going to make up for all the time she'd lost with him.

"Um, if you were never comfortable embracing your inner animal, why'd you decide to join the DCO in the first place?" she finally managed. "Didn't you think they'd expect you to use your shifter talents?"

He stopped tying his boots and shrugged. "This is going to sound stupid, but I didn't really give it a lot of thought at the time. John told me that I'd be using my talents to help people. That was good enough for me."

She smiled. Sometimes she wished she could see things as simply as Declan did. "It's not stupid at all.

And you do use your talents to help people. Your team is one of the best in the DCO. I should know; I write all the evaluations."

They finished dressing in silence, then repacked Declan's rucksack. She couldn't help looking around the cave. She was going to miss this place. It was where everything had come together for them.

He slung on his pack. "You ready?"

She sighed wistfully. "I guess so. Though if you wanted to stay here for another few hours, I wouldn't complain."

He chuckled. "I know what you mean, but the sooner we get out of here, the sooner we can get home and I can take you out for dinner like I promised."

That brought a moan of delight to her lips. "I see you've already figured out how to motivate me to get out of bed."

Declan pulled her into his arms. "Don't get me wrong. I much prefer to be in bed with you, but I want you in my bed at home. The only reason I'll be taking you out to dinner is so you can keep your strength up for all the things I want to do to you when we're in my bed."

She felt a shiver run down her back as much from his words as the blatant look of hunger on his face. God, she needed him again already.

"What kinds of things?" she asked softly.

He brushed her ear with his lips, his warm breath making her quiver. "For starters, a slow, sensual massage." As if to demonstrate, he glided his hand up her midriff to cup her breast through her T-shirt. "And after that, I'm going to kiss and nibble everywhere."

She caught her breath as his thumb grazed her nipple. "Everywhere?"

He lifted his head to look at her, his eyes glowing a soft rose color. "Everywhere."

Kendra bit her lip to stifle a moan. She was about ten seconds from ripping off his clothes and throwing him on the floor of the cave. "Let's get out of here. The sooner we get home, the sooner you can give me that massage."

Declan chuckled, then kissed her hard on the mouth before picking up their weapons. He handed one to her, then led the way to the cave's opening. She waited patiently as he parted the vines carefully, then listened and sniffed. She frowned at the water rushing by outside the cave, remembering how cold it had been.

"We should have waited to put our clothes on after we crossed the river," she grumbled. "They're going to be soaked again."

He grinned over his shoulder. "As tempting as skinny-dipping with you sounds, that probably wouldn't be a good idea. Don't worry. I'm planning on carrying you until we get out of the water."

Even though she knew Declan could carry her without any problem, it still didn't seem right. "But you'll get all wet."

"It doesn't bother me as much, you know that."

She opened her mouth to argue more, but he must have decided the coast was clear because he parted the thick wall of vines and hopped out of the cave with a splash of cold water. He looked around for a moment, then turned back to her.

"Come on." He slung his M4 across his back and motioned her forward. "I'm going to carry you, so get used to it. Now quit stalling."

Deciding that continued complaining on her part

would be more embarrassing than simply letting him carry her, she gave in and scooted to the edge of the cave opening, letting him scoop her up in his arms like she was a kitten.

Sometimes she forgot just how strong Declan was, but he carried her high above the water like he barely noticed her weight. She didn't talk to him as he moved downstream. He had that slightly distant look in his eyes that told her that he was focusing his senses—well, his ears mostly—outward, making sure there weren't any hybrids around.

She scanned the banks of the stream as much as she could, not that she expected to catch anything he'd miss. She was so caught up in the task, she barely noticed how far they'd gone until Declan stepped up onto the rock-covered bank. He scanned the area as he lowered her to the ground.

"Anything?" she asked softly.

He shook his head. "I don't hear a thing. I don't smell anything besides those damn orchids, either. They must grow pretty thick here around the water."

"Let's get back over that last ridge we crossed and on a northwest track," she said, moving ahead of him. "If we pick up the pace, we could be at base camp in a few days."

"Slow down." He chuckled as he caught up to her, trying to drag his carbine off his back and over his head at the same time. "I know you're eager, but let me get in front."

Kendra was so happy to finally have a clear path ahead of them that she wasn't as focused as she should have been on the jungle around them. If she had, maybe she would have realized everything was too perfect in those few seconds before the jungle floor erupted around them in a shower of dead leaves and sticks.

She brought her M4 up the moment she saw the hybrids coming out of the ground. The damn creatures had dug pits and laid in wait for them, somehow knowing she and Declan were hiding somewhere along the stream and that they'd come back this way.

Kendra didn't have time to understand why Declan hadn't known they were there—she barely had time to shoot. The hybrids were still springing out of the ground around them, so it was hard to tell how many there were, but there had to be at least half a dozen.

She got off a lucky shot, hitting the first charging hybrid in the head and putting him down as he rushed her. But before she could even get off another round, two more hybrids launched themselves at her. She heard a tree-shaking roar behind her and knew that Declan was fighting to reach her, but there was no way he would be able to get to her before the hybrids did. And she sure as hell didn't have enough ammo in her magazine to take down two of the raging creatures at the same time—not without being killed.

But that didn't mean she wasn't going to try.

She threw herself backward, firing a three-round burst before she hit the ground. She didn't target the hybrids—they were moving too fast for that—but instead aimed for the space directly above her, knowing that's where both the monsters would ultimately end up.

The move caught the first one by surprise, and he ended up sailing over her, but the other came down right on top of her. The impact drove the sliding stock of her

M4 into her ribs, crushing the air out of her lungs. But that didn't scare her nearly as much as the claws gripping her shoulders. She fought a tide of panic. The hybrid could literally rip her head off without much trouble.

Declan roared behind her, but the sound was drowned out by the snarls of hybrids. It sounded like he was being torn apart. Some part of her mind screamed that she had to get to him, but she couldn't. She wasn't even sure she was going to last long enough to help herself.

The creature on top of her bared its teeth, scrambling for a grip on her neck. She struggled for breath, trying to twist her M4 around and get it between her and the thing on top of her, but she couldn't. She squeezed the trigger anyway, praying it was pointed at something important.

Nothing happened. *Crap, the magazine must be empty.*

Knowing she was screwed but refusing to give up, she squirmed under the hybrid's heavy weight, shoving the hands away from her neck and shoulders at the same time she kicked with her knees. She didn't expect it to help—the hybrid on top of her outweighed her by a ton and was ten times stronger than she was—so she was shocked when the hybrid loosened his hold and rolled off her, taking her weapon with him.

Kendra scrambled back, wanting to put as much distance between the beast and herself. That's when she realized the hybrid was dead. For a second, she thought she'd gotten a lucky shot in, but then she saw that the barrel of her M4 was buried in the thing's chest. It had impaled itself on her weapon as it landed on her.

She didn't waste time considering her good fortune. Declan needed her help. She grabbed her weapon, kicking at the hybrid as she jerked hard. She refused to think about where the barrel of the M4 had just been, instead reloading it as quickly as she could. Snarls mixed with growls to become one terrifying sound somewhere behind her, and the hair on the back of her neck stood up as she shoved a fresh magazine into the gun.

Releasing the bolt to chamber another round, she turned around, expecting to see Declan with one of those large-bore needles shoved in him—or worse. But there was no needle. Just a lot of savage ripping and tearing as Declan and the remaining hybrids went at it, rolling around on the ground like a ball of living fury.

One of Declan's big fists shot out, connecting with one hybrid's jaw. The sound of breaking bone echoed around her, blood spraying from the creature's mouth. And yet, the hybrid barely seemed to notice the damage, leaping back in the fray to slash at Declan with long, ragged claws. Declan was bleeding all over, too, but he simply roared and kept smashing at the two creatures facing him.

Kendra tried to line up a shot to help, but they were moving around too fast for her to take it. She was just as likely to hit Declan as one of the hybrids. But there was no way she was just going to stand there and do nothing while he was slowly cut to shreds.

She aimed above them and squeezed off a three-round burst.

Both hybrids snapped their heads around at the sound of the bullets zipping over their heads. That was even more of a reaction than she could have hoped for, and it gave Declan the opening he needed.

He lashed out with his foot, his heavy boot catching the biggest hybrid square in the chest and sending him hurtling, to land on the ground ten feet away. Kendra was on the hybrid before it could get up, firing burst after burst into the thing's chest before shifting her aim and putting two rounds in the back of its head.

She loaded her last magazine as she turned back to Declan and the remaining hybrid. But the lone hybrid was no match for Declan, and he quickly gained the upper hand, smashing his fist repeatedly into the creature's chest until it stopped moving.

Then Declan was at her side, his eyes wide and terrified. "Oh God, you're bleeding!"

Kendra opened her mouth to point out that he was bleeding, too, but the words died in her throat as she looked down at herself. The front of her uniform was soaked in blood. Her hands tightened reflexively on her weapon. The hybrid she'd fought with must have gotten his claws into her after all. *But then why don't I feel weak from losing so much blood?*

It wasn't until Declan ripped open her outer shirt and sent buttons flying everywhere that she realized what had happened.

"Declan, I'm okay," she said. "It's not my blood."

He looked at her in confusion. "What?"

"It's not my blood," she repeated, then pointed at the hybrid who'd impaled himself on her weapon. "It's his. He bled out all over me."

Declan turned back to her, relief on his face. That was when she got a good look at him. His uniform had even more blood on it than hers, and most of it belonged to him. She swayed a little at the sight, suddenly lightheaded, and she reached for the tatters of his uniform top as much to keep herself from falling as to check on his wounds. She pulled the outer shirt aside and gently lifted the T-shirt underneath to expose dozens of wicked slashes. Blood flowed freely, running down his chest.

"Oh God. What do I do?" she moaned.

She'd put teams through hundreds of injury scenarios for training back at the DCO complex, but right now she couldn't remember a freaking thing she'd seen.

Declan grabbed her hands and gently uncurled her fingers from his tattered shirt. "It's not as bad as it looks. Right now we have to get out of here. Your gunfire is going to draw more hybrids."

Everything he said after, "It's not as bad as it looks," went right over her head. Because it looked really bad to her. She was pretty sure she'd caught a flash of rib in the wounds under his pecs. How the hell was he still standing?

"Declan, we can't go anywhere until I get the bleeding stopped."

But he dragged her away from the stream. "We need to go. Now. You can patch me up once we're somewhere safe."

She almost laughed. *Safe?* They wouldn't be safe until they were back home. But he was right. They needed to get out of here. She only hoped Declan was right about those wounds not being as bad as they looked.

Kendra was just about to break into a run to keep up with Declan, but he stopped beside the hybrid who'd impaled himself on her weapon. She frowned as he pressed one big boot into the thing's bloody chest, then the other.

"Get blood on your boots," he instructed. "Hurry."

She had no idea why he wanted her to do it, but she did it, even if it did make her feel ill. When she was done, he grabbed her hand and started moving. Instead of heading back up the ridge like they'd originally planned, he led her along the stream. Probably so they could make better time.

She glanced over her shoulder at the six dead hybrids and spent shell casings. She couldn't believe she and Declan were both walking away from that fight. But the victory hadn't come without a price. Declan was hurt much worse than he'd let on. Within minutes, he could barely walk without her help. They needed to stop so she could tend to his wounds, but she had no idea if they'd gotten far enough away from the ambush site yet.

"How did they find us?" she whispered as she took more of his weight on her shoulders.

"Those were the same hybrids who chased us into the cave yesterday." His voice was weak, his words barely audible. "The last one I killed was carrying a piece of your torn clothing. I could smell it on him. He was using it to track you. When we disappeared, they must have decided to lay in wait for us to come out of hiding."

She stumbled under his weight as he wobbled, but she got her feet under her and kept him moving. "How were they able to hide by the stream without you knowing it?"

She didn't mean the words to come out as accusing as they did, but Declan didn't even seem to notice. That scared her as badly as his stumbling steps did.

"They're smarter than we gave them credit for," he said softly. "They must have dug those holes by hand so I wouldn't hear them, then lined them with the same orchids we've been using to hide our scent. I couldn't smell them even when I was right on top of them."

"Hybrids aren't supposed to be that smart," she

insisted. "The ones we fought out in Washington weren't
much more than guns with feet and claws."

"Well, they've clearly gotten smarter."

She tightened her hold around his waist. "What was
the deal with putting hybrid blood on our boots?"

"It was the best idea I could come up with on short
notice," he rasped. "The orchids sure as hell won't work
anymore. I'm hoping they'll overlook the smell of an
injured hybrid."

There were about a dozen holes in that idea—
especially if the hybrids were smarter than they
thought—but she and Declan didn't have a lot of choices.

Kendra looked quickly at his chest. His torn clothing
was dripping with blood now. She had to do some serious first aid—quick.

"I think we've gone far enough, haven't we?" she asked.

He shook his head. "We've barely gone a mile and a
half. We need to keep going."

She didn't mention that at the slow pace they were
moving, they weren't likely to get much farther before
he passed out. Instead, she wrapped her arm around him
even tighter and tried to take up more of his weight.

Twenty long minutes later, Declan motioned her up
the slope to the left of the stream. "Up there," he mumbled. "There's a place to hide up there."

As she led him up the steep hill, she'd never been so
glad for his innate bear-shifter ability to find a hidey-
hole. Unfortunately, this particular hidey-hole turned
out to be a pile of dead trees that had fallen over some
boulders instead of a secluded cave. While Declan
leaned against a tree, she pushed the branches out of the
way. Underneath them, close to the rocks, was a nice

lean-to shelter. She took that part back about the cave. This would do just fine.

"Rub your bloody shirt around the outside," he said. "That will help hide our scent. Make them think one of their own dragged itself in here to die."

Kendra helped him inside the shelter, then did as he told her, praying that dying wasn't exactly what Declan was doing at the moment. When she was done, she left the uniform top shoved under a rock near the entrance of the lean-to. It was just too nasty and bloody to put back on.

She crawled in through the tangle of dead branches and found Declan lying flat on his back, his eyes closed. Her heart jumped into her throat. She scrambled across the rocks and dead leaves covering the floor of the shelter, almost whacking her head on a low-hanging branch in her race to get to his side. "Declan! Oh God, wake up!"

His eyes immediately popped open. "How can I rest with you shouting like that?"

Her breath exploded out in rush. "Dammit, don't scare me like that."

"Sorry."

She grabbed his pack from the corner where he'd pushed it and dug out the first-aid kit. Then she turned and started the horrifying task of getting his uniform top and T-shirt off. But the blood was drying, making everything one big, crusty mess.

"You don't have to do that," he said softly.

Tears stung her eyes as she cut open his T-shirt with the small scissors from the kit, then gently pulled the black material away from the gashes on his chest and abdomen. Taking off his shirt made the wounds bleed again, but at least she had them all exposed. They were deep, no doubt about that. But they didn't look as bad as she'd thought. She didn't see any white ribs, which she thought she'd seen before. She must have imagined them. *Thank God*.

Nevertheless, she got out some of the bigger bandages in the kit and tore them open. She could use them to put pressure on the worst of the wounds and stop the bleeding. She didn't have a clue what to do after that, but it was a start.

"This is probably going to hurt," she told him.

But when she pressed the four-inch square of white gauze down on the worst-looking gash, Declan only smiled at her. "You don't have to do that. I just need to get some rest and I'll be fine."

She ignored his male macho crap and applied a second bandage across the wound beneath his left pec, where she'd thought she'd seen his ribs peeking through earlier. Declan laughed at her this time. It sounded strained, but it was still a laugh.

"Kendra, honey, I appreciate what you're doing. But if you want to help me, then let me sleep. If I do that, my body will heal these wounds enough to let us keep moving."

She stopped what she was doing and frowned at him. "Seriously? You can just sleep this off?"

"Pretty much. Some of these went down to the bone, though, so it might take a while." He pointed at his chest. "I need to calorie load, then zonk out for a half a day or so."

She chewed on her lower lip. "You mean…hibernate? Like a bear?"

"Basically. I am a bear shifter, remember?" He gave her a small smile. "I'll be completely out of it for a while, though, so I'll need you to keep watch over me."

"You know I will." She chewed on her lower lip some more. What if he was making up the hibernation thing so she'd feel better? "Your file doesn't mention anything about being able to heal yourself through hibernation. How do you know it will work? Have you done it before?"

He grabbed her hand where it still held the bandage over his chest and gave it a squeeze. "Yes, I've done this before—a couple of times on missions. I never wanted anyone to know about it, so the guys kept it out of the official reports."

She took a deep breath and nodded. For the first time since they'd been ambushed, she actually had hope. "What can I do to help?"

"First, I need to eat and drink as much as I can. Then I need to sleep until my body decides I've healed enough."

Which, according to him, could be several hours.

Kendra dug through his pack and pulled out all the food she could find—three and a half energy bars and a roll of cherry-flavored candy.

"Is that all we have left?" he asked.

"Yes. And don't even try to talk me into eating any of it." She gently lifted his head and held the first of the bars to his mouth. "If you don't get better fast, I'm not going to need any food."

Declan frowned but didn't argue. He inhaled the power bars and the hard candy practically without chewing, then followed it up with half a canteen of water. When he was done, she rolled up one of his uniform tops and put it under his head as a pillow. Then she sat beside him and gently smoothed her hand over his forehead.

"My breathing and heart rate will slow down, so don't be afraid when that happens," he said softly.

She didn't like the sound of that. "How long do you think you'll sleep?"

"It's hard to tell. Twelve hours, maybe more."

That wasn't so bad. "Okay." She leaned over and gently kissed him. "Sleep tight. I promise I won't let anything happen to you."

He smiled at her, his eyes already drifting closed. "I know."

Less than a minute later, the sound of his deep, steady breathing told her he'd already drifted off. His breathing slowed little by little until she could barely see his chest move. She had to fight the urge to check to make sure his heart was still beating.

Kendra looked at her watch. Ten a.m. That meant it'd be dark before he woke up. It was going to be a long twelve hours.

She took off her bloody T-shirt and put on the only other clean one she had. It was wet, but it was better than being covered in blood. She sat back against one of the boulders and tried to relax. But that was easier said than done. Seeing Declan broken and bloody like this was tearing her up with a pain unlike anything she'd ever experienced. She dragged her gaze away from the bandages covering his chest with a muffled sob and focused on his ruggedly handsome face. She couldn't imagine a more beautiful man in the whole world, inside or out.

It was no surprise that she was in love with him.

She should have been shocked by that, but she wasn't.

Her feelings for Declan had grown in leaps and bounds every day they'd been out here. It was about time she finally admitted it. She only wished she'd gotten the chance to tell him before.

She blinked back tears. She couldn't think like that. Declan was going to be fine, and when his body was done healing, he was going to wake up, and they were going to get out of this jungle and go home. Together. And they would make it home. Fate would never be so cruel as to finally allow her to find the love of her life only to lose him.

Chapter 11

"THERE WAS AN ASS LOAD OF HYBRIDS ON THEIR TRAIL," Clayne said. "Half a dozen, at least."

Angelo swore. Now that Clayne and Ivy were following the orchid scent Declan and Kendra had been using to hide from the hybrids, they were finally making up ground. If they kept this pace, they could catch up to the pair by tonight or tomorrow. But the ass load of hybrids Clayne had mentioned threw a kink in that plan. They'd been lucky since the ambush yesterday, but if there were half a dozen hybrids out there somewhere just ahead of them, it was going to slow them down.

"Any chance it was only a random pack going in the same direction as Declan and Kendra?" Angelo asked.

Clayne shook his head. "No. The hybrids' trail is laid down right over Declan's and Kendra's. They were tracking them."

"How long ago?" Tate asked.

No one in the group had slept much since they'd started this risky mission, but Tate looked the worst. The anxiety was tearing him up as bad as the guilt, not to mention the lack of sleep.

Clayne shrugged. "Twenty-four hours ago. Maybe less."

Shit. It was hard to imagine Declan and Kendra getting away from that many hybrids.

"Declan and Kendra have stayed ahead of them this

long," Landon said as if reading Angelo's mind. "We have to believe they were able to keep it up."

Clayne looked skeptical but didn't argue. "I'm going to catch up with Ivy and Tanner."

The wolf shifter turned to go, but Landon caught his arm. "Be careful. And go slow."

Clayne nodded, then turned and ran. Angelo didn't have to ask what Landon had meant by that warning. If the pack of hybrids had already taken out Declan and Kendra, the rest of them could be walking right into another ambush. Everyone else must have been thinking the same thing, because they spread out without being told.

Clayne, Ivy, and Tanner led the way up a lightly wooded slope before disappearing over the crest. Angelo would have picked up the pace to catch up with them, but Landon ordered them to stay back until he got to the top of the hill and gave the all clear. But instead of waving them forward, Landon held up a clenched fist, then spread his hand wide. Angelo immediately dropped for cover. Around him, the other men did the same.

Angelo scanned the slope. *Shit.* There wasn't a tree or a rock big enough to hide behind within two feet of any of them. Not exactly the best place to get caught out in the open. He tightened his grip on his M4, ready to pull the trigger.

Up ahead, Landon glanced over his shoulder and waved them forward. Angelo jumped to his feet and ran up the hill, Tate and the others on his heels. Twenty minutes later, they were following Landon into the jungle to where Ivy, Clayne, and Tanner waited.

Angelo stopped and stared in amazement. The six dead hybrids lying on the ground around them were easy enough to figure out. What had him stumped were the six shallow graves that had been dug near the river.

"What the hell happened here?" Tate asked.

"Declan happened," Clayne said, a hint of a smile tugging at his mouth.

"Yeah, I figured that," Tate said. "I meant the graves. I seriously doubt Declan hung around to bury the bastards after they tried to kill him and Kendra."

"So what are the holes for?" Derek made a face. "Damn, are those flowers in there?"

It was Ivy who answered. "Yeah. The same ones Declan's been using to cover their trail. I think the hybrids hid in the holes so they could ambush Declan and Kendra."

"The orchid smell is so thick, Declan would never have been able to smell them," Tanner added.

Clayne growled. "Fucking bastards. Didn't matter, though. Declan kicked the shit out of them anyway." He nudged the hybrid closest to him with his boot. "He smashed this one to a pulp, and just about ripped the heads off those two over there."

"Declan wasn't the only one kicking ass." Ivy had moved over to the other side of the clearing. "Two of the hybrids were shot. It looks like Kendra stabbed this one to death with the barrel of her M4, too. Her scent is all over him but none of her blood."

"Damn." Derek laughed. "I knew Kendra was a badass."

"Looks like it." Tate grinned. "Let's go find them. They can't be too far ahead of us now."

Angelo was down with that. But Clayne and Ivy made no move to lead the way. Tanner stared at the ground.

"What's wrong?" Angelo asked.

Clayne exchanged looks with Ivy. "We don't know where they went."

Everyone stared at him.

"What do you mean, you don't know where they went?" Tate demanded.

"We can't pick up their scent," Ivy explained.

Tate frowned. "Can't you just follow the smell of those damn flowers like you've been doing?"

She shook her head. "We swept a hundred meter perimeter before you got here. We didn't pick up the scent of those flowers anywhere. The only thing we smelled were more hybrids."

"Shit," Angelo muttered. "How many of them?"

"A couple scouting packs," Clayne said. "Not as many as this bunch, but we're still talking at least three or four of them. No doubt, they're looking for Declan and Kendra, too. Hopefully, they're not having better luck than we are."

Tate swore. "What the hell do we do now?"

"Hang here while we try to pick up Declan and Kendra's physical trail," Ivy said.

We meaning her, Clayne, and Tanner.

"Again?" Tate scowled. "That took forever before."

"It's the best we can do right now," Ivy said.

And it was a hell of a lot better than they could do on their own, that was for sure, Angelo thought.

She gave Landon a long look, then turned to follow Clayne and Tanner in the jungle.

"You heard Ivy," Landon said. "We hang tight here until they get a bead on Declan and Kendra. Until then, let's make sure we're ready if any more hybrids decide to show up."

Angelo dropped his pack and pulled out his NVGs. The sun was already going down, and if recent experience was any indication, they were going to be in for another all-nighter.

―᷍᷍᷍᷍᷍―

Kendra hadn't checked Declan's wounds since the sun had gone down an hour ago, but they'd all closed up, even the deep ones. She never would have believed it was possible, but he really was healing himself. She knew shifters healed fast. She'd personally seen how quickly Ivy had recovered from the torture those freak doctors had put her through. But as bad as those wounds had been—punctures, scalpel cuts, pieces of skin sliced off—they'd been minor compared to the ragged claw marks crisscrossing Declan's body.

She didn't know how Declan had been able to keep this talent hidden from the DCO for so long, but ultimately she didn't care. He was going to live, and that was the only thing that mattered to her. It had been a long day in the cramped shelter waiting for him to wake up, and from how slow his breathing and heart rate still were, he was probably a long way from coming out of his hibernation.

She gently smoothed his hair back from his forehead. She'd figured out a while ago—when she'd laid her ear on his chest to convince herself that his heart was still beating—that her touch wouldn't rouse him. It had been beating…albeit very slowly. Since then, she'd held his hand, refusing to let go. Even that simple contact made her feel better.

As she sat holding his hand, she kept an ear out for

hybrids, but so far she hadn't heard any. And in between doing that, she'd daydreamed about all the things she and Declan might do once they got back home. Making love topped the list, of course. Followed by going out to dinner. Or maybe they'd just get takeout. That way they wouldn't have to leave her apartment—or his— for days. She wondered what his place looked like. Probably very rustic, with lots of wood and outdoorsy furniture. But mostly she just wanted to hang out with him and make up for all she'd missed with him in the past seven years.

Kendra was still smiling at that image when she heard a noise outside. Her heart catapulted into her throat. Just because she heard something, that didn't mean it was a hybrid. There were all kinds of animals out here in the jungle.

Pulse pounding, she slipped on her NVGs and quietly moved aside the branches covering the entrance to their shelter just enough to take a quick peek.

The trees along the stream were sparse enough to allow a little moonlight to filter through them and illuminate the scene. She covered her mouth with her hand to muffle a gasp. Two hundred yards away, a pack of hybrids were slowly crawling along the bank of the nearby stream, sniffing the ground. In the green back-light of the NVGs, the glow from the creatures' eyes was unmistakable.

She could definitely make out three of them for sure, but there could have been more. They were moving slowly, following the exact route she and Declan had taken earlier that day. As much as she wanted to believe that they'd keep following the stream and pass her and

Declan by, she knew that wasn't going to happen. It was only a matter of time before they reached the shelter.

She glanced at Declan. He was sleeping peacefully, completely unaware of the danger they were in. With her low on ammo and Declan in a self-induced coma, the fight would be over before it started. Once she was dead, the hybrids could do anything they wanted to Declan. She wouldn't let him be tortured the way Ivy had, not when there was something she could do about it.

Kendra flipped up her goggles and leaned over to kiss Declan hard on the lips. He didn't respond, but she liked to think he could sense her. "I love you, my big, gentle teddy bear, and don't you ever forget it."

She kissed him again, softer this time, then gently wiped away one of her tears that had fallen to his cheek. She wished she could write him a note, so he'd know what had happened to her, but there wasn't time for that, even if she had something to write on.

She traced her fingers along his scruffy jaw, regretting all the things she hadn't gotten a chance to say. But another clatter of rock on rock from down by the stream reminded her that she had no time for this. She grabbed her M4, dropped her NVGs back into place, and eased out of the shelter.

Kendra knew she couldn't go directly toward the hybrids. She needed to lure them well away from Declan before she tried to take them out. That way, if she failed—which was pretty likely—Declan would still have a chance. Best case, they wouldn't be able to find him at all. Worst case, at least she'd give him time to wake up.

She closed her eyes and tried to get a feel for which

way the wind was blowing. Ivy had taught her the trick of turning until you felt the breeze on your cheeks, and it pretty much worked. Fortunately, it didn't seem like the wind would carry her scent down to the hybrids. If she moved slowly and carefully, and didn't make any noise, she stood a good chance of getting away from the shelter without them realizing that she was there. As fast as her heart was beating, she'd be amazed they hadn't already heard it.

She turned parallel to the stream and headed away from the hybrids, which meant she was going in the same direction they were. Moving quietly along the rocky slope she was on proved difficult while wearing her goggles. The less-than-stellar depth perception the things provided made avoiding all the stones damn near impossible. But she did it, at least long enough to get out ahead of the slow-moving hybrids before slipping down toward the stream.

She turned to look over her shoulder. It took a few moments to find them in the dark. Three of them were crawling along the ground on their hands and knees, sniffing as they went, while a fourth walked beside them. *Crap*, she could recognize the one walking—it was Marcus's second-in-command. And he was leading his group of hybrid bloodhounds right toward Declan's hiding spot.

They were moving at a slow pace. If she was trying to escape, she very likely could have, but that wasn't what she was trying to do.

It was hard to tell for sure, but the hybrids were probably getting close to the section of the stream where she and Declan had headed up the slope to their makeshift shelter. If the creatures were locked on a good scent, they'd be turning up the slope any second.

She needed to get their attention before they reached that point.

Flipping up her goggles—she'd never be able to hit anything with them on—she hefted her M4 to her shoulder and sighted at the second-in-command. If there was one hybrid she wanted to kill first, it was him. She popped off one three-round burst at him. She didn't wait to see what she hit. She just dropped her NVGs back into place and took off running.

Being stealthy wasn't important now; moving as fast as possible was. She wanted the hybrids to know exactly where she was. And she wanted them to chase her.

Behind her, their growls got louder as they got closer. Their boots pounded the ground as they caught up to her. They were even faster than she thought. At this rate, they'd be on her before she got far enough away from the shelter.

Hating to do it, but knowing she had to slow them down at least a little, Kendra slid to a stop, then turned and lifted her M4. She had maybe fifteen rounds left, at most. She couldn't afford to waste one of them. She flipped the selector switch to semi and carefully lined up a shot at the first hybrid sprinting toward her. Well, as lined up as she could get it while wearing NVGs. She squeezed the trigger slowly, refusing to let adrenaline get the best of her.

She fired three carefully aimed shots, hitting at least one of them and making all four hybrids slow down. She got another forty or fifty feet before they were on her heels again. Not that she was complaining, but why the hell weren't they shooting at her? Were they so interested in killing her with their fangs and claws that they'd rather chase her than shoot her? She supposed she should consider herself lucky—until she thought about how painful those fangs and claws were going to feel tearing her flesh.

The chase turned into a crazy game of Red Light, Green Light as she turned around at random to shoot at the creatures. While it slowed them down, the game couldn't last forever. For one thing, she didn't have enough ammo. For another, she was getting tired much faster than the hybrids ever would. But she'd put a fair distance between them and Declan—maybe almost a mile. Would it be enough? She could only hope it was at the same time she pushed for more.

Then she heard her pursuers crashing through the jungle from her left and right, and she knew she'd made it as far as she could. They were flanking her in an effort to end the chase.

Kendra sped up, but it wasn't fast enough at this point. She was so damn tired. Her legs felt wasted while her stomach and chest were one solid cramp of protesting muscles. She didn't bother to turn and shoot again. She only had a couple rounds left, and she figured she was going to have a chance to use them at close range any second now.

She was so exhausted that it didn't even elevate her heart rate when a hybrid appeared out of the jungle ahead of her to block her path. She didn't slow, even as the thing crouched to lunge at her. She simply lifted her M4 and fired everything she had left—two whole rounds—at the second-in-command. Her hands were shaking so much, it was hard to hold her weapon firm, so she wasn't sure if she hit the thing or not. If she did, it must not have been in a critical area because it didn't flinch—or stop coming at her.

A fraction of a second later, another hybrid burst into the clearing from her right. She reversed her grip on her weapon. The short barrel was hot as hell in her hand, but she was ready to go down swinging.

Footsteps behind her told her that the other two monsters had arrived. Apparently, she hadn't hit any of them hard enough to put them down.

Her breathing ragged, Kendra swung her M4 as the hybrid leader in front of her leaped. She braced herself, expecting the hybrid to go for a throat slash and finish her quickly, so she was caught off guard when the thing casually reached out and ripped the weapon from her hand. It followed up with a dismissive shove that sent her sprawling to the ground.

She scrambled around on the dark, wet ground, looking for something to defend herself with, and came up with a rock about the size of her fist. It wasn't much, but she didn't have many options. She'd be damned if she'd just let them just rip her apart without fighting back.

She looked up, expecting to see all four hybrids descending on her at once, but they only stood there, claws flexing as they stared at her.

Kendra didn't think her heart could beat any faster, but it went into overdrive. She'd been scared before, but now she was freaking terrified. Thinking she was going to be killed while luring these bastards away from the man she loved hadn't taken much courage. But the thought of what these creatures had in store for her now—before they killed her—filled her with fear. What if they raped and tortured her to make her tell them where Declan was? Was she strong enough to hold out?

The hybrid leader came forward, his red eyes glowing in her NVGs. Kendra scrambled to her feet and lifted the rock she was holding. She wasn't sure if she should throw it or wait until he got closer so she could bash in his head. She decided to wait. If she pissed him off enough, he might kill her quickly.

But he stopped just outside her reach and stood there silently regarding her. She tried not to let him see how afraid she was, but it was damn hard. He was absolutely terrifying. His whole jawline was twisted out of shape, no doubt to make room for all those long, curved teeth. His ears were higher on his head, too, pushed there by the muscles on his shoulders. The thing's neck was equally thick, and she couldn't help but think of a huge saber-toothed tiger. The thing looked as if it could eat the rock she was holding as a weapon.

She lifted her chin and hefted her rock higher. "What are you waiting for? Come and get me, you freak!"

Her barb had no effect on the hybrid. He just kept staring at her. That was when she saw the blood running down one side of his chest. Damn, she *had* hit something with all that shooting. She supposed it was too much to hope the thing would suddenly drop dead.

"Where is the big man?"

Kendra was so shocked that the hybrid could speak with that mouth full of teeth, it took her a second to come up with a lie. All the time she'd spent with Ivy, Clayne, and the other shifters at the DCO had taught her that they could sniff out a liar. She had to assume that a hybrid could as well.

"He's dead." Even though it was a lie, the words were enough to cut her to the core, and her voice shook. She swallowed hard. "He died when your friends attacked us this morning. I've been hiding ever since."

She expected the hybrid to call her a liar or ask where Declan's body was. Even ask for details of exactly when and where he'd died. But the second-in-command did none of those things. He simply turned and motioned to the other hybrids.

"Bring her," he ordered.

Then he walked off.

The three hybrids were on her and had ripped the rock out of her hand before she even saw them move. She pounded at them with her fists and kicked at them with her boots, but they ignored her struggles. One of them simply picked her up and slung her over his shoulder like she was a bag of potatoes.

Kendra would have continued to pummel him with her fists, but then he started running, and it was all she could do to grab hold of his shirt to steady herself. Hanging over his shoulder made her feel dizzy, and she had to close her eyes.

Where the hell were they taking her? And what were they going to do to her once they got there?

She had no answer to either of those questions. But one piece of knowledge comforted her at least. They were moving farther and farther away from Declan with every step.

Kendra was practically unconscious by the time the hybrid threw her to the ground. She wasn't sure how long he'd been running. She only knew it had been too long. It felt so good to have the pounding in her head stop that she didn't even complain about the pain when she hit the stone floor.

She didn't know what was coming next, but she couldn't muster the strength to care. All she wanted to do was lie there until the earth stopped spinning. She reached up to touch her head and realized her helmet and goggles were gone. She must have lost them while that jerk was hauling ass through the jungle.

It wasn't until a hand touched her shoulder that she discovered her survival instinct was more intact than she'd thought. She shoved the hand away and scooted back, only to hit something.

"Relax," a male voice said. "I'm not going to hurt you. I just want to make sure you're okay. It looks like those things roughed you up pretty good."

Obviously, the man wasn't a hybrid. That fact alone was enough to snap her out of the fog she'd been buried in for the last…well, however long she'd been carried around on the back of that hybrid like a hobbit on an orc.

Kendra pushed her hair back from her face to see a gray-haired man kneeling beside her. He reminded her of her grandfather, except for the bloody rag tied around his forehead. Despite his kind eyes, she scooted back again, but whatever was behind her was still in the way.

"Slow down," Granddad said, reaching out to steady her.

A wave of dizziness swept over her. She shook her head to try and make the fuzziness go away, but that only made it worse. Then she realized the thing behind her was soft, squishy…and hairy.

She jumped and quickly looked over her shoulder. It was a body. A young guy, who looked like he might have been cute before someone crushed his throat. She scrambled away from the body on her hands and knees—the hell with her spinning head.

She dragged her gaze away from the dead man and looked around the room. Maybe thirty square feet, it had no windows, no furniture, and hardly any lighting to speak of unless you counted the two naked bulbs hanging from the ceiling. The door across the room, on the other hand, didn't look that cheap at all. No doubt it locked from the outside.

Kendra studied the other two men locked in with her and Granddad. Like him, they had graying hair and wore white lab coats. That probably meant they were scientists or doctors of some type. They looked just as abused as Granddad. One was holding his arm pressed against his chest like it was broken, and the other had bruises covering half his face.

She jerked her head at the body. "Who is that?"

"That's Jacob. He was my research assistant," Granddad said. "He complained about how we were being treated one too many times and those things killed him."

Kendra couldn't miss the sadness in the old man's eyes as he looked at Jacob's body, and her heart went out to him. When she'd seen the lab coats, she'd naturally assumed the men were working with Stutmeir's doctors, but if that were the case, why were they sitting in here with her like prisoners? More importantly, who'd smacked them around, and why was one of their fellow scientists lying dead on the floor at the hands of the hybrids?

"Who are you?" she asked.

Granddad held out his hand with a small smile. "I blame the stress of the situation for making me lose my manners, forgive me. I should have introduced myself before. I'm Harry Caswell. At one time, I was the assistant director of research at this facility." He motioned to the other two men. "And these two fine gentlemen are Albert Moline and Lester Tellarson, both senior researchers."

She shook each of their hands. "Kendra Carlsen."

"You must be one of the people Marcus has been hunting," Harry observed. "Guess he finally caught you."

Momentarily distracted from the other questions she'd been planning to ask—and figuring that this new subject sounded a lot more relevant—she jumped tracks to see where it would lead. "Who is Marcus? And why would he be hunting me?"

The three men exchanged looks; then Harry spoke again. "I really thought you would know. Marcus Roman was the head of security here. Well, until a couple weeks ago anyway. Now he's…well, I can only assume you haven't seen him yet. He's rather hard to miss."

Kendra could only think of one man she'd seen who fit that description. "Marcus is the leader of the hybrids, isn't he? Seven feet tall, muscles everywhere, and freakishly long fangs?"

The old man nodded. "Hybrid, huh? Interesting name, but it fits. I'm guessing you met him then?"

"Only at a distance," she said. "And that was scary enough. Do you know why he's after me?"

The man looked at her in surprise. "Not really. In fact, I was hoping you might be able to tell us what's going on. All we know is that Marcus has been raging around for the last few days, saying he wanted you and the man you were with captured. We never could get him or any of the others—what did you call them, hybrids?—to tell us who you were or what they wanted with you. But I get the feeling that Marcus thinks you'll be able to help him with his problem."

She sighed. Okay, so much for a quick, simple answer. "And what problem would that be?"

Harry grimaced. "I thought that would be obvious. He's turned into a monster with a serious lack of impulse control. I've seen him kill two of his own men just for asking him a question the wrong way. And he seems to be having a harder time getting his human appearance to return. As far gone as Marcus is, I think even he knows he's out of control. I just don't know how grabbing you or your friend is supposed to help him with that."

Kendra had a sinking feeling in her stomach that maybe she did. It hadn't been Stutmeir's doctors trying to get their hands on Declan's DNA in order to make a better hybrid. It had been a hybrid trying to get it so he could make himself better. It certainly explained why these three doctors were being held in this room—to do the research once Marcus had the DNA.

Thank God Declan was miles away from here, safe and sound in that shelter and getting stronger by the minute. Marcus would never get his hands on him.

Seated on the floor around her, the men were looking at her expectantly. She chewed her lower lip, trying to figure out what she could safely tell them. Probably not much. But she was going to have to trust them a little if she hoped to get out of here.

"I realize you don't know who I am, but I might have a pretty good idea what Marcus is after," she said after a moment. "I'm going to need to know everything to be sure though."

All three of the men nodded.

"If it helps get us out of here, we'll tell you anything," Harry said. "What do you want to know?"

Everything. But she'd start with something simple. "How did you end up down here in Costa Rica, and where did your hybrid formula come from?"

Harry shook his head. "None of us signed up for this, I can tell you that. We thought we were coming down here to conduct genetic research for the U.S. military. In the beginning, everything went fine. It was only a few weeks ago that it all went to hell. But before I get too deep into that, I think it'd be better if I started at the beginning."

Chapter 12

DECLAN WOKE UP FEELING LIKE HE'D BEEN HIT BY A train. But that was the way he always felt after coming out of hibernation. However, he was awake and his wounds had closed up; he could tell. That was the important part. But as he lay there getting his bearings, a lingering taste on his lips brought a smile to his face. He licked them and groaned at the delicious flavor that touched his tongue. Kendra had kissed him. Damn, that was something a man—or shifter—could seriously get used to. He closed his eyes and reveled in the sensation of what having her taste on his mouth meant to him.

Five seconds later, his eyes snapped open. If she'd just kissed him, why couldn't he smell her? He jerked upright, looking around wildly. She wasn't in the shelter. Worse, what little scent he could pick up told him she hadn't been in the shelter for a while—three or four hours at least. If he wasn't so freaked out by that, he'd marvel at how her taste had lingered so long after her kiss.

He closed his eyes and concentrated on what his ears could pick up. Had Kendra moved outside the shelter so she could watch over him? That was definitely something he could imagine her doing. But after thirty seconds of intense focus, he heard nothing to indicate that she was anywhere nearby.

Declan ripped off the bandages she'd so tenderly

applied to his chest that morning and grabbed his M4, then shoved his way out of the shelter, ignoring the snap and pop of branches as he pushed them out of his way.

Once outside the shelter, he spun around, forcing his eyes to sharpen as much as he could, trying to pierce the darkness around him and find the woman he loved. But he didn't see her anywhere. He tried using his ears again, slowing his breathing and kneeling on the ground so that he could pour everything he had into his only real shifter sense.

But while he heard the stream gurgling nearby, tree limbs and leaves brushing up against each other all around, and animals by the thousands, he didn't hear anything that would tell him where Kendra was. Or what had happened to her.

He fell forward onto his hands and knees with a growl. This couldn't be happening. He'd wasted years waiting for Kendra to finally see him. And now that she had, he'd lost her? The very thought that she might be gone left a dark, twisting hole inside that had him gasping for air and wanting to crawl back into the shelter and die.

Declan shook his head and pushed back on his heels, refusing to give in to his fear. All he knew at this point was that Kendra wasn't here. That didn't mean she was dead. He needed to figure out what the hell had happened before he gave up. Especially when there was a chance she was still alive.

He ducked inside the shelter long enough to grab his pack. There wasn't much in there of practical worth besides a few half-empty ammo magazines and the remains of the first-aid kit. But Kendra's extra clothes were in there, and he refused to leave them behind. When he found her, she'd want her stuff.

Back outside, he slowly circuited around the shelter, looking for any trace of Kendra's trail. Why the hell had she left the shelter in the first place? Obviously, the hybrids hadn't found them. If they had, they would have taken him, too—or killed him. That left only one logical explanation. Kendra had heard or seen the hybrids getting close to their hiding place and had slipped out to lure them away. It tore at his gut to know he'd put Kendra in a position of having to do something like that, but he knew she would without a moment's hesitation. If he had any doubt that she truly cared for him, he didn't after this.

Now that he was calmer, it didn't take him long to pick up Kendra's scent. It ran a route almost parallel to the stream. But even down on his knees, the scent was so faint he could barely smell it. And within twenty feet he lost it.

Declan growled in frustration as he retraced his steps back to the shelter and started again. But the end result was the same. He lost the trail before he'd gone more than thirty feet. His nose simply wasn't good enough to keep the trail, not with the constant breeze scattering her scent and the thousands of other animal and jungle smells distracting him. Worse, Kendra's boots had still been coated in stinking hybrid blood. Getting past that to find her beautiful smell was beyond his meager shifter ability.

He dropped to the ground again and roared. Anger consuming him, he pounded the ground with his fists and slashed at the nearby tree trunks with his nearly worthless claws. For the first time in his life, he needed his damn nose to work like any other shifter's nose, and it wouldn't. Why? Because he'd spent his whole life refusing to accept that he was a shifter, refusing to learn how to use the talents that would find the woman he loved. Now Kendra would pay for his stubbornness.

He backhanded the tree trunk to his right, foregoing the use of his claws and instead smashing it with his fist. The crunch of breaking wood was satisfying, but not nearly as much as finding Kendra's scent would have been. She was gone because he hadn't been strong enough to be the shifter she'd needed him to be. Not even twenty-four hours ago, Kendra had warned him that his inability to let go and accept his shifter talents would someday bring harm to someone he cared about. She'd been right.

Snarling, he lunged to his feet to tear into the trees to the left and right of him. It was stupid, foolish, and childish, but he couldn't stop himself. For the first time since he'd exposed his shifter side to Marissa, he gave into his fear and let the animal inside him out.

The fury exploded from him, blurring his vision and tearing one long continuous roar out of his throat. He lashed out at anything within reach, aching to destroy something, *anything* he could. He had no idea how long he raged like that, but when he let the bear inside him go, he was gasping for air in the sudden silence of the jungle.

He looked around, turning in a slow circle. Every tree within a fifteen-foot radius had been smashed to the ground and ripped to kindling. The uncontrolled violence of his tirade almost shocked him, especially when he looked down and saw that his claws were still extended.

No, his claws weren't just extended. They had shot out more than three inches beyond his fingertips. All he could do was slowly flex his fingers and stare in amazement as the curved claws moved back and forth.

Declan was so distracted by the sight, he almost missed that the jungle around him was no longer dark. He looked up in surprise. It was still at least an hour until sunrise, and yet he could literally see for a mile through what should have been pitch-black jungle.

Then, an even bigger realization hit him. He could smell *everything*.

There was something dead upwind of him, near the stream about three hundred yards away. A fish of some kind. The odor was unmistakable.

Farther away—maybe a mile—a jungle cat was eating a small rodent. Declan could close his eyes and almost point to exactly where the creature—a jaguar or ocelot—was munching its late-night sack.

The more he tried, the more scents he was able to detect. His mind categorized them without much thought, but then one scent reached his nose and immediately pushed every other one out. *Kendra*. He looked down at the ground, and it was like he could see every step she'd taken as she moved across the slope the shelter was on. He was able to separate the stench of the hybrid's blood from the perfume that was her own special mix of pheromones so easily he almost started laughing.

And he knew for a fact that she'd been moving on her own. There weren't any hybrid tracks overlapping hers.

Declan stood there, unable to believe it. He had shifted further and more completely than he ever had in his life. And the answer to how he'd done it was simple. The one thing he had never let happen had happened because he'd been more terrified of losing Kendra than losing himself.

He was sprinting across the ground before he knew his feet were moving, and he was running faster than he ever had. Yet, as fast as he was moving, he had no problem following the scent trail. He knew he could have closed his eyes and the trail would have still been just as clear for him.

He slowed when he reached the place near the stream where Kendra stopped and fired her weapon. The acrid smell of burnt smokeless powder was clear and obvious. His head tracked to the left, finding the three spent 5.56 mm casings. She had stopped and turned back upstream before firing.

That was when he picked up the smell of the hybrids overlaying Kendra's tracks. He couldn't stop the growl that emanated from his throat. *Damn it all to hell.* There had been four hybrids upstream of the shelter. Kendra had run down here, then fired at them, not to kill, but to get them to follow her.

She had done it to draw them away from him, just like he'd thought.

Declan ran even faster. Kendra had risked everything for him.

He found every place she stopped to shoot at the hybrids, luring them farther and farther away from him. And with every short stop, his fear grew. She hadn't even been trying to escape. She'd been sacrificing herself to save him. Tears burned his eyes, threatening to blind him, and he blinked hard.

Then he found the place where the chase had ended. He clearly saw and smelled the tracks of the two hybrids moving around in front of her, the other two herding her from behind. The scent of blood assaulted his nose and his heart lurched. But then he realized it wasn't hers. It had the brackish stench of blood that could only belong to a hybrid. She'd hit one of the bastards. Not severely though. There were only a few drops on the ground. But she'd gotten one. The image brought a smile to his face, and he felt the unfamiliar tug and pull as a mouth suddenly full of fangs longer than he was used to turned upward.

His nose led him to the rock on the ground, and he picked it up. Her beautiful, feminine scent cloaked the stone. But there was a trace of hybrid odor on it. Like the rock had hit the creature just long enough to leave a hint, but not enough to cover Kendra's scent.

The rock slipped from his suddenly nerveless fingers, fresh fear gripping him. This must have been the place where the hybrids attacked and killed her. His heart began to tear open, but then stopped when he realized there wasn't any blood—or anything else—on the ground to indicate that the hybrids had killed her.

Declan spun around, his nose not used to doing work this fine but quickly learning how.

Outside of this one spot, Kendra's scent diminished. It wasn't gone, but it was much fainter. He scanned the ground, searching for her tracks, but couldn't find any. Four sets of hybrid tracks headed away from the area, though. But one set was deeper than they'd been when they'd come into the clearing. Why? Then it hit him. The hybrid had been carrying Kendra.

He followed the tracks, his head digesting what his senses were telling him. It didn't make sense. The hybrids had attempted to subdue him with that damn needle, presumably to capture him, but they'd never seemed interested in taking Kendra alive. Back at the stream, it had appeared as if they were trying to kill her as quickly as possible.

Why take her now?

He considered and discarded several possibilities, until coming to the only one that was left. The hybrids thought he was dead and had decided they needed Kendra instead.

Declan raced faster, his mind going places he didn't want it to go. If they wanted Kendra alive, there could be only one reason. It was insane, but it was the only thing that explained why they would bother to take her. They intended to experiment on her. The doctors who had created the hybrid drug and tortured Ivy had Kendra and meant to do the same to her.

The roar that erupted out of him startled the jungle to silence. It probably carried for miles in every direction, but Declan didn't care. Let those hybrid assholes hear him coming. His claws flexed and he felt them extend even farther, sending stabs of pain through his hands that he relished. He felt muscles and bones moving and twisting as he ran, and he still didn't care.

He fed the rage, let it force the shift even further until he was almost lost in it. He didn't care if he ever found his way back to his human half again. He was going to find Kendra, and when he did, every hybrid that had even thought of touching her was going to know fear like they had never felt in their miserable fucking lives—right up until the moment he killed them.

—⁕—

"You still never said who you work for, Kendra," Harry reminded her. "Or how you happen to know so much about these hybrids?"

Kendra winced. She and the three doctors had been talking for more than an hour, during which time she'd been careful not to divulge too much critical information about herself or the DCO, instead keeping the conversation focused on them the whole time. But Harry and the other men weren't stupid. They'd already figured out that she'd dealt with hybrids before. If she wasn't careful, they'd end up learning more from her than she did from them.

That probably wasn't very likely, since she'd already learned enough to worry the hell out of her.

She gave them what she hoped was a disarming smile. "Hybrids—that's just a name I made up. And I really don't know that much about them at all."

Harry didn't look like he believed her, but at least he didn't call her out on the fact that she hadn't really answered either of his questions. That was good. Between worrying about what might be happening to Declan and trying to digest everything she'd learned in the last hour, she was too tired to expend any energy soothing Harry and his colleagues.

Her initial assumptions that this was another temporary research operation set up by Stutmeir's former doctors had turned out to be completely wrong. Not only was this facility far from temporary—Harry and his colleagues had been working here for more than six weeks—but they claimed they'd never heard of the doctors who'd tortured Ivy out in Washington.

Based on everything Harry, Lester, and Albert had told her, she'd come to a pretty wild conclusion—the people who'd created this latest hybrid pack were completely separate from those who had created the Washington State pack. Worse, she had a sick feeling in the pit of her stomach that the genesis for this latest hybrid process wasn't Stutmeir's work at all. It was the DCO's.

Harry and the other doctors, as well as everyone else who'd worked there, had been hired to come to Costa Rica and work on what they thought was a top secret Department of Defense genetics program designed to enhance soldier performance through the use of cutting-edge DNA manipulation techniques. It wasn't until they were given the boxes and boxes of background research that they realized the *cutting-edge techniques* involved the use of animal DNA. And the way Harry described the research information made it sound exactly like the technical reports the DCO had put together after the raid in Washington State. Even the color-coding on the edge of each report matched the way the DCO tracked intel sources. Even though the doctors and scientists had been shocked at the direction they were expected to take their research, none of them had complained, until things started getting too real.

"So when did everything go wrong?" she asked, still pondering exactly who in the DCO had betrayed them. The thought that Zarina had a spy on her team who was selling hybrid information was almost as scary as the hybrids themselves.

"About four weeks ago," Harry said. "When we were ordered to transition to human trials."

"No one ever said there would be any human trials," Lester interjected. The way he said it made Kendra think he felt the need to defend himself to her. "We were told that our work was completely developmental. It wasn't ever supposed to be used on humans."

Harry nodded in agreement. "Everyone thought that. Then we realized they weren't kidding, and that they weren't going to give us a say in the matter. The head of our research team, Dr. Mahsood, dismissed all of our concerns and ordered us to start administering our first batch of serum before it had even cooled. I have no idea why they suddenly started pushing so hard."

Had the DCO team's scheduled arrival for the training exercise accelerated their timetable to get the hybrids out of the lab and into the field?

"And that's where the camp's security force came into it, right?" she prompted.

This was the part of the story they'd gotten to when Harry had started pressing her about why she was asking so many question.

"They asked for volunteers and started with the guards. But it wasn't long before they were testing on the rest of the support staff," Albert explained. "It wasn't like we had a lot of options."

Kendra didn't bother to mention Stutmeir's preferred method of finding candidates to turn into hybrids — kidnapping homeless veterans.

"Marcus was the first in line," Harry added. "I have to

hand it to him. I thought he was a bully and a thug from the moment I met him, but he wasn't going to expose his men to a risk he wasn't willing to face himself."

Or he simply decided that if anyone was going to get turned into a super soldier, he was going to be the first in line. A big alpha male like Marcus probably thought he couldn't be in charge if he wasn't the biggest dog on the block. But Kendra didn't point that out.

Kendra hated to keep asking questions, but she needed information if she ever hoped to get out of this place. She had no idea why she'd been thrown into this room, but sooner or later, someone would come looking for answers from her. She had to have a plan by then.

"It went well in the beginning," Harry said suddenly. "Marcus and the other four volunteers went into…well I guess you would call it their hybrid state within an hour of the first treatment. The increase in strength, speed, and endurance was immediate and obvious. Improvements in vision both day and night, as well as the complete loss of pain receptivity, came later."

"Mahsood, and whoever he was communicating with back in the States, were ecstatic, and asked for additional volunteers," Lester added. "We wanted them to wait until we did some baseline testing and looked for long-term issues, but they wouldn't listen. That's when they started injecting the rest of the support staff. Mechanics, lab techs, medics…anyone they didn't think were essential to the test trials."

"Then someone started pushing for a field test to evaluate what we'd accomplished, and that's when we lost complete control of the project," Harry continued. "Marcus took over and before we knew it, they were

going out armed to the teeth, taking most of the guards
who hadn't been through the process with them."

"We found out later they attacked some military types
out in the jungle on an exercise," Albert said. "You and
your friend, apparently."

Kendra was about to ask what had happened to Dr.
Mahsood when the door slammed back against the wall.
Two hybrids strode in, looking bored and hungry. They
flexed their claws as they focused on her, and it was
hard not to cringe.

"Come with us," one of them said. While he was the
less animalistic of the two, she could still barely understand him.

She wanted to fight them but knew it wouldn't do any
good and might end up getting her killed. They seemed
to want her alive, and she wanted to stay that way. But
when she stood up to go with them, Harry and the other
men jumped to their feet faster than she would have
thought them capable of and moved to stand in front
of her.

"You're not taking her anywhere," Harry said firmly.

The hybrids tensed, their claws flexing again, their
eyes glowing a darker red. These two were seriously
on edge and seconds away from ripping the old men
apart. Knowing she couldn't let that happen, she
shouldered her way past the doctors and stopped in
front of the hybrids.

"It's okay, Harry," she said. "I'll go with them."

The hybrids almost looked disappointed that they
wouldn't have a reason to beat the doctors into submission.

Harry caught her arm. "You don't have to go
with them."

She gave him a small smile. "It's okay. Don't worry. I'll be back."

Kendra hoped she sounded more convinced than she felt. Turning, she followed the first hybrid out the door. The other one fell into step behind her as if she was some dangerous spy who might try to escape. If she thought there was even the slightest chance she could get away, she would.

They led her across an open space between the various other buildings that made up the research facility. The rising sun hadn't quite crested the ridgeline yet, so she couldn't make out much, but she saw enough to realize the place hadn't been built recently. In fact, some of the buildings looked as if they'd been here for a few years. Maybe it had been some kind of conservation center or something.

Even though escaping was probably going to be impossible, that didn't stop her from surveying her surroundings anyway. The wire fencing encircling the camp didn't bother her as much as the hybrids patrolling the perimeter. Getting past them would be difficult, even if she could somehow ditch her two guards.

But the hybrid in the lead was already walking up the steps to a building. He opened the door, then moved back and ushered her inside.

Kendra hesitated. It was almost completely dark in the building, except for the dim light coming from a small lamp on the table. At least she thought it was a table.

The hybrid gave her a shove that sent her stumbling into the room. She tensed, expecting something to pounce on her and rip her to shreds. But nothing tackled her and threw her to the floor. That should have been reassuring, but it wasn't.

She looked around warily. There was a large conference table in the center of the room, with half a dozen chairs around it. Along the back wall was a counter with a coffeepot and a microwave, as well as a small fridge. The tableau seemed out of place in the jungle camp.

Despite the everyday office vibe the coffeepot and microwave gave the room, there was an eerie quality to the place that had her checking every dark corner and shadowed crevice, trying to see who was in it with her.

That's how she found the second-in-command slouched over in one of those big conference room chairs, dead. There was dried blood all over its uniform shirt and down around the top of its pants. He must have bled out while sitting here, and no one had done anything to help. She glanced over her shoulder, but the hybrids who'd escorted her had already left and closed the door. Damn, these monsters were cold. It was like they didn't care whether anyone lived or died, even one of their own.

"Have a seat."

Kendra jumped at the deep, guttural voice coming from the other side of the room. She didn't need to see him to know it belonged to the camp's former head of security, Marcus Roman. She didn't think she'd ever forget the sound of it as long as she lived. She couldn't believe she hadn't seen someone his size in a room this small.

But then a chair on the other side of the table slowly spun around and the hulking hybrid materialized out of the darkness. Even sitting there awkwardly holding a glass of whiskey in his clawed hand, he was an imposing figure, and she had to force herself not to take a step back. She'd almost forgotten how scary looking he was.

He gestured to her side of the table. "You can take any seat—except for the occupied one of course."

She walked as far away from the dead body as she could and sat down across from Marcus.

He studied her with his glowing red eyes. She expected him to say something about the man she had killed, but it was like he didn't even know the body was there. "I never knew what they meant when they said an animal can smell fear. But I could smell yours the minute the men brought you into camp."

She wasn't sure what she was supposed to say to that, so she didn't say anything.

His eyes flashed a darker shade of red as he chuckled. She guessed it was a chuckle—with all those teeth, it was difficult to tell.

"You proved so hard to catch, I thought you'd be bigger."

He said the words so casually, she almost laughed. She'd expected him to say something more along the lines of, "Talk or I'll rip off your fingers."

But just because he hadn't threatened her yet, that didn't mean she wasn't in danger. This monster wanted something from her, or he would have ordered one of the lower-ranking hybrids to kill her already. Sooner or later, this conversation would get around to Declan or some other topic she didn't want to talk about. No doubt, his nonthreatening tone would change then.

She had to engage him a little, though, unless she wanted him ripping off her fingers in the next few minutes.

"Hiding is actually easier to do when you're smaller," she said.

His mouth twisted in what he probably thought was a smile, but it only made him look more menacing than he already did. "I suppose it is. But that doesn't explain how the big man you were with is so good at it."

She'd walked right into that one. "What big man?"

The smile disappeared, replaced by a menacing scowl. He set the glass down on the table with a thud. "Don't play dumb. I can smell him all over you. The big man like us, the one who's part animal."

It wasn't hard to figure out what he meant when he said he could smell Declan on her, and she felt heat suffuse her face. But it was the rest of what he'd said that really threw her for a loop. Marcus didn't realize there was a difference between hybrids and shifters?

"Where is he?" When she didn't answer, Marcus growled and slammed his hand down hard on the table. "Tell me where he is. Now!"

As if stunned by his own outburst, the hybrid ran his hand over his flattop and took a deep breath.

"I apologize," he said, all trace of anger gone from his voice. "I just want to talk to him."

She let out a snort. "Right. You and your men have been trying to kill us for a week, and you expect me to believe that you just want to talk? I don't think you and he would have a hell of a lot to talk about."

Kendra knew she should tread lightly, but this guy was too much. He'd kill Declan in a second if he had the chance, just like he was going to murder her.

Fresh flames kindled in the hybrid's eyes, and she braced herself, expecting him to launch himself across the table at her. Instead, he wrapped his clawed fingers around the glass in front of him, carefully lifted it to his mouth, and took a slow slip. He worked the rim of the glass around his fangs better than she'd thought he would, and by the time he was finished savoring the drink, his eyes had lightened again. This guy's mercurial mood swings made Tanner's seem mild in comparison.

He placed the glass down on the table. "You'd be surprised how much we'd have to talk about. Like how he does it."

Kendra frowned. "How he does what?"

Marcus's eyes narrowed, trying to figure out if she was being snide or simply stupid. "How he turns it on and off."

She had no idea what Mahsood or anyone else had said to entice Marcus so he would voluntarily let them inject him with an experimental drug. Probably that he'd come out the other side like some kind of Superman. But now he was stuck in this monster form with no way out. A small part of her almost felt sorry for him. But all she had to think about was the casual ease with which he'd ripped out one of his own men's throats simply because the guys had talked too much. The hybrid process might have given Marcus claws and fangs, but he'd made himself into a monster all on his own.

"It doesn't work that way," Kendra explained. "You're not like him. He wouldn't be able to teach you anything."

His lip curled back in a snarl. "Forgive me for doubting you, but I'd rather hear that from him. I'm going to ask you one more time. Where is he?"

"If you were so interested in talking to him, maybe

you shouldn't have sent all those things of yours after us," she shot back, the words out before she had time to think. "Six of them attacked us below the rapids in that river near where your men found me. They killed him."

Marcus surged to his feet so fast that the chair he'd been sitting in flew across the room and smashed into the wall. "You're lying!"

Kendra jumped. She wondered for a split second if hybrids had the ability to smell when someone was lying. But she immediately dismissed that notion. Hybrids seemed to share only the most basic traits with their shifter cousins.

"You're right. I'm lying." She wasn't sure why she got to her feet. Marcus was way too big for her to ever be able to look him in the eye. But that didn't stop her from putting her hands on the table and shouting at him anyway. "Because it makes complete sense for me to run around the jungle by myself instead of staying with the man who was keeping me alive out there!"

"If he's dead, then where's the body?" Marcus demanded.

"I don't know. He fell in the river and got carried away. Go look for him somewhere downstream."

Saying the words hurt her as much as they had the first time, but she was desperate to sell the fact that Declan was beyond their reach. She only hoped Declan was awake and gone by now. She needed to give him every extra minute she could.

The hybrid's eyes flared so brightly they seemed to light up the room more than the sun that was starting to peek in the windows. His claws dug into the conference table, and she thought he was going to tear right through it to get to her. She backed away, not caring if he could smell her fear.

"I guess I have no further use for you then," he said, the words a low, rumbling whisper.

Oh crap. She'd pushed too hard and blown the only chance she had to get away. This hulking killer was going to end this right here and now.

"Ruiz! Madsen!" he shouted.

The door jerked open behind her, and the two hybrids who had escorted her there strode into the room.

"Take her to the lab and give her the serum." Marcus's hellish gaze seared into her. "It'll be interesting to see what a woman looks like after going through the transformation process."

Kendra's blood turned to ice. She tried to run, but the two hybrids grabbed her arms and picked her up like she was a rag doll. She kicked and dragged her feet, but they ignored her struggles as they carried her across the camp.

Crap. She'd imagined Marcus doing some pretty horrific stuff to her, but she never thought he'd turn her into a hybrid. This was worse than anything she'd imagined.

Chapter 13

"WHAT THE HELL IS THE PROBLEM NOW?" TATE demanded.

Angelo ground his teeth as the DCO operative squared off against Ivy and Clayne. He knew Tate was scared shitless about Declan and Kendra, but so was everyone else. On top of that, they were all exhausted, thanks to pushing hard through the night. If anyone should be given a break, it was Ivy and Clayne. For whatever reason, Declan and Kendra's trail had gotten harder and harder to follow throughout the night. Ivy and Clayne had practically been crawling through the jungle on their hands and knees for the past four hours. They looked like a couple of zombies.

"We've lost Declan's trail again," Clayne said.

"How the hell is that possible?" Tate frowned. "We've been following it the whole night."

Clayne barely muffled a growl. "We've been following Kendra's, not his. If you'd been paying attention, you would have remembered me saying Declan's scent got all muddy and disappeared way back at that shelter we searched."

Angelo could understand why Tate might have missed that detail. The scene they'd found at the shelter had been confusing and scary as hell. First, there was the shredded uniform top covered in Declan's blood. Kendra's uniform top had been right beside it, covered in hybrid blood. And then, if those two things hadn't been bad enough, there was that patch of torn-up trees no one could explain. It looked as if a small bomb had exploded. By the time Ivy had announced they couldn't find Declan's trail anymore, hardly anyone had been paying attention.

It hadn't helped that neither Clayne nor Ivy had been able to explain what they meant when they said that Declan's scent had gotten *muddy*.

"Declan's scent just disappears right here in the middle of this mess," Ivy'd told them.

"So, now you've lost Kendra's scent, too?" Tate asked. "What happened, did her trail get all muddy, too?"

Clayne's eyes glowed gold in the early morning light.

Angelo stifled a groan. *Shit*. If Tate didn't shut the hell up soon, Clayne was going to clock him.

"No, it didn't get muddy," Clayne growled. "She was picked up by a hybrid and carried out of here."

"Then why the hell don't you just follow the fucking hybrid?" Tate shouted.

"Which one?" Ivy's eyes glinted green. She looked like she was angry enough to take a swing at Tate herself. "There've been at least half a dozen hybrids stomping through here in the last few hours, all moving in different directions. Which one do you suggest we follow?"

Tate's eye's narrowed. "How about the one that captured Kendra? Because I'm pretty sure that wherever she is, Declan won't be far away."

Angelo wasn't sure about that, but he wasn't going to be the one to point it out. Unfortunately, it looked like Clayne had chosen that particular moment to embrace the concept of tough love. Angelo shoved his M4 into

Derek's hand. On the other side of Ivy, Landon handed his weapon to Tanner. But before he and Landon could get between Tate and the two shifters, Carter interrupted.

"Guys. Hold up. I think I found Kendra."

Angelo jerked around to see Carter pointing at something in the distance. But instead of Kendra, he caught sight of a petite woman with long, brown hair and the biggest, most expressive eyes he'd ever seen standing about a hundred feet away. All he could do was stare back. She was freaking supermodel material.

"That's not Kendra," Ivy said.

"I'm guessing she's not a hybrid?" Landon whispered to his wife.

As if she heard them, the woman smiled. Angelo heard Carter groan behind him. He couldn't blame the guy. The woman had one hell of a gorgeous smile. But what was a woman who looked like her doing out here?

"I don't think so," Ivy said softly. "But she's wearing something that mostly masks her scent."

"Just because she's not a hybrid doesn't mean she isn't dangerous," Clayne said, not even bothering to keep his voice low.

The woman's smile broadened and she lifted her hand to make that universal *follow me* gesture with her finger. Then she turned and gracefully half ran, half leaped a few steps before stopping to look over her shoulder at them with those enormous eyes of hers and crooked her finger again.

"That answers the question about what she is," Clayne said. "She's a shifter, for sure. And I think she wants us to follow her."

Under other circumstances, Angelo would have

willingly followed her anywhere. She might be gorgeous, but they were in enemy territory. "What if it's a trick?"

"We're only going to find out if we follow her," Clayne said.

The woman gave them another smile, then bounded off again. This time, she took a half-dozen leaps, traveling a good seventy-five feet in a blink of an eye.

"Follow her? I don't think we're going to be able to keep up," Landon said.

"I can," Clayne said, and took off at a sprint.

Ivy glanced at Landon. "I'll keep Clayne in sight. You keep me in sight. I'll make sure not to lose you."

Angelo still wasn't sure chasing the freaking hottest-looking woman he'd ever seen outside of his best friend's wife through the jungle on a whim was a good idea. But Ivy didn't give them a chance to talk it over. One second she was there; the next they were all running after her.

Keeping everyone together at the same time, they maintained a defensive posture, and trying to stay with the much faster shifters was tough. With Carter's cracked ribs and all their other injuries, they simply couldn't move that fast. And the woman they were chasing was flat-out scary fast. Within a few minutes, it was damn near impossible for the others to keep a visual on Ivy.

Beside Angelo, Landon swore and ran faster.

"You two go," Tanner shouted. "Get ahead of us and keep an eye on Ivy. I'll make sure we catch up with you."

Angelo hated splitting up the group, but Tanner was right. He took off with Landon without hesitation. Within sixty seconds, they made up enough ground that they could at least see Ivy and Clayne and the mystery woman they were following. Though Angelo got the feeling she could have left them in her dust if she wanted to. He'd seen several of the DCO's shifters in action, but he'd never seen any of them run like her. Hell, she wasn't even running most of the time. She was bounding and bouncing like a frigging gazelle. It was like she was playing with Clayne. Every time he got within twenty feet of her, she kicked into another gear and extended her lead. He could hear Clayne's growls of frustration from where he was.

Up ahead, the woman disappeared from view. Angelo's stomach knotted as Clayne followed her over the slight rise, Ivy right behind him. If someone was planning to ambush them, this was the place to do it.

He and Landon had been doing this kind of shit together for so long that they didn't even have to tell each other to pick up speed; they both just instinctively did it. But when Angelo topped the hill a few minutes later, he skidded to a stop, which kept him from tumbling headlong down the sharp, rocky slope on the other side. A few feet to the right, Ivy and Clayne were crouched down behind several large boulders. The wolf shifter motioned for them to get down, too.

Without a word, he and Landon dropped and found cover while still moving carefully toward the two shifters.

"Where the hell is that human superball we were chasing?" Landon asked, breathing hard.

Clayne pointed to the right without taking his eyes off whatever he was looking at below, at the bottom of the slope.

Angelo looked in the direction Clayne had motioned,

and gulped. *Shit.* There was nothing over there but jagged rocks and scrub trees covering the edge of a cliff that skirted the ridgeline above the valley. Below that was a steep drop of at least a hundred feet. The only path the woman could have taken from here would have required her to jump from rock to rock in order to reach the top of the cliff, where it merged once again with the jungle. There was no way she could have traversed that path in the mere seconds she had between disappearing from sight and him and Landon getting here. It was suicidal.

"She pointed us toward the bottom of the valley, then skipped away across those rocks like a frigging mountain goat," Clayne growled. "I didn't bother to follow."

"No shit," Angelo muttered.

Ivy laughed. "I think Clayne is just pissed that a woman he probably outweighs by a hundred and fifty pounds outran him."

Clayne ignored the jab. "Yeah, well it looks like it was a good idea to follow the human superball."

Angelo guessed so. Below him, shrouded in trees and mist, were a collection of buildings surrounded by a patch-work collection of chain-link and low-stacked rock fencing. Even from here, Angelo could see hybrids. And right below the rocks where they were currently hiding, there was a goat trail that wandered through the trees toward the bottom of the valley. Whoever the woman was, she'd not only led them to the hybrid camp, but she'd also parked them right in front of the path that led up to the front door.

The sound of boots on rocks alerted Angelo that Tanner and the others had finally caught up. Ivy darted off to bring them in quietly, leaving Angelo with Clayne and Landon to recon the hybrid camp.

The compound was comprised of about a dozen buildings, with very little fortifications of any kind beyond those stacked rock walls. If they could get to those walls without being seen, they could use them for cover as they took out the hybrids one by one. Of course, if the hybrids saw them at any point, this was going to turn into a nasty house-to-house battle. With just the number of hybrids Angelo could already see below, that didn't seem like something they wanted to do.

Out of the corner of his eye, Angelo caught sight of Ivy leading the guys over the ridgeline. Tate sprinted over the moment he saw them.

"Any sign of Declan or Kendra?" he asked as he fought to slow his breathing.

"Nothing yet," Landon told him. "But that shifter led us here for a reason. If we're careful, we'll be able to work ourselves into a good position to see what's going on down there. Once we figure out where Declan and Kendra are, we'll pull back and come up with a plan to get them."

Tate's mouth tightened, but he nodded. "Okay. Man, you have no idea how hard it is for me to say this, but direct assaults and hostage rescue aren't what my team is trained to handle. So I'm going to trust you to make this happen, Landon. I know I've been bitching at you since you hit the ground, but I'm counting on you to get Declan and Kendra out of there alive."

"If they're still alive, we'll get them out," Landon promised.

"They're alive," Tate said firmly.

Angelo hoped so.

Landon waited for Ivy and the rest of the guys to gather around, then started laying out the team assignments and how each of them would approach the compound. He hadn't gotten more than ten words out of his mouth when the sound of automatic weapons filled the valley. A split second later, a loud roar echoed in the jungle.

"What the hell was that?" Carter asked.

Tate grinned. "Declan."

"Are you sure?" Landon asked. "I've never heard him roar that loud before."

Tate craned his neck, trying to see down into the valley. "Me either. But I know his roar anywhere. And there's only one thing I can think of that'd piss him off enough to make that kind of noise."

"Kendra's in trouble," Ivy said.

"Yup." Tate looked at Landon. "What now?"

Landon sighed. "So much for a plan."

Angelo couldn't help smiling. His former captain hated planning on the fly, but nobody did it better.

"We keep it simple," Landon said. "Angelo, you have Tanner, Butler, Carter, Derek, and Ivy with you. Get your team to that rock wall on the left side of the compound and hit them hard and fast. Make it noisy, too. I want you to draw everyone in that compound over to where you are. I'll come in with Tate, Brent, Gavin, and Clayne from your right. I'll delay until you're fully engaged, then come in and hit them from behind while they're focused on you. If we're lucky, we'll pick up Declan and Kendra as we're moving through the compound. Watch your sectors of fire along your right flank—that's where we'll be coming from. ID your targets. We don't know if there are any other friendlies in there besides Declan and

Kendra. Radio silence until contact." He looked around. "Any questions?"

Angelo shook his head. Around him, everyone else did the same.

"All right then," Landon said. "Let's go get Declan and Kendra."

As they started running down the narrow cliff trail, Angelo saw Landon quickly reach out and touch hands with Ivy. Just one touch, then his wife was sprinting ahead of them down the slope at a pace most of the others couldn't match.

Landon threw a meaningful glance Angelo's way. That simple look said everything his former captain couldn't put into words in front of the other men. *I put Ivy on your team because you're going to need her, but you'd better keep her safe.*

Angelo gave him a nod, then sprinted down the slope to catch up with Ivy. He, Ivy, and the guys with them would bear the brunt of the hybrid's initial onslaught, which meant they'd have to hold their own until Landon figured out how to hit the bastards from behind. People who'd never led troops into a fight wouldn't understand it, but Landon was sending his best friend and his wife in at the tip of the spear because he knew they were the best assets he had to get the job done. Soldiers understood those kinds of calls and would die for a leader who was willing to make them. Angelo would sacrifice himself before he let something happen to his best friend's wife.

—⁂—

Kendra's scent was getting stronger. She was scared. He could almost taste her fear in the air. Declan growled low in his throat as he ran down the path toward the buildings nestled in the valley below.

He'd been running at full speed for the past hour through the rugged, mist-covered terrain that made up this part of the Talamanca Mountains, and yet he wasn't tired. He was too damn furious to be tired. And his temper had only gotten worse when he'd found her helmet and NVGs a while back. She would have only given them up if she was tied up, hurt, or unconscious. The thought that those assholes had done any of those things to her filled him with so much rage, he could barely see straight.

The path flattened out at the base of the slope, but he was still carrying all the momentum from running down the hill as he came through the partially closed gate at the entrance to the compound. Three hybrids came out from the nearest building, their heads cocked to the side as if they'd heard the sound of his boots thumping down the path. Their eyes went wide when they finally saw him.

Declan's first instinct was to toss his M4 away and rip into the hybrids with his newfound claws. But he resisted the urge and instead fired into the trio while they were busy trying to get their own weapons pointed in his direction.

The two hybrids in the front staggered back as the high-speed ball rounds hit them in the chest. One slumped to the ground immediately, but the others came at him growling and snarling. Both had been hit and were bleeding, but not enough to go down.

He felt more than heard the hollow thump as the bolt of the M4 locked back on an empty magazine. He had a single full magazine remaining in his left cargo pants' pocket, but he dismissed the idea of attempting a fast reload in this kind of situation. The hybrids would be on him before he could even get the magazine out. Also, he wasn't sure his extra-long claws would allow him to handle the thirty-round magazine with much skill. Instead, he reversed his grip on the carbine and brought it down like a club on the head of the first hybrid he came to.

The military-grade weapon was never intended to handle that kind of abuse, and shattered in his hands. But then again, the human head was never intended to handle that kind of abuse either, and came apart pretty much the same way the weapon did.

The last hybrid only slowed down long enough to crawl over his buddy's body, but that was all the opening Declan needed. He batted the business end of the hybrid's weapon aside and shoved what was left of his own weapon—part of the upper receiver and the short assault barrel—through the thing's chest. He must have hit the creature's heart, because it stopped growling and fell backward to the ground with an extremely satisfying thud.

The entire fight had taken four or five seconds at the most, and yet he still fell like he was moving through molasses as he followed Kendra's scent. He couldn't see her, but he could hear her screaming. Icy hands gripped his heart. They were hurting her.

He should have scooped up one of the hybrid's weapons, but he didn't want to waste the time. He had to get to Kendra before it was too late. He skirted the corner of the building the three hybrids had just come out of and found himself in an open space in the center of the encampment.

Relief surged though him so fast he almost stumbled.

Two big hybrids were hauling Kendra between them, each with a wrenching grip on one arm. Their vicious clawed hands lifted her up so high that her toes couldn't even touch the ground. Not that she was trying to; she was too busy trying to kick them. But the look of terror on her face was clear. Wherever they were taking her, it scared the hell out of her.

The relief he'd felt earlier disappeared in a wave of fresh fury, and he charged.

The hybrids tossed Kendra aside with a snarl and reached for the rifles strapped across their backs. She bounced across the rocky ground to land in a tangled heap of arms and legs. The rage rolled up in Declan so hot that he didn't even try to silence the roar that erupted from his throat as he launched himself at the two hybrids.

They had no chance to get a shot off before he reached them, not that it would have helped them if they had. He was so mad that nothing would have stopped him from killing them.

Declan had rarely if ever used his claws in a fight. It had just never seemed natural, and up until a couple of hours ago, he'd never considered his claws long enough to be useful. That had all changed. He slashed his claws in a diagonal sweep across the first hybrid's chest, from left shoulder to right hip. He put every bit of power that his own muscled shoulders could give him into the strike, roaring again as his blow struck home with a devastating violence he'd never felt before.

The hybrid was dead before it hit the ground.

Declan didn't wonder why this new form of shifter

violence felt so right, so natural. He simply reached across the dead hybrid and ripped the other creature off his feet and threw him to the ground.

The hybrid immediately flipped to his feet, but Declan was just as fast now and had seen the move coming long before the creature even pulled it. The hybrid barely regained his footing before Declan was there to put him back down with a partially closed fist to the left temple.

As he fell to his knees, the hybrid took a blind swipe at Declan's midsection. If the strike had connected, Declan would have been gutted. But Declan blocked the strike with a low forearm, then brought another crushing blow down on the hybrid's head, this time directly on top. There was a sharp crack; then the hybrid slumped, lifeless, to the ground.

Declan had the urge to hit the son of a bitch half a dozen times for daring to touch Kendra, but he controlled himself. There were more hybrids—a lot of them— coming. He could both hear them and smell them.

He turned around to look for Kendra, praying she wasn't hurt.

She pushed herself up on an elbow and tried to roll over onto her back, but she was having a hard time managing it. As if sensing him, she turned to look his way. Her eyes locked with his, but instead of relief, there was only panic in them.

Before he had time to figure out what was going on in her head, a door on the far side of the compound flew off its hinges and crashed to the ground halfway across the camp. The huge hybrid Declan and Kendra had seen that first day stepped out of the building. He took one look at Declan, then swung his gaze on Kendra. The hatred in those red eyes nearly stopped Declan's heart. Mouth twisting into something that might have been a smile, the hybrid charged.

"Run!" Declan shouted at Kendra.

He didn't wait to see if she obeyed, but instead rushed the oncoming brute with everything he had. No matter what it took, Declan had to take down this asshole. Declan didn't know what had happened between Kendra and the hybrid, but his gut told him the creature would make sure she suffered if he got the chance. Declan wasn't going to let that happen.

Declan collided with the hulk at full speed, smashing into him like a linebacker on a football field. Declan felt something in his shoulder crack but ignored the brief stab of pain. Nothing was going to stop him from killing this monster.

By the time Angelo and his team reached the low stone wall along the left side of the compound, hybrids were there to meet them. The only saving grace was that most of them weren't carrying weapons. Not that it made fighting them any easier. If Ivy and Tanner hadn't been there, he and the other guys would have been dead a hundred times over. Those two were frigging amazing. If they weren't up to their necks in hybrids intent on killing them, Angelo would have enjoyed watching Ivy work. He'd never seen anyone move as fast as she did, literally spinning and ducking out of the path of incoming bullets, slashing throats here, ripping out hamstrings there. Hybrids might behave like berserkers, but apparently they weren't as stupid as Angelo thought, because they quickly began to avoid the section of wall she was on, choosing to try their luck elsewhere.

Tanner was amazing, too, but in a completely different way. He moved in a slower, almost hesitant fashion, like he was thinking about every move before he made it. But while he wasn't as graceful as Ivy, he still took down a lot of hybrids, only in a much bloodier fashion. Thank God he was on their side.

But even with all the advantages they had going for them—a good defensive position, enough ammo and grenades to get the job done, plus Ivy and Tanner—they were still losing. There were simply too many hybrids, and the flanking action he'd been expecting from Landon hadn't come.

"Landon!" Angelo shouted into his radio mic as he drilled a hybrid through the forehead. "You can make that appearance anytime now. No need to be fashionably late."

This was the first time they'd used the radio headsets since getting to Costa Rica, but he wasn't sure why they bothered. Landon hadn't responded to any of his calls for backup except to say he and the guys with him had their hands full and would get there when they could.

"We haven't even gotten out of the tree line yet," Landon yelled back over the open communications line. "I was hoping you'd draw most of the hybrids your way, but I'm guessing that part of the plan didn't work."

Angelo reloaded a fresh magazine before answering. "Your plan worked fine, Captain. We're facing four to one odds over here."

"Shit. We'll be there. Just hold on five more minutes."

In the silence that followed Landon's words, Angelo could hear the hollow booming sounds of grenades going off over the radio. "And by the way, I'm not your captain anymore."

Angelo chuckled. "You'll always be my captain. Now get the hell over here and pull my ass out of the fire, would you?"

"We're coming," Landon promised with that same grim determination Angelo had grown to trust. "Everyone okay on your side?"

"We're fine," Ivy answered. Her voice was so soft over the line that Angelo barely heard it. You'd never even know she was in the middle of a firefight. "What about you?"

"All in one piece," Landon said.

"Good. Make sure you stay that way," she said. "Don't do anything crazy, huh? We'll hold out until you get here."

Angelo appreciated Ivy's optimism, but he didn't think they were going to last the five minutes Landon and the other guys took to get there. He didn't say that, though.

"Okay, troops," he shouted above the din of automatic-weapons fire and snarling hybrids. "Landon needs us to hold out for a little while longer. He's run into some trouble."

Tanner turned and locked eyes with Angelo, and a knowledge that soldiers instinctively understood passed between them. The former Ranger knew they weren't going to be able to hold the hybrids until reinforcements got there.

Suddenly, Tanner's normally brown eyes flickered with a bright red glow. Then his teeth elongated and his claws extended. *Shit*. Angelo knew Tanner had been working hard as hell to rein in his hybrid nature and force down the violent impulses that took his self-control away, but someone had to slow down the hybrids and back them off, or none of them would be alive when Landon and his team arrived.

Tanner was over the wall with a roar that echoed in the jungle. On the other side of Ivy, Derek and the other Special Forces guys stared in disbelief, the hybrids forgotten for the moment. Luckily, Tanner's transformation and animalistic war cry stunned the hybrids, too. Tanner was in their midst before they had a chance to recover.

Tanner didn't even attempt to fire his weapon. Angelo wasn't sure he could with those long claws. Instead, he flipped his grip on the M4 in his hand and swung it like a club. When the weapon fell apart, he went at the creatures with claws and fangs. All Angelo could do was stare. He'd never seen anything like the way Tanner fought, unless you counted watching a show on Animal Planet. Tanner ripped into the hybrids like a lion in the middle of a pack of hyenas, bodies flying everywhere.

And yet despite the incredible damage Tanner inflicted on the hybrids, it didn't seem to be enough. He needed help.

Angelo slapped a fresh magazine into his M4, then stood up from where he crouched behind the wall. "Take it to them!" he shouted as he jumped over the only protection that had been keeping him alive, and ran into the fray.

He didn't look back to see if Ivy and the guys were following him. He prayed they were. If not, this was going to be the shortest assault in history.

—∾∾—

Kendra was on her feet stumbling after Declan even as he and Marcus smashed into each other. The sound was so loud, she was afraid the collision had killed Declan. But then he was back up and throwing himself at the gigantic hybrid again, roaring in a way Kendra had never heard in all the time they'd known each other.

When she'd first seen Declan, her heart had almost stopped. She had left him in that shelter so he'd be safe from the hybrids. And what the hell had he done? Walked right into the blasted compound and practically hand delivered himself to the monster that ran the place. She'd wanted to shout at him and ask him what the hell he was doing.

But she knew what he was doing. He was there to save her butt because that was just the kind of big, softhearted teddy bear he was.

Yet, while Declan's heart was the same as it had ever been, there was definitely something drastically different about the rest of him. She'd recognized it the second he ran into the courtyard. His eyes were blazing so vividly, she had no problem seeing them in the bright morning light. His jaw and fangs were pushed out almost as far as Tanner's when he was losing it, and his claws were almost as long as Marcus's. But what made her realize something big had happened to Declan was that roar. She'd never heard anything like it.

Though she had no idea *why* it'd happened, she knew *what* had happened—Declan had shifted more completely than he'd ever let himself shift before.

She stood there in awe as he squared off against the

bigger hybrid and shook off vicious blows that no other shifter in the DCO could have even survived. In return, he laid crushing hits to Marcus's shoulders and chest. Kendra had always known Declan could be a powerful shifter if he just let himself embrace his inner bear, but even she was stunned at the sheer power he displayed in standing up to the hybrid that had been hunting them for days.

Despite being terrified that Marcus was going to kill him, she was proud of Declan.

She knew Declan wanted her to run, but she couldn't. Besides the fact that she was just too sore right now—getting tossed ten feet through the air by a couple of hybrids could do that—there was no way she was going to leave him here to fight alone. Even though she believed in her heart that Declan couldn't lose, she had to stay to make sure.

Then she caught movement out of the corner of her eye that made her think maybe she was being a little too optimistic.

Three hybrids entered the courtyard, weapons down at their sides. *Crap*. Declan wasn't in a position to take on more hybrids—he had his hands full with one. If they joined in the fight, Declan wouldn't last.

She looked around for something she could use as a weapon. Her eyes locked on the broken bodies of the two hybrids who'd been dragging her to the lab, and the rifles they still had slung across their backs.

Ignoring the pain, she limped over to the bodies. She dropped to her knees beside the first dead hybrid and grabbed his weapon, trying to yank it off his back. But the corpse refused to work with her no matter how hard she pulled. *Dammit*. She jerked the sling strap off the front attachment point. She was getting the damn thing away from the creature if she had to drag him behind her.

Once she had the weapon in hand, she dug through the hybrids' cargo pants' pockets until she found all their extra magazines. There weren't many. Apparently, hybrids weren't fans of carrying too much ammo.

She was just dragging the weapon around to get into a shooting position as the three hybrids headed her way.

Kendra dropped to the ground behind one of the dead hybrids and threw the barrel of the weapon over the creature's chest, then grabbed the charging handle, praying the gun operated like the ones she was used to. She jerked the handle to the rear, feeling the bolt move with it. When it stopped, she let it go and felt the bolt slide forward with a satisfying thump. She hoped she'd just chambered a round properly. She didn't have time to aim, so she simply slapped her cheek to the stock and moved the rear of the weapon down until she was staring directly at the oncoming hybrids, then squeezed the trigger.

She discovered the hard way that she was on full auto, but while there was a solid *thump-thump-thump* against her shoulder, the rifle didn't jump around too much. Even better, the rounds she fired hit where she'd aimed, and the hybrid in front crashed to the ground.

One of the two remaining hybrids charged her, but his friend slowed long enough for her to get the first one, then shift over to pop the one who was having doubts. Knowing there were only a few rounds left in the magazine, she dropped it and put in a fresh one as she scanned the camp for more hybrids. Thankfully, there weren't any.

Kendra chambered a round, then spun to point the rifle at Marcus. Maybe she could get a clean shot at the big hybrid and put a quick end to this.

But that hope died quickly. Declan and Marcus were going at each other like a couple of deranged werebeasts, twisting and turning across the ground one moment, clawing and pounding at one another the next. She was too terrified of hitting Declan to even try and take a shot.

She'd seen a lot of shifters—and a lot of hybrids, too—fight, but none of them could match the pure, unbridled rage and violence of what she was seeing now. Declan and Marcus pounded and clawed at each other like something out of a prehistoric movie, growling and roaring at each other so loud the entire jungle had to hear them. She cringed as ribbons of blood hit the ground. Even if Declan lived through the fight, she wasn't sure he'd survive all the punishment he was taking.

Her heart squeezed in her chest. But there was nothing she could do, except wait and pray she'd get a chance to take a shot.

Kendra was just lifting the weapon to her cheek again when she heard the sounds of fighting on the far side of the camp. That had to be Tate, Brent, and Gavin. Who else would be willing to fight with a whole camp full of hybrids?

She opened her mouth to tell Declan that help was on the way, but he and Marcus smashed right through the side of a building. *Crap.*

Kendra looked over her shoulder again, wishing someone would come running around one of the buildings right that second. But they didn't. She was the only help Declan was going to get. She tightened her grip on her weapon and headed for the building and the fight inside.

Kendra got there just in time to see Marcus grab a huge computer monitor and smash it against Declan's shoulder. Declan barely noticed it. He simply lunged forward and raked his long claws across the hybrid's chest. Marcus ignored the pain the same way Declan had and brought his fist down on Declan's shoulder. It was hard to be sure over the growling, but Kendra swore she heard something break.

How long could a shifter, even one as strong as Declan, keep fighting at such a savage pace before he slipped up and let a fatal strike slip through? Kendra didn't know, and she didn't want to find out.

She darted behind a heavy desk and got her weapon into position. The time was coming when she was going to have to make a decision. She could keep praying that Declan would be able to end the fight without her getting involved, or take a shot she was uncertain she could make.

Chapter 14

ANGELO JUMPED OVER A DEAD HYBRID TO GET TO IVY, intent on making good on his promise to Landon about protecting her, and found Tanner, who was still in the grips of his own hybrid rage, stepping in front of Ivy just as three hybrids advanced on her. Angelo dropped to one knee, raised his M4 to his shoulder, and started taking slow, careful shots at the snarling monsters.

"What the hell are you two doing?" Ivy demanded, squeezing off a three-round burst over Angelo's head. "Get out of my way!"

"Fall back to the wall!" Angelo yelled over his shoulder. "Tanner and I will give you time to get to safety."

Ivy kept shooting over his head. "You stupid ass. Landon told you to do this, didn't he?"

"He never said a word," Angelo shouted. "Now hurry up and go. Carter's injured, and Butler and Derek need your help getting him out of here. They didn't sign up for this."

Angelo glanced over his shoulder, prepared to argue some more, but Ivy was already running across the rocky ground to where Derek and Butler were trying to get Carter up on his feet. Angelo dropped his magazine to the ground, loaded his last fresh thirty-rounder, and flipped to full auto, then threw a quick glance at Tanner. He returned Angelo's look, eyes flashing red as hell and claws flexing.

"You know, you're not so bad." Angelo wasn't sure Tanner could even understand him when he was in beast mode like this, but he grinned at the man anyway as he added, "For a Ranger."

Angelo made his ammo last as long as he could. When the bolt of his M4 locked back on an empty magazine, he dropped the weapon and pulled out his knife, then jumped to his feet. But before he could get in a jab, gunfire erupted from somewhere to his right. Tanner growled and crouched, clearly intending to launch himself at the hybrids.

Shit. What the hell was he doing?

Angelo sheathed his knife and jumped on Tanner's back, trying to keep him out of the line of fire, but all it did was freak out the ex-Ranger. Angelo ducked as Tanner reached back and tried to take off his face with those daggers that passed for claws. He'd be damned if he'd let go, though. More copper-jacketed rounds were coming their way. Landon's slow-ass help had finally gotten there. No way was he going to let Tanner die now.

More bullets zipped over their heads, taking out most of the remaining hybrids. The few who hadn't gone down ran for cover in the jungle.

Beneath Angelo, Tanner roared. One second the ex-Ranger was wiggling under Angelo's grip, the next he was tossing Angelo over his shoulder. Angelo hit the ground hard, pain shooting up his back and lancing through his skull. He opened his eyes just in time to see Tanner jump over him and tear off into the jungle in hot pursuit of the hybrids who'd escaped.

Double shit.

"Tanner, no!" Ivy shouted.

But it was no good. Tanner was way too far gone to come back.

Angelo closed his eyes and didn't open them again until he heard boots thumping in his direction. He blinked. Landon and Ivy were standing above him, concern on their faces. Angelo pushed himself up into a sitting position with a groan.

"About frigging time you showed up," he said. "I thought maybe you stopped for breakfast or something."

Landon reached down and helped him up. "Sorry about that. It took a lot longer to get here than I thought. You okay?"

"Yeah," Angelo said.

Well, except for the concussion. His head was still spinning.

Ivy punched Angelo in the shoulder—hard. The thump made him stagger back a step, which was a good thing, since she probably would have poked out his eye with the finger she was pointing at him.

"Don't you ever do anything that stupid again," she said. "No matter what Landon tells you, or doesn't tell you, to do! You could have gotten yourself killed."

Ivy gave Landon a hard look, then touched the rings on the necklace she wore hidden under her shirt before turning and running back to where everyone else was clustered around Carter over by the rock wall.

"What the hell was that about?" Landon asked.

Angelo opened his mouth to tell Landon that Ivy obviously didn't appreciate his chivalrous attempt to sacrifice himself for her, or the fact that Landon had put him up to it, but a roar from one of the buildings reminded him that their work wasn't done.

"You didn't find Declan?" he asked, picking up his M4 and falling into step beside Landon.

Landon flipped him a magazine, which he caught and smoothly loaded on the run. "Never got a chance. Had to come save your ass, remember?"

"Well, let's hope you didn't lose one friend trying to save another," Angelo said.

It wasn't hard to figure out where Declan was. If the growling and snarls didn't give it away, the big-ass hole in the side of the building did.

Angelo swore. What the hell kind of fight had the bear shifter gotten himself into?

Kendra darted across the room to see if she could get a shot lined up at Marcus and almost got crushed between him and Declan and the wall. She stifled a scream and quickly darted behind a filing cabinet. Throwing the barrel of her rifle on top of it, she sighted in on Marcus and started to squeeze the trigger. But almost as if he somehow sensed what she was doing, the big hybrid suddenly twisted Declan around so that he was the one in her sights instead.

Kendra clenched her jaw and aimed at the hybrid, but he moved out of her sight again.

Dammit!

She wasn't going to be able to wait for a perfect shot. But the way Marcus seemed to know what she was doing made it even more likely than ever that she'd end up hitting Declan if she did shoot. As if proving her right, Marcus jerked aside the next time she started putting pressure on the trigger.

What the hell was giving her away? Could he hear her squeeze the trigger?

Shifting the weapon, she took aim again, but this time she didn't sight in on Marcus, she aimed at Declan. It was dangerous to shoot anywhere in his direction, but she didn't have time to think about it. They were moving too quickly.

Kendra said a quick prayer, then squeezed the trigger. As she hoped, Marcus jerked Declan around...and put himself right in the path of her bullet.

She only grazed his leg, but the fact that she hit Marcus at all surprised the big hybrid so much that he twisted around with a glare. Lip curling into a snarl, he advanced on her.

Declan moved faster than she'd ever seen him move. He jerked Marcus around with one hand at the same time he slashed the hybrid's throat with the claws of the other. The hybrid went down but regained his feet just as quickly and came at her again.

Kendra stumbled back, falling over her own feet. She landed hard on her butt, her rifle sliding across the floor out of reach.

Marcus reached out and got a crushing grip on her boot, dragging her toward him. Kendra screamed and tried to kick him with her other foot, but she couldn't reach him. Marcus growled and yanked even harder.

A deafening roar echoed in the confines of the small room, and she covered her ears afraid they might actually burst. Eyes wide, she watched as Declan reached out and wrapped a hand around one of the creature's big fangs, then twisted his head all the way around backward. She squeezed her eyes shut, unable to watch.

And then there was silence.

Kendra opened her eyes to find Declan gazing down at her. His face was covered in so many scrapes and cuts that she could barely recognize him. But it was him. It was her bear shifter.

And his face wasn't the only part that was slashed up. There were similar cuts and gashes all over his arms, chest, and legs. There didn't seem to be an inch of him that wasn't injured. After seeing the way he'd survived the horrible gashes to his chest not so long ago, Kendra knew in her heart that he would heal from these wounds as well. But that didn't mean she didn't want to be there to wipe away the blood and pain anyway. The need to just put her hands on him and convince herself that he was okay was overwhelming.

She didn't wait for him to help her up, but instead of welcoming her with open arms, Declan took a step back. Then another. Kendra stopped, too. Fear flashed in his eyes and was quickly replaced by regret, and then sadness.

"Declan, what's—?" she began, but the words ended on a gasp as Ivy, Landon, and Angelo came charging through the hole in the side of the building.

There was silence as they all stared at her and Declan, then Ivy hugged her and mumbled something over and over that sounded like, "Thank God," but Kendra couldn't be sure. Her ears were still ringing a little from Declan's roar. She wrapped her arms around her friend and hugged her back just as fiercely.

Someone patted her back, and Kendra pulled away

from Ivy to see Landon grinning down at her. Behind him, Angelo was smiling, too. She stared in amazement as Clayne climbed through the opening in the wall. He was followed by Tate, Brent, and Gavin. Where the heck had they all come from?

Ivy pulled her in for another hug. "God, I'm so happy to see you."

"I'm happy to see you, too," Kendra said. "All of you."

She turned to see where Declan was, figuring that Tate, Gavin, and Brent would probably be hovering around him, but someone else put their arms around her, pulling her in for a hug and blocking her view. She hugged the person even though she didn't know who it was—he had risked his life to rescue her and Declan, after all. But when she stepped back, whoever it was cupped her cheek and kissed her hard on the lips. And it wasn't Declan. She jerked away.

What the hell?

Derek was smiling at her and saying something about being so happy that she was safe. She didn't quite hear exactly what he said, because she was busy trying to figure out why he'd just kissed her. Sure, they'd danced a few times at Ivy and Landon's wedding, but then again, she'd danced with a lot of people that night, including Angelo, and he hadn't kissed her.

Derek must have picked up on her vibe, because he quickly dropped his arms from around her and stepped back, running his hand through his hair. "Sorry about that. I, um, I'm just happy to see you safe."

She didn't know which of them felt more awkward. "No problem. Thanks. For coming to the rescue, I mean."

He nodded and probably would have said more, but

Tate, Brent, and Gavin showed up to save both of them from further embarrassment.

"Good to see you in one piece," he said.

Her lips curved. "Thanks to Declan."

Kendra scanned the room, looking for him. But her big bear shifter was nowhere to be seen. Her stomach clenched. Maybe his wounds were worse than she'd feared.

"Where's Declan?" she asked.

"He's out with Clayne, tracking down the hybrids who got away," Tate answered.

She understood that. Nobody liked the idea of a couple hybrids roaming around loose in the jungle. While chasing down rogue shifters—or hybrids—was technically part of Declan's job description, it still hurt that he'd left without talking to her first.

"Oh," she said.

Landon called out to Ivy from across the room. "Hey, Ivy! Angelo and I are going to check out the rest of the camp."

Kendra jerked her head up. *Crap*. Harry and the other doctors. She almost forgot. "Landon," she called. "The hybrids were keeping some doctors locked up in one of the small buildings on the other side of the camp. They were pretty beat up."

"We're on it," he said.

Ivy frowned at her. "You okay?"

Kendra gave herself a shake. "What? Yeah."

Her friend didn't look convinced. "Are you sure? Maybe Derek should take a look at you."

Kendra cringed. She'd rather not. "I'm fine, really. It's just…"

"Just what?" Ivy prompted.

Kendra didn't answer. She'd always confided in Ivy about everything. So why was she having such a hard time now? "Declan and I...well, we got really close out here. He got pretty beat up in the fight with the hybrid running the place and..."

"And you're worried about him," Ivy finished.

Kendra nodded.

"He's a shifter, remember?" Ivy smiled. "That means he heals fast."

Ivy was right. And if that's all it was, she'd probably only be half as worried as she was. But it was more than that. The fearful way Declan had looked at her right before Ivy and the guys had shown up, well, it had freaked her out. But how could she explain that to her friend when she couldn't make sense of it herself?

"Even so, I'll breathe easier when he gets back," was all she said.

To keep from going crazy until he did, Kendra tagged along with Ivy, Landon, and Tate to search the lab. Landon figured they only had a day or so before the Costa Rican government finally got bold enough to come see what all the shooting had been about. He wanted them to be long gone before that happened.

As she skimmed the files on one of the computers, Kendra filled Ivy, Landon, and Tate in on everything she'd learned from Harry and the other two doctors. She'd hoped the men would be able to tell the story themselves, but when Landon and Angelo found them, the doctors were already dead. All three of them had been shot in the head.

"You don't seem surprised that the doctors who were

working for Stutmeir aren't the ones who made these hybrids," Kendra said, glancing at Ivy and Landon.

"We've searched enough of their labs to know that this place doesn't look anything like those," Landon said.

"Which is too bad." Ivy tossed a folder down on the desk she was searching. "I was hoping to find Klaus and Renard when we kicked in the door—preferably dead."

Kendra silently agreed. Ivy would sleep a lot better knowing the two doctors who had tortured her were no longer a threat.

Tate looked up from the notebook he was reading. "So if Klaus and Renard didn't make these hybrids, who did?"

Kendra explained about the research files that Harry and the other doctors had been given. "The way Harry described those documents makes me think they came from the DCO."

Tate's eyes widened. "The DCO? Seriously?"

Kendra nodded.

He dropped the notebook on the table with a curse. "First, someone in the DCO purposely put my team in the middle of a hybrid ambush, for reasons we haven't figured out yet. Now, you're telling me it's possible that this same someone in the DCO set a group of doctors up here and gave them the research necessary to create the hybrids? Someone like John?"

Kendra didn't answer. Even after everything that had happened, she flat-out refused to believe John was involved. Ivy, Landon, and the others hadn't known John as long as she had. They hadn't seen how hard he worked to keep the Committee and people like Dick from turning the organization into something that would be capable of doing exactly what it seemed to be doing now. But how was she going to convince them of that?

"Maybe," Landon said, answering Tate's question.

Tate's face fell as Landon filled him in on what had been happening on the hybrid front, specifically their fear that Dick and others within the DCO were trying to replace shifters with hybrids, as well as what Landon had found while searching the DCO's classified records repository a few months ago.

"Wait a minute." Tate looked like someone had pulled the floor out from under him, then hit him with an axe handle. "Stutmeir was on the DCO's payroll? *We* funded his frigging research? How is that even possible? Stutmeir and his doctors were torturing people."

Landon traded a quick look with Ivy, but she shook her head. Kendra knew what that look meant, and Kendra couldn't blame her. There were obviously some things that Ivy wasn't ready to share, and the fact that she'd been one of the people Stutmeir's doctors had tortured was one of those things.

Tate dropped into the cheap, swivel desk chair. "And now, these same people have started a whole new hybrid program?"

"Or maybe some other group within the DCO," Ivy said. "We just don't know for sure."

Landon leaned back against the counter and crossed one booted foot over the other. "It can't be a coincidence that this is the exact part of Costa Rica where the DCO decided to send you guys. If there was a single rogue group within the DCO doing all this, they wouldn't have sent you down here."

Kendra understood where Landon was heading at the same time Tate did.

"Shit," he muttered. "So, the traitorous group of bastards in the DCO who employed Stutmeir got wind that a second group of traitorous bastards had a hybrid lab in this general area, then manipulated events to get us sent here."

"You and Declan said you thought someone had us conducting a grid search for something," Kendra pointed out. "Now we know what it was."

Tate nodded. "This lab."

"They were probably hoping the doctors would get nervous and abandon ship," Ivy said.

"But instead, the second group of traitorous bastards at the DCO decided to accelerate their program, and used your team to test their hybrids," Landon added.

"But the commander of the security force went nuts and took over the operation," Kendra finished. "God, that sounds absolutely crazy."

The muscle in Tate's jaw flexed. "So, what the hell do we do now?"

"First, we search every inch of this compound," Landon said. "I want to see if there's anything here that might tell us who from the DCO funded this program. Next, we collect information for Zarina. She's going to want to have details on these hybrids—pictures, blood and tissue samples, copies of any important-looking research. Maybe it will tell her who stole it from the archives. Last, we collect up everything that's left— every scrap of paper, every piece of equipment, and all the bodies—then we burn this place to the ground. I don't want anyone being able to use this particular hybrid process again. These hybrids weren't perfect, but they were better than the first group we ran up against. If these were second-generation hybrids, I don't ever want to face a third generation."

Kendra had to agree with that. "What do we do when we get home? There's going to be a debriefing."

"We tell the truth, or as close to it as we can get, anyway. That the camp and everything in it went up in flames during the fight with the hybrids," Landon said. "Until we know for sure that we can trust John, he gets nothing."

She hated lying to John. But if Landon was right about her boss, telling him what they really learned could get a lot of people killed. "And after that?"

"We figure out who really pulls the strings at the DCO," Landon said. "This hybrid program might have started with John or Dick—or hell, maybe both of them—but my gut tells me that someone on the Committee is involved, and we need to find out who."

Kendra's stomach churned. Going after the Committee made sense, but it was also the nearest thing to suicide she'd ever heard.

Kendra continued to pore over everything in the lab alongside Ivy and Landon while Tate rounded up the other guys so they could search the rest of the buildings. Landon was just calling John for a pickup when Kendra heard Clayne's voice outside. She hoped that meant Declan was back, too.

Tossing Ivy the flash drive with everything she'd found in her section of the lab, Kendra ran for the door. She sagged with relief when she saw Declan standing with Clayne…and Tanner? She hadn't expected to see him as part of this op. At the moment, though, she was too focused on Declan to wonder what the DCO hybrid was doing there.

Pulse racing, she closed the distance between them in record time and threw her arms around him in front of everyone. She was so happy that he was back safe, she didn't realize he hadn't put his arms around her. She immediately stepped back to search his face.

"What's wrong? Are you hurt?" She didn't wait for him to answer. "Maybe you should let Derek take a look at you."

"I'm fine."

"But he's a medic," she insisted. "He can—"

"I said I'm fine!" Declan growled.

Kendra jumped. From the corner of her eye, she saw Clayne give her and Declan a curious look. She bit her lip. "Okay. I just thought…"

Declan's expression softened. "I know. And I'm sorry. But I'm fine, Kendra. Really."

Was he? Because he sure as hell didn't seem fine to her. She nodded, blinking back tears.

"Okay, troops!" Landon called as he and Ivy came out of the lab. "We've got a pickup in two hours. Let's torch this place and get to the landing zone."

Kendra turned back to Declan, but he'd already walked over to join Tate and the rest of his team. She tried not to be hurt. He and Tate were like brothers. It made sense they'd want to catch up. She and Declan would talk on the flight home. As she watched them disappear into the building where he and Marcus had fought to the death a few hours ago, though, she couldn't help feeling that what she and Declan had shared had somehow been broken.

Kendra sat staring off into the dark interior of the C-17 cargo aircraft that was taking them home, slowly going over the last several hours and trying to figure out what had happened between her and Declan.

She'd hoped to talk with him on the way back to the States, but it hadn't worked out that way. Declan had been withdrawn and quiet since they'd left the jungle-shrouded labs yesterday morning. In fact, he didn't say more than two words to her the entire time.

Landon had pushed them hard to get to the extraction point on the Panama border that he'd set up with John. With all the injured people they were moving, not to mention the rucksacks full of hybrid DNA samples and lab reports, it had been damn hard getting to the clearing by the deadline. But no one had complained about the pace. They'd all been more than ready to get out of that damn place. She'd tried to stick near Declan during the hike out, but he'd disappeared into the forest, saying he wanted to make sure no one was following them. The excuse had seemed logical at the time, but with the way he'd been acting since, she now knew it had probably been a made-up excuse.

Two helicopters from the Panamanian Air Service had been waiting for them in a small clearing when they got to the extraction point. Her heart had crumbled a little more when Declan had gone out of his way to make sure he was on the other helicopter after she'd been buckled into the first one.

It hadn't gotten any better after they were quietly dropped off at some private facilities near the edge of the Panama Pacific International Airport. The place had food, showers, and doctors to take a look at their wounded. Everyone had laughed and joked as they cleaned up and got some warm food, but Kendra hadn't felt like doing either. The only thing she'd wanted to do was spend some quiet time with Declan. Unfortunately, he'd disappeared the moment they'd landed, saying something about needing to rest and heal up. She didn't have the guts to go after him, not if he was going to snap at her again.

She hadn't seen him again for six hours, not until they all boarded the C-17 Globemaster John had rerouted to their location. Even then, Declan had immediately headed to the back of the plane. The aircraft had been almost empty, and yet the place he'd chosen to crash was about as far away from her as he could get.

A short time after leaving the Panamanian airfield, she'd walked back to check on him, but he'd been in a deep sleep. It was obvious that Declan was still avoiding her for some reason, even if that meant sleeping all the way back to the States.

Kendra continued to replay the last few hours of their time in Costa Rica, looking for that one thing she'd done that had pushed him away, when Ivy slipped into the seat beside her.

"Hey, girlfriend," Ivy said softly. "I thought you'd be sleeping like everyone else, especially after the week you've had."

She shrugged. "I guess I'm too tired to sleep right now."

Ivy didn't say anything for a while, probably assuming she would continue. But Kendra didn't feel like chatting. Not about what was really bothering her anyway. She would tell Ivy about everything soon enough, but now wasn't the right time.

"You okay?" Ivy whispered. "Did something happen out in the jungle you haven't told me about?"

Yeah. She mused silently. *I fell in love with Declan*. But even though Ivy was her best friend, those weren't the words that came out. "I'm fine, really. I'm just thinking about what we're going to have to do when we get back. With John, I mean."

She could feel Ivy's gaze on her in the darkness and figured her friend knew she wasn't really being honest. But Ivy was intuitive enough to know that if Kendra wasn't ready to talk, she shouldn't push. She heard Ivy shift in her seat, then sit back with a sigh.

"I know it's going to be hard for you to sneak around behind John's back, but you understand why we have to do it, right?"

Kendra wanted to get Ivy focused on another topic of conversation, but she honestly didn't like this one any more than the previous. At least she could talk about this subject, though.

"Yeah, I understand why we have to do it," Kendra admitted. "I just wish we didn't. John has always been someone I looked up to. I have a hard time believing he's behind any of this."

"Me too," Ivy said. "But the fact is, we rarely know people as well as we think we do. And sometimes the people we think we know the best are the ones who can surprise us the most."

Ivy told her about the plan she and Landon had come up with to follow John, maybe even put a tracking device on his car, but Kendra wasn't really listening. Instead, she was thinking about what Ivy had said about how the people we think we know the best can surprise us the most.

Maybe that was the case with Declan. Maybe she didn't know him nearly as well as she thought she did, even after everything they'd gone through out in that jungle.

Chapter 15

IVY COULDN'T BELIEVE THAT SHE AND LANDON WERE actually conducting a surveillance operation on John. After all the red tape their boss had gone through to get them down to Costa Rica, then back out, it just seemed wrong. But Landon was right. If John was clean, that was great, but if he wasn't, they needed to know. Because their lives were being put at risk every day in the normal course of their jobs. If John was working another agenda, —possibly with people on the Committee—then the risk they were facing was even greater. One way or the other, they had to know for sure. She'd always thought of John as one of the good guys, but there was simply too much at stake to have blind faith in anyone right now.

As soon as they got back home, she and Landon bugged both his office in DC and at the training complex, as well as his car. In addition, they'd also followed him every night after work since getting back from Costa Rica. They figured that if he was going to communicate with anyone about what happened in Central America, he'd do it right after they got back, as all the traitors scurried around trying to cover their butts. While she and Landon were watching John, Clayne and Danica were watching Dick.

John didn't leave the training complex until nine, but unlike last night, this time, he didn't go straight home. Instead, he headed toward DC. Ivy assumed he was going to the office in town, but he took the Crystal City exit, then pulled into a twenty-four-hour parking garage.

"Great," she muttered as Landon parked along the curb a few hundred feet from the garage. "That connects to the shopping center. He could be going to any restaurant from there. Or the Metro."

She and Landon had just started down the street when their boss walked out of the garage and headed down the sidewalk along Crystal Drive in the opposite direction. But instead of going into a restaurant like Ivy thought he might, he walked directly to the Water Park and sat on the edge of the fountain.

Ivy and Landon stopped outside the steak house on the opposite side of the street and pretended to look at the menu. She frowned as John pulled out his smartphone, then leaned forward with his elbows on his knees to read it.

"Okay, that's not suspicious at all," Landon said softly. "No one sits outside to check his messages in forty-degree weather. I don't care how nice that fountain is."

It *was* nice, but Ivy agreed with her husband. "It looks like a predesignated meeting place to me."

She and Landon could only stare at the menu for so long before someone got suspicious, so after five minutes, they wandered to the next building. Ivy pretended to look at the dresses on the mannequins in the store window while Landon kept an eye on John. So far, no one had joined their boss.

"You think he made us?" Landon asked.

Ivy opened her mouth to reply when she caught a scent that made her head whip around. She sniffed the air, trying to pinpoint where the smell was coming from, then turned until she was pointing in the direction they'd just come from a few minutes ago. The wind was coming into her face from that direction, which explained how she'd picked up such a weak scent. Someone was watching them from upwind of their location.

Landon's hand was already on the gun under his coat. "What is it?"

"I'm not sure," she said. "A shifter, I think. But I've never smelled anything quite like it before."

Landon glanced at John. Their boss was still sitting on the edge of the fountain engrossed in whatever he was looking at on his phone. "That may be who John's here to meet."

"If the shifter catches our scent, he might bolt," Ivy said.

She and Landon quickly walked off the main street and ducked into an alley between a restaurant and the shopping center. They could still see the fountain from where they were, but between the nearby Dumpster and the swirling wind, she didn't think the other shifter would be able to pick up their scent.

A few seconds later, a tall man in an overcoat walked slowly down the opposite side of Crystal Drive. He stopped at a few stores but didn't go inside. Like he was window shopping—or checking for a tail.

"Is that the guy you smelled?" Landon asked.

She shook her head. "I can't be sure. The wind works against us as much as for us back here."

They edged closer to the entrance of the alley as the man continued down the street. He stopped and leaned one shoulder casually against the wall at the entrance to the running trail, hands in his pockets, his eyes locked on John.

"What the hell?" Landon asked. "Is he here to talk to John or not?"

Ivy didn't have a clue, but a few moments later, the man abruptly turned and started back down the street the way he'd come.

"Shit," Landon swore. "Stay on John. I'll follow Overcoat."

Ivy caught his arm. "I don't get a good feeling about the guy in the coat. We either follow him together or stay with John."

Landon didn't argue. Or hesitate. "We follow Overcoat then."

They waited until the man passed the alleyway, then slipped out to follow him. At the crosswalk, he moved over to their side of the street, then continued heading toward where they'd parked. A few blocks later, he turned off Crystal Drive onto a smaller side road.

She and Landon got to the corner just in time to see the man turn again, this time darting into an alley. Then they heard the sound of running feet.

"Shit," Landon muttered. "He made us already."

Chasing a guy, especially one who might be a shifter, when they didn't know a damn thing about him probably wasn't the smartest thing in the world, but she and Landon didn't have much choice. This whole op was a bust if they didn't get a good look at him.

She and Landon cautiously peeked around the edge of the building. The alley was a dead end. Overcoat was nowhere in sight. Ivy pulled her weapon. Beside her, Landon did the same. Since she had a better sense of smell, her husband let her lead the way, but he stayed close. Ivy's nose led her straight to the back corner of the alley.

She shoved her gun in the holster at her hip. "He climbed the wall. I'll go after him."

"Not without me," Landon said. "I don't have claws, remember?"

"But I do," she reminded him.

Her husband scowled. "I don't like it. This could be a setup."

She'd already considered that. "I know, but my kitty senses aren't tingling. First hint of trouble and I'm off that roof like a shot. I promise."

Landon's jaw flexed. "Okay. But be careful."

"I will. Head around to Jefferson Davis to see if he comes out that side."

Landon kissed her hard on the mouth, then disappeared down the alley.

Ivy extended her claws just enough to get a purchase on the cracks between the bricks, then climbed. She got to the top of the three-story building thirty seconds later. That was more time than the strange smelling shifter had taken to scale the same building. Whoever the guy was, he was a better climber than she was, and faster, too.

His scent was easy to pick up on the roof, mostly because it was so unique. Ivy pulled her SIG and followed it, careful to scan the rooftop as she went.

The trail didn't lead to Jefferson Davis like she thought. Instead, it led her along the rooftop parallel to Crystal Drive. She was forced to cross several low walls and navigate around a couple of HVAC units before she ran out of buildings. She leaned over the edge of the roof

she was on. Below was a cross street between Crystal
Drive and Jefferson Davis. There were hardly any street
lamps, and no stores to speak of. No one would have
seen the guy climb down. He could be five blocks away
by now.

Dammit.

Ivy holstered her gun and slipped down the wall to
the street, landing lightly on the sidewalk in front of a
darkened shop window. She sniffed the air and groaned.
No wonder the mysterious shifter had come this way.
The wind whipping down this street would make picking up a scent trail nearly impossible. The guy was good.
He'd known there was another shifter on his trail.

She'd just pulled out her cell phone to let Landon
know where she was when her kitty alarm went nuts. A
split second later, she felt a prickling sensation along her
back as someone dropped down soundlessly behind her.
Crap. He'd somehow hidden on the wall and waited for
her to climb right past him. What the hell kind of shifter
could camouflage himself so well?

She breathed in, imprinting his strange scent on her
memory. That was when she picked up another scent,
one more familiar. She'd smelled it on the slim woman
from the jungles of Costa Rica, the one who'd led them
to the research compound.

Ivy forced herself to relax, ready to twist and slash
at his face before diving to the side and drawing her
SIG. She didn't know who this guy was, but he'd made
a mistake if he thought he could sneak up on her just
because her back was turned.

But the sudden pressure of something round and hard
pressed into her back stopped her cold.

"Don't move, Ms. Halliwell."

His voice was a slow, sibilant whisper in her ear, and for some strange reason, her body obeyed his command without any conscious thought on her part. She bit back a hiss as the fog cleared and forced her head to start working again. She transferred her weight to her toes, ready to spring sideways.

"Stop that," he ordered in that same eerie whisper, and she froze again. This time, he didn't give her time to gather herself before he continued. "I have no desire to shoot you or your partner."

Was it just her imagination or had the man said *partner* with just a bit too much emphasis?

"Then what are you going to do?" she demanded.

"Warn you."

That cold voice didn't reassure her at all. Many people would consider a bullet in the back a very effective warning.

The man chuckled softly. "I don't have much time. Your partner is racing around to this side of the block as we speak, so I'll be brief. Trust John, or you'll get him killed. And though you don't understand it yet, he's the only thing keeping you and the other shifters alive right now."

Ivy frowned. That didn't come across as the warning she'd expected. It didn't make a hell of a lot of sense, either. She turned her head ever so slightly, trying to get a glimpse of the man holding her at gunpoint.

The pressure against her back increased, and she immediately jerked her head around to face the window again. Down the street, boots pounded the pavement, getting closer. *Landon*. The shifter heard it, too, and turned his head toward the sound, allowing her to see his reflection in the dark glass for the first time. Unfortunately, the street lamp that illuminated the window also wreathed his face in shadows. Her eyes shifted to pick up more light.

He must have sensed her gaze on him because he turned his head slightly to look at her. And in that moment, she saw his face—dark blond hair, angled brows, high cheekbones, an aquiline nose—and his eyes.

Ivy's breath froze. She'd never seen eyes like this on any man—or any shifter. They were a wash of orange and yellow that shown clear, even in the dim reflection of the window. But while the color was shocking enough, the pupils made shivers run up and down her spine. They were cold, black, and partially slitted. Not like her own cat's eyes, but more like a lizard's. It was the freakiest thing she'd ever seen.

She had no idea how long they held eye contact like that, but then the man blinked, and she involuntarily jerked away. Maybe *blinked* wasn't the right word. But what did you call it when an inner set of thin, clear lids closed over the eyes from side to side?

The shifter laughed softly. "Trust John, Ms. Halliwell. Everything depends on him."

Behind her, the air fluttered, then the reflection in the window was gone.

Ivy was still standing there staring up at the roof when Landon ran up to her.

"What happened?" he asked.

She didn't move. Any thought of trying to follow the shifter fled her mind the second she'd seen him scale the wall. He covered two stories in less than five seconds.

She didn't want to think about how easily a man like that could get around a city like this. She and Landon would never even get close to him unless he wanted them to. And that was exactly what had happened. He'd let them follow him, then split them up, letting her move right past him without her ever seeing or smelling him just so he could give her a warning she didn't understand.

"Ivy?" Landon took her arm, gently turning her to face him. "What is it? What did you see?"

"I have no idea," she said.

Kendra hadn't seen or heard from Declan since they'd gotten back two days ago. She'd called, texted, emailed, even gone to his apartment, but no luck. He was avoiding her. If it was any other guy, she would have thought he regretted sleeping with her. But her gut told her there was more to it than that.

He wouldn't be able to avoid her forever. Tonight, everyone was meeting at Ivy and Landon's apartment so the couple could fill them in on the strange shifter they'd run into when they followed John the night before. So far, Clayne and Danica had arrived. So had Tate, Gavin, and Brent. Derek and Angelo would have been there too, but the two Special Forces soldiers were already on their way to Tajikistan with the rest of their team. The only one who hadn't shown up yet was Declan.

Maybe he was just running late.

Or maybe he really was planning on avoiding her forever.

She'd be damned if she'd let him.

She picked up her glass of iced tea and walked over

to where Tate was talking to Clayne by the sliding glass door that led out onto the terrace. They stopped in mid-conversation to greet her with, "Hey."

"Hey," she said. "Sorry to interrupt."

"You weren't. We were just talking shop." Tate took a swig of beer from the bottle in his hand. "What's up?"

She smiled. "Not much. Just wondering where Declan is. I thought he'd be here already."

Tate shared a look with Clayne. "He's not coming."

Her hand tightened on the glass. "Why not? Is he okay?"

Declan had eaten four MREs, then gone into hibernation the minute they'd boarded the plane for the trip home. By the time they'd touched down in DC, his wounds had completely healed. *Oh God. What if he had a relapse or something?*

"He's fine," Tate assured her.

The words should have made her feel better, but instead they only made her stomach clench more. "Then why isn't he here?"

Tate stared down at his beer bottle for what seemed like forever. When he lifted his head to look at her again, there was sympathy in his hazel eyes. "Kendra, Declan is leaving the DCO."

She had to put her hand against the wall to steady herself. It felt like someone had just kicked her in the stomach. "What? Why?"

Tate shook his head. "I don't know. He won't say. I was hoping that you'd be able to tell me. I got the feeling that something happened with you two out there in the jungle."

"Nothing happened." Unless you counted falling in

love. Apparently Declan didn't. "Do you know where he is?"

"At his place," Tate said. "Probably packing."

Kendra's hand started to tremble so much she almost spilled iced tea all over the wool area rug. She set the glass on the mantle above the gas fireplace. "I have to go see him. Tell Ivy and Landon I left."

She didn't wait for either man to reply, but just scooped her purse up from the floor in the entryway where she'd left it, then grabbed her coat from the nearby closet and hurried out of the apartment. Ivy'd already filled her in on the mysterious shifter and his cryptic message anyway, so she wouldn't be missing anything. Except Declan if he left. There already felt like there was a hole in her heart.

Kendra was halfway to the elevator when Ivy's voice stopped her. She turned to see her dark-haired friend hurrying down the hallway, her brow furrowed in concern.

"I saw you leave," Ivy said. "What's wrong?"

Kendra didn't feel like standing there talking when Declan could already be leaving, but Ivy was her best friend. She deserved to know what was going on.

"It's Declan," she said. "He's quitting the DCO."

Ivy's eyes widened. "Are you sure?"

She nodded miserably. "I can't let him go, not after what happened between us in Costa Rica." Tears blurred her vision. "How can he leave when I'm in love with him, dammit?"

"Maybe he doesn't know."

Kendra frowned. "Of course he does. I told him!"

"What did he say?"

She opened her mouth but then winced. "Nothing. He

was sort of unconscious at the time." At Ivy's shocked look, she added, "He was injured and went into hibernation to heal…don't ask. Anyway, I told him I loved him before I left the shelter to lure the hybrids away from him."

Ivy already knew that part of the story, so she didn't have to rehash it, thank God.

"What am I going to do about Declan?" she groaned. "I won't let him leave, even if I have to hold him at gunpoint."

Ivy smiled. "That's one way to handle it, but probably not the best. If Declan is like every other man on the planet, being subtle isn't going to work. Tell him exactly how you feel and exactly what you want."

Her friend made it sound so simple. Kendra squeezed her keys so tightly they dug into her palm. What if the reason he was leaving was because he already knew how she felt, and he didn't feel the same? The thought hurt too much to contemplate, much less articulate.

She swallowed hard. "I'm sorry I can't stay for dinner."

Ivy gave her a hug. "Don't worry about it. Go tell Declan you love him."

Kendra's head spun as she drove to Declan's apartment. She replayed everything that had happened in Costa Rica. Everything had seemed so perfect in the cave. Where had it gone wrong?

She was still trying to figure it out when she rang his doorbell thirty minutes later. There was no answer, just like the other two times she'd stopped by.

"I know you're in there, Declan, and I'm not leaving until you open this door and talk to me," she called. "I'll just keep ringing the bell until your neighbors call the cops. And when they come, I'll tell them you haven't been at work for days and that I think you may be hurt. I'll convince them to kick in your door. You know I can do that."

No answer.

Kendra rang the bell again, holding it down longer this time. When that didn't get the response she was looking for, she banged on the door with her fist.

Still no answer.

She muttered a curse. If he thought she was going to let him walk away that easily, then he didn't know her very well. She dug in her purse for her iPhone, ready to go through with her threat and call the police when the door suddenly jerked open.

Declan stood there barefoot, wearing a pair of low-slung jeans and nothing else. His hair was damp and he had the perfect amount of stubble on his jaw. He looked good enough to eat. The gashes that had covered his chest were so faint she could barely see them unless she really looked. And gazing at all that muscle right now was way too distracting. It was all she could do not to reach out and run her hands over him.

"I was in the shower," he said.

"Uh-huh." Considering he was half-dressed and his hair was slightly wet, he probably wasn't lying about that. But she seriously doubted he had been in the shower the other times she'd stopped by. She looked pointedly at the muscular arm he had braced on the doorjamb blocking her way, then back at him. "Can I come in?"

Declan was still for so long that Kendra actually considered whether she could duck under his arm before he could stop her. But then he stepped back. That was a relief. For a minute there she had visions of him picking her up and putting her outside like Fred always did with the saber-toothed cat on *The Flintstones*. There wasn't much she could have done except followed Fred's example and pounded on the door…again.

She looked around. While Declan's place definitely didn't have a woman's touch, it wasn't the quintessential bachelor pad, either. The hardwood floor and neutral palette with its touches of blues and greens gave the place an outdoorsy feel that fit him.

"What do you want, Kendra?"

She turned to see him standing in the entryway, regarding her with his arms crossed over his chest. The cool, detached tone in his voice made tears spring to her eyes. But she kept it together.

"We need to talk," she said.

"About what?"

What the hell did he think they needed to talk about? "About why you're leaving the DCO."

Declan scowled and muttered something under his breath. "Tate told you."

"He shouldn't have had to. I should have heard it from you, Declan." She stomped across the room to stand in front of him. "I'm here now, so go ahead. Tell me why you suddenly decided to leave."

He brushed past her. "It's time for a change."

She'd been working at the DCO long enough to know a lie when she heard it. She took a breath, keeping her gaze fixed on the door as she willed herself to stay calm. Getting into a shouting match with Declan wouldn't do anything but make them both mad. But even if what he said wasn't true, it was still hard to take. She'd risked her life to keep him safe in that damn jungle. She closed her eyes and counted to ten, then turned to face him.

"You were supposed to take me out to dinner," she reminded him.

"I only said that so you'd eat that stupid power bar," he growled.

She didn't believe that. "Is that why you made love to me, too?"

He looked at her sharply. "You know it wasn't."

"Then how can you just leave?" she demanded, her voice rising. "If this is about Derek kissing me, it was nothing. He and I danced a few times at Ivy and Landon's wedding…"

His eyes went wide.

Oh crap.

"You can't tell anyone Ivy and Landon are married, Declan."

"You know me better than that."

"I thought I did, but now I'm not so sure." She walked over to stand in front of him. "Declan, why are you leaving? I thought what we shared in Costa Rica meant as much to you as it did to me."

She thought for a moment that she'd finally broken through the wall he'd rebuilt around himself, but then he shook his head.

"I'm sorry, Kendra," he said softly. "It's just better this way."

She stifled a scream. Better? How could leaving her make anything better? She opened her mouth to ask him that very question, but then she remembered Ivy's advice.

Tell him exactly how you feel and exactly what you want.

She ran her hand through her hair. "Declan, I don't understand any of this, and if you really want to walk out on the DCO—and me—there isn't much I can do to stop you, but I'm going to have my say before you go."

"Kendra—"

"Dammit, Declan, I love you!" So much for taking the calm approach. "I've loved you since that morning I woke up on your chest in that cave. And I don't want you to leave."

She wasn't sure what she expected him to say or do after a proclamation like that, but a reaction of some kind would have been nice. Instead, he just stood there, looking sad and forlorn. She steeled herself. Here it came, the part she'd feared, when he told her he didn't feel the same.

"I'm sure you think you do, but it doesn't matter," he said quietly.

Kendra didn't know which part of that sentence was more condescending—the part where he decided she only thought she loved him, or the part where he decided that laying her heart on the floor at his feet didn't matter to him.

She moved closer until she was only inches from that big, perfect, muscular chest of his. Then she poked him with a finger.

"Don't you dare patronize me," she shouted. "If I say I love you, then I love you. I've never said those words to another man in my life, and I won't stand here and let you throw it back in my face. And as for it not mattering, well, it sure as hell matters to me!"

His lips quirked ever so slightly, but he didn't smile. Which was a good thing. If he started laughing at her, she'd smack him.

"I didn't mean to sound patronizing, Kendra. I really didn't," he said. "I know that you feel what you feel. All I'm trying to say is that in our case, being in love isn't enough."

Okay, that was…confusing. "What's that supposed to mean?"

He didn't answer.

"Declan, please talk to me," she begged.

He gently brushed her hair back, allowing his hand to linger there for just a moment before letting it fall to his side with a sigh. "I'm saying that you don't have to pretend for me. I saw the expression on your face when I showed up in the hybrid camp. I saw the fear and panic plain as day. It wasn't the first time I've seen that look on a woman's face, but it sure as hell will be the last, I promise you that."

What did he mean about her pretending? And what did her reaction to seeing him in the hybrid camp have to do with any of this? If she remembered correctly, she'd been overwhelmed by a dozen different emotions at that time. And yes, fear and panic had definitely been among them.

That's when it hit her. This had nothing to do with her or how she'd looked at him that day. The whole drive over here she'd been trying to figure out what she'd done wrong. Trying to imagine what she could have said that was so bad it made Declan feel he had to leave the DCO to avoid being around her. But the one thing she'd never imagined was that Declan was leaving because he thought she was scared of him. He thought his worst nightmare was happening all over again, only this time it was her instead of Marissa, and this time he decided to be the one who ran. Crap, why the heck hadn't he just told her all this?

She put her hands on her hips and tipped her head back to look at him. "Declan MacBride, if there's one thing I thought you would have already learned about me, it's that I'm nothing like your ex-fiancée."

His brows furrowed. "This isn't about her."

"It's not? It sure seems like it is to me." She snorted. "You go all shifter trying to protect a woman you care for, like Marissa. Then you see something that looks like fear and panic in my eyes, and decide all on your own that I suddenly don't want to have anything to do with you and your fangs and your claws — like Marissa."

She didn't realize that she was poking him in the chest with her finger again until he caught her hand in his to make her stop. She pulled away from him angrily.

"But this time, instead of waiting for the woman to bail on you, you decide to bail first. I bet you thought it'd be less painful for you that way, huh? Well, it's not going to happen, Declan. I'm not going to let you walk out on us because you're worried I can't handle your inner bear."

Declan arched a brow. "Are you honestly going to stand there and tell me that you weren't freaked out when you saw me? That you weren't absolutely horrified?"

She closed her eyes and counted again. She wanted to scream. He could be so dense! When she got to ten, she opened her eyes and leveled her gaze at him.

"Was I freaked out when I saw you? Hell, yes. Was I horrified? Definitely. But was it because I was scared of you? No." She took his hands in both of hers. "I was scared because I'd left you in that shelter the night before to save your life. And there you were, practically hand-delivering yourself to the very people I was trying to protect you from, the ones who wanted to capture you and experiment on you. What you saw on my face was pure and total fear. I was terrified they'd grab you and torture you like they'd done to Ivy. Marcus practically admitted to me that was what he planned to do if he ever got his hands on you."

Declan's hands tightened around hers. "I thought that was why you left me alone in the shelter—to lure the hybrids away."

Tears welled in her eyes. This time she didn't blink them back. "I would rather have died than let them get their hands on you."

He reached up and caught the tear rolling down her cheek with his thumb, tenderly brushing it away. "When I woke up and realized you were gone, I…I sort of went nuts. I was so scared when I couldn't find your trail. That's when I finally completely shifted."

She stepped closer and rested her palm on the part of his pecs she'd poked earlier. "I'm sorry I frightened you like that. But I'd do it again if that's what it took to keep you safe."

He cupped her cheek. "There isn't anything I wouldn't do to keep you safe, too."

"Including leaving the DCO because you thought it was best for me?" she asked.

He nodded. "I couldn't understand why someone like

you would want to stay with someone like me. Not after seeing me like that."

She took his big hands in hers again, holding on to them tightly. "Someone like me would want to stay with someone like you because I love you. You were willing to pull down all the walls you'd built around yourself and be the shifter you were always meant to be to save me. That's the kind of someone you are to me, and it's all that matters. I love you. Is that so hard to believe?"

He lifted their joined hands to his lips and kissed her fingers. When he raised his head again, there were tears in his eyes. "Yes, it is hard to believe. But I'm glad. Because I love you, too."

Then his mouth closed over hers and he was kissing her so hard she could barely breathe. But she didn't complain. She kissed him back just as fiercely. She'd missed him.

"So, we're good, right?" she asked when he lifted his head. "You're not going to quit the DCO?"

He grinned. "No, I'm not going to quit."

"Good."

She snuggled against him, but he caught her chin and tipped her head back. "Now I have a question for you."

"What?"

"You and Derek?"

The question had come from so far out in left field that it took her a moment to get her thoughts together. Then she realized she better not hesitate too long because if she didn't know better, she'd swear Declan looked jealous. Which was cute but also possibly dangerous. She'd just pulled their relationship back from the brink, she didn't want it going south again because Declan thought she had a thing for another guy.

"Derek and I met when he and the rest of Landon's old Special Forces team went to Washington to help rescue Ivy. Like I said, we danced a few times at Ivy and Landon's wedding. That's all. The moment he kissed me, I immediately shut him down and let him know I'm not available." She made a face. "Something you would have known if you'd hung around a few minutes longer."

Declan chuckled, then shook his head. "I still can't believe it."

"Believe what?" she asked.

"That Ivy and Landon are married."

She groaned. Oh, *that*. "I was serious before. This is more than top secret. If you leak a word of this, Dick will split them up and—"

"I'm not going to say anything," Declan promised. "Besides, I've known that Ivy and Landon were more than partners for a while." He grinned down at her. "You know, you have a lot of secrets. At some point real soon, you're going to tell me all of them."

She'd gladly tell him anything and everything. Well, everything except the matchmaking software she came up with. And no way was she typing her name in there, either. She didn't need some computer to tell her that Declan was her soul mate.

"I will," she told him. "At least as much of it as I can tell you without betraying confidences. But I'll tell you everything I can, as long as you promise you're going to stick around to hear all of it."

"I'll be here." He cupped her face, his thumb

brushing her cheek. "Although, if we're going on missions together, we're going to have to learn to sneak around like Ivy and Landon."

She laughed. "We don't have to worry about that. I don't think I'll be going on any missions anytime soon. I've decided I like being an office drone a lot more than I thought."

Declan grinned. "Good. Because I want my ring on your finger where everyone can see it. Including Derek."

Her breath caught. "Ring? As in wedding ring?"

"Yeah." He wrapped his arms around her, pulling her close. "If you don't mind being married to a bear."

Kendra laughed. "I don't mind at all."

"I was hoping you'd say that." He gazed down at her, his blue eyes turning that same beautiful rose color they had in the cave. "Then what do you say we go into the bedroom and celebrate?"

She went up on tiptoe to kiss him long and lingeringly on the mouth. "I say, lead the way."

Declan did better than that. He swung her up in his arms and carried her there. She caught a glimpse of a big four-poster bed and a huge built-in bookcase as he set her down on her feet, but she was too focused on him to pay much attention to the decor. He undressed her slowly, kissing each and every part of her body as he exposed it, leaving her quivering and weak-kneed by the time he was done. She clutched his shoulders, afraid she'd fall if she didn't hold onto something, but Declan was already urging her back on the bed. She lay on the pillows, watching as he unbuttoned his jeans and pushed them down. Then he was on top of her, bracing his weight on his forearms as he covered her mouth with his.

Kendra wrapped her arms around him. Had it only been a few days ago that they'd made love like this in the cave in Costa Rica? It seemed like years.

She cooed as her trailed scorching kisses along her jaw and down her neck, shivering when his teeth scraped against her skin. No, not teeth, *fangs*.

She grabbed his head, gently urging him to look at her. He gazed down at her in confusion, his eyes glowing like the setting sun.

"What is it?" he asked.

"I just wanted to see your face," she said softly. "Your fangs are out."

His eyes widened, and she caught the panic in them before he quickly looked away. She cupped his cheek, gently bringing his face back to her. He didn't meet her gaze.

"Declan, look at me," she entreated. "Please."

He did, slowly. His eyes were almost back to their natural color, and his fangs had retracted nearly all the way. She couldn't see much more than the tips peeking out. Knowing he was hiding that part of himself made her want to cry all over again.

"Declan, when I say love you, I mean *all* of you, including your shifter half," she said. "You never have to be afraid to show me that side of yourself, especially in the bedroom. Okay?"

He started to say something, but then stopped and swallowed hard. She waited for him to try again, but instead he kissed her so hard she could barely think much less remember what they'd been talking about. When he finally lifted his head, she saw that he'd unleashed his inner bear again.

"Thank you." She smiled up at him. "Now I want you to stay just like that while you make love to me."

He did, not shifting back until he made her scream with pleasure and they were both lying back on the pillows gasping for breath. Kendra knew because she'd been gazing into his eyes when they both came.

"You're going to wear me out," he said huskily.

She smiled as she snuggled up to him. "Shifters don't get worn out."

"Maybe not, but they do get hungry." He lightly ran his fingers up and down her arm. "And I'm a bear, so I get hungrier than most."

"Then maybe you should make good on your promise and take me to P.F. Chang's."

"Sounds good to me," he said. "Though as hungry as I am, I might have to order one of everything on the menu."

She laughed. "They have a very large menu."

Declan rolled her over with a sexy growl, settling himself between her legs again. "I have a very big appetite."

Yeah, she was learning that about him. Kendra's reply was muffled against his mouth as he kissed her. *Mmm*, maybe dinner could wait a little longer.

Epilogue

Somewhere in Tajikistan

MINKA PAJARI WATCHED WARILY FROM HER SEAT ON the cold stone floor as the two guards talked softly among themselves outside her cell in a language she couldn't understand. Normally, that wouldn't be enough to make her uneasy. But the doctors who'd turned her into the monster she was had been away for a few days, and something told her those vicious thugs were coming up with a new way to torment her. They'd always been mean to her, throwing rocks and poking her with sticks, putting vile things in her food and water bowls, but things had gotten worse after she'd killed their friend.

She hadn't wanted to do it, and in some ways, she hadn't. It had been the animal inside her defending itself that had caught the rock the man had thrown at her and sent it whistling back to hit him in the head. But the other men didn't care about that. Their friend was dead and they wanted to make her suffer.

Today was different, though. She didn't know whether it was the rapid beating of their hearts or the sudden acrid, bitter smell of their sweat that made her nose wrinkle in disgust. Either way, she knew they were growing tense with the anticipation of violence and that they meant to hurt her badly this time. Without the doctors here to stop them, they might very well kill her.

Not that she cared very much whether they killed her or not. Death might be a blessing. But she feared the pain the men would inflict on her before they ended her life. Because when they hurt her like that, the animal inside her came out.

Even though she'd come to accept some aspects of the animal the doctors had put into her blood—the hearing that allowed her to know when the men were about to strike, the sense of smell that warned her when the doctors were coming back to continue their tests, the eyesight that let her see the rats and bugs near her in the darkest part of night—overall, she still hated what she'd become.

The rage inside her was a living thing, coming out whenever it wished, no matter how hard she tried to control it. Even now, the animal purred in the back of her mind, wanting the men to come close, so she could tear them to shreds for everything they had done to her.

Minka closed her eyes and tried to find a calm place, tried to will the animal to go back to sleep. She had learned the technique from the female American soldiers when she worked as a translator. Yoga, they called it.

But then the metal door of her cell smacked against the wall. She opened her eyes just in time to see the two men burst into the room with their newest torture devices—long black sticks that crackled and sizzled on one end like the electric wires that fell to the ground during storms in her small hometown.

She remembered what those sticks felt like from the last time they'd tormented her with them, and so did the animal. It came out with a hiss and she sprang to her feet, long claws slashing at the sticks in an attempt to keep them away.

But the animal's fast reflexes couldn't overcome the advantage Minka had given the men when she'd closed her eyes and tried to shut out the monster. Even as she knocked one stick away, the other found its target, thumping into her stomach and sending her whole body into spasms on the ground. She yowled, trying to drag herself away from them. But there was nowhere to go. They backed her into a corner, jabbing her with the things until all she could do was lie there in a twitching, sobbing heap.

Even then the men didn't stop. They only laughed and prodded her until her vision went black at the edges. She was right. They were going to kill her.

Minka didn't know she was alive until she came to later. She was tied to the bars of her cell, thick rope around each wrist keeping her upright. The metal dug into her breasts, and she tried to pull free but couldn't. Her legs, on the other hand, weren't bound at all. She realized suddenly that her left ankle felt lighter than it had in a very long time. She looked down and saw that the men had removed the heavy metal manacle that had kept her chained to the floor every day and night since she'd been there. Why had they done that?

Dread crept into her, making her shiver. She cocked her head to the side, listening, and heard movement behind her. She twisted her head to look over her shoulder and saw her two captors staring at her with a look she hadn't seen on their faces before. Her heart began to pound. She'd seen that look on other men before, men who hurt women and took what they wanted from them.

Her captors grinned at her and unbuckled their belts.

That was when Minka knew the evil men had something more horrible in mind for her. They had tied her to these bars so they could do anything to her that they wished without her getting her claws on them.

Tears sprang to her eyes and though she tried to blink them away, more took their place. She'd been ready to die, but while she was sure they would kill her when they were done with her, she wasn't ready to let them take her this way. It was more shame than she could accept. She refused to submit to it, and the animal inside her refused as well.

Minka threw her bare feet up and onto the bars right below where her wrists were tied. She planted them firmly, then yanked with every fiber of her being. Either the ropes would break or her arms would come off, she didn't care which.

She howled with all the rage inside her. The ropes snapped and then she fell free of the bars. She didn't even know if she still had hands, much less arms until she twisted in the air and landed firmly on all fours. She jerked her head up, flinging her long hair over her shoulder. The man closest to her was staring at her in confusion, his mouth hanging open. He wasn't laughing now.

The second guard swore and came at her with his crackling stick.

Without the metal manacle around her ankle, she was freer to move. She leaped sideways, avoiding the stick the man thrust at her, and slashed with her claws, finding flesh.

The man dropped the stick with a shout that made the animal inside her rejoice. She dropped onto all fours

again to lash out and ripped out his hamstrings so he
couldn't get away. But there was still her other captor
to contend with.

Minka turned around. The second man was already
out the door and halfway down the hall. She caught up
to him before he got more than ten feet and leaped on his
back, crushing him to the ground. She dug her claws into
his back and sank her teeth into the junction of muscle at
his neck and shoulder.

The man cried out and struggled, but she pressed all
her weight into her claws, digging them in even deeper.
His pulse throbbed under her teeth. One savage jerk
could finish this man forever.

But the animal hesitated, almost as if it was asking
her for permission to continue.

Minka faltered. These men had tormented and tortured
her for a very long time. They had wanted to do things
to her that no man should ever do to a woman. They
deserved to die. But for reasons she couldn't explain, she
couldn't give the animal the approval it sought. With a
growl, she retracted her claws and her fangs.

She glanced over her shoulder at the man still in the
cell. He was curled into a ball on the floor, moaning.

Minka hit the door running and didn't stop. Around
her, the night was completely dark, or it would have
been if not for the animal allowing her to see through its
eyes. She tried to get her bearings, but nothing looked
familiar. There was no mistaking the mountainous terrain of her homeland, though. She was still in Tajikistan.

She was barefoot, her shirt was torn, her skirt was
ragged, and she had no food or water. But she was
going home.

Tears of joy filled her eyes and overflowed onto her cheeks. After being a prisoner for so long, she was finally going home.

Tajikistan

ANGELO RIOS GLANCED AT HIS WATCH. THE TEAM
needed to get moving or it'd take all day to get back
to camp. Their A-team had been doing a recon sweep
back and forth through the rugged terrain of southern
Tajikistan when they heard about a small town near the
mountain pass that had been hit hard by a recent storm.
Repairing buildings damaged by high winds and torren-
tial rain wasn't the kind of work Special Forces usually
did, but Angelo and the new lieutenant, Brad Watson,
figured it'd be an easy way to gain a little goodwill with
the locals, which definitely *was* an SF mission.

He squeezed the last of the cheese onto a cracker
from his MRE—meal-ready-to-eat—and shoved it in his
mouth, then stuffed the empty wrapper into his rucksack
and swung the pack over his shoulder. The rest of the
team got the message and did the same.

"So, tell me this," Derek Mickens said as he tightened
the straps on his own ruck. "What does that big bear
shifter have that I don't?"

Angelo chuckled. The guys had been ribbing Derek
ever since they'd heard his crush Kendra Carlsen—now
MacBride—was having twins with her husband Declan.

Angelo was about to point out that the DCO's resident
bear shifter had seventy-five pounds of muscle and six
inches on Derek, not to mention a face that didn't scare
small children, when screams of terror from the far end
of the village they'd just helped rebuild silenced the
words in his mouth.

Angelo had his M4 in his hands and was running toward
the sound even as the rest of the guys spread out behind
him, checking for incoming threats. He rounded the corner
of a dilapidated building and was heading down a dirt road
lined with more crumbling buildings when a man covered
in blood ran toward him. Two more men followed, fear
clear in their eyes and blood staining their clothes.

At first Angelo thought it was an IED—an impro-
vised explosive device—but that didn't make sense. He
hadn't heard an explosion. He slowed down anyway,
worried he was leading the team into an ambush.

One of the men pointed behind him, shouting something in Tajik. Angelo's grasp of the language was pretty
good, but the man was speaking way too fast for him to
make out what he was saying. Then he figured it out.

Monster.

He opened his mouth to ask where the "monster"
was, but the man was already halfway down the road.
Angelo picked up the pace only to skid to a stop in front
of a mud-covered shack a few moments later. He knew
he was in the right place because there was a guy who
looked like he'd been sliced up by Freddy Krueger on
the ground in front of it.

Angelo got a sinking feeling in his gut. He'd seen
damage like this before.

He jumped over the dead guy and was through the

door before he even thought about what he was doing.
Thinking only slowed you down in situations like
this anyway.

Angelo raised his M4, ready to pop the first threatening thing he saw. If he was right about what had attacked
those men, it would take multiple shots to kill the thing.

But what he found stopped him cold in his tracks.
Derek and Lieutenant Watson skidded to a stop right
behind him.

There wasn't a square foot of wall space in the one-
room shack that wasn't splattered with blood, and in the
middle of it stood a pretty, dark-haired woman, gazing
down at two dead men at her feet. Her shirt was on the
floor beside them, one of her bra straps was torn, and
her skirt was ripped. Her feet were bare and covered in
dirt, and he thought there were tears on her cheeks, but
he couldn't be sure since her long, dark hair hung down
around her face almost to her waist.

Angelo felt a rage build inside him like nothing he'd
ever felt before, and he was torn between staying where
he was and going after the rest of the men who'd tried
to rape her and killing them, too.

He glanced at her hands, hoping to find a knife there
and praying he was wrong about what she was. But
she didn't have any weapons. Unless you counted the
wickedly sharp claws on each slender finger. And given
the amount of blood in the room, those hands certainly
qualified as weapons.

As if just realizing he was there, the woman lifted
her head to look at him with glowing red eyes. She
growled, baring her teeth and exposing some seriously
long canines.

How the hell had a hybrid turned up in Tajikistan? More importantly, what the hell was he going to do with her?

"What the fuck is that thing?" the lieutenant asked hoarsely even as he raised his carbine and sighted in on the woman's chest.

The woman growled again, louder this time, and crouched down on all fours, like she was getting ready to pounce on them.

Shit. Things were about to get ugly.

But instead of leaping at them, her eyes darted around, like she was looking for a way past them. Unfortunately, they were blocking her access to the doors and the windows, and she knew it. For some reason he couldn't explain, Angelo suddenly didn't see a hybrid monster like those he'd fought in Washington State and down in Costa Rica. He saw a woman who was scared as hell.

"Derek, get everyone outside and away from the building," Angelo ordered softly, never taking his eyes off the woman. "We're freaking her out."

"Freaking her out." Watson snorted. "Are you kidding me? She's the one freaking me out."

"Outside, LT," Angelo ordered again, more firmly this time. "Trust me on this one."

He knew the lieutenant wanted answers, but right now, he didn't have time to give him any. Behind him, Derek was herding the officer toward the door.

"LT, remember when we told you that you'd be seeing some weird shit in the field that they never mentioned in school?" Derek asked. "Well, that weird shit just started. But trust Angelo. He knows what he's doing. He's dealt with these things before."

Their voices faded as they moved outside.

The woman's eyes followed Derek and Watson until they disappeared from sight, then slid to Angelo. He slowly lowered his weapon and carefully set it on the floor. Then he raised his hands and spoke softly in Tajik.

"It's okay. You're safe now. No one is going to hurt you."

The red glow in her eyes flickered, then began to fade. Angelo let out the breath he'd been holding. Maybe he'd be able to get out of this situation without killing her. He couldn't explain why that mattered to him all of a sudden. She was a hybrid and clearly out of control. Many might consider killing her to be a mercy, and the only sure way to keep her from killing again.

But from what he'd seen, the woman had a pretty good reason to attack those men. And more importantly, Angelo knew for a fact that not every hybrid was beyond reach. Tanner Howland from the Department of Covert Operations was one of those. Not only had the former Army Ranger learned how to control the rages that defined his kind, he'd learned to harness that rage to save a lot of people down in Costa Rica several months back. Angelo was pretty sure he wouldn't be alive if it weren't for that one particular hybrid. If Tanner could do it, who was he to say that this woman in front of him couldn't get herself under control, too? She certainly seemed to be trying.

Angelo kept up his calm chatter, reassuring the woman that she was safe, and soon enough, her eyes turned to a normal, beautiful brown. There was still some anger there, but there was also confusion, maybe even hope.

Raised voices echoed outside, drowning out Angelo's soft words. The villagers had worked up their courage and come looking for blood. The woman's head snapped in that direction, and like a light switch being flipped, the veil of calmness that had descended on the female hybrid disappeared.

She tensed, and he watched her face as anger warred with what he could only describe as frustration mixed with honest-to-goodness fear. As each of those emotions appeared, her eyes changed from red to green to brown, over and over in a dizzying display like nothing he'd ever seen before.

But then, just as it seemed like she might have a chance, the internal struggle was over and the woman leaped at him.

Every instinct in Angelo's body screamed at him to lunge for his weapon, or at the very least pull out his knife. But he ignored his instincts and instead set his feet for impact, blocking her slashing claws with his forearm, then ducking down and tackling her. It wasn't the nicest way to treat a woman, but considering the fact that she was trying to kill him, he decided she'd just have to forgive him.

He twisted at the last second, letting his shoulder take the impact. He'd planned to immediately roll his weight onto her, hoping to keep her from getting away by pinning her to the floor like a wrestler, but the hybrid didn't give him a chance. She spun in his grasp, trying to break his hold on her. He wrapped his arms around her, doing his best to trap her clawed hands safely against her breasts as he pulled her back down. She twisted in his arms again, trying to sink her teeth into his shoulder.

He hugged her tightly to his chest, whispering over and over that it would be okay, that she was safe, that no one would hurt her.

When she buried her face in his neck, he just about freaked, sure she was going to tear out his throat. He resisted the urge to shove her away and go for his gun, instead continuing to talk to her. Unbelievably, she didn't bite him. She kept struggling to free herself, though. But after a few moments, she went still, all the fight gone.

Angelo glanced down at her. Her cheek was resting against his chest, her eyes closed, and her fingers curled into the front of his uniform. He wasn't sure if she was asleep or had simply passed out from exhaustion. Either way, her breathing was rhythmic and even. The sight of her made his heart ache, and he gently brushed her hair back from her face. This close, he was finally able to see past all the dirt and blood. While he'd thought she was pretty when he first saw her, now he realized that she was absolutely beautiful—and vulnerable looking as all hell.

"Damn, Tex-Mex," Derek said from the doorway. "You're good with the ladies when you want to be."

Angelo didn't laugh. "Get on the satellite phone and call Landon. If you can't get him, try Ivy or Clayne. Tell them where we are and that we've stumbled on a hybrid. We need a priority airlift to get her out of here. And whatever you do, don't let LT get on the line to the battalion."

COMING SPRING 2016

WOLF TROUBLE

XANDER HAD TO PICK HIS JAW UP OFF THE FLOOR OF
the training room when Gage introduced the newest
member of the SWAT team. He didn't know what
to expect, but it sure as hell wasn't Officer Khaki
Blake. Tall, with an athletic build and just enough
curves to fill out the SWAT T-shirt, she had the biggest brown eyes and softest looking lips he'd ever
seen. She had her dark hair pulled back in a bun, so
he couldn't tell how long it was, but he'd bet money
it fell past her shoulders. She smelled way too good to
be believed, too—like a slice of frosted spice cake in
a uniform.

Shit. He was practically panting. If he didn't get a
grip soon, he was going to start frigging drooling.

He gave the other guys a covert glance to see how
they were dealing with her scent and was stunned to see
that none of them seemed to be reacting at all. Why not?
His nose wasn't that much better than theirs. He knew
for a fact that several of the other guys—Cooper and
Brooks specifically—could smell a hell of a lot better
than he could.

Maybe everyone was so mesmerized by finally

getting to see a female version of their kind that the rest of their senses had stopped working.

Gage had left it up to Xander to fill the Pack in on what had gone down at the meeting with Deputy Chief Mason while he'd headed home to pack for his trip to Washington State. While the guys had been pissed that the top brass was playing politics with the team, they'd been intrigued at the idea of adding a female werewolf to the Pack.

They'd bombarded him with dozens of questions, none of which he could answer. Was she as fast and strong as they were, or did her abilities manifest themselves in completely different ways? Would she be as aggressive as they were and able to handle herself in a fight? Were there more like her out there, or was she the only one?

Not all the questions were so general. Brooks wondered what she would look like, Max wanted to know if she would smell like them or more feminine, and Becker... Well, Becker just wanted to know if she liked to wear yoga pants. God, that kid had an obsession with those things.

Xander had told them the only truth he knew—that no one outside of Gage knew a damn thing about female werewolves. And Xander wasn't so sure how much their commander knew, either.

While Xander had been lost in thought, Gage turned the floor over to Khaki, who was currently explaining how much she appreciated the opportunity to be in SWAT.

"I know I won't be handed anything, but I look forward to proving to every one of you that I belong in the Pack and on the team." She spoke in a light, lilting voice that nevertheless easily filled the large classroom. Xander could definitely pick up the Midwest accent, mixed with a little West Coast flavor. "I'm not asking for anything from you, but a chance to do just that."

Xander surveyed the room again, trying to read expressions and body language. Some of the younger guys like Becker, Cooper, Max, and Remy seemed ready to accept her. And while the rest of the team was projecting a cautious wait-and-see attitude, no one appeared to be flat-out against her yet.

That was a relief. From what Gage had told him about Khaki, she seemed like a good cop. But getting accepted into the Pack was an uphill battle for everyone new to it. Just ask Max and Becker—the two most recent additions to the team. Being a woman was going to make it even harder. It would be damn near impossible if some of the guys were already dead set against the entire concept of a female on the team before she even started.

Khaki's scent wafted across the room to tease his nose again, more insistently this time. Xander took a deep breath through his mouth, hoping to clear his head. It seemed to work—until she and Gage walked over to him.

Xander pushed away from the desk he was leaning against to stand up straighter. This close, he could see that her eyes weren't merely brown. They had little flecks of gold in them, too. He had no doubt she'd look even more amazing when she shifted and her eyes turned completely gold.

"I'm giving Officer Blake the afternoon off to go apartment hunting, so you won't be able to start training right away," Gage said. "But I wanted to make sure she got to meet her squad leader before she took off."

Xander was so busy figuring out how to breathe without overdosing on her scent that it took a minute for Gage's words to register. When they finally did, he just about had to lean back on the desk again to keep from falling over. He'd just assumed Khaki would be assigned to Mike's squad. Which was stupid, he realized. Xander had one less team member than Mike, so now they'd be even. But Mike was more patient than Xander, and far less brusque. Or maybe it only seemed that way because Mike thought before he spoke, whereas Xander tended to blurt out the first thing that came to mind. Regardless, he wasn't the best person to train Khaki.

Even if he was, he couldn't. She smelled too damn irresistible. He'd never be able to concentrate for more than a minute at a time, much less be objective about anything.

Khaki smiled and held out her hand. Xander shook it, trying to ignore how smooth and warm her skin felt in his rough mitt.

"Sergeant Dixon told me a lot about you, Corporal," she said. "I'm looking forward to learning from you."

Xander returned her smile, unable to help himself. "Welcome to the team."

Thank God the rest of his squad came over or he might have stood there gazing into her eyes for the rest of the day. He released her hand and stepped back as Max, Hale, Becker, Cooper, Alex, and Trevor crowded around Khaki, asking her where she was from and how long she'd been a werewolf. That was when reality kicked back in and reminded him that the woman he'd just spent the past fifteen minutes mentally undressing was going to be on his squad, and that he was going to be her supervisor.

Shit, he was in so much trouble.

COMING AUGUST 2015

Acknowledgments

I hope you enjoyed reading *Her Wild Hero*! After meeting Kendra and Declan in *Her Perfect Mate* (Book One in the X-Ops series), I knew they were going to end up together. Which was why it was so hard to keep it a secret when readers asked which guy the DCO's resident Jill-of-all-trades was going to fall for. But Kendra and Declan's story is just beginning. There are some fun surprises in store for them throughout the series! You'll also get to hang out with all your other favorite characters, including Ivy and Landon, Danica and Clayne, and John and Cree, as well as some others you haven't met yet.

You probably noticed that we spent a lot of time with Angelo in *Her Wild Hero*. That's because his book is next in the series. I can't wait for him to get his happily ever after!

Oh, and I can't forget about Mickens! You'll be seeing him again, too!

This whole series would not be possible without some very incredible people. In addition to another big thank you to my hubby for all his help with the action scenes and military and tactical jargon; thanks to my agent, Bob Mecoy, for believing in me and encouraging me and being there when I need to talk; my editor and go-to person at Sourcebooks, Cat Clyne (who loves this series as much as I do and is always a phone call, text, or email away whenever I need something); and all the other amazing people at Sourcebooks, including my fantastic publicist Amelia, and their crazy-talented art department. The covers they make for me are seriously drool-worthy!

Because I could never leave out my readers, a huge thank you to everyone who has read my books and Snoopy Danced right along with me with every new release. That includes the fantastic girls on my Street Team, as well my assistant, Janet. You rock!

I also want to give a big thank you to the men, women, and working dogs serving in our military, as well as their families.

And a very special shout-out to our favorite restaurant, P.F. Chang's, where hubby and I bat ideas back and forth about storylines and come up with all of our best ideas!

Hope you enjoy the next book in the X-Ops series, coming soon from Sourcebooks, and look forward to reading the rest of the series as much as I look forward to sharing it with you.

And if you love a man in uniform as much as I do, make sure you check out my other action-packed paranormal romantic suspense series from Sourcebooks called SWAT (Special Wolf Alpha Team)!

Happy reading!

About the Author

Paige Tyler is the *New York Times* and *USA Today* bestselling author of sexy, romantic fiction. She and her very own military hero (also known as her husband) live on the beautiful Florida coast with their adorable fur baby (also known as their dog). Paige graduated with a degree in education but decided to pursue her passion and write books about hunky alpha males and the kick-butt heroines who fall in love with them. Visit www.paigetylertheauthor.com.

She's also on Facebook, Twitter, Tumblr, Google+, Instagram, and Pinterest.

Her Perfect Mate

X–Ops
by Paige Tyler
New York Times and *USA Today* bestselling author

~~~

He's a high-octane Special Ops pro

When Special Forces Captain Landon Donovan is pulled from an op in Afghanistan, he is surprised to discover he's been hand-picked for a special assignment with the Department of Covert Operations (DCO), a secret division he's never heard of. Terrorists are kidnapping biologists and he and his partner have to stop them. But his new partner is a beautiful, sexy woman who looks like she couldn't hurt a fly—never mind take down a terrorist.

She's not your average Covert Operative

Ivy Halliwell is no kitten. She's a feline shifter, and more dangerous than she looks. She's worked with a string of hotheaded military guys who've underestimated her special skills in the past. But when she's partnered with Special Agent Donovan, a man sexy enough to make any girl purr, things begin to heat up…

~~~

Praise for *Her Perfect Mate*:

"A wild, hot, and sexy ride from beginning to end!"
—Terry Spear, *USA Today* bestselling author

For more Paige Tyler, visit:

www.sourcebooks.com

Her Lone Wolf

X-Ops

by Paige Tyler

New York Times and *USA Today* bestselling author

Leaving him was impossible...

It took everything she had for FBI Special Agent Danica Beckett to walk away from the man she loved. But if she wants to save his life, she has to keep her distance. Now, with a killer on the loose and the stakes higher than ever, the Department of Covert Ops is forcing these former lovers into an uneasy alliance...whether they like it or not.

Seeing her again is even worse

The last thing Clayne Buchanan wants is to be shackled to the woman who broke his heart. She gets under his skin in a way no one ever has and makes him want things he has no right to anymore. All he has to do is suffer through this case and he can be free of her for good. But when Clayne finds out why Danica left in the first place, everything he's tried to bury comes roaring back—and there's no way this wolf shifter is going to let her get away this time.

"Dangerously sexy and satisfying." —Virna DePaul, *New York Times* bestselling author of the Belladonna Agency series

For more Paige Tyler, visit:

www.sourcebooks.com

Don't miss book 4 in *New York Times* and *USA Today* bestselling author Paige Tyler's super-hot X-Ops series...

Angelo and Minka's story

On a mission in Tajikistan, Special Forces team leader Angelo Rios didn't expect to run across Minka, a rogue hybrid shifter on the run. Something about the wild, desperate beauty stirs him deeply. Angelo's instinct is to protect her—body and soul—while duty dictates he turn her over to authorities.

Praise for Paige Tyler's X-Ops series:

"Nonstop action and hair-raising storytelling done well." —*RT Book Reviews*

"A thrilling suspense, great characters, a steamy romance. Wow, just wow!" —*Fresh Fiction*

"An action-packed thrill ride from start to finish. I can't wait for the next installment." —*Night Owl Reviews*, Top Pick!

"Dangerously sexy and satisfying." —Virna DePaul, *New York Times* bestselling author

For more Paige Tyler, visit:

www.sourcebooks.com

Hungry Like the Wolf

SWAT: Special Wolf Alpha Team
by Paige Tyler
New York Times and *USA Today* bestselling author

—⁓—

She's convinced they're hiding something

The team of sharpshooters is elite and ultra-secretive—they are also the darlings of Dallas. This doesn't sit well with investigative journalist Mackenzie Stone. They must be hiding something…and she's determined to find out what.

He's as alpha as a man can get

Gage Dixon, the SWAT team commander, is six-plus feet of pure muscle and keeps his team tight and on target. When he is tasked to let the persistent—and gorgeous—journalist shadow the team for a story, he has one mission: protect the pack's secrets.

He'll do everything he can to protect his secret

But keeping Mac at a distance proves difficult. She's smart, sexy, and just smells so damn good. As she digs, she's getting closer to the truth—and closer to his heart. Will Gage guard their secret at the expense of his own happiness? Or will he choose love and make her his own…

—⁓—

For more Paige Tyler, visit:

www.sourcebooks.com

Wolf Trouble

SWAT: Special Wolf Alpha Team
by Paige Tyler

New York Times and *USA Today* bestselling author

———∿∿———

He's in trouble with a capital T

There's never been a female on the Dallas SWAT team and Senior Corporal Xander Riggs prefers it that way. The elite pack of alpha-male wolf shifters is no place for a woman. But Khaki Blake is no ordinary woman.

When Khaki walks through the door, attractive as hell and smelling like heaven, Xander doesn't know what the heck to do. Worse, she's put under his command and Xander's protective instincts go on high alert. When things start heating up both on and off the clock, it's almost impossible to keep their heads in the game and their hands off each other…

———∿∿———

Praise for Paige Tyler:

"A wild, hot, and sexy ride from beginning to end! I loved it!" —Terry Spear, *USA Today* bestselling author of *A SEAL in Wolf's Clothing*

"Hot, action-packed, and sexy as hell!" —Sara Humphreys, award-winning author of *Vampire Trouble*

"Wow, just wow!" —*Fresh Fiction*

For more Paige Tyler, visit:

www.sourcebooks.com

In the Company of Wolves

SWAT: Special Wolf Alpha Team
by Paige Tyler
New York Times and *USA Today* bestselling author

The new gang of thugs in town is ruthless to the extreme—and a pack of wolf shifters. Special Wolf Alpha Team discovers this in the middle of a shootout. When Eric Becker comes face to face with a female werewolf, shooting her isn't an option, but neither is arresting her. She's the most beautiful woman he's ever seen—or smelled. Becker hides her and leaves the crime scene with the rest of his team.

Jayna Winston has no idea why that SWAT guy hid her, but she's sure glad he did. Now what's a street-savvy thief going to do with a hot alpha-wolf SWAT officer?

Praise for Paige Tyler's SWAT series:

"Bring on the growling, possessive alpha male... A fast-paced and super-exciting read that grabbed my attention. I loved it." —*Night Owl Reviews*, 5/5 Stars, Top Pick!

For more Paige Tyler, visit:

www.sourcebooks.com

Jaguar Pride

Heart of the Jaguar
by Terry Spear
USA Today Bestseller

An impossible mission...

JAG Special Forces agents Huntley Anderson and Melissa Overton are hot on the trail of poachers when they're suddenly saddled with two jaguar shifter cubs. They have to locate the parents, pronto—but who's going to babysit in the meantime?

A lifetime of possibilities...

Huntley is a rough, tough jaguar shifter and an all-business agent, but he's not going to let two abandoned youngsters come to any harm on his watch. Seeing her super-manly partner try to get the playful cubs under control stirs up some unexpected desires in Melissa, and she begins to feel like Huntley's not the only one who's in over his head...

Praise for *Jaguar Hunt*:

"Terry Spear's Heart of the Jaguar series gets better with each book... A fantastic read." —*The Romance Reviews*

For more Terry Spear, visit:

www.sourcebooks.com

Way of the Warrior

A romance anthology to benefit
the Wounded Warrior Project

Eight passionate love stories about amazing military heroes by bestselling authors:

Suzanne Brockmann   Julie Ann Walker

Catherine Mann   Tina Wainscott

Anne Elizabeth   M.L. Buchman

Kate SeRine   Lea Griffith

**To honor and empower those who've served,
all author and publisher proceeds go to the
Wounded Warrior Project.**

The Wounded Warrior Project was founded in 2002 and provides a wide range of programs and services to veterans and service members who have survived physical or mental injury during their brave service to our nation. Get involved or register for programs and benefits for yourself and your family online at www.woundedwarriorproject.org.

For more information, visit:

www.sourcebooks.com